What People Are Saying About

The Eighth Sea

The Eighth Sea has been described as hard to put down, a deep and enduring romance, a plot filled with unexpected twists and the characters hard to get out of one's mind…an inspiring journey into the unknown.

"*The Eighth Sea* paints a haunting picture of true anguish, survival, adventure, the will to live against all odds, new life, and the hope that only God can provide. It is a very compelling read."

—Sue Mallory, Author of *The Equipping Church*

"From the moment we meet a mother and daughter separated by an ocean of longing and despair, we're hooked. Nancy Sprowell Geise weaves an epic tale of love, loss, hope, and determination. Through her unforgettable characters, we discover that no matter what happens in life, we can find our way to our Eighth Sea. With belief, perseverance, and trust, life can show us our way home."

—Donna Mazzitelli, Writing With Donna

"*The Eighth Sea* pulls and pulls at your heart. Over and over, the golden threads continue to weave a tapestry until the very end. As readers, we never forget stories like *The Eighth Sea* that give us hope and characters such as Brenna who embody our deepest need – to find our place in the world, our way home."

—John Forssman, English Teacher

"*The Eighth Sea* has the dramatic feel of a great movie combined with the depth and emotion of a true epic novel. I couldn't put it down. I found myself reading it through the night. I will think about this story and Nathan and Brenna's romance for years to come."

—Sally Robinson, Worksmart USA

"There is so much to recommend about *The Eighth Sea*: a unique set-up, a great heroine, a tragic back-story, and great settings. I'm deeply connected to the characters' emotions and motivations and love the historical romance of it all. Nancy Sprowell Geise is the real deal."

—Trai Cartwright, Craftwrite

The Eighth Sea is a must read for individuals and book clubs alike. This story will remain with you as you make your way through your own Eighth Sea.

The Eighth Sea

Dear Alice -

It's been a joy

meeting you at Curves!

Blessings as you find

your own 8th Sea!

Nancy S. Meise

2012

The Eighth Sea

by Nancy Sprowell Geise

The Eighth Sea

Author photo by Crystal Geise, www.crystalgeise.com
Front cover art by Susan Jenkins, www.susanjenkinsart.weebly.com
Edited by Donna Mazzitelli, Writing With Donna
Book design, production and back cover by Veronica Yager,
www.yellow-studios.com

ISBN: 978-1468108194

Printed in the United States of America

For Doran, who is my "Nathan"

St. Christopher, West Indies 1769

His agonized cry splintered across the jagged cliffs and with the wind was swept out to sea. She was gone. He couldn't breathe. He was supposed to keep her safe. He had failed.

Life stopped...for her...and now for them.

He heard a bird singing. How could it be singing? There is no life.

Emily walked toward him...her lips moved...she was saying something... something he didn't want to hear...couldn't bear to hear. He watched helplessly as she collapsed in the sand.

Chapter One

St. Christopher, West Indies 1788

Brenna saw the man's fist, clenched and trembling, and knew he wanted to hit her. She sensed his hesitation. *He's remembering how hard I hit him back the last time.* Although four years had passed and she had been only fifteen, she knew he had not forgotten. It had taken him nearly a fortnight to recover.

"Thief!" bellowed the man again, shaking a coin in his dirty claw of a hand.

Her vision blurred with rage. "It's what I've earned!"

"Earned? I'm gonna see you in chains for this!"

"Where's the rest of it?" she demanded and snatched at the coin. She did not care about his threat. With the money gone, her punishment was complete.

"Somewhere ye'll never get yer hands on it," he laughed and jerked his hand away.

Brenna felt bile rise in her throat. She ran from the shack, into the pouring rain, and retched. Grasping a broken gatepost for support, she waited for the courage to enter the barn.

Water pooled at her feet as she stood over the hole in the barn's dirt floor where she had so carefully hidden the old box. As she feared, the tin was gone. A cry escaped her. *How? How did he find it?* Brenna felt something brush against her leg and dropped to the ground as a large, golden-haired dog looked up at her. "Oh, Honey! It's gone. All of it!"

Brenna Findlay closed her eyes. *Seven years,* she thought, fighting back tears. Seven years of rising before dawn, harnessing the mule, loading her cart with fruits and vegetables, and hauling it three miles down the mountain to the island's capital…seven years of working every day without exception…seven years of planting and harvesting the fields…seven years of peddling produce, saving the meager tips that grateful customers occasionally slipped into her hands…seven years of returning after dark, knowing she would do it all over again in a few hours…seven years of envisioning the day she could leave.

Another wave of nausea threatened. She inhaled and tried to stop it from consuming her. Before tonight, she had saved nearly enough money to leave. Now, it and the dream were gone. She pulled aged straw beneath her but found no comfort on the uneven mound. Wet and shivering, she moved closer to the dog for warmth. Listening to the steady rain, her mind raged. *What am I going to do? I can't start over. I can't.*

At dawn, Brenna's tired eyes remained open. She breathed deeply and tried to summon the energy to rise. Sliding open the barn's dilapidated door, she gasped. Water was ankle deep in every direction. Brenna had no idea how she would be able to move the cart through the mud when she had barely been able to do so yesterday, before this latest rain.

She squinted at the dreary sky; though still raining, the early morning light fought to break through. She knew that going to the market today would be a waste of time. Her full cart from yesterday was evidence that most patrons had no interest in buying produce in such weather.

Brenna looked at the decrepit cottage beyond the flooded field. With the money gone, she no longer saw the point of working. Yet, despite how dismal the prospect of doing so now, it was more appealing than staying here. She gazed at her cart and then at Honey. "At least we don't have to pick any more produce." The dog wagged her tail. "Honey, I know you want to go, but you can't. It's miserable out there."

Even before last night, Brenna had been dreading this day—the anniversary of her mother's death. Each year it unearthed the pain, fresh and raw. Now, with the money gone, it was even more unbearable. She yearned to run back through the years—into her mother's embrace to a time when she had been loved. Instead, Brenna struck a match to the lantern in the windowless tack room and waited for her eyes to adjust. In the dim light she found the mule's halter, rope, and brush and carried them into the stall. Gently, she rubbed the nose of the old grey beast and began to brush his mane. Her hair fell against his neck. She frowned at the sight of it, tangled in straw, and knew hers must look much worse than his. Brenna stopped and glanced at the brush again. Shrugging, she touched it to her own hair and began combing.

Five hours later, and for the fourth time, the cart was stuck axle deep in the heavy mud. Sobs racked her body as she sat on the side of what had been a dirt road before the rains began. Never had she been so wet, so cold, so tired.

She no longer cared that she was sitting in the mud. In her brown threadbare dress, she looked more like a rag doll than a girl of nineteen. Her dirty hair hung like yarn over her mud-splattered shoulders, with individual strands plastered against her face and neck.

Seven years, thought Brenna, of the last time she had known such sorrow. It seemed longer. The memory was as clear as if it were yesterday. Oddly, it was as though it were someone else's yesterday. It, too, came with a driving rain. She closed her eyes against remembering and the sickening knot deep within, but the sight of her mother's frail coffin lying on its side in the deep hole, being pounded with mud and rain, came anyway.

"Straighten it out," she begged the two men as they pitched in shovelfuls of wet earth. "Please straighten it out!" The men, methodical in their task, ignored the girl's pleas. Frantically, she looked for anyone who would make them stop. The few mourners who had earlier stood with Brenna through a driving rain were gone.

With heads bent low against the gale, the two men continued to slam their spades into the wet mound, heaving mud into the grave behind them. Realizing they did not care enough to listen, Brenna slipped into the pit. Her trembling legs straddled the uneven casket as she pushed aside the muck. She clasped her hands around the jagged front corner and pulled. She could not lift it. Straining, she jerked harder and harder. Nothing. Desperate now, she dropped to her knees, then to her stomach, and pressed her wet body across the roughly hewn casket. Stretching her arms as far as they would reach, she hugged the crate and pulled. Still nothing. Again and again she tried to move the wooden box—oblivious to the pain—the rough surface rubbing raw the skin on her cheek and arms. She paid no attention to the rain or the pelting dirt. She felt her mother's body shift within the box. A strangled cry left her lips. "Mother, Mother," she whispered. She held her breath and listened. Brenna lay frozen. The soft rhythmic thumping of her own heart was the only response she heard. Somehow, some way, she hoped her mother could hear it too. Then pain seized her. She cried out. Something hard had hit the back of her head. She touched her fingers to the wound and felt the warmth of blood; a fist-sized rock slid off her shoulder. She did not care. She was losing the battle. She could not leave her mother this way. Wildly, she pulled at the casket. Heaving, she pressed her face against the cold box. "Oh, Mother," she sobbed. "I can't do it!"

Hearing her voice for the first time, the two gravediggers turned, mouths agape at the sight below them of the young girl embracing the casket. She was covered in mud and blood. When she lifted her head they saw her huge, sad, and pleading eyes.

Growling obscenities, the larger of the two men slammed his shovel down and turned to leave. But he stopped when his toothless friend slowly rubbed his hand across his bristled beard, saying, "Well, now, just a minute." After studying the girl, he said hoarsely, "My father used t' say, 'If'n ye don't stand fer something yer nothin' but wastin' space.' Seems to me, this wee lass has made her stand. I'm just thankin' God we didn't bury her alive." The man looked hard at the girl's tear-stained face, "All right, I think we best set about giving yer mum a proper burial."

Sitting in mud, drained of all energy, Brenna could scarcely believe she had once been that stubborn child. She watched the water flow off her skirt and wondered if in some way these were the same raindrops which had fallen on that fateful day. She felt in some measure as if it had been raining ever since. Brenna halfheartedly squeezed the water from her skirt. In a happier time, she would have found humor in trying to wring the soaked fabric while it was still raining. Not today.

A light ocean wind began to blow. Brenna lifted her head and imagined she could hear the sounds of her mother's voice—loving whispers from long ago. She closed her eyes and could still feel the strokes of her mother's gentle hand brushing her hair, telling Brenna she was grateful her daughter had been raised on such a beautiful island, the beauty of which she now emulated. Her mother laughed as she softly rubbed Brenna's golden strands against her own cheek, saying her hair had soaked in so much of the equatorial sun that on cool twilight evenings like tonight, it cast a luminescence. Her mother said her skin was perfect, like the glossy-smooth surface of the beach after a delicate wave washed ashore.

Brenna looked at her mud-covered arms and hands and wondered—if her mother were here now, would she even recognize her daughter?

She realized her mother had been right. Her world was very much like the island itself, only not in the way her mother had described. Rather, hers was a life of isolation. Most of the young white women of St. Christopher filled their days with dancing and gaiety. None of that was true for Brenna. Her life more closely resembled the lives of the area slaves who worked the cane fields.

Brenna tried to determine the hour. "Mid-morning at least," she groaned. Most of the time her trips from the fields to the village took her two hours, for although the island rarely had a day without rain, the sun was also quick to shine, leaving the path virtually dry. Not this day with its great curtains of rain. She had never seen it like this. The dirt roads were now one long ribbon of mud, making travel by cart nearly impossible.

Normally by this time, she would have sold most of the day's produce and been on the return trip. As it was, she had traveled less than a quarter of the distance to the village and she was exhausted. Brenna dropped her head. Her body shook with sobs of fatigue, heartbreak, frustration, and most of all, loneliness.

The people of the island generally left their doors and windows open wide to welcome anyone passing. At Brenna's cottage, her father demanded their doors and windows remain closed. Brenna realized long ago that her father's warped sense of pleasure had centered on making her life miserable. Determined to never give him the satisfaction of knowing he had succeeded, she constantly struggled to remain dry-eyed. But now, she was unable to stop the tears. For the first time in her life, she knew defeat. True and utter defeat, for it came from deep within.

Brenna touched the bracelet on her wrist. "If you're ever scared or lonely, Brenna," her mother had whispered a week before her death, "I want you to remember your bracelet. It's God's reminder that he's with you…even when it seems he's not. And Brenna, he'll help you, but he'll never force his way into your life…he's a gentleman in that way. He'll wait until you ask. Brenna, you must ask."

She swallowed hard at the memory and her failure to honor her mother's dying wish. Not once had she been able to bring herself to pray. Brenna remembered when she and her mother used to do so every night before they went to bed. Since her death, Brenna sensed that if she prayed, it would be an admittance of fear and loneliness and a victory for Harley, her father.

Brenna knew if her mother were here now seeing the depth of her despair what she would want her to do.

Brenna covered her face in her wet hands. "If you can hear me, God, I don't know what to do. Please help me. Show me what to do."

Shrouded in misery, Brenna was oblivious to her surroundings and to the fact that the rain had ceased when a voice above her said,

"T'would appear, madam, your tears do little to aid the soggy state in which you now find yourself."

Brenna's back stiffened at the sound and she turned to see who had invaded her privacy. She lifted her head and knew that the image of the stranger before her would forever remain imprinted upon her mind. Perhaps it was the sunlight as a single beam filtered through the dreariness and centered squarely upon horse and rider. Or possibly it was his green eyes, vibrant and pure, yet turbulent like the calm of the sea while a brewing storm gathered just beyond the horizon. The lines of his body were as long and straight as the beams of a soaring mast. His tan skin was as flawless as a finely tailored sail and his teeth were nearly as white. There was a tough aura about him, as if he had experienced much; yet when he smiled, as he was doing now, she saw a glimmer of the carefree young boy he must have been.

As the wind blew through his black hair, she watched him closely and sensed he was free—more than anyone she had ever known. For a brief moment, she wanted him to ride silently away, preserving forever this image.

Her fixation halted as his gaze touched hers. She flushed with embarrassment at her open inspection of him, acutely aware of the difference between them. He, clean and dry in his calf-length overcoat and leather boots, mounted atop a magnificent bay, and she, in her wet and tattered muslin dress, sitting in the mud. To her further humiliation, her nose was running and she had no handkerchief. A strange expression of humor tinged with sympathy pulled at the corners of his mouth and crept into his eyes.

Determined to salvage some remnant of pride, Brenna's eyes met his, challenging. Her look seemed to bait him, for he said in jest, "As I was saying, I do not believe your tears will do much to improve the situation in which you now find yourself. In fact, I have found that tears rarely do much except fuel one's own pity."

Her embarrassment turned to rage. All the despair, anger, and disappointment of her life seemed to culminate in this moment. The man represented everything she wanted yet would never know. A landslide of emotion consumed her. She glared at the stranger. Too angry to speak, she stood, marched toward her mule, grabbed its lead, and began forcefully tugging on the rope.

"Perhaps you'd be in need of a little assistance and I'd be most honored to aid such a fair maiden in distress," he said playfully.

"Distress!" cried Brenna. "Why, you boorish cad! I'd take no bloody help from you even if I needed it…which I do not!"

"Ah, so the lady can speak," laughed the man lightly. "And at long last I thought I'd found the perfect specimen, a speechless female!"

"Why you…rogue!" spat Brenna, her eyes narrowing angrily.

Unable to stand any further humiliation, Brenna was determined to be rid of the stranger before he could do further damage to her pride. Facing the mule, she placed her feet as firmly as she could in the mud and gave a forceful tug on the lead. The action worked. The cart and mule lurched forward and sent Brenna sprawling backward. She landed unceremoniously, sending forth a wave of mud.

"Oh, m'lady," howled the stranger, "Are you all right?"

Brenna was once again too furious to speak, and to add to her indignation, one of her wooden-soled sandals was missing. Anyone else would have cared little for the old sandal, but it was the only pair she owned. Beyond caring how she looked, Brenna pushed herself up and began to paw through the thick muck.

She realized her attempts to find the sandal were futile and looked up to see horse and rider handily guiding her mule toward a more solid portion of the path. By the time she breathlessly caught up, they were stopped; the mule casually munched the tender grass as if nothing out of the ordinary had happened. She flung globs of mud from her arms and hands and looked helplessly for something to wipe them on. She resorted to her filthy skirt. Too humiliated to feel any appreciation, she grabbed the rope from the stranger who was now laughing so hard he could barely stay seated on his mount.

"Any time I can be of service, ma'am," he said and tipped his hat with a mocking bow. "May I accompany you to town? I don't know how you got this fa…"

"No. Please just leave." Brenna looked away so he would not see her hot and angry tears.

The man hesitated, then reached into his pocket, pulled out a handful of coins, and offered them to her. "As payment for improving what otherwise would have been an entirely uneventful day…and hopefully…so that you may secure a new pair of shoes."

Brenna fought the impulse to snatch the needed coins. "Keep your money, you swine!" As soon as the words were out, she wished she could suck them back in. She realized that of the two, she quite accurately fit that description. With her jaw clenched nearly as tight as her hand around the lead rope, Brenna turned and angrily began to pull the mule down the slippery path, struggling to disguise her lopsided gait.

Nathan Grant watched intently until the young woman rounded the corner. When he finally stopped chuckling, his brow narrowed.

He winced, recalling her tears and filthy dress. He thought of her missing shoe and realized he had been unintentionally crass. His attempt to lighten her mood with humor had utterly failed. *Why didn't I at least ask her what was wrong? And why wasn't I more tactful in trying to give her my pocket change? Perhaps I ought to follow her and offer some true assistance.* Then, recalling her anger, he sensed there was nothing he could do or say now to persuade her to accept anything from him.

He rubbed his hand across his chin and thought back to the first moment when she looked up at him. *There's something familiar about her.* He wondered if he had seen her at one of the waterfront taverns making advances toward a fellow seaman. *'Tis a shame we're leaving so soon, for I'd rather enjoy seeing her again.* Tinged with guilt by his less than gentlemanly behavior, he sighed slightly, turned his horse, and rode on.

The shack was as black as the sky when Brenna wearily opened the door. "What's taken you so long?"

Brenna did not need to see Harley to know he had been drinking nor was she in any mood to deal with his foul temper. Without speaking, she walked past him toward her room. She wished she had stayed a second night in the barn.

"Ya deaf, girl?" He struck a match to the lamp's wick and revealed his angry twisted face. "I said, what took ya so long? I've been waitin' for my supper and I be wantin' it now!"

Brenna ignored his ranting. He was clearly drunk. Brenna felt her chest tighten at the thought of where her precious savings were being spent.

"Answer me! Answer me!"

She turned and faced him squarely. "Had I not spent hours dragging the mule through the mud, I would have been here long ago…and had it not been for the last ship buying the entire load, the whole day would have been a complete waste of time."

"You lazy hussy," Harley's voice shook with disgust. "I'd wager you spent yer day lyin' with the waterfront scum just like that tramp, Helen!"

"Pox on you! Say what you will about me, but I will listen no more to your lies about my mother! She…"

"Your mother? Helen ain't your mother." He laughed at the look of confusion spreading across her brow. "Ah, don't understand now, do ya? Well, as I said in case you missed it, you ain't her daughter. Nor mine, thank God!"

"You don't know what you're saying."

"You! Yer the brat of some vagabonds who *sold* you when they were passing through! They wanted nothin' to do with no stinkin' female!"

Brenna hated that she could not stop listening.

"You, thief, were worthless to them except…for the jingle of the coin. Just like yer worthless to me!"

Sold. The words ripped through her. For Brenna, who had spent years watching slaves being sold at the block, knew there was no greater humiliation. She spun to face him. "It's not true!"

"Callin' me a liar, now are you? You should thank me, you ungrateful wench. If I hadn't *bought* you, who knows where you'd be. Whorin', I'd bet! If'n ye ain't already!" Then, with dark eyes narrowing, he sneered through his rotting teeth, "You owe me!"

You owe me. Brenna's mind reeled. How often had she heard that from him? Never understanding why he said it, his words were now beginning to make sense.

"I only bought you," he hiccupped and then took a long drink from his bottle, "because that half-crazed Helen forced me. She was hysterical 'bout the bastard babe of a French sea-dog she had lost givin' birth. The fool actually thought you were hers…a reincarnation of her lost brat! Said ye were gift from God! Hah! Curse from the devil more like it!" He wiped his mouth with the back of his dirty hand, "So," he slurred, "I bought you. Far more than ye've turned out to be worth! Why'd you think you had it so easy? You bein' a gift from God, Helen demanded you had to have it all! Why, you're nothin' but an undeservin'…"

Brenna ran from the cabin. Harley pulled the cork off another bottle, belched loudly, then shouted after her, "An' tomorrow we're gonna sell that bracelet! Oughta bring a boatload of mighty fine port!"

Brenna did not feel the branches rip her clothing as she tore through the thick underbrush nor did she give thought to the rough surface punishing her bare feet. She did not stop until she reached the sandy shore. She dropped to her knees and realized Honey had followed her. The dog moved next to her.

She raised her head. The black night had given way to a blanket of brilliant stars. *Sold!* She wanted desperately to deny the words, but they explained too much. *I should have known! How else could a father treat his child with such hatred? 'You owe me!' How many times have I heard that from him?*

Brenna scooped up handfuls of sand and let the grains run through her fingers. *Could Mother have had a child with another man? She must have been desperately lonely to have done so.* Brenna could understand such loneliness. She wondered if her mother had wanted to escape the brutal man as much as she did now.

Brenna never understood her mother when she told her that she was "a gift from God." Helen's words now made sense, if her mother actually believed she was somehow her lost baby brought back to life. *Was Harley telling the truth? Could her mother actually have believed such a thing?*

Brenna stroked Honey's soft fur. Her thoughts turned for the first time to another woman—a woman Brenna did not know existed until now. *What kind of a person could she be, this other 'mother' of mine? A mother who would sell her baby, not in hopes that someone would be better able to love and care for me, but for money! And what kind of person could have sold her child to a man as wretched as Harley?* She tried to imagine a face but could visualize nothing. Furiously, Brenna wiped her hand against her wet cheek and vowed. *If I meant so little to you…then the same shall be so for me. Dearest mother, whoever you are, you shall never again bring forth my tears!*

Chapter Two

Charleston, South Carolina

Emily brushed aside a tear as a soft Carolina breeze touched her face. She rubbed her hand along the smooth rail of her front porch and wondered how many thousands of tears she had shed, overcome by the same sick emptiness. She scanned the night sky searching for answers that would never come.

Can you hear me, little one? Can you see me through the stars? Does it make sense where you are? Does any of it?

"My darling, it's late and it's chilly," said Weston from behind, wrapping his arms around her.

Emily had not heard her husband join her.

"What's wrong? What's on your mind?" His words were tender. When she did not respond, he said softly, "It's okay." *Brenna was on her mind. Brenna was always on her mind.*

With an arm around her shoulders and his gait marred by a slight limp, Weston walked with his wife out of the cold night air. As he pressed the door closed, he wished he could so easily close the door on the past and forget the demons of that fateful night…nineteen years earlier…

St. Christopher, West Indies 1769

Dusk was quickly spreading over the waters of the West Indies. Weston and Emily stood with the ship's captain on the deck of *The Sea Bird* and observed the brilliant sunset. Emily cradled their seven-month-old daughter Brenna in her arms.

"Have you been sailing long, Captain Higgins?" Weston asked of the stout man.

"Aye. Most of me life." His voice was heavily laced with an Irish accent. "Made me first voyage when I was but eleven. Hired on as a boatswain. That'll be thirty-eight years now."

"Thirty-eight years! That's a long time for any man to be at sea, Captain." replied Weston in admiration.

"Aye, that it is."

Emily unwound her squirming daughter from the confines of the yellow quilt and asked, "Do you ever yearn for a more settled life, sir?"

"Nay," he laughed, "'fraid none of me friends could stand me 'round that long! An' I'd guess there'd be more salt water in these old veins now than blood." He pulled his gray, chest-length beard and said proudly, "Yea, I've sailed jest 'bout every kind o' packet known, from sealers to merchants. An' seen jest 'bout every coast there is, from the Falklands to Greenland."

"Some of your adventures must have been terrifying," said Emily.

"Ah, there's been many o' close call, but none like the night off the coast of Spain when me packet broached, an' let me tell ye, the luck o' the leprechaun t'was on me side that night. T'aint no other explanation for that frigate on her side, then suddenly correctin' herself!" He rubbed his thigh. "Nearly lost me leg in that one, but the surgeon aboard t'was a good one an' didn't have need o' 'is hatchin' knife after all."

Weston looked at Emily and knew the captain's tale was doing little to help her growing apprehension about the voyage. He, too, would be relieved when they stepped onto the American shore. Captain Higgins had informed the nearly seventy passengers prior to leaving England that since they were departing late in the season, they might be in for rough sailing. Mercifully, the voyage had been uneventful. Despite his interest in the captain's tale, Weston's thoughts rested solely on his wife who had given up her efforts to cradle Brenna and now held her upright so the infant could view the rolling waves beyond the rail.

My wife, Weston thought, admiring the graceful way she held her head against the ocean breeze and her long, dark hair blowing with the wind. He still could not believe she had chosen him. Slightly shorter than he, Emily stood several inches taller than most women. He had never seen anyone of such pure beauty, yet it was her remarkable two-toned eyes which most intrigued him. A thick, black line divided the two distinct colors of her eyes…a deep rich blue and a bright luminous aqua green. Rarely did a stranger meet Emily without commenting on her unique eyes. Weston was pleased their child, like the two generations of women before her, had inherited the beautiful Irish eyes. The baby was given the name of her beloved grandmother, Brenna, after Emily's mother.

Weston saw a bond between his wife and child that went well beyond their eyes. The love between this mother and daughter was deeper than he had ever witnessed. The terrible accident that claimed the lives of her parents two years earlier had been a brutal reminder for Emily of the fragility of life. In turn, she channeled the love and closeness she had shared with her mother to her own child. Hour after hour Emily cradled her baby and savored each tender moment. Brenna's gaze softened when she looked into her mother's eyes. Weston knew it was a force that time or space would never sever.

A glint of gold flashed off baby Brenna's wrist. He touched the soft skin beneath the bracelet they had put on her tiny wrist in celebration of her birth. The bracelet's woven gold chains were designed to be unwound as she grew. At the time, they debated whether they could afford such an expense, but after they saw the treasure with its special inscription, they knew it had been the right decision. The sacrifice brought them joy.

"My husband saw it as well, didn't you, Weston?"

"I'm sorry, dear. What?"

"I was telling the captain about seeing the sails of another ship in the distance earlier today."

"Yes. We both spotted it, but it was too far off to make out her flag."

Captain Higgins hesitated in his response as he sighted two small birds. The captain pivoted to look over the ship's stern at an ominous mass of dark thunderclouds rolling toward them. He frowned and said absently, "Our watch spotted the vessel as well. Ye need not fear; looks as though she's an American merchant ship. Most likely she'll be at our heels until we reach St. Eustraluis."

"St. Eustraluis?" questioned Weston, unaware of a scheduled stop.

"Aye, 'tis a small rocky island where we'll dock shortly before headin' for the Colonies."

Oblivious to the gathering winds, Emily's gaze remained locked on the western horizon where the sea and sky flowed together with no discernible edge—both catching the fiery red and vibrant orange hues of the dying sun. She said breathlessly, "I've never seen a more beautiful sunset."

"Aye, that 'tis, mum, an' normally such color in the evenin' sets me mind at ease, but that," he said and nodded his head at the sky in another direction, "that…aye…we may be in for some weather yet if them clouds continue buildin'." He motioned to the fast-moving dark clouds and said, "Never like to see 'em swirling like that." He pointed over the tall mast, "See 'em birds…high flyin' storm petrels? Generally only catch sight of 'em when a brewin' gale forces 'em to descend. Hum," he added, twisting the long end of his beard, "like it better when they t'aint nowhere to be seen." Abruptly, he turned to leave. "Best take yer family below, Mr. Emerson, 'fore they get wet." Hurriedly, the captain moved away and Emily noticed for the first time the vessel's expanded sails and the choppiness of the water. The tranquility of their voyage was soon devoured as a wall of darkness spread across them like ink pouring from a tumbler, chasing away the final rays of the dying sun.

"T'would appear Captain Higgins was right," said Emily minutes later. She pressed her hand against the small, thick porthole. "It's raining." She wished she could wipe away the raindrops for a better view. "Oh, Weston, I don't like this."

"He's been sailing all his life, Emily."

"Yes, and how many times has he almost gone down? Something tells me, t'wasn't the luck of the leprechaun on his side. More likely he's like a cat. The question is…how many lives has he got left?" Emily looked at her husband and then again through the porthole, "You sense it too, don't you?"

Weston's silence confirmed her fear. He joined her at the small window. The moisture against the porthole evoked Weston's memory of a snowy winter evening ten months earlier…

Sheffield, England, 1768

A swirling wind rattled the shutters of their small cottage. Weston looked out at the desolate, snow-covered valley.

Behind him, Emily removed a small box from a wooden chest. "I wanted," she said with a mischievous smile, "to share this with you when it was more complete, but I can't wait another moment."

Weston grinned at his young wife's excitement. He had been aware for some time that she was working on a secret project.

"As you know, this gift is for our baby."

"'Our baby,'" Weston marveled, words he never thought he would hear.

Emily guessed his thoughts and pressed his hand over her enlarged abdomen. "This girl's going to be strong and enduring."

Weston smiled at her confidence that the baby was a girl. With her knack at intuition, he had no doubt of the gender of their unborn child.

"Since it appears we'll be leaving here shortly, I wanted to create a gift of her heritage."

Weston winced. The prospect of uprooting his wife and child and taking them to an unfamiliar land still bothered him; yet, after months of weighing their options, they always reached the same conclusion. In England, their dream of owning land was not possible. Because she was a female, Emily had not been entitled to her late father's estate, and since Weston's father had had no land of his own, there was no inheritance. Their only chance of ownership would be for the king to grant them such a privilege. Since neither had any royal connections, they had no such opportunity. In England, they could only envision a future of unfulfilled toil. In America, they believed they had a chance for something more.

"You've certainly aroused my curiosity." Weston nodded at the gift.

"I've started making a blanket."

"A blanket?"

"A quilt actually."

"You must be counting on this strong and enduring child being tiny," chuckled Weston, noting the size of the box containing the blanket.

"Not quite that small," laughed Emily. "It's still in pieces." She opened the box. "Enclosed are six blocks."

"Blocks?"

"Sections rather. Each tells a story and when pieced together they will form a quilt." Emily handed him the first square, "This one's dedicated to your parents."

Weston ran his fingers over the finely embroidered scene. A woman watched as a man wearing a miner's cap entered a mine. Weston was surprised by a sudden tightening in his throat. The memory of a day, many years past, came flooding back.

"Daddy, please don't go in again," begged the teary-eyed boy and grabbed his father's arm. James Frances Emerson looked into the pleading brown eyes of his eight-year-old son. "It's my job, Wes."

"But, Daddy, please!" cried the boy, unable to comprehend his father's reasoning. "Don't do it! Don't go into the dragon's mouth!"

James set down his pick and knelt next to his son. "I've been thinking about your nightmare, Wes, and you're right. In many ways, this shaft is like a beast that can devour those who disrupt it. And, like your nightmare, it can be cold and dark…and even at times fiery." James took hold of both his arms and held Weston at arm's length. "I know this is hard to understand. But I have no choice, son. Every man must do his part."

Weston knew he had lost the battle and helplessly watched his father scoop up his pick and disappear into the dark shaft. With shoulders slumped, Weston slowly walked up the path to the shack on the hill. He squinted in the noonday sun and looked at the lifeless, gray cottage before him.

How different you are, he thought somberly, *from our home in Pontypridd.* Pontypridd, Wales, was the only true home Weston had ever known, in the happy days when his mother was alive. That home had vibrant blossoms of red and white roses that concealed the uneven foundation of their one-room mining shack. Inside, a rug, tediously woven by his mother from rags, covered the threadbare couch and checkered blue curtains hung neatly in the paneless windows. No one would have guessed his mother created them from a tattered bed cover she found discarded in a nearby ditch. Weston shook his head and knew his mum would not have been pleased that he and his father left their home in Pontypridd immediately after her death. From Caerphilly to Llanelly, the father and son roamed for nearly three years, never staying longer than four or five months in any of the mining camps. Weston often wondered if his father hesitated to remain in any one place for fear he might find a comfort that would somehow be disloyal to his wife's memory.

Six years after he begged his father not to enter the mine, Weston looked at his dying father.

"I want you to promise me," James had whispered, his labored words barely audible, "that you never work the mines."

Weston closed his eyes, unable to bear the sight of his father lying on the cold, flattened remains of a corn husk mattress. Weston had seen often the tormented, suffocating deaths of other coal miners after years of breathing coal dust. Yet, he was unwilling to accept that the man before him, his skin tinged with blue, his eyes hollow, was dying. He held his father's limp, swollen hand and remembered when they were strong.

"Son?" James' voice was a rasp. He waited for Weston's reply.

How can I promise him I'll never work the shafts when already I should be doing so with all the other boys my age? It's the only life I know.

"Father, I..."

"I told you once..." interrupted James, his trembling hand covered his mouth with a blood-stained handkerchief. "I told you once..." He coughed forth more blood. "I had no choice. I was wrong, Weston. We all have a choice."

"But…"

Determined to finish, his father moved his swollen tongue over his parched lips. "I never had much to give yer mother, but I gave her my word that her only child would never know this blackened torment." He coughed again. "I must have your word, son. It must end here."

Two days later, Weston watched the snow-covered pine coffin being lowered into a shallow grave. It was his fourteenth birthday. A light mist emerged from the grave as the cold air brushed the damp soil. Weston flinched and thought he felt the distant heat from a dragon's maw.

"Thank you, Emily," said Weston hoarsely, "for including my parents in your quilt."

"I'm grateful, Weston, that our child is a part of them. I just wish I could have met them."

"They would have loved you," replied Weston, gratified he had been able to honor his father's request. He never worked the mines.

"And this one," said Emily, handing him a second square, "represents my father."

Weston looked at the embroidered outline of a horse and an anvil. "Dale would have liked this; he was a fine blacksmith."

"Yes, he was."

Weston suppressed a smile, for he knew Emily's next words. She did not disappoint him.

"You know," she said in the same manner she always did when she spoke of her father, "people brought their horses to him from all over England, for he was able to shoe those that no other farrier would touch. It was as though the animals sensed his kindness. I guess that's why my mother was drawn to him as well."

"Ah, your mother," grinned Weston. He was so pleased that he'd had the chance to know Emily's parents before their deaths. "Your mother, Brenna Kate, was a rare woman indeed! I know of no other lady who would have left her country when she was sixteen to marry a man she had known only three weeks!"

"I think that was the Irish in her. She said she knew my father was the man of her dreams the first moment she saw him. Anyway, this block is for her and the homeland she so dearly loved." Emily placed the block with a finely stitched flag of Ireland in Weston's hand. "I really miss them, Weston."

He rubbed the back of his wife's neck. "I know." Weston recalled how happy he was when he learned that Emily was with child, for a gaiety had returned to her that he had not seen since before the death of her parents. He had begun to fear it was gone forever. Emily was in the wagon with her parents when it tumbled down a steep ravine. Both her parents were crushed by the wagon. Emily was thrown free but she landed hard against a massive boulder. She spent weeks in bed recovering with Weston by her side.

Weston and Emily were overjoyed and amazed when Emily learned she was pregnant, for the injuries she sustained in the accident gave them little hope she would ever be able to conceive. Even the doctors considered the baby she was now carrying a miracle child.

"I only wish my parents could have known their granddaughter," said Emily of her coming child.

"I have a feeling perhaps they do."

She removed another piece of fabric and immediately brightened. "Any guess at this one?"

Weston looked at the fourth block bemused. "Can there be any doubt? It's the bridge in Sheffield where the most beautiful girl I'd ever seen cost me the best fishing pole I'd ever owned."

"Well," she said, laughing and poking him gently, "if you hadn't been standing in the middle of the bridge, that horse would never have gotten between you and the rail!"

"And if you had kept a tight hold on the lead of the mare your father was trimming, a wild, careening horse would never have charged down the road in the first place!"

Emily smiled, leaned forward, and kissed him lightly on the cheek. "I might add, if you hadn't lost your pole, Father would never have invited you to dine with us."

"A fishing pole for a wife," Weston grinned, his eyes sparkling, "there are many t'would say I drew the shorter straw."

Emily threw back her head and laughed heartily. Finally recovering, she removed the final block from the box. "You have to use your imagination with this one."

"Let's see, it looks as though the view is from the bow of a ship, with the outline of land ahead." Weston smiled. He knew immediately what that land represented—their new beginning. "And with luck, a vessel we will be aboard within the year."

Weston looked at the five blocks spaced next to one another on the small pine table and hugged his pregnant wife tenderly, "It's beautiful, Emily."

"I need to get it completed, for the baby will come to depend on it for comfort and safety."

"She just keeps pulling away."

Weston could see Emily's frustration as Brenna refused to nurse.

"I think she knows I'm nervous."

"Would it ease your mind if I go topside to see if I can determine whether the storm is easing?" It had been over an hour and Weston was eager to do something besides wait out the storm in the ship's stuffy cabin.

"Yes, thank you. I'll change Brenna's under-cloth. Perhaps that will encourage her to settle."

Weston pulled the wool cap over his head.

"But be careful, Weston."

When he stepped onto the deck, Weston was hit by a powerful wind. He tucked his head against the gale and heard the captain's barked orders. "All hands! All hands! Man yer positions and stay there! Wooldridge, Brady, Beaudry! Anchor yerselves to the wheel! It's gonna take the strength of Job t' keep her in position! We're in fer a whale o' one!" The winds settled momentarily as Weston heard the continued shouts of the captain, "An' the rest of ye, reef the sails! An' hold tight to yer axes! We may be hackin' some timber tonight!"

Weston felt a tightening lump in his chest at the unsettling words. With a cold rain slapping his face, he sought the captain. "Can I be of assistance?" he shouted.

The captain turned, a look of surprise on his face. He shook his head and yelled back, "Best ye be tendin' to yer family. No, wait!"

Weston moved toward the captain.

"A prayer or two," he yelled. "That's what ye can do."

Weston nodded and retreated to his quarters, relieved Emily had not heard the captain. He took a deep breath and opened the door.

Though he had tried to mask it, he knew she saw his fear. He brushed water from his wet shoulders. He saw the difficulty she was having trying to balance. "Here," he said and patted the blanket next to him, "sit with me. I'll take Brenna." He cradled Brenna, bundled in the special yellow blanket, and tried to ignore the vessel's erratic movements and its terrible groans. He was about to tell Emily that it sounded like the ship was caught in a cherry pit vise slowly being crushed when he thought better of it.

With his free arm pressed tightly around Emily's quivering shoulders, the two listened as the occasional raindrop became a pounding sheath of rain against the deck above. The howling wind deafened, unlike any they had ever heard. The ship tossed so violently, Weston feared the hull would crack. Helplessly, Weston and Emily prayed for the return of the familiar pitch of the vessel as it bobbed and lurched. Both cried out when a huge cask smashed through their wooden door, followed by a surge of water. Their belongings tossed about in the dark clutter of debris.

"Oh, Weston! We're going down!"

He shouted back, "No! It's just a cask broken free of its moorings!" He braced himself against the violent gyrations of the vessel and covered his wife and child, knowing that man was no longer in control of the ship. He begged silently, "Please don't let us go down!"

Powerless, passengers and crew waited for calm in the unrelenting storm. For nearly two hours, the ship waged its battle for survival, fueling Weston's hope that it might soon end, when an eerie pause—a merciful stillness cast over them. Then it hit. So violent was the jolt that Weston felt as though a child had picked up a toy ship in a bottle, lifted it high over his head, and then slammed it to the ground. An explosive light and deafening roar reverberated through the vessel. Weston, Emily, and child were thrown to the floor. Weston rose to his knees and looked at his wife's huge, terror-filled eyes and knew the sickening truth—they'd been struck by lightning.

Weston grabbed his wailing daughter and, with Emily, lunged toward the door, clambered up the narrow companionway stairs, and onto the slippery deck. Acrid smoke penetrated the damp air, burning their eyes and nostrils. Both cried out, unable to believe the horror before them. A man lay face down at their feet, the back of his skull partially missing. Blood surrounded him and trailed overboard as the ship listed severely port side. Above them, the mast and rigging hung in scarred fragments ablaze.

Weston turned at the guttural cry behind him. One of the crewmen stood with ax in hand and frantically hacked at the remnants of yardarms that had fallen around him. Realizing the futility of his actions, the man tossed aside his ax and disappeared through the smoke and rain toward the stern of the ship. Chaos seized the passengers as they fled toward the lifeboats, trampling those fallen. Men yelled for their wives, women screamed for their children, and the heartbreaking shrieks of the young were carried away by the howling wind.

Seeing the scores of people who were piling into the four lifeboats at the mid-section of the ship, Weston grabbed Emily's arm. He pulled her toward the stern where a small boat just off the rail hung suspended by several lines at deck level. They were the first to reach the craft. Weston thrust Emily and the blanket over the side and intended to hand Brenna to her once she had found her balance. He then would be free to help lift others into the boat so it could be released by its pulleys and lowered into the water.

"Quickly," Emily screamed, "let me have her!" Emily reached to grab Brenna when the ship lurched forward and the towering mainsail crashed onto the deck and severed the lifeboat's ties. The tiny boat plunged bow first into the turbulence below. Weston clutched Brenna tightly as they slammed onto the deck and began sliding toward the water faster than the ship was sinking. Weston clawed at the wood with his free hand, yet he was unable to stop the slide. He felt his legs scrape over the ship's edge. He yelled wildly and braced for the fall when the ship's rail lifeline brushed his hand. He grabbed it. With one arm holding the rope and the other holding Brenna, the two dangled precariously against the ship's slanted high side. With every ounce of strength he had, Weston clenched the rope. The muscles in his back and shoulders burned, and his arm felt as though it was being wrenched from its socket. Sheets of rain blurred his vision. Weston squinted toward the sea and made out the vague outline of a lifeboat. With the ship's deck quickly sliding below the dark water, Weston realized what he must do. Had he been able to use both hands, he would have eased his way down the ship's tilted side and into the water. With the baby in his arms, he was unable to do so. He gripped Brenna tightly, slid his hand over her tiny nose, closed her mouth with his palm, and pressed her face firmly against his chest. Using his feet as leverage, he pushed hard off the side of the ship and released the rope.

Cold water engulfed them. It was several seconds before he was able to kick his way back to the churning surface and away from the ship. He held Brenna high in his arms and used his legs to guide him toward the lifeboat he had twice glimpsed. The distance to the boat was not great, but the waves made the task nearly impossible. Though he carried her as high as he was able, Weston knew Brenna was in grave danger. With every swell, the waves submerged them both, and she emerged seconds later coughing and spitting up the salty water. Time seemed to stop. He was desperate to swim faster, yet he could not. Finally, the boat was nearly within reach. Fearing its wild motion might strike them, Weston kicked furiously, trying to stay at a distance.

"Emily! Emily!" He heard no response. Certain the high winds prevented her from hearing him, Weston lunged forward and grabbed the side of the small boat. He pulled himself up with one arm and swiftly shoved Brenna over its steep edge with the other. Cold fear spread through Weston as his eyes swept the empty craft.

"Emily! Emily! Emily!" he screamed, his words unheard even to himself. The wind and waves roared around them. He pulled himself inside the boat. With his lungs burning, Weston's eyes frantically searched the water surrounding the boat. He could see nothing. Throwing himself toward the opposite side of the pitching craft, he scanned the surface, yelling her name, knowing she was a poor swimmer. The raging conditions would never allow him to find her. He raised his fists to the blackened depth and screamed out, "No!"

Weston saw wild thrashing in the dark water. "God, please….!" He stood to leap when a prolonged lightning strike flooded the boat with light. Brenna's face was pasty white, her lips blue. Weston forced back a scream. Grabbing her, he turned her over and pounded her back. She coughed, spewed water, and trembled violently. Next to her was one of the severed ropes used to lower the boat from the ship and next to it lay the quilt. Weston hesitated as he again glimpsed the flailing person in the water. He knew Emily would not want him leaving Brenna like this…exposed and shivering. He grabbed the blanket, turned it inside out where it was still dry, and tightly wrapped it around his daughter before sliding her under the wooden bench. Firmly, he grabbed the rope and dove into the water.

The rope, Weston realized as he swam toward the direction where he had last seen the splash, was his only link to the lifeboat and his daughter. Carefully, he let the rope slip through his hand, creating enough slack to swim but never letting it leave his grip. Weston's pace did not falter, despite the fatigue, swallowed seawater, and the rough line ripping the flesh on his hand. None of that mattered. With his left hand he knew he held the life of his young daughter; in his right, the hand he would use to reach out for his wife. As he swam, Weston prayed continually for her to stay afloat. Exhausted, he fought on and finally spotted her.

"Emi… Emi…" he struggled, trying to cry out for her to swim to him. Instead, he choked down only more of the salty water. Emily was nearly within reach. But the rope had come to its end. Holding the rope in his right hand, he extended himself as far as he could. It was not enough. Frantically, he tugged on the rope, trying to pull it and the boat toward him. Nothing happened. Wildly, he pulled harder on the rope, against the waves. The boat seemed to move in his direction. Emily was so close. He strained to reach her. Then without warning, the vessel, which rose atop a large swell, fell down the backside of the wave. The rope jerked from his grasp as Weston felt Emily's hand in his.

The American merchant ship, *The Lucretia,* came to the aid of *The Sea Bird's* burning wreckage. One of the ship's crew spotted Weston and Emily in the rolling sea clinging to a piece of the ship's mast and immediately sent a retrieval boat. Only one of the five lifeboats was rescued by the American merchant ship, but it was not their daughter's. The storm ended quickly, fueling the Emersons' hope that the tiny craft carrying their daughter might have stayed afloat. As the night waned, Emily and Weston never left the deck, straining against the guardrail and searching the black water for any sign of the small boat. The moon's light, partially obscured by the thick clouds, was of little help. Weston extended a lantern at arm's length over the rail but found that it only further impaired his vision.

The first streaks of dawn gradually erased the darkness. Weston pulled a damp blanket over Emily's shoulders and looked into her swollen, tear-streaked face. "Emily, go lie down. You're exhausted."

"No. I won't. I won't leave her out there! Oh, Weston!" she sobbed and fell against him, her voice hoarse from hours of yelling into the darkness for Brenna. "She'll be crying for me and I'm not there! I'm not there!" Abruptly, Emily pushed away from him, leaning heavily against the rail. Her coarse voice was barely audible, "Brenna! I'm here! Brenna!"

Weston wanted to cover his ears, to block out the pain he heard in his wife's voice. He wanted to cover his eyes and escape the haunting images of Captain Higgins and their other new friends aboard *The Sea Bird* who had been lost. *Was it really only last night we were all laughing together at dinner? How could it have all changed so quickly? Oh my God, how?*

While the search dragged on, Weston forced his mind to imagine the moment when they would find Brenna and everything would be okay. His trembling hands clutched the ship's rail in a desperate struggle to hold off yet another wave of despair threatening to engulf him. He closed his eyes. He knew he needed to collect himself and be strong for Emily. Slowly, he let out a breath and opened his eyes, willing his thoughts to calm. He forced himself to picture Brenna nestled peacefully in her blanket, being rocked by the life boat. Captain Burdick had said it was possible the lifeboat carrying Brenna might have beached itself upon the near island of St. Christopher or its sister island, Nevis. Weston tried to put out of his mind the captain's other words that in the unlikely event the craft survived the storm with no one to bail out water, it was highly improbable the unmanned boat would maneuver itself safely around St. Christopher's rocky shores. The craft's only hope, the captain had said, was to wash ashore on St. Christopher's tranquil western coast. If it came ashore anywhere else, there would be little hope.

Three hours later, Weston Emerson's agonized cry splintered across the rocky cliffs of St. Christopher, and with the wind, was swept out to sea. He sank to his knees in the sand and slowly untangled a sea-soaked cloth from a jagged piece of lifeboat lumber. Trembling uncontrollably, he clenched the tiny blanket to his chest.

"Not her! God Almighty! Not her!" Desperately, Weston scanned the clouds for an answer. "Take me instead! Please, take me! I'm her father. I was supposed to keep her safe! Please, take me instead!" Realizing the futility of his pleas, Weston buried his face, his tears spilling on to the tattered remnants of the blanket. In an instant, his world had been swept away like the vanishing grains of sand beneath his knees.

He pressed the torn cloth against his cheek and recalled Emily's loving words that the baby would come to depend on it for comfort and safety. Violently, he flung the cloth to the sand, unable to stand its betrayal.

A bird sang overhead. *How could it be singing when there was no longer any life?*

Emily, who had run in the opposite direction in the search, was making her way toward him. "Weston...please...please...No... No!"

She collapsed on the beach.

Chapter Three

St. Christopher, 1788

Continuous dark curtains of waves crested and then dissolved, silently touching the shore. Brenna wondered how many miles they had traveled to reach their destination with so slight a glance. She sighed, feeling the weight of the decision she had made. She knew she no longer had a choice…everything good in her was decaying and would be destroyed if she stayed. She could not let Harley's evil, or *that* of the parents who sold her, have such victories. She would leave the island and the only life she had ever known…no matter the obstacle…no matter if she died trying.

Where will I go? And how? Brenna pulled out the coins in her pockets and grimaced. Although it was far more than she had ever earned in one day, it was still the only money she now had. She returned the coins to her pocket, raised her wrist to her mouth, spat on the dirty bracelet, and polished it with her skirt. The touch of it calmed her as it always had. She still had many questions about the bracelet whose strands she diligently unwound every few years to accommodate her growing wrist. *How had Mother ever acquired the funds to purchase it and why did Harley permit her to do so?*

Since her mother's death, Harley had threatened daily to sell it. Brenna was surprised he had not already done so. Her only insight as to why he had not yet made good on his many threats was that once, when she was about seven, she overheard her mother and Harley arguing over it. She heard her mother say that the bracelet was a gift from God, and if he sold it, a terrible curse would come upon him. Brenna never saw any evidence that the man was a believer in God, but she suspected some lingering fear of that threat was the only reason the bracelet was still in her possession.

She read the inscription. *To our beloved miracle, Brenna. Luke 19:10.* Brenna wondered again why her mother had chosen the Irish name and the Bible verse. Her mother had often read her the verse: *For the Son of Man is come to seek and save that which was lost.* Helen had told Brenna that she once thought Brenna was lost but then found and that she was a miracle. Brenna was always perplexed with the explanation, but in light of what she had learned last night, that Helen had thought she was her baby somehow returned from Heaven, it made more sense.

Brenna covered her bracelet and imagined her wrist without it, having instead the coins it would bring. She considered the wrath her mother must have endured from Harley over its purchase. *Is selling it the only way I can secure a portion of my passage?* Brenna knew her mother would encourage her to sell it if it meant her happiness. Yet, when Brenna realized that by selling it, she would be selling a part of her mother, she knew she could not do it.

Funds or not, Brenna knew she had to go. *If only I was a man and could get hired working a ship.* Three years ago, after realizing it would take several more years to accumulate enough money to buy passage, she had thrown herself at the mercy of several sea captains and begged to be hired. The few who took the time to listen told her variations of the same argument: that a woman's presence aboard would cause more trouble than it was worth. Although no one would admit to it, Brenna suspected their main reluctance was the persistent rumors among such men that a woman aboard would bring bad luck to the ship and crew.

Some of her pleas to be hired had been met with deaf ears; their responses ranged from uproarious laughter to those who offered to bring her aboard as "entertainment for the crew." She was repulsed at the thought. Selling her body was an option she would never consider.

Despite the futility of her quest, Brenna had not been deterred and continued to press her case at every opportunity until local officials had threatened to deny her access to the wharf if she continued to harass the seamen. Knowing she could not afford to lose her produce sales, she had reluctantly abandoned that approach.

Brenna thought now of the people who indentured themselves to wealthy landowners for passage abroad in return for as much as seven years of work. *I've already been sold once. I won't let it happen again!* She knew, too, that enslaving herself to anyone would be too similar to the life she was leaving. *No! Never again!*

Brenna dug her feet deeper in the sand and listened to the soothing waves. Her thoughts focused on the only other way she knew to leave the island. It was dangerous at best—stowing away aboard an outgoing vessel. She remembered the American ship that had purchased her produce earlier in the day. The jingling change in her pocket was proof of that sale. She had been paid well above the value of the goods. She recalled the friendly gentleman who was in charge of the ship's cargo. He said he was rewarding her heartily in appreciation for her service to his ship, despite the wretched weather.

Brenna wished she had paid more attention to his words about the ship's departure and prayed it had not already left. Brenna stood and brushed the sand from her arms and legs. She had made her decision. She did not care where it was going, so long as it sailed.

Harley's loud snores broke the silence of the tiny cabin. Brenna cautiously made her way across the floor and tried desperately to let only the outside edges of her feet touch the warped boards. She knew the chances of him awakening from his drunken state slim; nevertheless, she tried to soften every step, never more aware of the sound produced by the squeaky floor boards. Harley snorted loudly and rolled over. Brenna froze. It was several moments before his rattling resumed. She moved toward a chair and his neatly folded clothes. She had washed those four days before and was glad they were still untouched, unlike the dirty heap on the floor. She grabbed the folded shirt and breeches and moved toward the kitchen where she stuffed a cheese round, two loaves of bread, and a small water jug into a sling sack and pulled it over her shoulder. As she did, she paused, struck by the thought of how this simple act reminded her of the hundreds of mornings in the past when she packed enough food to last her through her day's work.

To the rear of the kitchen was her straw cot. She frowned angrily at the empty night stand. Harley had taken the lantern again. She grabbed her small, thin blanket and tossed it over her arm. In the darkened cottage, Brenna saw only one more item she needed and she shoved it snugly upon her head. Quietly, she stepped out into the damp night.

Brenna opened the barn door and was once again greeted by Honey who looked as though she had just settled in for the night. She lit a candle, found a piece of parchment and a quill, and wrote, "Seth Penoyer wants to buy the mule." Their neighbor had told her just last week that if she decided to retire the animal in the near future, he would like him as a pasture companion for his rambunctious young horse. Seth was a good man and would treat the mule well and she knew Harley would be eager for the money. She wished Seth's wife did not have a fierce aversion to dogs so she could leave Honey with them as well. Brenna tacked the note to the barn's door.

"Come on, girl," she said gently to her dog. Together they walked down the narrow lane as they so often had in the past. With only a thin moon, the night was unusually dark. The two companions made their way down the mountain's slippery path toward the island's capital, Basseterre. Brenna was grateful the rain had stopped. The path was still muddy, but she found the walking much easier without the cart. Even the brilliance of the star-studded sky did little to light the way. Brenna had walked this route so frequently that she knew every stone, root, and turn in the path. She knew each shrub and tree she passed. She stopped frequently, trying to shake the mud from between her bare toes; she wished she had her sandals. As she walked, she imagined the orange orchards, the coca trees, and the tall palmettos swaying in the gentle breeze. She could hear the wisp and creaks of the country windmills as they turned and wondered if she would always remember the little things about her life on the small island. Would she recall the beautiful shrub that opened every afternoon at the same time each day? Would she remember how difficult it was to look at the large bunches of crimson flowers when the sun was shining because the plant's brightness hurt her eyes?

Brenna knew exactly when she passed the Knapps' cottage to her right. She could picture the old couple out working in their garden, almost as if they were there now. Brenna realized that everything was the same as it had been most of her life. After tonight, all that would change. She sensed she would never again walk this path.

Brenna guessed it to be near midnight when she entered the quiet outskirts of the village. A light shone through one window in a stone public building. She knew the dockyards would not be so calm and it was unwise for any young woman to be spotted alone. She ducked behind a tall building and quickly slipped off her worn dress into Harley's oversized clothing. She imagined his fury upon waking and realizing that not only did she still have all the earnings from the previous day's sale, but she had taken some food and his clothes as well. It would never occur to him that these were a pittance compared to the life savings he had taken from her last night. He would be positively thunderous, undoubtedly believing she had fled to the waterfront, expecting her to be "Whorin," as he so often accused.

And why? Why did he never believe me when I said I had never been with a man? In truth, she had never even been close. Although an occasional man had tried to persuade her a bit too zealously, Honey's growling did much to convince such men that she was not quite so tempting after all.

Brenna could not fathom women actually taking them up on their offers. She found such men, so eager to be with any stranger, repulsive. Brenna frowned at the memory of the face of the stranger who pulled her cart from the mud. She was irritated at her thoughts, the same unwelcome thoughts that had occurred to her several times today. She was determined to shut her mind to the encounter with him, yet, his mocking expression and broad grin came filtering back anyway. *There's no time for such nonsense!* Brenna stuffed her tangled hair into the floppy hat and made her way past Pall Mall Square. She hoped she looked the part of a lad in his early teens in baggy clothes with a dirt-smudged face. Not having slept the night before, she was exhausted when she finally came to an alley behind a row of waterfront taverns. Through the night air came laughter, slurred voices, and the banging of someone playing the piano. The smell of stale brew mixed with the sea air gave a foul odor to the hearty celebrations. Despite her fatigue, Brenna quickened her pace, uneasy at the prospect of encountering any drunken seamen.

A short time later, Brenna was relieved to see the large ship she had sold her goods to earlier in the day. With a tightening throat, she kneeled down and whispered some of the most difficult words of her life, so much so that she contemplated not leaving. "Well, girl, here you are, back where you started." Brenna stroked her dog's head. "If there were any other way, I'd do it…you know I would. But I can't stay here." Brenna was crying so hard that she could barely see the dog. "I can't…stay…and you can't go. I can't keep you hidden…there's…there's just no way…and the food and water…I don't know if there will be enough for me to survive, let alone both of us…and if we're caught…" Brenna swallowed hard. "You've got a better chance of surviving here than on any ship." She realized as she said the words the truth of them for her as well.

Honey's soft brown eyes gazed up at her so intently that Brenna wondered whether the dog actually understood her words. "And, girl, you can't go back to the cottage. Harley always hated you and I won't be there to protect you." Brenna wrapped her arms tightly around the dog's neck and forced out the words, "You have to stay here." Brenna rested her head against Honey's and whispered, "I love you. If there is ever a way, I will find my way back to you, I promise. Mother always told me the Lord will save that which is lost." Brenna laughed through her tears. "And I don't know if this saying applies to dogs, but I have to believe that it does. I pray you will not stay lost for long. Please, please stay safe. You've been the best friend I've ever known."

Unable to hold back her sobs, Brenna forced herself to walk away. She choked out the words she hated to say, "Stay, girl, stay." She did not need to look back; she knew Honey would obey and not follow. Brenna could not bear the thought of how long the dog would remain there waiting for her master to return.

Ten minutes later, with her heart aching for her friend, Brenna neared the dock she sought. As each step drew her closer, her heart quickened, and her stomach tightened. She knew what she was doing was unlawful and if she were caught the punishment would be severe. Imprisonment or even death was possible.

So as not to be spotted by the ship's gangplank guards, Brenna crouched low behind a bush. She knew the two men were posted not only to guard against possible stowaways and to protect its now-loaded hulls of cargo from thieves but also to insure that none of the crew left the ship for one last night or two on the town. When it was time to cast off, many first-time captains had costly delays; their crews scattered from gambling houses to stockades. Any captain worth his salt knew it was wise to keep his men aboard a day or two before they set sail. *The captain of this ship is obviously no fool. If only I had a way to distract his men and get on that plank.*

Half an hour later, Brenna was still scheming a diversion when an opportunity presented itself. A woman in a ruffled red velvet dress, cut so low Brenna thought her large breasts might burst free, staggered toward the ship. Fully intent upon boarding, she was abruptly met by the two guards.

"Halt," commanded the larger of the two, "no one is permitted to board this ship without the consent of the captain."

"Ahh," slurred the woman, "well, that's exactly where I was heading. Ye see," she said hiccupping, "I was coming by to give yer captain a little going away present, if ye knows what I mean." The woman winked.

The men looked skeptically at each other and then at the scantily clad woman. The smaller of the guards said quietly, "I can't see the captain takin' a fancy to her. But," he said as if he were uncomfortable with the decision, "maybe we ought to let her on. After all, we're going to be a long time at sea and the captain might enjoy…"

The larger man interrupted in a voice louder than was necessary, as if convincing himself, "The captain ordered that no one be permitted aboard. Now get yerself gone, woman!"

"But ye don't understand, I ain't just no one. I'm his girl!" And with that the brunette lunged toward the plank. Four arms stopped her, but she was not easily denied.

"Take yer bloody hands off me!" the woman yelled as the men dragged her away amid abusive protests and flailing arms and legs.

Brenna was quick to seize her opportunity. She dashed from behind the bush toward the plank and onto the ship's lantern-lit deck. After years of helping to load her produce aboard ships, Brenna knew exactly what to do and where to go. She found the hatch and opened it. Then, with the agility of a cat, she quickly scurried down the steep companionway steps to the vessel's second level. Rounding a tight corner, she found the next set of steps. She repeated the process, descending through the ship's deep hull, each level darker than the one before. With each turn, she was relieved she did not see evidence of the quarters of either a carpenter or blacksmith who often occupied such lower levels. Uncertain where she was, Brenna shuffled into a small compartment where a rough line brushed against her ankle. She guessed she was in the room where the spare ropes and sails were stored. She wished she had her lantern for she could see nothing. Fumbling, she piled several sails under her for a soft pallet.

She listened for any near voices and tried to still her fears. *What have I done? What am I going to do now?*

Through the blackness she strained to see, but the darkness was complete. She realized the irony of how the black void surrounding her mirrored how she felt about her future—she had no idea, no inkling, no glimmer of what lay ahead. Only darkness. Brenna pressed her body against the uneven pallet and forced back the threatening tears. Two hours later, she found the sleep she had sought so long.

Chapter Four

A sliver of light seeping through a crack far above proved vastly inadequate. Despite her grogginess, Brenna sat up quickly. Like a child lost in a crowd, wide-eyed and bewildered, she scanned the blackness and tried to remember where she was. The queasiness within told her she was not on solid ground.

Sailing, Brenna realized, rolling from side to side. As the disorientation ebbed, the horrible events of the previous day filtered back. Everything she had believed about her life was far from reality. Helen was not her natural mother, Harley was not her father, the island no longer her home. And her birth parents, instead of loving her, had sold her.

As the moments passed and the ship continued its rhythmic swaying, Brenna wished she could see the island. She wondered if it was still in view, growing smaller on the horizon, as the ships she used to watch sail away. She had spent hours pretending she was aboard those ships. Today, she felt no excitement for the dream. This was no childhood fantasy. She was leaving the only home she had ever known. Although St. Christopher held many painful memories for her, she forced herself to focus on the happy times too. She recalled the hours she passed on the beach as a child playing on its smooth sand, chasing the waves that swept in and out with the current. She remembered being very young and playfully dashing through the narrow, winding footpaths of the forest as fast as she could run. Exhausted, she would collapse on the jungle floor, filling the leafy canopies above with laughter. When her panting eased, she would lie still, sheltered by the lush ceiling overhead. Closing her eyes, she would listen through the quiet to the rustling of the towering trees far above for the call of some distant bird. If she waited long enough, she would hear the snap of bamboo from an aged stalk that had finally lost the battle of time.

Later, she would venture to her favorite place. She was seven when she first made the discovery deep within the forest. She had followed the sounds of rushing water and come upon a small stream. Wondering about its origins, she fought her way through dense vines and over a series of large boulders. Brenna tracked the thundering sound when suddenly the forest opened before her to reveal the most surprising and stunning sight she had ever beheld. She was surrounded by a circular veil of water cascading across the towering cliffs high above and at her feet, a pristine mountain pool. The brilliant aqua-colored water shimmered spectacularly with the hues of the wild orchids and fanning ferns that covered the surrounding rocks. Brenna found peace here. For the next five years she came often and nestled on its warm sand beach and swam in its cool water. To her knowledge, she was the only one who knew of the hidden pool and she told no one about it.

Brenna shivered at the dampness of the hold and wished Honey was here. Tears filled her eyes thinking about her. She smiled, despite her sadness, and remembered the first time she had seen the pup ten months earlier. She had just finished selling the last of her produce when she rounded the corner into an alley. There, trying to lick the spilled contents of a broken jar of honey, was the scrawniest, dirtiest puppy Brenna had ever seen. The very tip of her tail was missing from some apparent mishap. When Brenna looked into the big black eyes of the abandoned pup, she wondered if this is how she too must look to strangers. An instant bond was formed. Brenna could not leave her newfound friend.

In the months that followed, Honey changed from a scraggly, weak puppy into a bounding, carefree dog, her coat taking on a golden shine. The dog, like herself, was left to eat a diet of mainly fruits and vegetables from the garden. A goat provided the household with milk, some of which Brenna churned to butter. Both dog and master's diets lacked meat. Occasionally, Brenna traded some of their produce for fish or poultry. With the increase in Harley's drinking and his appetite often nonexistent, he forbade her from trading for the more expensive items, and the meat hooks in their smoke hut hung empty more often than not. Most of the time, she went to bed after only eating fruit, a raw vegetable, and a slice of bread or cheese.

Harley required Brenna to keep a detailed log of all her produce sales and tracked it against what returned with her each day. Each evening, he would take every coin the sales produced. She had kept the tips secret. Brenna had no idea how he recently discovered that she had been earning them.

While Brenna sold her produce at the busy market, she was followed closely by her ever-present, short-tailed, golden dog with big white paws. Her last day on the island had been an exception.

Honey had earned a reputation among the seamen. Not only was she protective of her owner but she was also known for her unusual ability to sit up, as a small dog will do to beg. But Honey was no small dog, and scarcely a passerby failed to make at least one amusing comment on the hound's antics.

Brenna thought back to before Helen died, before she worked the produce fields, when she had the time to roam freely throughout the island. Looking back, she realized she had acquired a great deal of knowledge during those early adventures. She learned the art of buying and selling through bartering with many of the local sailors for their daily catch. On the island's shore were the Black Rocks, remnants of Mt. Misery's violent eruptions. It was here where she loved to climb and explore.

From the vivid stories of the island's volatile past she learned history. There was Bloody Point, where over a hundred and fifty years earlier, the British and French fought a vicious battle against the Carib Indians for possession of the island. Over two thousand Indians were killed, and she was told that the island's rivers ran red with their blood. The battle for control of the island changed when the British and French broke their alliance in fighting the Indians and became bitter enemies with one another. For a time, long before she was born, the

French controlled the northwest and the southeast ends of the small island, while the English held the center. Brenna could not envision how the people managed under such split alliances.

The massive British-built Brimstone Hill Fortress still stood—evidence of the continuing struggle between the French and British. As a child, Brenna feared the dominating structure sitting atop a huge cliff. It smelled of sulfur and scores of black-iron cannons aimed outward. When she was thirteen, the cannons were no longer silent. Thousands of French troops rallied to take the fortress. Badly out-manned and low on ammunition, the British were forced to surrender. The island was soon abuzz with news of the British loss. Like so many of the islanders, Brenna rushed to the scene and watched in amazement as the French soldiers respectfully stood at attention while the English soldiers marched proudly out of their fort and down the hill. Brenna peered cautiously from behind a tree and was dismayed by the site of one curly, redheaded British soldier who moved past her. He held his shoulders high and his back straight, he stepped with determination; yet, upon closer inspection she saw that his face was stained with tears. This forbidding soldier had been crying! He seemed so young and vulnerable at that moment. Brenna could still remember the soldier's face as clearly as if he were before her now.

The French victory at the fort was short-lived. The ceremony was repeated the next year when the British took back the fort. Brenna wondered if the redheaded soldier ever returned. For as long as she could remember, there had been a great tension between the French and British colonists, which occasionally flared at the docks. Harley had always hated the French, but he was too self-absorbed in his drinking to participate in the British struggles against them, and Brenna's isolated life did much to insulate her from the severest turmoil.

Next to exploring her hidden pool, her favorite times were when she made the exhilarating treks to the peak of Mt. Misery. It was always there, while the wind blew through her hair and she looked at the water far below, that Brenna felt the same feeling…an overwhelming loneliness and a yearning to find what lay beyond the blue water forest.

And now, God willing, I will know, thought Brenna as she rolled over on her pallet. Brenna wondered if her family life had been different, would she have been content to live her life there. But, as it was, although she had grown up on its shores, she never felt as though she fully belonged. The sense was inexplicable to her even now.

And am I to wander like those sailors who sail all their lives, not for the sake of adventure and profit, but rather to find the one place they can call home? Is this to be my fate also? The thought crossed her mind that if this were to be her future, it would be a loss to no one but her. Brenna felt a deep ache knowing if she were to die on this journey, no person in the world would know or care. For Brenna, this was the ultimate loneliness.

She opened her eyes and strained to see. Sighing softly, her thoughts moved to the uncertainty she faced, but unlike last night when fatigue overcame her, she was not afraid. She reasoned that what was ahead could not possibly be as bad as what she was leaving behind. Yesterday, her life had little meaning. One day was like every other, and the monotony was stifling, especially to a young woman of nineteen. She was certain of only one thing: today would not be like any other. Today she was plotting a new course.

The vessel lurched and the movement brought Brenna's thoughts back to the ship. *Where is she headed?* Brenna recalled the colors she displayed, one star circled by twelve others. *She's American. But what's her destination now? Is it to the Colonies to sell the goods of the West Indies, or is she heading southward briefly before crossing over and catching the northeast trade winds and sailing to one of the many ports in Europe?* The thought of spending months amidst this cold darkness sickened her and she prayed they were headed for a much nearer American port. Brenna hoped it was America for other reasons as well. She had heard sailors' tales of the great American wilderness that demanded the best in a person. To Brenna, America represented freedom, something she had not known with Harley.

Brenna sat upright. *Whatever the destination, my opinion is irrelevant for I cannot affect the ship's course. My only choice is to face each day, each obstacle, as best I can.*

Brenna knew the most pressing problem she faced was supplies, for regardless of the ship's course, it was bound to be a long time before she would arrive at any port. The food and water she brought with her would last no more than a few days, and the darkness of the hull would make it difficult to find the supplies she needed. Knowing fresh food would be kept in the base level of the hull where it is the coolest, Brenna's first concern was to find where the water casks were stored and some place she would be able to relieve herself. She decided to begin her search for water immediately and slowly pushed herself off the floor. The uneasiness in her stomach quickly forced her back down. She removed a piece of stale bread from the sling, chewed it slowly, hoping to calm her stomach. When she was finished, she again drifted quietly off to sleep.

A bright light and voices woke her. They were not muffled but loud, and they were coming closer.

"Aye," came a husky voice, "that one should do fer now. Here, give me a hand. This cask may be small, but she's bloody heavier than the ship's anchor!"

Brenna's eyes were wide and her body motionless as three men walked past the opening to her compartment. She desperately hoped they were not retrieving any ropes and sails. With the lantern lit and the hatch open, the hold was considerably lighter. Brenna pressed hard against the floor. Moments later, grunting and panting, the men passed the compartment opening. It was not until several seconds after darkness resumed that Brenna let out the breath she did not realize she had been holding. From the man's complaint of the heaviness of the cask she hoped it might have been filled with water. She was pleased with her luck when she entered the compartment next to the rope and sail room and felt the broken tar seal of a water barrel already opened. Extending her arms, she searched the room and found it stacked high with such casks. She removed a small tin cup from her sling, dipped it in the cool water, and drank greedily. Satisfied at knowing the location of the water, she decided to search for a safer hiding place nearer to the fresh food supplies. Knowing the compartment would be chilly, she returned to the rope room and reached to take one of the ship's extra sails with her for bedding. She touched the rough cloth against her cheek and considered the risk. The loss of such an item would be too easily missed and a subsequent search likely. She sighed softly, left the sail behind, and continued her descent to the next and lowest level.

Moments later, a smile spread across her face as she entered the hold where she smelled the familiar aroma of vegetables. Brenna knew this lowest hold was probably the safest for her hiding, and she was thankful she would only have to climb to the next level to retrieve water. Her smile vanished when she gouged her shin against something sharp. She felt warm, moist blood trickling down her leg. When she had recovered enough to move forward, she curled her toes to keep from breaking them and extended her hands for protection. She stopped when she touched a stack of crates. Next to it was another, then another, and then another. The containers varied in size and form. Each stack was supported by an array of ropes. Everywhere she turned, there was yet another rope crossing her path, so many that Brenna began to feel like a moth caught in a spider web with nowhere to escape. She had seen such ropes often when in the lighted holds but had never given them any thought. They now seemed to create an unending web of trouble. When she finally made her way to the ship's slanted side, Brenna let out a cry as she tripped on a rope tie and slammed her head against the side of a crate. Reeling with pain and frustration, she kicked the crate. Its hollow sound puzzled her. Her anger dissipated as her curiosity grew to know the contents of the tall wooden box bolted to the side of the ship's wall. Finding a latch, she opened the crate's door and was amazed to discover a wooden privy opening to a holding box.

Why on earth is there a privy down here when most sailors simply use the heads in the bowsprits? Brenna swept her hand through the mass of spider webs crisscrossing the structure. She had heard that an occasional ship provided such privies in the transport of military soldiers, but she believed them rare. Whatever the reason, Brenna was immensely grateful for its presence, for until now, she feared she would merely have to find a spot in a corner.

After searching for a secure place to lie down and have the best chance to remain hidden, Brenna found a nook in the furthest corner of the hold surrounded by two large oblong crates. As she curled up on the hard keel planks, she realized this lowest hold, submerged deep within the water, was far colder than she had anticipated. She was thankful she had her blanket to cover her, but she wished she had another to cushion the wooden floor. In her rush to leave last night, such a thought never crossed her mind. She wished desperately for a little straw with which to make a pallet. If she could locate the livestock aboard, she might be in luck. However, she knew if there were any sheep, goats, and poultry aboard, they were apt to be housed on the poop deck, inaccessible to her.

What troubled her most about staying in the hold was the thought of mice and rats. Brenna shivered at the mere thought that some might be near. She had heard horror stories of stowaways dragged from hulls with their fingers and toes missing, the work of hungry rodents. Brenna hastily moved a discarded rail pin she had found earlier closer to her side. She fervently hoped she would never have to use the makeshift club. Three hours later, Brenna shrieked and jumped to her feet as she felt the brush of animal fur against her arm. She clenched the pin high and was ready to strike the varmint when she realized her error. Laughing with relief, she slid back to the floor and stroked the curious feline. Brenna wondered why more captains did not have the good sense to use cats in the holds, minimizing rodent destruction to their supplies. *Whoever you are, Captain, I'm forever in your debt!* Brenna felt again for the cat, but it was gone as deftly as it had come.

When she woke, Brenna began again the task of bumping her way through the dark maze. Four hours later, she was bruised, cut, and beyond frustrated with her inability to find her way through the darkness, yet she had one bit of luck. She had found two discarded burlap bags that she used as a pallet. Although irritating to her skin and nearly flat, they were slightly better than the hard, cold floor, and they enabled her to use her small blanket as a covering. She was angry at herself for not having brought her two other dresses for warmth. After a few bites of her hard cheese, she stood and continued trying to learn her way around the hold.

While it was nearly impossible to determine the time, Brenna estimated that several days must have passed before she was able to move without constant fear of injury. She smiled when she discovered some of her own vegetables that she'd sold to the ship's cargo man. The carrots, onions, turnips, and celery were a welcome treat, yet despite an aggressive search, she was unable to locate any of the oranges, limes, pineapples, and coconuts she and other peddlers had sold to the ship. Fresh or pickled, she simply could find no hint of any fruits. Brenna pursed her lips in disappointment. Disappointing too was the lack of meat or fish to be found. She searched diligently for any trace of salted or smoked meats, but this, too, proved unsuccessful. With great reluctance, Brenna realized the stores of meat, fruits, and cheese must be kept in another of the ship's holds. Even hard tack proved elusive, and yet, she knew it must be aboard since she had never heard of a ship underway without a large stock of such biscuits.

In addition to the problem of enough varied food, Brenna quickly discovered another—the water. With the vegetables, she was careful to take only a small portion from several different sacks and barrels. She felt certain they would not be readily missed. The water though was different, for the diminishing level in the barrel that the crew kept unsealed for their use when in the hold could not be disguised. She wished she could take a little from each barrel, but she did not have this advantage. Brenna knew once the seal of a cask was broken, its water had to be used before another was opened or the water would foul. So she waited every few days for the crew to tap a cask, taking as little as possible. She prayed that the slowly disappearing water would go unnoticed. Frequently, as Brenna dipped her cup into the deep barrel of cool water, she craved taking more to use to scrub away the grime on her body that had accumulated. But she was fearful to not take any more than was absolutely necessary. Reluctantly, she resolved that she would be filthy for the duration of the voyage.

She quickly discovered that even more than the provisions, endless time was her biggest enemy. Periodically, she was able to hear the ringing of the ship's bell signaling a change in the watch, but in the continual darkness it was impossible to know whether the ringing meant it was dawn or dusk. A few times, she faintly heard a whistle blow and knew it must be the boatswain awakening the crew, but she could not hear it frequently enough to determine the hour. Day and night merged, and Brenna began to feel as though she were wandering aimlessly through a fog with no beginning or end. Occasionally, crewmen entered her hold to carry away another crate or cask, yet these sporadic visits were not consistent enough to gauge the time. During these intrusions, Brenna pressed her body as hard as she could against her meager pallet, willing herself to remain unseen.

Although she had no way of knowing the number of days they had been at sea, Brenna sensed that it had to be over a fortnight when she could no longer stand the confinement. The uneasy tension welled to the point that she feared she was losing her sanity. Suddenly, the mildew-laden air seemed thicker, her pallet harder, and the hold smaller. She started to sweat and could not breathe. *I have to get out,* she gasped, gulping hard and trying not to vomit, *if only for a moment. I have to have fresh air.* Recklessly, Brenna clamored through the maze, scrambled up the stairs, and ducked into the rope and sail room where she had spent her first night aboard. She waited until no light filtered through the cracks overhead. Silently, she moved up the levels of the narrow companionway steps and stopped when she reached the closed hatch. Pacing footsteps on the deck above quickly diminished her enthusiasm. Realizing the danger of such actions, Brenna scowled at her foolishness and lack of control. Shakily, she retreated. Over the next few days, whenever she felt the pressure building to go topside, she forced herself to breathe slowly and deeply. She closed her eyes and envisioned that she was back at her hidden mountain pool. Although it took measured concentration, it usually worked. On the occasions when it did not, she found herself dashing toward the privy, vomiting violently.

Every time Brenna awoke, she felt as though she was locked away in a forsaken prison. She began to empathize with the blind and the deaf of the world, for it was as if she were both. With the extreme darkness, her eyes were only slightly able to adjust. She memorized the number of steps it took her to get from one crate or rope to another and learned when she should change direction.

The silence was the worst of her torments. Day after day, she heard nothing but the creaking and sloshing of the vessel as it eased its way through what appeared to be calm waters. Never before had she realized how much daily human contact meant to her. Even though her life on the island had been isolated, until now, she never understood how the everyday pleasantries, the "good mornings" and smiles from strangers walking past on the street, had sustained her. She pledged she would never forget or take them for granted again. Brenna was greatly disheartened that the cat proved so elusive and had appeared only twice. She suspected he must have been a favorite of the crew as well and thus his time was well occupied.

Hour after hour, Brenna listened to the slap of the waves against the ship and was mesmerized by the creaks and moans of the well-seasoned timber. She anticipated each list of the vessel as it pressed through the water. She strained to hear any excited shouts from the crew indicating their voyage was nearing its end. To her profound disappointment, she heard none.

During these long hours, she thought often of Helen. She had been a loving mother who did everything in her power to ensure her daughter's happiness, yet she was not happy in her marriage. From the time she was a young girl, Brenna had known there was something very wrong between Helen and Harley. To this day, Brenna could not understand how her mother ever married such a man.

Brenna, alone in the cold dark hold of a sailing ship, had no way of knowing that nearly twenty years earlier, Helen had fought her own battle for survival.

St. Christopher, 1769

Helen stared at the back of her sleeping husband and trembled. *How much longer can I hide this from him?*

Even in his sleep, Harley terrified her, for Harley was not a forgiving man. He had always resented any man who could better him, and Helen knew the knowledge of another man impregnating his wife would be his ultimate humiliation. Seeing all too often where his wrath combined with spirits could lead, Helen prayed she would be safely off the island before he ever guessed the truth. As she had done every night for the past several months, Helen arose from the straw berth and pulled the belt of her cotton nightdress loosely around her waist. She stepped onto the wooden porch of their small hut overlooking the sea. The air was heavy with the smell of salt as Helen stared at the eastern horizon where she had last seen her beloved Peter sail.

Oh, Peter, where are you?

She listened to the sound of the lonely waves rolling in at high tide and wondered if Peter was awake and thinking of her. She willed her thoughts across the waves. *Please come home, Peter, please. I'm going to have your baby.* Helen closed her eyes. She could see Peter as if he were standing before her now. His regiment was shipping out for what he said would be an eight-week duty. His blue eyes were so soft and gentle. He cupped her chin in his hand and kissed her, "You're the sweetest woman I've ever known, Hélène, and as I stand before God, when I return I'm taking you away with me. You'll not live another day with that brute!"

As her vision fixed upon the black waters, Helen knew Peter had every intention of fulfilling his promise, yet she had waited nervously as the eight-week absence became fifteen. "I know you love me, Peter," she whispered, "Please come home. I need you." Reluctantly, Helen recalled that she once had believed Harley when he too told her he loved her.

Harley came into Helen's life suddenly. When she first met him, he had just arrived from London and to a lonely woman of twenty-nine who had never left the island where she was born and was fearful she would never marry, he represented excitement and adventure. He came to St. Christopher, he told her, as a hired foreman to a large tobacco plantation. He seemed to be a good man. She cared nothing of his promises of a life of ease; she just wanted someone to love and someone who would reciprocate that love. Two months after his arrival on the island, Helen became his wife.

Hours later, after their wedding ceremony, the bride anxiously waited for her bridegroom to join her. Helen's grand dreams of love and marriage were shattered when her husband appeared and she saw him for what he truly was. The Harley before her was not the gallant man she believed but rather a staggering drunk who immediately berated her with a series of insults. When he realized she was crying, he struck her fiercely. Terrified of what he would do once in her bed, Helen was greatly relieved when he never approached her. Later, when he had consumed even more port, he admitted his impotence. She soon realized the man she married was not only a drunk but a liar. There was no position as foreman; he had traveled to this island only to avoid an English debtor's prison. Helen berated herself for foolishly ignoring her doubts. She soon understood his reason for marrying her—to gain access to the small dowry her parents had set aside before they died for her betrothal.

In the years that followed, Helen's life was a nightmare. On several occasions, after deciding she could no longer endure her life, she decided to flee. But her fears always stopped her. Where would she go? What would become of her? Would God punish her for breaking her vows?

Helen dealt with her unhappiness by keeping to herself—until she met Peter. She would never forget the moment he entered her life; it began as she fed the gulls.

A light offshore breeze danced with the hem of Helen's gray muslin skirt billowing toward the sea. She raised her arm and tossed a handful of small breadcrumbs into a flock of sea gulls. Battling one another, the birds tumbled amid the surf and flew away greedily with the soggy morsels.

"They're actually quite aggressive, n'est-ce pas?" came the flowing words over her shoulder, heavily laced with a French accent.

"Aye, but they're also free, bound to no one or no place," replied Helen, drawn to the kind voice.

The handsome sailor looked into her big brown eyes and said softly, "Oui. But having no restraints also has its price."

Helen sensed in him a goodness she had rarely seen. The two remained silent, locked in their private regard for one another.

"What's your name?" he asked finally, breaking the spell.

"Helen."

"Ah, Hélène. The name of my mother's sister."

"And you?"

"Peter."

"Where are you from, Peter?"

"Paris. Montfermeil, actually. A small village just outside Paris."

"And now?"

"On leave from Fort-de-France on Martinique. Have you been there?"

Helen shook her head.

"Never? Pour quoi? The island is so close. Is it the tensions between the British and the French?"

Helen shrugged, "No. I've never left St. Christopher." Seeing his surprised expression, she turned toward the sea and explained, "There has never been anywhere else for me to go."

A look of sadness touched his face but vanished quickly as he said brightly, "I've brought wine and cheese. Would you care to join me?"

"Nay, I'd best not."

"S'il vous plait, for I've dined alone every day this week."

Excitement swept through Helen as she felt for the first time in years a spark in her lifeless existence. Timidly, she accepted his offer.

In the weeks that followed, Helen made arrangements to be with Peter as often as she dared. Harley, as usual, was preoccupied with himself and unaware she was spending more time in the village. Initially, Helen felt no guilt about her meetings with Peter, for everyone, she rationalized, needed companionship. But it was not long before Helen was forced to admit that she had fallen in love. Peter was everything Harley was not. He was giving, caring, honest, and he loved her.

Seven weeks after they first met, Helen surrendered the battle that had waged within. On a secluded beach with the waves rolling in at their feet she became one with him. The woman, who had been married for three years and never given herself to a man, was finally shown what it was to share such love.

The following morning, Peter sailed for Martinique to rejoin his crew. Vowing to return, he reluctantly said goodbye. He never knew he left her with child.

Helen pulled the robe tighter over her shoulders. As the night breeze flowed across her face, she wished she could feel the movement of the child.

A path of tears spilled down Helen's cheek. She thought of the shame her father, a man of the cloth, would have felt at her adultery and of her plans to abandon her legal spouse. Helen, who had tried all her life to please her father, could not bear the thought of his disappointment. *I never meant to break my vows, Father! What I did was wrong! I should have asked for an annulment long ago, but if I had done so, he would have killed me! Please,* she pleaded to her father, long since dead, *you must know that if I stay with him, I'll perish! Please, please, Father, understand that Peter is my only hope for happiness!*

Later, as the sun's light broke through the overcast sky, Helen wiped away a light film of dust from her small looking glass. She frowned at her swollen lids and realized that for the health of Peter's baby, she must force herself to sleep soon. *But how, when I'm afraid of sleeping?* Helen, who was known for talking in her sleep, lived in constant fear she might cry out Peter's name and give away her secret, bringing forth Harley's wrath. Each night, she battled against sleep until the early hours of dawn when, exhausted, she gave up the struggle.

Staring at her round face and dark brown eyes, she wondered, *Oh Peter, is it me you see when you close your eyes? Is it me you yearn to pull into your arms at night? Is it…*

"Why are these platters still soiled wench?" demanded Harley, stomping into the kitchen. Then, not waiting for her reply, he continued, "I've been gone over an…what…and ya ain't even dressed!"

"I know. I…I…was just a bit tired."

"Tired? I'm the one that's gone all the way to town 'n back and you're tired!"

"Harley, please," said Helen, wishing he had stayed away all day, "just let me get dressed and I'll be getting about my duties."

"'Tis 'bout time!" he barked, adjusting his trousers.

She glanced at her husband and wondered how she could ever have married him. Sitting at the kitchen table, removing his foul stockings, Harley was dressed in the same oversized brown cotton shirt and trousers he wore every day. Helen had long since given up trying to persuade him to wear any of the tailored garments she had sewn. Nor had she had any more success at convincing him to groom himself. His nails were broken and dirty, his hair matted, and because he was unable to grow a full beard, his face was a gritty patchwork of uneven gray stubble. Helen could not help comparing Harley to Peter. She loved the touch of Peter's smooth skin just after he put it to the razor's blade and the lemon scent of his sandy-brown hair. She smiled as she recalled the life bubbling in his light blue eyes and the clarity with which he viewed the world.

Harley grimaced as he examined his large toe, its nail red and moist with infection. She paid little attention as he swore at his ailment, but she stiffened at his offhanded remark, "The French lost another one. Don't know why it is they…"

"Another what?" interrupted Helen, her chest instantly tightening.

"A ship, of course."

"Which one?" Helen barely recognized her own strained voice.

"Don' know. Heard t'was posted yesterday. Didn't bother to look, can't read them bloody French names any…"

Helen did not hear any more as she raced from the cottage and down the trail toward the village dock. She did not stop until she reached the platform where she pushed through a small gathering of citizens reading the notice of the "missing and presumed dead." Without her magnifying glass to aid her poor vision, Helen was unable to read the notice. She clasped the arm of the man next to her and gasped, "Peter…Peter Loegél. Is he…is he there?"

"Ah, let's see. Peter Loegél, yeah. Aye, sorry mam. He's third on the list." Helen heard no more and fell to the dirty wooden planks.

Her eyes slowly opened. A large black woman towered over her. When her vision cleared, Helen recognized Anna, a well-known slave in the market.

Anna patted her gently on the wrist and said, "Don't ye fret, Mrs. Findlay. Yer husband's been summoned."

Harley walked slowly behind the lad who had rushed into his cottage moments earlier. He was unable to fathom a reason for Helen's faint or for her peculiar behavior of running away an hour earlier in her sleeping gown. He stepped through the open portal of the dockside hovel and stared at her ashen face.

"I'm pregnant," she murmured. She hoped he would vent his fury by taking her life.

Darkening rage flooded his neck and engulfed his face. "You whore! I should've known!" He raised his hand to strike, but froze as another emotion consumed him. "Who is he? I'm gonna kill the…"

"You've got your revenge," said Helen flatly, "he's dead."

The sun's descending light cast a hazy glow through the dirty window of the slave's shack. Helen lay motionless on the strawless berth. Peter stood before her in a small boat, drifting toward open sea. Seeing his lips move but unable to understand what he was saying, Helen cried out helplessly, "Wait! Wait! I can't hear you! Please! You can't leave me again! Take me with you!" He faded as his words reverberated through the shell of her body, "Take care of my baby, Hélène! Take care of our baby!"

Jarred, Helen sprang from the berth, her heart pounding and her body covered in sweat. She slowly sank down again. Uncertain whether what she had just experienced was a vision of Peter or merely a dream of a fatigued mind, she realized it did not matter. The child, Peter's child, was her sole responsibility now. "I will not fail you, Peter," she whispered, hugging her abdomen, her last physical tie to Peter, "As the Lord is my witness, I will not fail you!"

Harley did not mention the incident or the baby again. She wanted desperately to believe his claims of having given up drinking and hoped he had finally realized that her marriage certificate did not bind her to him regardless of his actions.

Three weeks after learning of her treachery, Harley watched his wife sleep. He pounded his fist repeatedly in the cradle of his empty hand. With every fiber of his being, he loathed her for what she had done, yet there was one he hated even more, the man who had made a fool of him by impregnating her. He yearned to clench his hands around his neck and squeeze the life from him. *But, no!* He was denied even this, as death had already found the French dog. Harley hoped the man had suffered as he died. With great effort, he hid his wrath in front of Helen. He knew if she were aware of his wrath, she would flee and his revenge would remain unfulfilled. If he could not punish the man, he vowed he would make the man's child pay. As the weeks became months, he masked well his seething hatred for the child.

Helen awoke at dawn with a deep ache in her back and knew it was time. She asked Harley to bring the midwife. He told her he would summon her as soon she was showing signs of being closer. Throughout the day the pain in her back became unbearable and she was certain something was terribly wrong. She pleaded with Harley to go immediately. Instead of running out the door as Helen had fully imagined he would do, she watched in horror when he pulled the ale jug from under his chair, drank from it slowly, and spat, "You got yerself into this. You can get yerself out, alone!" And with that, he left the cottage.

When he returned the next day, he fully expected to see the wench nursing the bastard's baby. The sight that greeted his bloodshot eyes as he stepped inside caused him to bolt, retching. He would never forget the sight or the smell. It was the stench of death.

In time, Helen's body recovered, but her mind did not. She ate little, slept less, and spoke to no one. From before light to after dark, she sat on a large boulder overlooking the ocean. To her, the sea was the beginning and the ending of life, for her life revolved around it; from the food she ate to the people who came and went with it. Week after week, Helen stayed on the beach, rocking back and forth in monotone prayer, begging for forgiveness and for life to be given back to her child.

So it was on a September dawn in 1769, Helen sat alone on the rocks just above the cliffs. Distantly, she heard a faint, undistinguishable sound. Standing slowly, she squinted against the rising sun. Several yards off shore was a small boat. Distracted and confused, Helen heard the sound again, a cry. It sounded like a baby.

A baby? A baby? In the boa…

"My baby!" Helen shrieked and fell to her knees. "Thank you! Thank you, blessed God! Thank…" Then with a jolt, she remembered the reef.

"No!" she screamed, and scrambled down the steep cliff, terrified she would be unable to reach the boat before it crashed against the rocks. "I won't lose you again!" She plunged headlong into the water, furiously struggling against the powerful waves. Her drenched cotton dress wrapped around her legs and pulled her backwards. Undeterred, she fought her way forward. Minutes later, an exhausted Helen reached the craft. She hoisted herself up against its side. Her labored breathing stopped when she looked into the boat. Lying just as Weston had left her was Brenna. Helen felt the boat's rope brush against her side. She pulled it hard until she was able to get to standing depth. Struggling to find her balance, she fought to steady the boat as it moved toward the fierce rocks. Helen scooped up the child, leaving behind a yellow blanket, a blanket that had helped to protect the infant. She paid no heed to the rising surf when it caught the tiny boat and carried it toward the massive rocks. She did not hear the wood shattering as the craft broke apart.

Helen cradled the baby and walked toward her cabin, her gentle movements clearly displaying the love she already felt for the child. She stepped as if she carried a delicate piece of coral. She kissed the baby tenderly upon her forehead and carefully opened the door of the shack. "He's forgiven me! He's forgiven me!"

Harley did not need to ask what she held in her arms; he could plainly see the child.

"Where?" he asked dumbfounded.

"The sea. He's given my baby back!"

The baby began to wail. Helen slipped a damp muslin gown from the chilled body. Helen was not surprised to see that the child was a girl, for she was certain this was her baby girl brought back from Heaven. Helen gasped when she saw the bracelet around the tiny wrist. Helen grabbed her magnifying glass. Giant tears swelled in her eyes as she read the inside inscription, "To our beloved miracle, Brenna. Luke 19:10."

"Brenna," she whispered. "*He* named her Brenna."

Brenna rolled from her side to her back, then to her side again. She wished there were some way to get comfortable. It simply was not possible.

Why did you do it, Mother? Why did you ever marry a man such as Harley? You were the most generous person I've ever known. How could you have settled for so much less in a mate? You deserved more than a spouse who barely took the time to look in on his dying wife.

"Ma'ma, please." pleaded twelve-year-old Brenna to her mother as she had every day for over a week, "Please, please wake up! I'm frightened and I don't know what to do!" Suddenly, Helen's eyes fluttered open and in a shallow, thin voice said, "Remember, Brenna. God is with you, even if you can't feel him. *He* saved you before. *He'll* do it again." As quickly as her eyes had opened, they closed and never reopened.

The next day, after forcing the gravediggers to straighten the casket, it had been the sound of dirt and sand hitting the coffin that she could not bear. Brenna had pressed her hands over her ears and ran as fast as she could away from the valley to her hidden cove where she fell to the earth, choking in anguish. She remained there for two nights alone, not eating or drinking. Finally, recalling her mother's words that she wanted Brenna to be happy no matter what the future held, Brenna wearily left her secret hideaway. She never returned. Without Helen, she knew there would be no peace, and without peace, there would be no happiness.

Weak and exhausted, young Brenna staggered back to her cottage. Once inside, she reached into her smock's pocket and withdrew its contents. Brenna stared blankly, momentarily unable to comprehend what it was—the dirt and sand that had fallen on her as she tried to straighten the coffin. She opened her fingers, the soil spraying onto the floor.

When she entered her mother's room, she had no tears left to cry. Her hands and legs trembled as she gathered Helen's belongings: three dresses, one pair of shoes, wire spectacles, a magnifying glass, and a worn leather Bible. Brenna sat on her bed and tenderly stroked the Bible. A poem, written in Helen's hand and dated four days before she lost consciousness, was tucked between its pages. It was dedicated to Peter.

"CITY ON THE HILL"

There is a city, a peaceful city,
where naught but peace and silence dwell;
What communion have the dwellers
or if any, none can tell.
There is no war for wealth or fame;
or grasping avarice or ill will;
Nor mawkish pride nor slander…in
that fair city on the hill.

I am tired of the valley, of its
struggles, toil and care;
Since my task is nigh completed,
the rest of loved ones I long to share.
Yet fluttering heart have patience,
thou shalt reach the goal, be still:
There's a green spot that awaits
thee…in that city on the hill.

Brenna read the poem silently and then whispered, "I know you've found that city." She had no idea who Peter was, but she sensed that now Helen was with him.

A book and light enough to read by would have been a welcome blessing to help pass the hours she spent in the dark hold. Brenna desperately wished she still had Helen's special poem and Bible. She still felt the horror of the night a drunken Harley had thrown them into the stove. Her fingers still bore the small scars of the burns she sustained in trying to save the precious treasures, but they had already turned to ash.

With no books to occupy her, Brenna had to rely on her mind. She wondered how the crew spent their time when not on active duty. She pictured them cleaning their weapons, swabbing the deck, napping in their hammocks, and drinking their daily ration of grog while they played backgammon and cards with the other seamen.

Once, as she dozed, Brenna dreamed she was back on St. Christopher running through the forest just like she had as a young child, pretending a wild beast was after her. But this was no child's game she played, for the entire forest was ablaze. Choking on the smoke-filled air, she ran to the beach. The clear ocean water before her turned to a red, boiling bed of lava. Frantically, she searched for an escape, but there was none. Smoke and fire were everywhere. The searing sand burned through the sole of one of her sandals. Brenna knew there was no escape, when a man appeared upon a huge steed and raced toward her across the fiery beach. With a swift swoop, he lifted her next to him and as they rode, horse and riders rose gracefully above the island inferno and into the clouds. Brenna felt the even rocking motion as they climbed higher and higher. With a start, Brenna awoke, realizing it was not the horse's gait she felt, but the motion of the ship. Although the dream faded, the face remained clear. It was the face of a man she had met only once before. Brenna did not wish to remember that meeting. *And why does this stranger appear in my dreams? Why does he haunt me this way?* She repeatedly asked herself the same question. Every night since she had seen him when her cart was stuck in the mud, he invaded her dreams. Irritated, Brenna tugged the damp blanket over her shoulders.

Brenna shivered in the darkness and pulled the threadbare cloth tighter. The chill was continuous now. *It must be summer but it's hard to believe.* In her dark, isolated world, the seasons no longer held any meaning.

As the long days mounted, even Brenna's imagination could not continue to carry her. With each day, her body began to revolt against the lack of nourishment. Vegetables and water were not enough for her already slender form. The continual ship's movement added to her misery. What had been an occasional bout of stomach discomfort turned into continual agony. Her head throbbed, her stomach cramped, and every part of her body ached. She wanted only to sleep, but even that was difficult. She now wished she could vomit in hopes of relieving some of her inward pain, if only for a moment. But her body did not give in to even this one wish. It seemed to be responding to its need to retain its meager contents. Chilled one moment and covered in sweat the next, Brenna knew she was no longer in control. She was soon vaguely aware of the vicious cycle that had begun. The more ill she became, the less strength she had for collecting and eating food. The less she ate, the sicker she became. When she did gather the strength to climb the steps and tap water, she began taking more than she needed to avoid having to make the effort again. At one point, not being able to stand the searing pain in her head, Brenna doused her blanket and wrapped it around her pounding head. Crawling back to her corner in the hold, she regretted the impulse and longed to have the blanket for warmth. Covered in feverish sweat, yet trembling violently from the cold, Brenna curled up tightly against the flattened burlap.

Time passed in a hazy, fitful sleep. Brenna woke only long enough to press her water cup against her parched lips.

Distantly, she heard the hatch close as three of the ship's crew left after completing the routine of removing one barrel in exchange for an empty one. She knew the truth. *I'm not ever going to leave this place.* As the realization dawned, she was filled with a deep despair more painful than the physical pain in her body. She agonized over the same questions that had bothered her for years. *Is there nothing more? Is there no purpose for my life? No plan? No reason? Why, dear God? Why have I been put on this earth? Has my existence meant nothing more than to die a meaningless death where no one will know, no one will care?* With hot tears stinging her eyes, Brenna knew that she had to find the energy to make her way topside and plead her case to the ship's captain.

Shakily, she pushed herself off the planks and everything around her started to spin. She reached for a crate to brace herself. When she opened her eyes, she was on the floor with a stabbing pain just above her right ear. She touched the wound and felt warm blood. She waited, trying to clear her thoughts. She grabbed a rope to pull herself to her feet, but again she fell. For the first time, Brenna cried out, praying that the men would come.

South Carolina

Her feet were cold. Her breathing was labored. A thick fog gripped her body. Emily felt herself floating, propelled toward something she wanted but dared not face. She knew it was out there, through the heavy fog and just beyond her grasp. The glimmer of gold flashed in the fog and then disappeared. The cry came again, a baby's cry, far off, yet clear. She heard water slapping against wooden planks. The fog thinned. Before her, a small boat was slowly filling with water and in the center, a baby. The baby was crying for her. The fog grew thick again and closed. The shimmer of gold reappeared on a wrist reaching upward, seeking help, its other hand moving to stop the rain from falling on its face. Suddenly, the arm begging for help changed. It was not that of an infant; rather, it was slender and sleek. It was a woman's wrist.

"Brenna!" cried Emily. The cry jolted her and she gasped for air, as if breaking to the water's surface from a great depth. She was cold, shivering violently in her damp sleeping gown. Weston was startled awake.

"Again?" he asked and turned toward his wife.

"Oh, Weston," said Emily. Her voice quivered uncontrollably. "Why is this happening to me? Why now?"

Unable to explain his wife's dream, the same dream that had plagued her for over a month, Weston pulled Emily firmly against him and stroked her soft hair.

Emily felt the sweat above her brow and closed her eyes. In the cradle of Weston's embrace, she forced herself calm. As the darkness of the predawn faded, the two remained locked in one another's arms, but the haunting image of the bracelet and the slender arm reaching out for her would not leave Emily.

She could find no reason for her recent anxiety over the loss of her daughter so many years ago. In the first years following Brenna's death, Emily had been inconsolable to the point of not wanting to live. Her mind raged against God, against the "why" of it and hundreds of "what ifs." *What if we hadn't boarded that ship…what if we had tried a different lifeboat…what if…* Unable to find solace in any of these, Emily had spiraled into great despair, feeling as though she were immersed in a deep pit, with no escape.

Then, three years after losing Brenna, an unexpected gift arrived. Emily's aunt, her father's sister in England, in preparation for her move to London, was packing her attic and discovered a box of Dale's childhood keepsakes. Aunt Carol knew that her brother would have wanted his daughter to have his treasures. Aunt Carol immediately had the box shipped aboard an American bound vessel. Inside the box, Emily had discovered one of her father's journals. She caught her breath at his penned thoughts regarding life and death, dated when he was twenty-two…

Luke 19:10
"The Son of Man seeks us out and will save those who are lost."

After considerable contemplation of this passage, I find comfort knowing that the Lord is active in His perusal of us. While mysteries abound, I know with certainty that Christ is a man of His word. He does not deceive nor play with our minds. And while I am resigned that tragedies will happen on this earth, I know with certainty, death is not the end. I instead steady my mind on the beautiful things of His created world…the flowers in the spring…the warmth of a fire…the sky at dawn…and most especially, the love in our hearts and… in our capacity to love. I know that the creator of such goodness will have even greater joys awaiting us in Heaven. And oh what splendor awaits us! Praise be to God for all that is…the wonders of the here and now…and the yet to be experienced in the life-ever after!

Emily had always known this verse was her father's favorite because he had quoted it often when she was a child. It was the reason she had asked Weston if they could use it for the inscription in their baby's bracelet.

The gift of her father's journal and his uplifting words were the spark Emily needed in deciding to go on living. They helped her come to better terms with the loss of her parents in the wagon accident and the loss of her baby. When she read his words, something deep within Emily shifted. She recognized the truth in them. She also realized the best way she could honor the memory of her parents and Brenna was to cherish her own life and not allow death to have the final victory by destroying her. She had decided then and there that she would go on and find whatever joy she could. She would celebrate and rejoice in every part of life…and be thankful that she had once known a daughter's love…even if that love came only in the loving gaze of an infant. She would not let death have the victory of destroying that love nor the happiness she had shared with her little baby.

In the years since reading her father's words, Emily had found that peace knowing her daughter was safe and protected in Heaven.

Now, in the wake of yet another nightmare, Emily could find no such contentment. She could not understand why she was suddenly plagued with fear over her daughter's well-being. It simply made no sense.

Two days after she first tried to rise and leave the hold, Brenna no longer had the strength to continue the fight. With trembling hands, she pulled her cap over her head for warmth. As her weak body rolled listlessly with the ship's motion, a quiet resignation settled upon her. A light smile touched her lips as she surrendered to the inevitable. *Please, just let me sleep.* Explosively, Harley's face appeared before her and she knew that her death would mean his triumph. She ached at the terrible realization.

As she lay on her side with her arm cradling her head, Brenna became aware of a pressing weight against her cheek hurting her. She slowly recognized its source—her bracelet. It had never caused her pain before. She turned her head to ease the pressure and its inscription came to mind. *For the Son of Man has come to seek and save that which was lost.*

She tried to move her lips, *"Please, if you really do exist, save me. Please, don't let evil win."*

The ship lurched and forced Brenna on her back. Something caught her eye. She squinted. In the seams far above she saw a light. She had noticed a distant dim light there before, but she had never seen a pattern. Now, the light was strong and brilliant. Its shimmering rays formed a perfect cross, pulling downward, reaching her broken body. Brenna closed her eyes. She could not remember how cold or pain felt. She had never known such warmth…such peace…such love.

Chapter Five

"It's open, Thatch, come in," responded the captain to his supercargo.

"I'm sorry to be botherin' ye, Captain, I can see yer busy."

The captain placed his pen in its well, stood, stretched, and turned from his ledger where he had spent the better portion of two hours working.

"Thatch," he replied, "whatever you have to say, I'll be interested in hearing."

"Well, sir," answered the man sheepishly, "I'd be more eager to discuss this matter with ye if'n I had some proof in the matter."

"And which matter might that be?"

"Well, I…I," stammered the man uncomfortably as his fingers twisted his hat in his hands. "I believe someone's stealing from ye, sir," blurted Thatch boldly.

"Stealing. Stealing what?"

"Supplies, sir."

"Thatch," said the captain with a small laugh, "I find that hard to believe. I have always believed my men to be well fed."

"Aye, Captain, t'would agree. Yer ship is by far the best provided for that I've ever had the good fortune to serve, but nonetheless, something's amiss. 'Twasn't until recently that I noticed the water."

"The water?"

"Well, sir, I've always kept a watchful eye over our fresh water. When I was a lad aboard *The Edgewood,* the crew nearly killed one another after someone maliciously contaminated over three-quarters of the ship's water supply with seawater. An entire crew nearly died from lack of water while surrounded by nothin' but. Anyway, the water aboard is something I am very careful 'bout."

"I realize and appreciate that, Thatch. Now what's the problem with ours?"

"Well, lately, some of the casks are not as full as they oughta be. 'Tis not much, mind ye, but there's definitely something wrong. Some crew member is most likely sneaking into the hold and taking it freely—whether to bathe or drink, I know not."

"And have you any clues as to who this culprit might be?"

"Nay, sir, and I've been keeping an open eye on that hold, but I haven't been able to catch him yet."

"Thatch, would it be possible we've acquired a passenger from the last port perhaps?"

An affronted Thatch responded, "Nay, sir! I personally checked all supplies coming aboard, and I can tell ye in no uncertain terms that no one got past the posted watchmen! Nay! Much as I hate to admit it, it 'as to be one of the crew."

"Thank you for bringing this matter to my attention. And Thatch, I wasn't doubting your ability. In the many years you've been sailing with me, we've yet to take along a stowaway. That's a remarkable record."

"Thank ye, sir." Embarrassed with the compliment, Thatch left the captain's quarters.

Half an hour later, three of the ship's crew were surprised when their captain appeared and personally wanted to join them in retrieving a produce barrel. Although they knew this captain frequently assisted his men in tasks a captain usually would have no part of, even *he* had never volunteered for this menial task. The three looked skeptically from one to another when the captain said he planned to stay in the hold after they left.

Although he had a lantern in hand, its wick remained unlit. The darkness was complete. The only noises were the continual creaks of the ship as it rolled from side to side and the water sloshed against its planks.

Surely, my hunch was wrong. For certainly no one could endure this stifling environment for as long as we have been at sea. Still, I find it hard to believe one of my men would steal the water when it is so readily available to them.

The captain had decided to wait in this particular hold after considering that if he were a stowaway and wanted to avoid the ship's crew, the most logical place would be the hold at the bottom of the ship where crew traffic would be minimal.

Twenty minutes later, the captain, deciding he was truly alone, took out his flint and steel to light his lantern and leave when he heard the moan. He waited. It came again.

Without opening her eyes, Brenna wondered if the Son of Man were indeed coming to take her away, for a light penetrated her closed eyelids, becoming increasingly brighter. She felt neither fear nor relief. She was too sick to care and too weak to open her eyes, but she knew this was not the same light she had just experienced. She did not struggle when she was lifted over a shoulder and carried from the darkness.

Nathan Grant could scarcely comprehend what he had seen. There, toward the farthest corner, crumpled on the cold floor of his ship, was the shadowy figure of a young lad. Even in the dim light, Nathan knew by the pasty white color of the skin that he was extremely ill. When he lifted the lad over his shoulder, however, Nathan realized immediately that he'd been mistaken. This was no male. The man's clothing and the slender physique could not hide the fact it was a female he carried.

No one spoke to the captain as he made his way from the hold to his quarters carrying the stowaway. The stern look of the captain's face challenged anyone to speak.

Perplexity turned to astonishment for the captain when he laid the girl upon his berth and removed her hat, releasing her dirty, matted hair.

"My God!" he cried in utter disbelief. "What's she doing here?" Several seconds passed as he stared, mouth agape, at the sight of the pale, thin, young woman occupying his berth, the same woman he had met the day before leaving St. Christopher. He frowned deeply when he saw dried blood on one side of her head. He was relieved after a closer inspection showed no evidence of a deep wound. *She must have followed me onto my ship. But why? And why didn't she come to me sooner, before nearly dying in the hold? Didn't she know I would have helped her?* Nathan realized this was no time for questions. He hurriedly covered her and then raced from the room in search of his first mate and trusted companion. He did not search long, for Iestyn was already heading toward the cabin. The spry sixty-two-year-old man missed little on this ship and in less than two minutes, word had been shouted to him that the captain had personally taken an apparent stowaway to his quarters. Iestyn wasted no time in racing to his aid.

Seeing the man in the passageway, Nathan pulled him inside his cabin and closed the door.

"As you can see, Iestyn, we've acquired a guest, and a rather sick one at that."

"Aye, half-starved I'd guess," responded the first mate and rubbed his hand through his thinning brown hair.

"I want you to tend her. See that she's well fed and kept warm. Right now I'd guess she's in immediate need of some liquids; soup broth of some sort may be in order. Oh…and let's see she gets a good dose of vinegar and plenty of lime juice and sugar. We don't want to lose her to scurvy now."

"Aye, Captain," spoke Iestyn, the whites of his eyes tinged yellow with time.

"And Iestyn," said the captain, looking down at the gaunt and chalky-white face of the sleeping girl, "several of the crew saw me carry her here, but I'm assuming they believed her to be a lad. Let's keep it that way. They're an excellent crew, but a woman aboard would just be adding temptation where no temptation is needed. And the last thing we need is for them to head down the nonsensical road of thinking we're in for bad luck."

"I think that wise, Captain."

"I don't like the deception, but in this instance…" he said, pressing the back of his hand to her cheek, not liking its hotness, "I feel…" Nathan was about to say he felt an obligation to protect her after his behavior on the island but instead said, "as far as the men are concerned,

I want them told that we have quarantined the *lad* for the remainder of the voyage as a precaution until we determine if our wee interloper is disease free." Nathan picked up a cloth, held it above his copper basin, and poured water from his pitcher over it. After wringing out the excess water, he moved over to his berth, and placed it gently over her forehead. The young woman moved slightly but did not open her eyes.

"Don't ye think the men will find it a might peculiar that ye are givin' up yer personal quarters t' a stowaway?"

Nathan adjusted the cloth and then looked from the girl to Iestyn. "Well observed. It may prove helpful if the crew believes even I am leery enough to stay away. It ought to keep their curiosity at bay. I think the girl will be left alone." Sighing heavily, he wished she would awaken. He had so many questions he wanted to ask. "As much as I would like to speak with her myself, I think you're right. It's imperative the crew not observe me having any contact and for them to see that you are the only one permitted to go near these quarters. Once she's recovered enough to speak, you can convey her story to me as I am most eager to hear it."

"Aye, sir."

"And Iestyn, anything…anything she needs…see that she gets." The captain stopped, remembering how she had turned down his offered coins on the island. "Even if she asks for nothing. If you think it will help her, see that she gets it."

"Ye have my word, sir."

As he left, Nathan had no doubt his first mate would take exceptional care of the girl. He knew Iestyn to be one of the most trustworthy men he had ever known.

Three quarters of an hour later Brenna's eyes remained closed, but sensing she was awake, Iestyn spoke as he lifted Brenna's head and neck, "Here, missy, sip this."

The aroma of chicken broth filled her senses. The thought of eating sickened her. She turned her head away.

"Come on, lassie, I know ye won't be wantin' it now, but soon, ye'll be beggin' for more."

Brenna was later able to recall very little about the first few days she was in the captain's quarters. She was seldom awake, and when she was, she thought little of her circumstances. The few times she had the strength to open her eyes, she saw a kindly, older gentleman tending to her. His gentle words and thoughtfulness touched her deeply, yet she did not have the strength to speak. Last night when she tried, no sound came forth. She knew, though, that when the man looked into her grateful eyes he understood, for he smiled warmly, telling her there would be plenty of time for words later.

When her thoughts began to clear, Brenna still found it hard to believe she was alive. She had been prepared to die. She remembered the warmth of the light of the cross. *Had it all been a dream?* Brenna knew better. She sensed that she had glimpsed something for which she was not yet to know…of something yet to be. Whatever it was that she had experienced, she closed her eyes and said a deep prayer of thanks, for her life…for the warmth of the light and for a hope she had never before known.

Five days after she had been discovered in the hold, Brenna tried to stand. Steadying herself against the berth, she waited until her fear of falling subsided. Slowly, she began to move about the room. There was no doubt it was the captain's quarters, evidenced by the large freestanding globe and brass instruments. The room was practical and well-organized. Beside the berth were a plain wooden sea chest and a heavy strong box.

A small stove was the room's heat source and next to it was a worn leather chair. She moved to the captain's desk and saw an open book, a large feather quill, an ink well, and a candle. Behind the desk were a rack of neatly rolled charts and shelves with rows of leather-bound books.

In the room's center was a highly polished table with four stout chairs. A mug tray and a large lantern were suspended over the table. A tinder box and a deck of playing cards rested on the table. In the room's farthest corner was an empty brass tub and next to it, a large copper basin and matching pitcher. At the stern was a built-in bench with two small portholes at eye level. Most of the furniture, with the exception of the chairs, was bolted to the smooth, wooden floor. Two framed items decorated the walls—a large map marking trade winds hung near the room's entrance and on the wall near the dining table was a picture of a dark ocean at night, its waves reflecting the shimmering shafts of a low-lying moon. Brenna moved closer to view the intriguing picture. The scene was peaceful and serene, yet aglow with life, as if the amber hues of the moon's rays had extracted the heat from the earth's very core. A soft light fell across the sea and was carried toward shore. Brenna was uncertain how long the painting held her, but she was struck by an overwhelming desire to meet its creator.

Hesitantly, Brenna sat down in the large, comfortable chair. Her eyes moved across the room and she thought about her lifeless island shack. This room was everything the shack was not. She sensed its master, whoever he was, must have spent a great deal of time aboard, for the quarters carried a sense of belonging. She rubbed the soft leather of the armchair and closed her eyes. *Who is he, this man who allows me to stay in his own room? And where is he? And why does he deem me, a common stowaway, worthy of sleeping in his bed? Why would he permit this? It makes no sense!*

Years of living with Harley taught Brenna that trust was not something easily gained. *Surely, there must be a reason behind such generosity. But what? And why did he not just leave me to die or throw me in the ship's irons? He most certainly is under no legal obligation to aid a stowaway and a thief! What possible reason could there be for him to bring me here?* An uncomfortable answer brushed her mind. She was, after all, a woman aboard an all-male ship. In her many efforts to leave St. Christopher, she had been offered such an option more than once.

A seeping anger began to fill her. She moved back to the porthole and stared at the calm sea beyond. Dispiritedly, she tapped her head against the glass, wanting another explanation. *Is this your form of payment? Well, Captain, if that is your intent, you will have to throw me to the sharks before that will happen! And Iestyn? Could this seemingly good and kind man be party to the captain's plan? Was it really possible?*

Brenna nearly cried at the thought that Iestyn could be part of the deception. She found it hard to imagine, and yet, why else for such kindness?

Brenna yearned for the resolve to reject all of the comforts she was being bestowed...the food, the warmth of the berth, even the tender words, if they were offered in ruse. Yet, she knew she was not strong enough to do so.

Her temples pulsed with anger. *So Captain, if you want to shower me with kindness, I will accept what you offer, but I shall play no part in whatever charade this may be until your intent is clear. I will become well and strong for my sake, not for your future pleasure! And somehow, some way…if you or your men decide to force your hand with me…I will flee…I don't care if I have to swim! I was a work slave most of my life! So help me God, I shall never become a pleasure slave to you or your men!*

In the beginning of her recovery, Iestyn did everything he could think of to try and persuade her to speak to him. He repeatedly asked her questions—her name, her origin, how she came to be on the vessel, and how she survived as long as she did in the hold. When it became apparent she would not talk, Iestyn responded, "Well, that's okay, missy, I suspect when ye've got somethin' t' say, ye'll speak. Actually more of us should take lessons from ye. Like me mother always said, 'If'n ye can't improve on the silence, don't.'"

Although Brenna chose not to speak, Iestyn compensated the void well. He continued to talk to her as he worked about the room. Despite her determination not to do so, Brenna enjoyed the conversation, one-sided as it was, for in the weeks she spent alone in the hold she had craved someone to talk with. There were times when she desperately wanted to suspend her distrust and open up to the man, but her recall of the possible motive for his kindness forced her into continued silence.

"Your dinner, Captain," said the first mate cheerfully as he entered the captain's quarters, now the smaller stateroom.

"And has our 'guest' eaten yet this evening?" Nathan rose from his desk where he had been recording an entry in the daily log.

"Aye, sir, she's just now finished." Smiling proudly, he added, "An' even though she tried not to show it, I could tell she loved the Wales cake I asked the cook to make special fer her."

The captain raised his brows and arched his back slightly. "Ah. You've obviously taken a liking to the girl. 'Tis not often you'll reveal your mother's special recipe."

"Aye, sir, actually I rather like the lass."

"And her health?"

"Her fever has passed and she now seems t' spend most of her day sleepin' soundly, instead of tossin' and turnin' as she was doin' the first couple of days."

"Has she spoken to you yet?"

"Nay, sir," He lifted the tray lid and revealed a plate of barded beef, potted cheese, and some warm bread. "I don't think she's one to trust too easily."

"Well, Iestyn, if anyone can win her confidence, it's you. I'm certain that in no time she'll be chattering away and talking far more than you care to hear."

"Thank ye, sir, but I don't know. She appears t' be quite stubborn."

Nathan recalled the rainy day when he first met the girl. "No doubt, even to her own detriment."

"An' why do ye say that, Captain?"

Nathan bristled. He recalled his less than gentlemanly behavior toward the island girl and how she had suffered even more since. He was angry at himself. He surmised it would not be long before the girl conveyed the encounter to his first mate. He was surprised she had not already done so. And yet, she was such a puzzle, that girl. Nothing she did made any sense to him. He could not understand why she was now punishing Iestyn with her silence when all the man was trying to do was help her. Nathan realized, when it came to women, he understood little. Yet, of all the women he had ever known, she was one of the most perplexing. He wondered how long he would have to wait before he learned more about her. Until then, he would bide his time.

"How do ye know she's stubborn?" repeated Iestyn.

"It's evident that as sick as she was, she did not surface from the hold," replied Nathan. He realized as he said it, that it was very much the truth.

"Well, I'd have to agree with ye there. I can't imagine how she did it. Quite a remarkable woman, I'd say."

"When the young lady has strength enough to do so, I think she would enjoy a warm bath." He recalled the unpleasant aroma that assaulted him as he carried her from the hold. "Heaven knows," he added sarcastically, "she could use one."

"I'll see to it." Iestyn left the captain to his meal.

Nathan picked up his fork and began to eat but found he had little appetite. He could not stop thinking about the young, mysterious woman who was at this very moment sleeping in his bed.

Who is she? Why did she follow me aboard my ship? Is she in some sort of trouble? Is she running from the law or perhaps even a husband?

He finished his meal, picked up his quill, and dipped it into the well to complete his entry in the log but soon put the quill down. He was unable to get the girl out of his thoughts. *She is indeed remarkable to have survived in that hold for so long. What kind of a woman is she who did not come to me? She must have known I would have helped her, as I tried to do on the island. Could it possibly have been her pride that kept her from doing so? Surely not! But why then did she not make herself known? I knew from the first moment I saw her weeping that day in the rain that her pride had been badly bruised…but to let pride stand in the way of her life? If that had been the case, Lord have mercy on any man who's foolish enough to fall victim to her charms!*

Nathan smiled slightly as he wondered why he worried about some poor unknowing chap when her welfare was now his concern.

He tapped his palm firmly against the desk. *What am I to do with her? If she were a man, I could easily press her into service to work off what she owes. Or, I could turn her over to the authorities in Bristol when we arrive, but what would be the point? Make her pay for her actions against this ship?* Nathan almost laughed at the notion. It was plain the girl had suffered enough, not only aboard his vessel, but from the obvious nightmare of a life she led on the island. He recalled his callous reaction to the girl with her cart stuck in the mud. It had bothered him ever since. Though he had instructed his supercargo later that same day that if a white woman selling produce appeared at the quay, he was to purchase her entire load and pay handsomely for it, it had done little to ease his nagging sense that he should have done more to help her. He was pleased when Thatch found him the next day and told him the lass had indeed appeared…in the pouring rain…and they had purchased her load. Still, Nathan knew he should never have left her there struggling with her cart, despite her objections. *But what, what am I going to do, follow around every needy woman in every port of call?*

Unable to comprehend his feeling of responsibility toward the girl, Nathan closed his eyes. *Who forced you, island girl, to sell produce? Where's your family?*

He rubbed his hand over his chin. *Clearly, she's endured enough, but what am I going to do with her now?*

Three quarters of an hour later, Nathan liked his solution. He would ask the girl if she were interested in an assignment in the home of the Gauleys of Bristol. The couple, now living in a country estate just north of the city, might be in need of a good maid. She was obviously accustomed to hard work and would, if she agreed, be a fine addition to the Gauley's staff. As for their part, the Gauleys could not offer a better household in which to work; there was scarcely a friendlier or more respected family in the community. They would see to it that the girl be given a clean room, with plenty of fine food and the opportunity for days off. Since he was a close childhood friend of Nathan's father, Nathan was confident Mr. Gauley would entertain the idea of hiring the lass.

Pleased with the decision, Nathan donned his light overcoat and left his quarters.

Rarely had Brenna experienced anything as soothing as the soft fragrance of the scented bath water. And never had she been so pleasantly surprised as when Iestyn asked if she felt up to taking a bath. "A bath," she whispered. For weeks, she had longed for a bath to soak off the grime and filth covering her body.

This is heavenly, she sighed to herself, lounging in not her first tub of water, but in her second. Iestyn had tapped on her door shortly after she had scrubbed off most of the filth using boiled sea water and asked if she might now enjoy relaxing in a clean bath of fresh water. She was overwhelmed by such generosity and, with a broad smile, gladly accepted. While she stood wrapped in a towel behind a partition, Iestyn changed her water.

"By the way, mum," said Iestyn preparing to leave, "I brought ye some fresh sheets, a sleepin' gown, a pair o' the captain's trousers, a scarf ye can use to hold 'em up…an' a couple o' his shirts. Know it ain't right, but hope ye don't mind wearin' a man's clothes…least they're clean."

Brenna suppressed a laugh, for men's clothing was what she came on board wearing and were the only garments now to her name.

"An' now, missy, I'll leave ye to bathe before yer teeth start t' chatterin'."

Iestyn, even if you are simply acting, right now, I'm glad of it!

When Brenna entered the tub for the second time, she discovered Iestyn had left a scented bar of soap, which she used gleefully to scrub and lather her long, tangled hair. She sank slowly into the water until it reached her chin, closed her eyes, and let her mind and body rest, washing away all feeling.

Two hours later, Iestyn tapped lightly on her door before entering with a dinner tray. "I thought ye might enjoy…" Iestyn's tray tilted as he stared directly at Brenna who sat in the captain's chair reading a book, her golden yellow hair cascading over her shoulders. "Ma'am! I ain't never…I can't believe…" bumbled Iestyn. "Forgive me manners, but I 'ave truly never been so stunned in all me days!"

He straightened slightly. "Why, I knew there was a fine young lady behind that dirt, but, mum, if'n I do say so, men's clothing or not, yer but the vision of an angel. Ye surely are a sight for these tired ole eyes."

Regaining his composure, Iestyn set the plate of beef stew and cheapside cakes beside her. "Here, ye must be starving."

Brenna was as much surprised by Iestyn's compliments as she was embarrassed, yet she also feared them. She prayed he would not relay to the captain his belief that she was now somehow fit for duty.

"Now, ye sit there an' eat, an' don't ye be worrin' 'bout nothin'. I'm here t' take care of ye."

Tears of gratitude filled her eyes as she looked at the man who, acting or not, had in a few days shown her more warmth than she had known since before Helen's death.

Bowing deeply, Iestyn shuffled from the room, but not before Brenna saw the dampness in his eyes as well.

As Brenna's strength and health returned, so did the anxieties about her fate. She learned the captain had personally carried her from the hold and into his cabin, but he had never returned. *Why does he not at least come to speak with me? Why hasn't he demanded some sort of repayment?* Then, recalling how horrible she must have looked…and smelled…she thought it might not be all that surprising he'd had no interest in her in such regards. She hoped that was the case.

Brenna pulled the collar of his shirt to her face, inhaled deeply, and enjoyed the faint scent of the fabric. *Perhaps I've been wrong. Maybe he fears catching something dreadful from me. But if that is so, why would he allow me to occupy his quarters?*

One afternoon, Iestyn entered the room carrying a slice of cheesecake made from the nut of cocoa. "Ye surely are a sight on this fine day. I just can't get over how ye've recovered. Remarkable really, when ye think back to the condition ye were brought to this room. I still can't get over how ye could possibly have survived down there as long as ye did. An' t' think…of all voyages t' hit a terrible patch o' em' doldrums like we did! No wind for nearly three weeks! Worst I've ever seen! Anyway…all that extra time fer ye…in that terrible dark hold…such is no place fer anyone an' certainly not a lady like yerself! An' how ye even managed to get yerself aboard has us all baffled. Ye know, mum," he spoke, bending closer to Brenna as if to let her in on a secret, "in the thirteen years the captain has sailed, he ain't never once had a stowaway. That's a remarkable record, unheard of actually."

So, I've broken his precious record! Brenna wondered what punishment awaited her.

Eight days after she took her first bath, Brenna looked around the cabin. She was restless. She was weary of playing cards by herself, and she had read most of the books on the captain's shelves from *The Practical Navigator and Seaman's Daily Assistant* to *Finding the Latitude and Longitude at Sea.*

The words of her tutor, Mr. Middleton, spoken many years ago, sounded in her mind. "Books are the window to the world, and it is up to you to see that the window is opened." The word "you" was actually intended for Decker, the only son of the wealthy landowners, the

Watkins. Helen, who had worked as the personal cook to the Watkins for over five years, persuaded her employers to permit young Brenna to attend the tutorials of their son Decker as a "silent student." In exchange for her daughter's lessons, Helen had agreed to work an extra day each week. It was the only day she previously had free.

Thanks to Helen's sacrifice, Brenna began her studies at the age of six. Every day she sat silently in the back of the private school house, forbidden to speak. She was to listen and listen she did. Even at six, Brenna sensed she was being afforded a great privilege few girls were fortunate enough to receive. She was determined her mother's sacrifice not be in vain. She listened, studied, and wanted to question, but her hand always remained at her side.

Mr. Middleton provided her with proper books, chalk, and slate. And she was permitted to use the family library. Although she was not allowed to bother Mr. Middleton, he did frequently pass by her desk and, after observing her work, would nod his head and say, "Notable. Quite notable!"

Although Mr. Middleton worked exclusively with Decker on his speech, repeatedly stating the importance of proper communication, Brenna paid close attention. Each day, when she left the classroom, she spent hours practicing how to speak like her teacher.

Her mentor had traveled widely and spent much of his life in Europe. His accounts of Rome, Paris, Vienna, and London intrigued Brenna, and she had hoped to see some of the places he described, but her fascination intensified during his teachings of the American Colonies. Mr. Middleton had once spent three months in Boston visiting his sister. He had found no pleasure in what he described as the "uncivilized land." He said his sister spoke of some fine and cultured cities elsewhere in the Colonies, but he cautioned that they should not be confused with the great cultural cities of Europe.

Young Brenna, however, did not know about such culture. She was fascinated with his tales of the hearty souls who left their homes, possessions, families, and friends. Mr. Middleton said such behavior was reserved for fools and outcasts. Brenna, though, felt a strong connection with them and wondered if they, like her, were searching for something they could not define. *Do they also lie awake at night wondering, why am I here? Is there nothing more?* She was inspired by the

Colonists…the young and the old, willing to risk their very lives for a chance to find the answer. *No, Mr. Middleton, the only fools are those who never dare to search.*

For as long as Brenna could remember, she had longed to go to America. Now, as she looked around the ship's quarters, she felt that dream slipping away. She had surmised long before that they were sailing for Europe. Iestyn confirmed her suspicions earlier in the week.

"And do ye be havin' kinfolk in England, mum? Is that why ye boarded *The Grace*?" He asked this as he did all his questions, as if he were expecting an answer. Realizing again that she would not reply, he sighed, "Ah well," he said opening the heavy door, "I guess 'tis none of me business anyway. Oh, an' I nearly forgot." He reached into his pocket and withdrew a small leather pouch. "Captain found these when he went back t' have a look at where ye'd been sleepin' in the hold." Iestyn shook out the contents on the table. It was the money from the sale of produce to this ship.

England. So, I will be seeing the favored land of Mr. Middleton after all.

As time passed and the captain never appeared to demand physical payment, a new sense of fear began to sweep through her. *Prison*, common for sea criminals not immediately hung.

Brenna rubbed her crossed arms and tried to dispel her growing unease. She discovered this morning the reason the captain had not come to see her. She overheard Iestyn speaking to a man outside her cabin. Miles, as Iestyn called the man, wanted to enter the quarters to retrieve a chart. Iestyn stopped him and said that even the captain still would not do so for fear the stowaway may still pose a health threat. When she heard his retreating footsteps, Brenna sighed in relief. As long as the captain feared her, she would be safe from his unwanted advances. Still, she was concerned and knew she had yet to face punishment for her crimes against the ship.

She picked up a copy of Daniel Defoe's *Robinson Crusoe* from the sideboard and began flipping its pages. She had already read it while on board and could not keep her thoughts on the words. Instead, she set the book in her lap, her mind drifting back to a time shortly after the death of her mother.

"I told you the girl can do the work!" shouted Harley at Mr. Watkins. "You can work her all day and all night for all I care! God knows she ain't worth nothing otherwise!"

The sharp words pierced Brenna who listened from behind the inside of the cottage door.

"Your wife was a loyal, hard worker, and we're all very sorry for her death, but as I have repeatedly told you, Mr. Findlay, the position is not fit for a child! It's been filled."

"But you can't do this to us!" protested Harley. "You can't throw us out with no bloody warning!"

Brenna had never heard Mr. Watkins raise his voice the way he was doing now. "I would hardly call three months 'no notice,' and had it not been for your child, you would have been asked to leave long ago. My wife, however, could not bear the thought of turning Brenna out."

"Ah, dearest Brenna," sneered Harley, his voice laced with sarcasm, "how I must remember to thank the brat!"

"You, sir, are a despicable human being and not worthy to father any child, let alone one so sweet as Brenna!"

Sensitive about his infertility, this insult infuriated Harley far more than Mr. Watkins could ever have known.

"You slitherin' snake! I'm gonna…"

"Eight o'clock on the morrow! I shall bring in a new family to occupy these quarters. I will expect you to be gone."

"And if I ain't?"

"Then I shall turn you over to the authorities. Mark my words, for they are not spoken lightly."

Shortly after sunrise the next morning, Brenna closed the door to the home Helen had filled with love. She spent the next few weeks in horror and disgrace while Harley openly tried to sell her at the quay to outgoing vessels. When the authorities were alerted, Harley was threatened with imprisonment if he did not stop. Three weeks later, a drunken Harley returned to the underside of a bridge where they had stayed since leaving the Watkins' plantation. He boasted that he had coaxed a former island slave to drink and then a game of cards after the man told him about his recent fortune—his former master of forty years had surprised him when he granted him his freedom with a gift of six acres, a barn, and a shack on the side of Mt. Misery. Harley had won the game.

Two days later, Brenna watched with despair as the man, his shoulders slumped, shuffled out of his home. Brenna knew that if hopelessness had a face, she was seeing it in the old man.

For the next seven years, when Brenna closed her eyes each night, she wondered about the man who should have been sleeping there instead of her. She despised Harley for what he had done to him and wondered if anyone else saw the dark pall she did, hovering over the farm, each time she looked at it.

"Ma'am," whispered Iestyn as he quietly opened the door to Brenna's quarters, "I'm sorry if I'm botherin'…" He stopped. Brenna was asleep in the chair next to the stove, an open book in her lap.

"Quiet," yelled Thatch to the crew as they gathered on the poop deck, "the captain's got an announcement."

"Thank you, Thatch, for the fine introduction," grinned Nathan, suppressing a chuckle. "If my calculations are correct, we should be seeing shore within forty-eight hours."

After the outbursts calmed, the captain continued, "I know several of you have friends and business you need to attend to while in Bristol…"

"We know McGuire took care of enough business for all o' us last year when we was here!" shouted one of the men to the snickers of the rest.

"To continue…" said Nathan, looking directly at the man who had interrupted him. The man scratched his curly crop and lowered his gaze. "I expect this stay to be much shorter than the last time we were here. I hope to have completed all our business and be heading toward home short of two fortnights."

Again came the whoops and hurrahs of the crew, many of whom had family and called the Colonies home.

"That'll be all," said the captain as he headed toward the bow of the ship. Iestyn intercepted him on the way. "May I have a word with you, sir? In private?"

"Certainly. What's on your mind?" asked Nathan as he closed the door to his cabin a few moments later.

"Well, sir, I know 'tis not my place to ask, but what I'd been wantin' t' know is, what do ye intend to do with her?"

"I assume you're referring to our name-unknown stowaway?" Seeing Iestyn nod, Nathan paused. He knew Iestyn had taken a liking to the girl and that undoubtedly she had sent him on this fact-searching mission and whatever he said would be relayed to her. He fought a threatening smile, glad she had finally shown her hand. He was eager to see what tactic she would use in pleading her case. Iestyn had always been completely loyal to him. Now, he was doing the girl's bidding

Surely he knows me well enough to know I shall be fair with the girl. But as he looked at his first mate, he saw no such assuredness in Iestyn's expression. *Remarkable.* Meaning only to jest with him for doubting him, Nathan's eyes looked squarely at his first mate. "Iestyn, she boarded *The Grace* illegally and stole the provisions of the crew as would a common thief. Therefore, with our island stowaway, I intend to see that justice is done."

"But, sir, ye're bein' cruel and most unfair!" Iestyn lowered his brow and with a tone laced with anger said, "The woman's been through a great deal…'tis plain to see…if only ye'd give her a chance! I'm certain she'll do whatever she can to make it up to ye. She's a good woman, far better than the likes o' that woman ye've been courtin' in England!"

Nathan ignored his first mate's last comment. "You said the woman here has been through hard times. I was unaware that she has spoken to you. What has she revealed?"

"She hasn't, not directly that is. But the evening that ye first brought her t' yer quarters, she was feverish and delirious…an' she cried out in her sleep."

"Really? And what was it she said in her dreams that gave you such insight into her suffering?"

"Well, she said, 'No! Tell me I wasn't sold!'"

"Sold?"

"Aye, sir, she said, 'sold,' which leads me t' believe she's runnin' away from an indentured contract. May be it's how she came t' be on the island in the first place. An' now, after livin' as a slave, she's trying t' get back t' her home in England. I would guess that's why she came aboard this ship…learnin' our destination an' boardin' us."

"That's an interesting theory." *And one that would explain the reason behind a white woman selling at the open market.*

Nathan recalled his brief conversation with her on the island. He remembered thinking at the time that she had a bit of an unusual accent—British with a very slight island dialect…a much lighter one than he was accustomed to hearing on the island. Her words were polished, as if she had exposure to formal English studies. *But that obviously could not have been the case or else she would not have ended up selling produce.*

"Well, Captain, I do hope ye reconsider. She deserves a lot better than the life she's led. An' Captain, I tell ye, the woman has the face of a magical princess."

Raising his eyebrows, the captain replied, "As you've said…repeatedly, and one that's undoubtedly cast her spell on you."

"When ye see her ye'll know what I mean." Iestyn looked knowingly at the captain.

When the captain did not respond, Iestyn added, "Believe what ye will, but I'm telling ye, she's the loveliest sight these ol' eyes have ever seen, even wearin' yer clothes! An' she wears them a mite bit better than ye, I might add," he laughed heartily. "An' speakin' of eyes, hers are the most spectacular shade of blue and green. Two completely different colors. T'aint never seen any other like 'em or more beautiful."

Nathan recalled the woman he had seen on two previous occasions—covered from head to toe with mud, then filthy, half-starved, and unconscious. He could not imagine the girl being the ravishing sight Iestyn described. Yet the man's word had always been as good as a king's ransom and his judgment of character better than anyone Nathan had ever known. Nathan's curiosity was aroused almost to the point of taking the chance of his men seeing him enter her cabin before they docked.

The sun was level with the horizon when Iestyn entered Brenna's quarter carrying a large white box, "Good morning, missy. As ye've probably heard from the rustling overhead, the watch sighted the soil of England several hours ago. 'Twon't be but a few moments an' we'll be headin' into the mouth of the River Avon an' ridin' the six o'clock tide into one of me favorite ports in all the world, Bristol."

Brenna had been standing at the window since she awoke. His announcement was of little surprise.

"I guarantee, a busier place ye'll rarely have seen," he commented, set the package on the berth, and joined Brenna at the porthole. "Why, I've seen this port so crowded that I could have easily crossed the width of the Avon by simply steppin' across the decks of the ships lined up to dock. Ah, Bristol," he said with a sigh, glancing outside, "I'm glad t' see that ye haven't been shut down by them pirates."

Iestyn saw Brenna's look of surprise.

"Aye, pirates. Now, thankfully, most of the piratin' activity in these waters ended nearly sixty years ago. Recently, however, a small band o' cut throats have been plaguing this area."

When she was on St. Christopher, Brenna had heard whispers of such activities in Britain, but she had not considered the possibility that this ship was in danger.

As if reading her thoughts, Iestyn laughed lightly, "But ye have no need t' fear. Nay, mum! There t'aint no one, not even the biggest of fools, t'would mess with this ship. She's fast, well-gunned, and with a crew that's the envy of the King himself."

He looked out the window and smiled contently. "Bristol. Ye might say I grew up here. I was born in Wales, but spent me young years in Ireland. That probably helps ye understand my peculiar dialect, if'n ye've noticed it."

Brenna smiled in acknowledgment. His blended accent had always puzzled her.

"Anyway, after I left Ireland, I got me first job as a shipwright right over there. See that dry dock?"

Brenna smiled again. She recognized the signs of a long tale and was happy for the diversion.

"This town's renowned ye know, for buildin' some of the finest ships in the world—hard work though 'tis. I started as a caulker, packin' oakum in the planks. A tedious job, but 'tis what keeps the ship afloat. I tell ye, there ain't nothin' like the feeling of Launchin' Day when a huge crowd gathers 'round to see the hull put to sea. I can still feel the knot in me gut each time we launched a vessel as I stood holdin' me breath waitin' t' see if the craft would hold her own.

"Anyway, after havin' me fill of caulkin', I took the position of sailin' aboard the new vessels durin' their shake-down an' assistin' in any repairs they might need. I finally decided t'was much easier ridin' these hulls than buildin' them, so I hired on permanently. Several years later, I met Captain Grant, the finest sailor I've ever known, an' offered my services. An' if ye need any proof of the captain's abilities, jes' take a look out there, an' I guarantee nearly every other ship will be in tow by horses pullin' the vessel in and out, for this channel's a tricky one. Takes many o' those packets three or four tides t' come ashore. But Captain Grant guides this ship like no one else. Ye ought t' stand sometime at the wheel an' see jes how difficult t'would be to maneuver a ship of this size, yet the captain does it deftly. Ye see that small inlet over there?" he asked, pointing. "Well, when I was a lad I watched as the bowsprit of a vessel tryin' to turn stabbed clean through…a horse…that was standin' dockside! If'n I hadn't seen that poor creature danglin' from the front of that ship with me own eyes, t'aint never would have believed it! Still have nightmares about it."

Brenna flinched at the thought of the poor horse's demise.

"Ye'd never see *The Grace* havin' that sort of trouble, no mum, not with Captain Grant at the wheel." Moving closer to the porthole, he said, "Let's see now, perhaps I can spot for ye the spiral of St. Mary's Radcliff. Nope. Guess ye can't see it from this angle. Maybe when ye deboard, for 'tis definitely worth seein'. St. Mary's Church is reputed as the fairest parish church in all of England, an' I'd have t' agree."

I hope I have the opportunity to see it as well—and not just its prison walls!

"Bristol," Iestyn said fondly as he rose, "brings back happy memories." Then, with a chuckle he added, "Though the same might not be said for those who disappeared from here." Noting Brenna's look of confusion, he explained, "A series of underground caves crisscross beneath much of the waterfront here. Rumor has it, some have connections with a few of the local merchant establishments, an' when a ship is havin' trouble fillin' her roster, a few strong arms enter the inns, an' pick out whatever able-bodied men they choose, drag 'em through the caves, and press 'em into service. I've known many a sailor who didn't come t' the trade by choice." Iestyn noticed her look of shock and added, "Not those aboard *The Grace*, mind ye. Nay, with the fair treatment and fine wages the men get aboard her, there's a waitin' list to crew! I beg yer pardon, mum," said Iestyn, his ears growing hot with embarrassment after realizing how close they were to docking at Cannon's Marsh and how long he had talked, "I nearly forgot why I was sent. The captain has informed me that he'll escort ye t' shore after the crew has taken leave."

Ah, so that's it! He'll wait 'til no one else is aboard to come at me. Then he'll either try to accost me or personally escort me to the gaol! You may believe him to be a fine man, Iestyn, but he's surely not one to be crossed as I've done!

Iestyn picked up and removed the lid from the box he had earlier set on the berth. He grinned broadly. "The captain apparently had this tailored on St. Christopher fer…a friend…but he felt ye have more need fer it than she." From one side of the box, Iestyn removed and gently shook out a yellow satin gown, its bodice dotted with pearls with a matching yellow and black silk petticoat. The opposite side of the divided box contained small, black hand-gloves, black suede slippers, and a wide-brimmed yellow bonnet with a black plume.

Brenna looked wide-eyed at Iestyn. It was the most beautiful gown she had ever seen.

"And the captain wanted me t' tell ye that the slippers, although probably not the right size, are his present t' ye t' replace the one ye lost. He said ye'd know what he meant."

Brenna did not know, and the look on her face showed her confusion. Iestyn simply shrugged his shoulders in response.

He must have noticed that I didn't have any on when he carried me from the hold. He's certainly observant.

"Well, if there's nothin' else, I'll leave ye to change."

"Iestyn," said Brenna softly as he turned to leave.

At the sound of her voice, a huge smile consumed Iestyn's face. "Ah, lassie, I knew ye could speak, an' what a fair voice at that. What 'tis it now?"

Brenna bit her lip. "What do you think he'll do to me?"

Iestyn looked uncomfortably at the floor. "Well, mum, I was wonderin' 'bout that myself, an' I broached the subject with the captain a short while 'go."

"And his response?"

"Well, as ye may know, these matters are frequently left up t' the captain of each vessel," answered Iestyn, avoiding her question.

Brenna sensed his hesitation. "The truth, Iestyn, please I need to know. What exactly did he say?"

Iestyn looked helplessly at the woman who finally trusted him enough to ask. Dispiritedly, he responded, "He said he would see t' it that 'justice is done.'"

Brenna felt she was going to be sick. Momentarily, she wished she had been left to die in the hold; at least that way her torment would have been over.

"Mum, I know how that must sound. But I've known this captain fer a long time, an' I can honestly say that a finer and more just man I've never met." He moved to the painting of the serene, moonlit ocean. "Do ye honestly believe that anyone with such a stroke of the brush could be anythin' less?"

"The captain did this?" Brenna was incredulous.

"Aye. He's quite talented." Iestyn opened his mouth to add that he was convinced the captain would see to it that no harm would come to her, but he closed it when it occurred to him how hollow his words would sound after what he had just told her about seeing that justice would be done. He did not believe the captain would allow harm to come to her, and yet, where this woman was concerned, the captain's actions were highly peculiar. He realized he could do nothing more to reassure her now.

He decided to seek out the captain again. He was determined to return here and set the poor woman's mind at peace.

As he turned from the painting to leave, Brenna reached out and took his hand in hers. "Iestyn, I've been unfair to you. I've questioned your motives at every turn, and I was wrong. You've been the kindest gentlemen I've ever known." Lightly, she brushed his hand with a kiss. Brenna was almost as surprised as Iestyn, for the kiss had been a natural reaction to a trusted person for whom she cared. Iestyn reluctantly left the cabin, but not before Brenna was able to see his broad smile and his face flushed with color.

Fine man indeed! She thought angrily of Iestyn's words about the captain. *Fine man who is making sure that 'justice is done'!* She wondered nervously what justice *that* justice would be.

She looked down at the beautiful gown lying on her berth and mused about the woman who would not be seeing it. The buxom woman on St. Christopher came to mind. She wondered how many other such women must there be in his ports of call. *Does he furnish them all with such extravagant gifts? If so, he is most likely a man of dwindling funds!*

Absentmindedly, Brenna lifted the gown and stroked the soft satin material against her cheek. Despite her unwillingness to accept anything else from him, Brenna could not suppress her glee as she slipped into the dress; it was the most beautiful she had ever seen. As she began fastening the numerous tiny hooks, she was grateful they were on the front of the gown. Once she had secured the last of them, she pulled tight the bodice lacing to help tailor some of the fabric snugly around her waist.

Brenna looked in the mirror and gasped. It was as though she were looking at someone else. Since Helen's death, she had been forbidden from purchasing any new material. She could not count the number of times she had cut and pieced scraps of cloth to her existing clothes to accommodate her growth over the years.

The yellow gown draped low across her shoulders, showing more cleavage than she had ever displayed. Brenna tried in vain to pull the material slightly higher. As she turned, her eyes widened at the low dip in the gown. She had never publicly shown any of her back, and she felt her cheeks grow hot at the mere thought of Iestyn seeing her in this, let alone the strangers of Bristol. She spun in front of the captain's mirror and decided her favorite part of the dress was the way it cascaded over her hips and then flared wide to the floor. Her smile widened as she envisioned dancing in it.

Brenna's beam quickly faded as she realized who she had imagined her partner in the dance to be...the handsome island stranger. She was angry that even now she was unable to keep the man from her thoughts, especially on this day when she should be thinking about prisons, certainly not ballrooms!

She looked again about the captain's quarters. *Why do you insist I wear the gown? Is it so you won't find me so repulsive if you try to force your way on me? Is that your motive, dearest Captain? I will not be taken by force!*

Brenna moved to the painting once again. Her anger subsided and she was filled with doubt. *Could the man who created such beauty be capable of attacking anyone? Yet, why else would he be giving me this garment? It certainly isn't for journeying to prison! What's he up to? What does he want from me?* Her eyes opened wide as a thought occurred. *He's going to sell me! The food, the baths, everything! Of course! He's going to sell me to the highest bidder, just like Harley tried to do! This captain is trying to barter me off as some high-priced whore! And I've been helping him—eating, bathing, and now dressing well!* Brenna wanted to rip the dress off. Instead, she moved to the small bench at the porthole and sank down.

Nearly an hour passed, and still Brenna had no idea of what she would do once they docked. Unable to tolerate the waiting, she rose and stared out at the images of the city beyond. Iestyn had been correct. Bristol was the busiest place she could ever imagine. The quay was alive with activity as *The Grace* sailed inland. Wagon loads of sacks, casks, and barrels were being loaded onto vessels of all sizes. On the pier, three ladies looked as though they were out for a morning stroll while several businessmen stood casually talking to one another. Brenna watched as a young mother struggled to carry her baby in one arm and a large basket in the other. Two men, several feet apart, twisted twine together in making rope, while nearby two young boys teeter-tottered on a board across a barrel. A horse, hoodwinked to prevent it from shying, was being led onto a ship's plank. For these strangers going about their daily lives it was just an ordinary day. For Brenna, unless she found a way to escape, this would be the last day she would know freedom, facing the ultimate in human degradation, being sold for pleasure. If she fought, which she would, she would be shackled and thrown into some forsaken prison.

As she sat observing the world outside her room, Brenna froze in horror at the sight outside her window. Praying her eyes deceived her, she pressed her face closer against the inside of the glass. "Oh, no!" she whispered and then closed her eyes to the horrendous sight. "Oh, please, no!"

Brenna had heard of this but never before had she been witness to it. Suspended over the water were five metal cages, and hanging in three of the cages, were human remains. "Sea criminals, just as I am." She knew the convicted were hanged and their decomposing bodies strung up over the docks, remaining there for weeks as a deterrent to other would-be offenders. *God in Heaven, no!* Violent sobs consumed her as did a wave of nausea.

What's taking them so long? We've been docked for hours. She had a long time to consider her possible fate…imprisonment or being sold. After recovering from the shock of the dead bodies, she had decided that with the captain wanting her dressed in such finery, it was more likely he intended her to be sold rather than imprisoned. *Perhaps the captain is speaking with some locals now, trying to work out a lucrative deal for my sale.* The thought did little to soothe her as all the nervous waiting from the last few weeks culminated in these last few hours.

Brenna jumped at Iestyn's brisk knock at the door. "He's ready for ye now, mum."

Sighing heavily, Brenna touched the coins she had left on the captain's berth. Though it was nowhere near what was owed for passage, she hoped the captain would understand it was all the money she had. She looked at her bracelet, wondering again if she should leave it as payment.

"*They wouldn't want you to do it.*" Brenna turned sharply. The words in her head had been so clear, they sounded as if spoken by someone else. *Where did that thought come from? Who is* 'they'? Brenna could make no sense of her inner thoughts, but she knew she would have to find another way to repay the captain. She would not part with her bracelet.

Weakly, Brenna stood. She knew she must keep her composure if she was going to find an opportunity to escape. Dispirited, she looked around the cabin one last time and felt a pang of loneliness, as if she were leaving a friend who had been of great comfort. As she moved, she felt the hard steel of the letter opener tied to the outside of her shin beneath her dress. She prayed she would not need to use the weapon in her defense. Determined not to let the captain know she had been crying, she piled her hair and slipped the large yellow bonnet on her head. Fearing her strength fleeting, she shakily unlatched the door.

Iestyn gasped and then smiled a bright, crooked smile. "If'n there's ever been more of transformation as ye comin' from the hold t' now, I don't know what it could be! I jes' can't take it in! Oh," he laughed, "wait 'til Captain sets his eyes on ye! He's in fer the shock o' his life!"

With her head held high and a face masking the raging turmoil beneath, Brenna walked down one level of stairs and toward the man standing at the ship's rail looking out upon the city. She paused. It was obvious he was the captain, but somehow even with his back to her, he did not look like the wretched ogre she had imagined would be waiting to greet her. Instead, the man stood tall, lean, and straight. He appeared at ease on this ship, and his clothes, although slightly sea-worn, were finely tailored.

With her golden hair tucked beneath her bonnet and its brim swept low across her brow, Brenna pulled her shoulders back, took a deep breath, and moved toward him.

Slowly the man turned.

Nathan's eyes widened. *My God! That's the girl I carried from the hold?* He nearly laughed aloud at the thought of what a charade she must have played these last few years on the island selling produce. *Indentured contract or not, some eager fellow would gladly have paid off her contract if they had but taken the time to see through her dirt and rags!* Nathan studied her closely, wanting to see her full face. *Who does she remind me of?* He was not sure if it was the way she carried herself or the tilt of her head, but there was something very familiar about her.

"You? You're the captain of this vessel?" Brenna exclaimed incredulously.

"And this you didn't know?" said Nathan with equal skepticism.

"Of course not! How could I…I…" Brenna could not even form the words. *Surely, he must have recognized me from the produce wagon when he carried me to his quarters.* Momentarily, Brenna's fears eased. *After all, hadn't he said something when we were on the island about being of service?*

Oh, why hadn't I held my tongue? Maybe he'd be more willing to help me now. But obviously that's not the case, for had it been, he would not be taking me now to see that 'justice is done'! And if he intended to help me, surely he would have sent word through Iestyn!

The captain moved closer. Brenna felt her heart pounding so hard she wondered if he were able to hear it. She recoiled when he boldly took her by the arm with one hand and with the other gently removed her bonnet, allowing her thick hair to fall. But it was not at her hair that he stared. It was her eyes.

Brenna did not understand the look the man was giving her, but she realized this was the moment for which she had been waiting. She jerked her arm from his grip and bolted down the ship's plank and onto the shore of England.

Thunderstruck, Nathan stared in disbelief at the inscription on the broken chain bracelet now in his grasp.

"Oh my God! Brenna! She's alive!"

Chapter Six

Bristol, England

Brenna ran, knowing only that she could not stop. She ran through the crowded, narrow streets. She did not pause to scrutinize this city and compare it to the villages of St. Christopher. She thought of nothing but getting as far from the ship and its captain as her legs would take her. Brenna did not notice the surprised looks she was attracting as she fled up the cobblestone streets adorned in yellow satin. No one stopped her when she bolted across a footpath, running as though her life depended on it. She did not notice the heads that turned to watch her race past with her skirt lifted high, revealing far more leg than was acceptable.

She ran until the burning in her lungs would not allow her to go up another hill. Exhausted, she fell against a high stone fence where, with hands on her knees, she bent over and gulped for air. Brenna looked around for the first time and realized the distance she had traveled was much greater than she imagined, for she was far from the port sector of town in an affluent neighborhood. A row of red brick houses lined one side of the street while sandy-colored brick homes adorned the side where she stood. Each home had a small, immaculately tended garden.

It was several moments before she hesitantly peered from behind the wall, fearful the captain was close behind. She let out a long sigh of relief and looked in every direction. Had it not been for a group of children that approached as she ran from the landing dock and then stopped behind her, she was certain her escape would not have been successful. She had glanced back over her shoulder long enough to see the head of the captain surrounded by children. She knew she was fortunate as well that there had not been any remaining crew about when she made her escape.

She grasped the wall, still feeling the sway of the ship. *I can't believe it! I can't believe he's the captain! How is that possible? The same man with those mocking eyes who laughed as I searched in the mud hole for my…*

The shoe! So that's what Iestyn was referring to when he said the captain was giving them to me as a gift to replace the one I had lost! He was mocking me even then! Furious, she wanted to fling the gift shoes out of sight but restrained. Although they were too large, she was relieved they had stayed on her feet at all. She looked down at the slippers and saw they were ripped and shredded. They had been meant for gliding around a ballroom, not for racing across city cobbles.

I don't believe it was him! He's the captain! In her years of working at the wharf, Brenna had observed captains from around the world, but never had she seen one such as that man. For the most part, captains were rough, sea-battered, often uneducated men who had worked their way up through the ranks to captain. Generally, they spent most of their lives at sea. This man dressed well, spoke well, and was, without question, the most handsome man she had ever seen. She shoved her foot farther into the loose shoe and wondered, without resolution, why she was so irritated by his appearance.

His expression when he removed her bonnet bothered her. She leaned against the wall until her heavy breathing became lighter. *He looked at me as if he recognized me. Not just our encounter on the island once before, for obviously*, she thought, looking down at the shoes, *he had already made that connection. No, it was something different.*

Brenna also could not identify precisely why, but for an instant, just before she fled from his grip, she had a feeling that in him she had a friend. *Friend indeed! Who are you fooling, Brenna? He's no friend. If he were, he would not have been ready to march me off his ship and see that 'justice is done' by peddling me off to the highest bidder!* The image of the three bodies hanging over the water flashed through her mind. Her eyes darkened. *And how many men have you sent to such an end, Captain?* Brenna realized this man could be a dangerous adversary if his laughing eyes and handsome demeanor concealed his true nature.

She knew if she were to evade the captain now, she must take several steps to avoid detection. The first was her appearance. Dressed as she was, she was surely an easy target to remember and identify. Secondly, she had to leave Bristol.

She made a decision to achieve her two immediate goals in the business district. Large beads of sweat had formed on her brow and upper lip. She wiped them away with the back of her glove. She had not noticed before just how warm the temperature was nor had she any idea what day or even month it was. She guessed it to be fall. She looked around at the abundance of trees and noticed the leaves were not only green, but yellow, orange, red, and brown. She remembered Mr. Middleton describe how in cooler climates the foliage changed each fall. Brenna was amazed to see it firsthand.

Uncertain which direction to turn, she spotted two young women coming toward her, a short stocky woman using a closed umbrella as a cane and a fair-headed woman pushing a baby's pram. When they came within speaking distance, Brenna asked, "Excuse me, but I seem to have lost my way. I'm new to town, just visiting my uncle, and I want to go shopping. Could you please direct me to the nearest market area?" The two women looked at one another with disbelief.

Brenna wondered what she said that was so wrong. The woman pushing the carriage answered, "You mean to say your uncle actually permitted you to walk? Why on earth did he not send for a carriage or sedan chair?"

"Ah…he ah," stammered Brenna, "I just arrived by coach from a long journey and was tired of being cooped up, so I persuaded him."

"Well, I can't understand a man of our neighborhood allowing you to do so and unescorted too! Who is this man?"

Annoyed but not exactly sure what to say, Brenna answered by saying the first name that came to mind, "Johnson. Iestyn Johnson."

"Iestyn Johnson," replied the stocky woman. The two women looked perplexed at one another. "I don't believe I know him. Where does he reside?"

"Ladies, please," said Brenna, trying to conceal her growing irritation, "as I said, I'm lost. I have come a far distance already from his home and if I don't get on my way, he'll certainly call a search. Would you please direct me?"

Obviously taken aback by Brenna's affront, the blonde woman said politely but disapprovingly, "King Street is a popular area. Along with several merchant shops, you'll find the library and the Theatre Royal."

"Is that near the quay?" Brenna asked apprehensively, wanting to avoid the captain and his crew.

"It's fairly close."

"I ah…generally have better luck shopping away from the dockyards. Is there another area where I might find a clothier's shop?"

The woman looked skeptically at her friend and then back to Brenna. "I can't imagine your resistance to the busiest sector of town, however, if you insist, there's always Christmas Steps."

"Christmas Steps?"

"It's a narrow corridor built on steps and lined on both sides with shops."

"How do I get there?"

"Well, let me think. Follow Park Row there past Brandon Hill to Stony Hill Road. Stony Hill will take you directly to Christmas Steps."

"Thank you for your help, ladies," Brenna replied and quickly began to walk toward the east.

In parting, Brenna heard one of the women say, "Well! If her uncle is already worried, why on earth would she be heading off now?"

The smug response came from her friend, "'Tis obvious by her manners that neither she nor her uncle lives in Clifton! Did you hear her accent? Most peculiar! And her eyes! Two-toned! Have you ever…"

Brenna smiled, unable to hear any more. *If only you knew how truly far away I am from living here!*

Nearly an hour later, Brenna ducked into the first clothier shop she saw on Christmas Steps. It was an exclusive woman's apparel shop filled with fine fabric and accessories. It was the most splendid shop Brenna had ever seen. She was immediately approached by a tall, slender woman wearing a gown of black and white. She appeared stiff in both attire and personality. Brenna did not know how best to approach the subject.

"May I be of some assistance, madam?" asked the woman with an unusually raspy voice, eyeing Brenna closely. Her look of admiration changed when she saw Brenna's feet.

Sheepishly, Brenna placed one foot over the other. Then, not wanting to waste more time, she blurted out, "I wish to make a trade."

A glimmer of disappointment spread across the woman's face. Brenna stood uneasily as the woman looked around for the box she would have used to carry in the garment she wished to exchange.

"I'm sorry but we do not have a policy of trading." Then, with curiosity in her tone, she asked, "What had you hoped to trade?"

"This gown," said Brenna. She pulled the skirt taut so the woman could see its handsome fabric.

"That!" exclaimed the woman. "Heaven forbid! You don't mean to say you want to sell the clothes off your back?"

She studied Brenna's expression and seeing it unchanged, the woman cleared her throat. "Well, I see. This is unusual. What did you have in mind to trade it for?"

"Another more casual dress and the money to make equal the trade."

"Money?" spoke the woman, unable to hide her disbelief. "How much money do you propose?"

"That'll depend on the garment."

"And which of my competitors made the gown?"

Brenna thought she heard a note of jealousy in the woman's tone.

"It was a gift."

"Oh, I see," said the woman in a slightly haughty tone, "and its tailor you do not know?"

"Nay," replied Brenna, her agitation growing. She peered out the window, fearful some of the captain's men might be searching for her.

"Well, since I do not know its origin and the quality that went into its making, I'm afraid that…"

"You know as well as I that it's a fine garment, one that would turn a fair profit for you."

"But of course, it's been worn."

"Once," replied Brenna curtly, omitting that she had just run miles in the dress.

"Very well," sighed the woman dramatically, as if she had finally been persuaded. "I'll make the trade and we'll settle the exchange after you select the fabric you want. I'll get my tape and make the necessary measurements."

Hesitating, Brenna said, "That won't be possible. Do you happen to have any dresses already prepared?"

"You want a gown measured for someone else?" questioned the woman in disbelief.

"Aye. I need it immediately."

"I see," replied the woman, frowning with disapproval. "I'm afraid I don't...ah, just a moment." She tapped her quill against the counter. "Let's see. Two or three years ago, I tailored several gowns for a woman whose husband was sent to debtors' prison before she was able to return for them. I believe they are in the back. Would you like to examine them?"

"Please," nodded Brenna, eager to be out of the captain's dress.

The clothier returned from the back of the shop carrying two large boxes and quickly wiped away the dust from them. She said haughtily, "I've heard of a designer in Paris who's encouraging a line of pre-made clothes, but I don't know anyone who would carry them." She opened the first box and added, "I can't believe such a concept would ever be successful. It's ridiculous to imagine anyone entering a shop and coming out wearing a gown cut to fit the masses!"

Fifteen minutes later, the woman was unable to mask her surprise when Brenna did just that, emerging from the powder room in a plain, brown dress designed for travel. "This is just what I was hoping for." The brown, cotton waistcoat with matching skirt had no distinguishing ornaments.

"I thought you might decide on the much more fashionable ball gown instead of one so plain."

"Not today, thank you. Would you also show me your bonnets, shoes, and glov...Oh no!" cried Brenna and grabbed her wrist. Her bracelet was gone. She sank despondently into a nearby chair. She had worn that bracelet every day she could remember—through rough play as a child and hard labor as an adult. The golden band had survived her temptation to sell it and it had survived Harley. She swallowed hard, trying to keep grief from overcoming her. Ten minutes later, despite having enlisted the aid of the shopkeeper and the two having rummaged through the store, Brenna knew the bracelet was gone; she thought it must have happened in the scuffle with the captain. *Strange that it came off so easily in his hand.* Brenna brushed aside her tears. The bracelet was her one possession and her only physical tie to her past and her mother. Her wrist looked empty without it, and without it she felt even more alone.

Brenna closed her eyes, unable to stand the sight of her vacant wrist, but she knew she did not have the luxury of mourning its loss now. She forced herself to concentrate on escaping.

It was clear, even though she was acquiring the dress, shoes, hat, gloves, satchel, and money, the woman was by far getting the better end of the bargain. Years at the docks taught Brenna the tricks of the bargaining trade, but in her current circumstances she felt she had no alternative but to accept. She wanted to threaten the woman with going to another shop. She felt certain the shop attendant would quickly have a change of heart, but Brenna did not have the time to argue.

Gloomily, Brenna stepped from the shop in her new attire with two shillings in her pocket. The clock on the wall in the shop struck four-thirty as she left. She knew if she were to leave this city today, it would be best to go before dark.

She walked across the River Avon Bridge and southward on Saint Thomas Street. As she made her way, Brenna felt slightly more at ease in her change of clothes. She paused when the distant sound of church bells echoed softly across the hills of Bristol. She was suddenly overcome with a great urge to stop, find that church, and enter its sanctuary. Instead, she forced herself onward and hoped that one day soon she would be able to return.

Brenna picked up a crumpled newspaper carelessly discarded on the side of the road. The date above the nameplate read September 24, 1788. Brenna was correct; it was fall. She skimmed the front page of the "Felix Farley's Bristol Journal." A story from Portsmouth caught her attention. It told of a man who admitted to killing his wife by jumping on her. Horrified by the thought of the grisly murder, Brenna rounded a corner and headed east away from the docks.

She wished Honey were here to help ward off any trouble and to keep her company. *You've had plenty of time to wonder why I've let you down.* Brenna shook her head as if to close out the pitiful image of her dog lying half-starved on the side of the road waiting for her master to return. She said a silent prayer for the dog that some loving soul had taken her in.

A slender, young lad leaning against a hitching post caught her attention. He held a gray kitten. She paused momentarily to ask him if the paper she held was current.

"No, ma'am, that's last week's 'Journal.' Today's the second of October." Then smiling broadly and revealing three missing front teeth, the boy beamed, "I oughta know. It's my birthday!"

"Happy Birthday! And I wish you a long, wonderful life!" smiled Brenna, but her smile quickly faded. *A long and wonderful life—if only I could hope for so much.*

Brenna moved toward the outskirts of town, having no idea where the road would lead. The hills and valleys surrounding the city were steep and abrupt and covered with fine woods, frequently revealing a red sandstone earth. Brenna wished she had time to enjoy the beautiful fall evening, but she was wary of anyone spotting her. Each time she heard the distant tap of horses' hooves she ducked behind a tree or shrub and waited for the travelers to pass. She considered hailing one of the carts and asking for a ride, but a woman traveling down a road unescorted at dusk was certain to arouse suspicion. She decided against taking a ride until she spotted two oxen slowly pulling an ancient wagon brimming with straw. An elderly farmer drove the plodding team. Since it was nearly dark, Brenna felt she might be able to slip onto the back of the cart just after it passed the tree where she stood. It occurred to her that again she would be traveling without the permission of the owner, but as with the ship, she rationalized she had little choice. Several moments later, Brenna cuddled in a soft bed of straw and the driver was none the wiser.

As the cart slowly rolled over the uneven ground, the rocking motion made her feel she was once again on the ship. When the last remainder of daylight disappeared over the countryside, she wondered how far they were going and if they would ride through the night. She did not worry the oxen might lose their footing in the darkness. She sensed that, like her mule, the team and its guide had traveled this road often in darkness and in light. No longer able to see anything but the bright stars overhead, Brenna gently closed her eyes and slept.

She had no idea how long she had dozed, but when she opened her eyes, she noticed it was not nearly so easy to see the stars, for an occasional oil-lit lamp diminished their shine. She peered cautiously over the seat and saw the driver was gone and the oxen stood tied to a hitching post between a small church and an inn. Brenna gazed around but was able to see little. The buildings on the street lessened the bite of the night wind. She pulled more of the straw over her and tried to go back to sleep, but this time, sleep did not come easily. When she closed her eyes, the face of the captain was before her. *Blast him! Must he ruin everything? My pride, my freedom, my bracelet, and even my sleep!* Night after night aboard the ship, she dreamed about the man. In each dream the circumstances changed, but always the captain was there. *What is it about him? And what's wrong with me? He's trying, at this very moment, to see that I'm either sold as a whore, imprisoned or...or put to death!* Brenna squeezed her eyes tightly in an effort to close the man from her thoughts.

The darkened sky slowly slipped away and soft-colored clouds rose on the eastern sky. Brenna had watched each moment of it. Her mind had not permitted her to sleep for the remainder of the long night. The air was crisp and cool and the unfamiliar scents filled her senses, unlike anything she ever experienced on her tropical island. She recalled Mr. Middleton describing fall. "Such vast aromatic compositions fill the air...as though all the other seasons were blended in a large vat...the lingering fragrance of a summer's rose, the freshness of a springtime rain...the cool scent of a snow yet to come...and above it all, harvested crops and burning leaves. Ahhh, there's truly nothing else like it in all the world."

Brenna had thought Mr. Middleton's expression of fall poetic, and now she understood why he felt such affection for the season. She knew, too, that on such a glorious morning, after sleeping the night on a bed of straw, she should feel cleansed and at peace. But she felt no such peace. Instead, she was stiff, tired, hungry, and terribly irritated. *And I hope you, dear Captain, slept just as poorly, anguishing over the loss of your prisoner!*

Although she knew it early, Brenna decided she had better get clear of the cart before anyone spotted her. She slid to the ground, stretched, and brushed off the clinging straw. She was glad she had kept her hair pulled back and tucked into her new bonnet.

Brenna knew immediately she was in Bath. Mr. Middleton spoke often of his favorite English city. Brenna now understood why the city was known as the "White City." The buildings lining both sides of the street were white. All consisted of a stark, smooth stone. Brenna walked to the end of the neatly cobbled block and saw the name "Broad Street" etched into the cornerstone of a building. She thought the street was aptly named, for it was much wider than the streets she had seen in Bristol. Brenna was amazed at the size of all the structures she had glimpsed over the last two days.

As she stood before a church called Saint Michael's, Brenna realized just how famished she was. Wishing there were some better use of her coin, Brenna sighed and walked back toward the nearby inn.

Brenna stood in front of the mirror of the Saracen's Heads wash room and pulled tight the material of her skirt, hoping to smooth out some of the wrinkles. She poured a fresh pitcher of water into the basin and splashed away the dirt that had accumulated during her night's ride. Brenna's long hair tumbled from beneath her hat when she removed her bonnet. Using the brush on the stand to pick out some of the straw, she combed her hair smooth. She completed her toiletries by securing the loose coiffure with her brown ribbon and again donned her bonnet.

The inn was quiet on this morning, but there were a few patrons scattered about the cozy common room. She selected a small round table where to her left was an elderly couple and to her right were three men not much older than herself. Two of the men were talking and laughing while they ate. The third, a lanky, brown-haired man with gaunt cheeks and deep set eyes, continually stared at her. Uncomfortable, Brenna turned her back to the man, slowly sipping her tea. The aroma filled her tired body and immediately she began to feel better. But the thought of the man behind her made it difficult to fully relax.

Surely, he cannot be one of the captain's men looking for me here! The serving maid brought her order of eggs, sausage, and a basket of freshly baked bread. The meal filled the void, but surprisingly, Brenna noticed its taste did not compare to the food she had eaten aboard the ship.

Iestyn told her more than once that the cook was one of the finest on the seas. Iestyn said the captain aspired to hire the finest men and treated them fairly and with respect. In return, Iestyn said his crew was fiercely loyal, which eliminated the need for extensive retraining for each voyage. *If I were captain, that's precisely how I would try to operate.*

A female captain? It was an idea she had never considered, and as she sipped her tea, she could not suppress a smile.

"Ye look as if ye be needing a little company, missy," said a voice interrupting her thoughts. As she turned, Brenna realized the young man who had been the cause of her earlier discomfort was pulling a chair up next to hers. His disheveled appearance and the foul smell of his breath, now too close to her face, made his presence even more distasteful.

"No, thank ye, sir. I'm waiting for my husband," replied Brenna, quite relieved he was not one of the captain's men.

"Looks like she don't want no part of ye and who could blame her?" said one of the man's companions. "Why don't ye just leave her alone? Yer just wasting yer breath."

"I was just keeping the lady company," said the man, glaring at his friend. Then turning to Brenna, he added, "Now why would a husband allow such a pretty thing like you to be left alone?" He stroked her arm with his boney fingers and said, "Maybe ye'd prefer a man who'd pay closer attention to ye."

"My husband is most possessive," said Brenna curtly and jerked her arm away. "I assure you he will be most unhappy to find you here. I feel it only fair to warn you now that…"

"Ye heard the lady," said the man's friend. He grabbed the pesky man by the arm and yanked him toward the door, "we don't need no troubles, mate. 'Member what happened the last time?" He looked over his shoulder and added, "Even if she is handsome." The third patron followed reluctantly behind.

Brenna looked about the room, hoping no one else noticed the encounter. The elderly couple glanced her way and quickly turned to one another. Thinking about the rude man, Brenna realized dourly, *He does present a problem that I'm sure to encounter as long as I wander aimlessly about unescorted.*

After she paid for her meal, Brenna had only one shilling and few pence remaining. She knew she had to secure employment at once. She also needed to get away from such public places, for it was possible the captain might even be searching for her in Bath.

Surely, he'll consider the possibility that I left Bristol, and Bath is a logical site. The cities can't be more than ten miles apart. No, the captain will not have ruled this city out by any means. Surely, though, he will realize it's not worth his time and purse to search the countryside for a mere stowaway. He'll most likely turn the matter over to the authorities. No doubt he's already left word of what his directive is for my punishment if I'm captured.

Brenna decided she was going to solve none of her problems by sitting in the inn. She rose to leave and spotted a notice board bolted to the wall beam next to the front door. Brenna read through the variety of notices, including public meetings, Boxing Day at Boxall, and vessels and cargo being auctioned. One small item caught her attention.

"Governess needed for child. Experienced and referenced only. Room and board provided. Send papers and inquiries to Malcolm Stone, *Royal Crescent.*"

It was precisely the type of position she wanted. She also realized it was doubtful she would be hired, for she had no references and no address. Yet, knowing she had nothing to lose, she inquired immediately of the proprietor for directions.

"Excuse me, sir. Are ye the inn's keeper?" Brenna asked of the tall, middle-aged man standing behind a large desk.

"No, madam," came his sophisticated voice, "that would be Mr. Bell. He's not here at the moment. May I be of some help?"

"I need directions to an area called Royal Crescent. Have you heard of it?"

"Heard of it?" said the man, looking at Brenna skeptically. Seeing her bewilderment, he added seriously, "You must be new in town."

"Aye. I just arrived last night."

"Ah, well, that explains it. I thought everyone had heard of the Crescent."

"What is it?" asked Brenna.

"It's best if you experience it for yourself. I will tell you this, however, the Crescent is described as an 'elliptical form,' quite renowned for its architectural superiority and home to more than thirty families."

"How do I get there?"

"Go north here on Broad Street. Turn left on George. Take a right on Gay Street. Go up the hill and through the Circus…"

"The circus?" Brenna asked confused.

"Nay, not the kind of circus of which you are thinking. This Circus is a group of buildings with elaborate columns. Once you get through the Circus, turn left on Brock Street and it will lead you straight to the Crescent. You'll be hard pressed to miss it."

Brenna turned from Broad Street onto George Street and observed several small shop merchants busily setting up goods on vending stands that lined the street. Taking in the sights rather than watching where she walked, Brenna jumped sideways when she nearly collided with a rotund baker exiting his shop. He carried a large tray of steaming hot, sweet-smelling, baked goods.

"Oh, I beg your pardon, sir!" exclaimed Brenna.

The man recovered quickly and smiled. "Fer such quick reactions and fer saving me hours o' rebaking, dear lady, I'll let ye have one of my special scones."

"Thank you," smiled Brenna to the kindly man whose face was heavily etched with the lines of time. "I've never been one to pass up freshly baked pastries." Brenna took a bite of the warm, lemon-flavored scone and said, "This is delicious! Thank you!"

"Yer quite welcome, and I must say that if it had been left up to me, we most surely would have bumped into one another. I'm afraid my ole bones just don't move like they did in my younger days."

"Why is it," questioned Brenna, changing the subject as she looked down the street, "that the other side of this street is so elevated while this side is so low?"

"Elevated so the promenaders won't soil their finery when they parade."

"Promenaders?"

"Oh, ye haven't seen it yet?"

"No," replied Brenna puzzled, "I'm newly arrived in town."

"Well," spoke the man, "I'd never seen anything like the parading either before coming to The Bath. Every morning precisely at ten, the gentry of the town, all dolled up in their finery, parade before one another along this street for the rest of us to watch."

Unimpressed by the thought of watching such an event, Brenna asked skeptically, "Every morning?" Seeing him nod, she then asked, "Don't they have anything better to do?"

He howled, "Aye, my sentiments exactly! And that ain't even the half of it! Just wait! A more pompous society ye'll never have seen!"

He saw her look of confusion, "The gentry here all adhere to a strict code of conduct."

"I see," said Brenna and swallowed the last portion of the cake.

"Aye," continued the jovial baker. "Each morning, the gentry go immediately to the Pump Room for their daily dose of mineral water, followed by bathing in the spas, rub downs, and I hate to think what else. At ten sharp, they promenade at one of several designations in town. From eleven to twelve noon they'll be in church at the Abbey. Then it's back to the Pump Room again and from there another parade before dining. After an early dinner, they'll be off either to the theatre or the Upper Rooms for balls and card parties. Everything will end exactly at eleven p.m., even," he added with a twinkle, "if it's in the middle of a dance! They follow this same routine every day!"

"I've never heard of such structured lives!"

"Nay, neither had I." The baker scratched his chin and added, "This is a strange group all right!" Then, before Brenna could respond, he smiled, showing several brown and missing teeth, "Wait till ye see some of their parading clothes! I'd describe 'em, but ye'd never believe me! But I will tell ye this," he moved closer to Brenna, "some of their houses had to be fitted with extra high entrances so the ladies, with their tall an' fancy hair styles, can get into their homes!"

"Surely you jest!" exclaimed Brenna.

The baker laughed loudly and replied, "One t'would think so, but as I stand here now, 'tis the gospel truth! And not only that," he said and inched even closer as though letting her in on a secret, "once the ladies get their hair all dolled up, they go to unbelievable measures to keep them in place, including," he grinned, "sleeping in a sitting position all night and doing so fer weeks! Can ye imagine what might be growing inside them masses after so long!"

Brenna immediately thought of how long she had been forced to go without washing her own hair.

Noting the woman's repulsed expression and realizing he had talked more than he intended, he asked, "Where are ye off to?"

"The Royal Crescent, to put in for a position."

With a ripple of laughter, he responded, "Ah, well then, ye'll be right in the heart of it!"

"Really?" asked Brenna, uncertain she would want to work for such people.

"Ah huh, the Royal Crescent is where the cream of the gentry folk live." Still chuckling but calming slightly, he added, "There are plans in the making for a row of houses to be built just west of the Crescent. And do ye know why?" When Brenna shook her head, he responded triumphantly, as if this last statement exemplified all he had just told her, "As a wind break! The sole purpose of putting up the buildings is to block the wind from blowing the ladies' skirts while they parade on the lawn in front of the Crescent!"

Brenna frowned at the possible reception she would receive when she knocked on the door of the Royal Crescent. "Have you ever heard of Malcolm Stone or his family?"

"Can't say I've heard of him, but I can tell ye that many of the families of the Crescent are quite friendly once ye look beyond the façade of what they wear…and their daily rituals."

"I hope so." Brenna realized she hated to leave her newfound friend and said reluctantly, "Unfortunately, I have to be going. Thanks again for the cake and the enlightenment."

"Anytime," he said sincerely, "and if I were able to afford the coin, I'd hire ye myself! I hope ye will stop by again soon, will ye? Who knows, maybe I could use your help then. Until such time, I hope ye find whatever ye are looking for."

So do I, thought Brenna. She turned and walked up Gay Street, praying she would find the Stone family kind, loving, and in need of her services.

Brenna stopped when she realized she had entered the Circus. Never before had she even imagined anything like the series of massive buildings, nearly identical in appearance, arranged in a circle. All were made of the whitestone she had seen so much of in Bath. In the center of the Circus was a large, open space covered completely with cobblestones. Coaches crossed the paved lawn while a handful of ladies, men, and children walked in various directions. Two men carried a sedan chair, whose curtains were drawn, obscuring the occupant. Brenna had seen several of these small carriages in both Bristol and Bath, and she decided she would never feel comfortable riding in one, even if she could afford it.

She left the Circus and moved along Brock Street. Brenna's eyes and mouth opened wide at the sight of the building before her. She knew immediately how the Royal Crescent got its name. The building was in the shape of a huge arch, resembling a perfect crescent. Staring at the vast building, Brenna wondered if she had heard the man at the inn correctly. *Thirty families live here? On St. Christopher this could be home to hundreds of families!*

The homes, each several stories high, were connected to one another, creating one enormous building. The smooth, stone structure brilliantly reflected the golden morning sun. The building overlooked the spacious expanse of a two-tiered lawn. Cattle, sheep, and horses grazed on the lower level. The upper level was a finely manicured lawn. Brenna laughed as she recalled the baker's story and decided the higher lawn must be where the gentry paraded.

Curious as to which one was the Stones' home, Brenna asked the only person she saw, an elderly woman standing on her front steps.

"Excuse me," called Brenna from behind a black, wrought-iron fence on the sidewalk. "Could you direct me to the home of Malcolm Stone?"

"Certainly," she said pleasantly, "it's the one with the burnt orange door."

Brenna noticed that the only features distinguishing the houses from one another were the color of the front doors and the design of their foot scrapers and door knockers.

Nervously, Brenna looked up at the large door of the Stone home and drew in a deep breath. Apprehensively, she announced her presence with a firm knock. A formidable gentleman who Brenna guessed to be in his late forties, wearing a powdered wig and black waistcoat, greeted her.

"Yes?"

"I wish to speak with Mr. Stone, please."

"I am sorry, but Master Stone is not here. What message do you wish me to relay to him?"

"No message, sir, but would it be all right if I waited for his return?" Brenna hoped she would not have to wander around Bath for hours.

"I am sorry, but that would be some wait. Mr. Stone is out of the country and is not expected back for several weeks."

"Oh, I see," said Brenna, her tone heavy with disappointment.

"Stanford, show her in," said a female voice from inside.

The butler did not conceal his surprise. "Follow me." He led Brenna through the wide stone entry and into an elaborately decorated drawing room. A woman twice Brenna's age and size, with short, curly black hair, sat on a gilt-wood chair with a plate of truffles in her lap. The chair was dwarfed by the woman's enormous frame.

"What manner of business do you have with my husband?" she asked bluntly.

"Well, mum," said Brenna cautiously, "it was in response to the governess position I saw posted. Is the position filled yet?"

"No," said the woman. She motioned for Brenna to take the seat across from her. "Didn't you understand that all applications were to be posted to this address?"

"Yes. But you see I need a position immediately."

"And why is that?" asked Mrs. Stone, popping a truffle in her mouth and licking the melted chocolate from her fingers.

"I just arrived in town, and I wish to begin as soon as is possible."

"As I said, all inquiries were to correspond by post. My husband intends to make his decision after reviewing all the applications upon his return. I will take your name and information and you shall be contacted within the next several weeks."

"Thank you, but that won't be necessary." Brenna stood to leave and curtsied. "Thank you anyway for your time."

"Let me see your papers," said Mrs. Stone suddenly.

"I have none."

"No papers? You mean you have misplaced them?"

"No, mum, I have none."

The woman leaned forward slightly and asked, "Am I correct in believing then that you have no references?"

"It's true."

"And have you no experience as a governess?" asked the woman in disbelief.

"None," replied Brenna honestly.

"I've never heard of such nonsense! You have no papers, no experience? Why then do you propose I hire you?"

"I think I would be good with children."

"You don't know for certain? Have you had no exposure to children?"

"No," said Brenna, her unease growing.

"My husband would be most displeased at me hiring a governess without his approval." She ate another truffle. "Your accent is one I can't identify. Where are you from?"

Brenna recalled the story she had carefully rehearsed. "I was raised on an island in the West Indies. Since the passing of my mother, I came to England to start a new life."

"You arrived then from London aboard the Flyer?"

"The Flyer?" questioned Brenna, unable to hide her ignorance.

"The London Flyer. Surely you've heard of it?"

"No, mum. I was in London only a short time." Brenna had hoped to avoid deception, but she knew of no other way to keep the woman from knowing she landed in Bristol.

"The Flyer's the fastest coach there is," said the woman as she tried cumbersomely to reposition herself in the chair. "It can make the hundred miles in one night."

"One night!"

"You came by wagon then?" questioned Mrs. Stone. "And it took you, what? Three, four days?"

"Three," lied Brenna.

"What has brought you to The Bath?"

Brenna was pleased to still have an audience with the woman. "Coming from a very small island, I found London quite overwhelming. I was told that in Bath there is opportunity for employment and the city is not quite so large. So, here I am."

"I beg your pardon," said Mrs. Stone indignantly, "but this town is never to be referred to as just plain Bath—it is *The* Bath. Do not err again in my presence."

"Yes, mum," said Brenna sheepishly, puzzled by the woman's irritation. Then, recalling the rituals described by the baker, Brenna began to understand.

"I must say you've certainly made a wise choice, for anyone who is anyone," she said haughtily, "eventually finds their way to The Bath. We have here the ultimate in elegance: the Abbey, our Assembly Rooms, the mineral baths, the theatre, and hospital. Why, what more could anyone want?"

Thinking Mrs. Stone's words sounded practiced, Brenna said, "It seems like Ba… The Bath has much to offer."

"Indeed! Now, I believe we were discussing your qualifications."

"I know that by hiring me," volunteered Brenna, "you would be taking a risk. I am very willing to work on a trial basis. If you are not pleased, I will leave within the week."

"That sounds agreeable, considering," said Mrs. Stone as she ate the last truffle on the plate, "we've been without a governess for some time and frankly I'm sick…" She thought better of her choice of words, "I don't think the lapse is good for Scott."

"Scott is your son then?"

"Yes, and I must warn you that he is most exasperating. Are you certain you can handle him?"

"I'll try," said Brenna, thinking Mrs. Stone's ill feelings toward her son probably contributed to part of his "exasperating" behavior. *What have I done by accepting this position? A disinterested mother and a belligerent child! How to handle myself?*

"Well, then, if you're going to be under my employ, there are certain things you must know. Firstly," she said. Mrs. Stone withdrew a key hanging by a chain around her thick neck and unlocked the tea caddy, "As you know, tea is very expensive, and even though it is my husband's trade, we do not have it flowing freely about the home. It, as well as the cheese and chocolate, as you can see, is always kept under lock and key, and no servants," she peered over her spectacles and looked directly at Brenna, "including you, shall have access to this. Understood?"

"Yes, mum." said Brenna politely. "Your husband is in the tea business then?"

"His shop is in Pulteney Bridge."

"Pulteney Bridge?"

"It is a wondrous bridge crossing the River Avon and lined with glorious shops such as ours."

"I see."

"As I was saying, I run a highly ordered household. You, Mrs. Twedt, the housekeeper, and Stanford are the only employees who, when absolutely necessary, are allowed access to the front entrance and main staircase. At all other times, you shall use the servants' door and rear stairwell."

"And if I may ask, how many servants do you have?"

"Let's see," she said, counting on her fingers, "there is Stanford, Mrs. Twedt, two housemaids, a kitchen maid, and the cook. Six, I believe; you'll be the seventh."

"Seven!" exclaimed Brenna, finding it hard to believe it took the efforts of so many to service one household.

"Yes," frowned Mrs. Stone, "'tis not nearly as many as I'd like. I would like at least one chamber maid and another cook, but it's all my husband will permit." Then, under her breath she added, "Tight as he is with the coin!" The woman struggled to rise. "Well, now, I've already missed my session at the baths and there's parading to do. Stanford, show Miss…? I don't even know your name."

"Brenna. Brenna Findlay." Immediately, Brenna realized her folly. She had meant to use another name. She knew that if the captain had her bracelet, he also would know her name was Brenna. She had spoken carelessly. *Oh well, hopefully Brenna is a more common name here than on St. Christopher.*

"Show Miss Findlay to the governess' quarters. And your trunks, when will they be delivered?"

"I have none. I'm afraid they were stolen on my journey from London."

"Stolen?" Mrs. Stone added, "Good Heavens! Don't tell me the pirates are at work on the roads as well? What is this world coming to? 'Tis no wonder you were so eager to find employment."

Chapter Seven

"It makes no sense!" stormed Nathan as he paced the small confines of his cabin. "We know she entered the shop in the unmistakable yellow gown and left in a common brown, but Brenna could not have gone far without notice; her appearance would never afford her that!"

"I agree," said Iestyn. "But it's been three weeks and we've searched this town inside out, sir. I don't know how we've missed her."

"Then she's left Bristol," said Nathan and forcefully dropped his ledger against his desk.

"But, Captain, she had no money."

Quizzically, Nathan looked at his first mate, "And do you so quickly forget she paid little heed to that fact before she left St. Christopher and boarded *The Grace*?"

Iestyn's face flushed hot. "Then, where do we go from here?"

"We will search until we find her," replied Nathan sternly.

"But that could take months."

"That's a real possibility."

"Keeping the crew for such a duration," argued Iestyn, "will be most costly to ye, sir."

"I appreciate your concern, Iestyn, but that's of little consequence to me now. I repeat, we shall search until she is found. I am not leaving England without her!"

His first mate looked crestfallen. "My apologies, Iestyn. I shouldn't have taken my anger out on you. It's me I'm angry with. How could I have been so careless to let her get away in the first place?"

"Don't worry, sir. I've jes' never seen ye so upset. But ye can't blame yerself. Ye had no way of knowin' the lass would bolt and be so difficult to trace."

"Nevertheless, it was irresponsible on my part, for if there is one thing I should have learned about her is that she's never, never to be underestimated!"

Nathan spoke so sharply that Iestyn flinched, "Oh, I did a superb job in leading her to believe she was being escorted to her death! When will I learn? Brenna is a survivor!"

"Captain," said Iestyn softly, "'t'wasn't yer fault."

"Oh, but it is my fault! And my apologies will mean nothing to Emily and Weston if anything happens to their daughter now!"

"Yer being entirely too hard on yerself."

Nathan's steely green eyes stared out the porthole. Why hadn't he reached out and simply grabbed her? When he finally recovered after realizing who she was and started after her, a large classroom of young children had stopped at the end of the pier to study his ship and momentarily blocked his exit. Once he was able to get through, he had frantically scanned the crowded street for a sight of the woman in yellow. She had simply vanished from view.

"I wonder where the lass is?" Iestyn asked simply as he left the captain.

Nathan tapped his head on the glass. *God, if only I knew! Where is she? What would I have done in her place? Brenna, please tell me you haven't stowed away on another ship! I'll never find you if you have. Surely you wouldn't have done that! Not after your miserable experience in the hold of this ship! You've got to still be in England. But where?*

Captain Nathan Grant sank dejectedly into his chair. He still could not believe Brenna was alive. He relived again, as he had over and over, the moment when he first learned the truth. The thought brought sweat to his brow even now.

Although her hair was a different color and she was much younger, when he looked into her eyes, it was as if he were looking at the woman who had been like a second mother to him—Emily Emerson, his own mother's best friend.

Countless times he had heard the story of the golden-haired baby tragically drowned during a shipwreck off the coast of St. Christopher some twenty years past.

As he lifted her bonnet and saw her eyes, there was no doubt the girl was the Emersons' daughter. Nathan could not believe he failed to notice the resemblance the first time he saw the girl on the island, for the similarities were remarkable. Any doubts he had were immediately overcome when he saw the bracelet and its inscription. The stowaway aboard his ship, the woman who nearly died during its journey, was Brenna Emerson. The facts were too overwhelming to be merely coincidence.

The captain had since told Iestyn the incredible tale of Brenna, separated from her family and presumed dead all these years. Iestyn had heard Nathan speak of Emily and Weston, but he had never met them.

Now, as he stood looking helplessly about his quarters, Nathan unrolled one of his charts and studied the English countryside. *Where are you? What are you doing? You survived the ship wreck, but how? Who found you? Why did you end up selling produce like a common slave? Why did you leave the island? Were you running out on an indentured contract as Iestyn speculated or are you in some sort of trouble?*

You fool! You could have known the answer to all these questions when she was aboard this ship had you simply talked to her! All that time…I had her right here! First, I wanted to be sure the crew thought I was afraid to go near her over disease threat…and then I wanted to wait until she asked to speak to me. And why did I think she would ask to talk to me when her pride nearly let her die in the hold, just so she wouldn't have to? How could I have been so stupid?

Nathan fought the urge to crumple the map and rip it to shreds. Unable to stand the confines of his cabin and the lashings of his mind, Nathan picked up a stack of papers from his desk and stormily set out in search of his helmsman.

Five minutes later, he spoke to the man on the foredeck. "Miles, I want you to take eight of our men and ride toward London. I want you to distribute these bulletins at every public point along the way, including inns, stage stops, city posts, everything. If she went toward London, somebody had to have spotted her."

"And when we reach London?"

"Continue doing the same. No location is to be missed."

"Captain, London is immense. It could take months," said Miles, hesitating.

"Then it will be some time before I see you again."

"Come on, Miss Brenna," said the boy of ten who playfully tugged on her arm as they stood outside the Orchard Street Theatre, "they'll start the show without us!" Brenna did not hear what the child was saying as she stared at a notice posted next to the ticket booth. Over and over she read, in hopes she might somehow alter its message.

"A six thousand pound reward for information leading to the location of a young woman named Brenna. It is of the utmost urgency she be located. Description: Approximately 20 years of age, tall, slender with long, blonde hair. Two-toned color eyes. Complexion—fair. Last seen in Bristol, England. Contact Captain Nathan Grant of the American ship, The Grace, anchored at Cannon's Marsh, Bristol."

Brenna felt she was going to be sick and her legs as though they were made of seaweed and would not support her. *Six thousand pounds!* Her mind screamed. She ripped the bulletin from the board and squeezed it in her hand. *What sort of folly is this? He couldn't possibly intend to pay such a reward! It's a fortune!*

"Come on," the boy repeated himself. Then, seeing the stricken look on her face, he paused. "What's the matter? You're whiter than milk."

Brenna pulled her hat low over her face and in labored gasps said, "Nothing, I…I'm just a little tired. Let's go on or they'll start without us."

"But that's just what I said!" Scott replied and followed behind.

Once inside the darkened theatre, Scott quickly seemed to forget his bewilderment and became enthralled with the performance of

The Romance of Bluebeard. Brenna paid little heed, for her all-consuming thought was of the notice and its implications.

Four weeks since I've last seen the captain, this Nathan Grant, and still he hunts me. Why? And six thousand pounds, it's ridiculous! He couldn't possibly intend to pay such a king's ransom! Is his pride so injured he'll stop at nothing to capture me and see that 'justice is done'? What am I going to do? I'll leave Bath and go so far that he'll never be able to find me! But where? She trembled. *Think! Where will I be safe? Nowhere. There's no place I will ever feel safe.* She rubbed her throbbing temples. *Oh, if only he were reasonable, I would turn myself in and pay him all my earnings since arriving in Bath and then work toward paying him off the remainder. But, obviously the Yankee is unsound! He has to be to offer a reward like this!* She twisted a lock of hair. A thought struck her. It just might work. *At least it's better than doing nothing!* Sighing softly, somewhat relieved, Brenna turned her attention toward the performers and the boy at her side who was completely unaware of the turmoil within his teacher and friend.

"Oh, Miss Brenna, this is such fun! Can we come again next week?" whispered Scott enthusiastically between acts.

"Well, that'll be up to your mother." She recalled Mrs. Stone's warning before they left that if Scott's clothing were damaged at the theatre, he would never be permitted to come again. From their position in the balcony box seats, Brenna now understood why the theatre posed such a problem to the patrons' clothing. For the majority of the audience, who watched the performance as they stood in the pit below, were splattered with candle wax that dripped from the overhead lamps. Brenna found it hard to believe those people each paid two shillings to stand in the pit and have their clothes ruined. She was glad the Stones had seasonal box seats.

"Do you think Mother will let us come back?" Scott asked anxiously.

Brenna looked at his wax-free clothes. "I don't see why not."

The smile that spread across the youngster's face was evidence enough of his feelings toward her. As she looked at him now, Brenna found it hard to believe this was the same child to whom she was first introduced just a month before. She would never forget their first encounter.

"No I won't!" The defiant voice of a young lad filtered through the five-story home to Brenna's attic chambers. "Father said I won't have a governess until he gets back!"

"And I've told you, you have no say in the matter! She's already hired!"

"Well, wait 'til Father finds out what you've done!"

An eerie sensation filled Brenna. She wondered how one so young had learned the art of cruelty so well. Her thoughts were quickly forgotten by the slam of a door and an angry, muffled reply, "I don't care! I'm not going to like her or do anything she says!"

Brenna waited for his temper to ebb. *What am I doing here? I have no qualifications for such a position. How will I handle him when he already resents me?* Brenna took a deep breath and gently knocked on his door.

"Well, it's not locked," came the gruff response from within.

"Scott?" asked Brenna pleasantly and poked her head around his door. A slightly plump, brown-haired boy, whose nose and cheeks were covered with freckles, sat on the floor. "I'm Brenna. I'm pleased to meet you."

"Well, I'm not pleased to meet you," mumbled the boy coldly.

"So I've heard," said Brenna as she sat down next to him. "I'm sorry you feel that way, but I don't know what to do about it. I've been thinking. I understand you're not happy with this arrangement, but frankly there's not a whole lot either one of us can do. You're not in a position to get rid of me, and I have nowhere else to go. I need this job. So, as I see it, we have two options, we can either both be very bitter about the situation and end up miserable or we can try and make the best of it."

The boy paused, then, slightly more upbeat said, "Well, at least you're honest. It's more than I can say for my other governesses." He looked at her for the first time. "Your eyes are kind of prett…strange." He quickly corrected himself. "Why don't you have anywhere else to go? Don't you have a home?"

His question hit her harder than she anticipated. She recovered and repeated the story she told his mother hours before and felt a pang of guilt when he had just commended her for her honesty.

Excited to learn she traveled from a small island in the distant waters of the world, Scott quickly forgot his prior resentment and asked enthusiastically, "An island! What's it like?"

"St. Christopher is…"

"St. Christopher?" interrupted Scott, "Is that the name of your island?"

"Yes, although some people call it St. Kitts."

"St. Kitts," said the boy, barely able to contain his excitement, "I've even heard of it! What's it like?"

"Well, it's very beautiful, but very different from Bath, excuse me, The Bath."

"How?"

"Well, it's very warm and green. There are mountains and miles of black and white beaches."

"Black and white? Like pepper?"

"No, not mixed together, but separate."

"Separate, you mean some are all black and others all white?"

"Exactly," she smiled.

"Why black?" he asked, his eyes growing wide with fascination.

"From the volcanoes."

"Volcanoes!" he exclaimed, jumping to his feet. "Have you ever seen one erupt?"

"No," she laughed lightly, "thank goodness."

"Oh," he sounded disappointed, "well, what else can you tell me?"

"Hum, let's see, well there are plants and flowers so big and colorful they're impossible to describe. And the monkeys…"

"Monkeys!" he said, nearly shouting, "I've seen drawings of them!"

"Yes, monkeys," she laughed. She remembered the toll they wreaked upon her produce until she had Honey to fend them off. "But on St. Christopher, they're troublemakers, destroying gardens and fields."

"Did you ever play with them?"

"No, they're wild."

"Never?" he asked, as if wishing to change her answer.

"No," she smiled, "never."

"One of my teachers told me about a sailor who came back from one of those islands. And the sailor said they have these island trees that are so vicious, even one look at them and you will go blind, forever!" The boy looked suspiciously at Brenna's eyes. "You must not have seen any of those."

Brenna could not suppress her laughter, "I think they were talking about the manchineel tree."

"That's the one!" The boy was wild with enthusiasm. "So it's true!"

"Well, they're dangerous, but just looking at them won't make one go blind. But its fruits are very poisonous."

"Poisonous! Did you ever eat one?"

"No, thankfully! But what is strange is what happens if you're standing beneath the tree and it starts to rain."

"What happens?"

"It starts to drip this odd sap and once you touch it…"

"Once you touch it, you go blind?"

"Actually, I heard of it happening once to a visitor, but their sight eventually returned. But mainly what it does is burn your skin. I only did it once and that was lesson enough for me."

The boy's mouth gaped open at what he was hearing. "What are the people like? Barbaric?"

"Do I look barbaric?"

He shrugged sheepishly, picked up a small wood soldier, twisted it in his fingers, and replied, "I guess not."

"Actually, they're very much like the people here."

"Are they all slaves?"

"No, not all. People from all over the world live there, including many from Europe. But, unfortunately yes, there are many slaves as well."

"Unfortunately? Why do you say that? Didn't you like being around them?"

"I don't like seeing anyone denied freedom. And I especially abhor people paraded in shackles and chains."

Brenna's thought trailed to Cundy, a slave from the large Montgomery plantation. She smiled at the many hours she had spent bartering with the fine and witty man. He repeatedly succeeded in arguing her down to less than half her asking price on produce.

Scott's forehead wrinkled slightly, "Does everyone on St. Christopher feel like you?"

"No, I'm sorry to say, but I'm certainly not alone in my beliefs. There are many people…of all color…rallying against it."

Scott slid back to the floor. "Do you think slavery will ever be stopped?"

"I really don't know," she said truthfully, "and if it is, it won't be without a fight. But of one thing I'm certain, people will only tolerate oppression so long."

Brenna looked at Scott in the dim, candlelit theatre. She found the change in him over the last few weeks remarkable. It was apparent the boy had long been neglected by his father, who spent most of his time working abroad, and by his mother, who displayed little interest in her son and instead spent her days between the spas and parading. Brenna had quickly realized the boy was lonely. She understood how painful it was for one so young to feel that way. He had simply needed someone to talk to and for someone to take an interest in him.

Most of Mrs. Stone's attention toward her son came as criticism. As a result, the boy had grown angry. Brenna discovered during a conversation with him a couple days after they met that he seldom left his home and had no real friends.

"Scott," Brenna said earlier that Saturday morning as they sat eating porridge, "would you like to invite some of your friends to come over for a game of bowls?"

"I don't like bowls," he said bitterly, "and even if I did, I wouldn't play them with any of my friends."

"Oh, I see," said Brenna, "and why is that?"

"Because I don't have friends. I don't like any of them, and they don't like me."

"Why?"

"They say I'm ugly." Scott shrugged, but the hurt that flickered across his face belied his nonchalant tone.

"You're not ugly Scott. Not on the outside and not on the inside. And you do know, Scott, the only thing that matters is what is on the inside."

"Sure, that's easy for you to say, looking like you do." Then, realizing he had paid her tribute, he quickly added, "being so bony and all."

Brenna suppressed a smile. "I'll never forget a gentleman who lived on St. Christopher by the name of Sam Ogden. Only he was known to everyone as Saddleback Sam."

"That's a strange nickname."

"Yes, until you saw him. His back was curved as though it belonged to a swayback horse. Yet, he was the most remarkable man I've ever known."

"Yeah, why is that?" asked Scott. He blew on his hot porridge and pretended little interest.

"Well, when strangers looked at him, they immediately turned their heads to hide their disgust. His back was the least of his problems. Scarred from a fire as a child, he had no nose, was missing an ear and an eye, and the skin twisted over his face was stretched as tight as the skin over a drum."

"I would look away too," Scott said, wrinkling his nose.

"Yet Saddleback Sam, who had more reason than anyone I've ever known to be bitter, was exactly the opposite. I never heard him say an unkind word, and he would do anything to help another. He sat dockside for hours telling us children stories. When I was about your age, he told us how fortunate we were to have been given a spot on this earth and how it was our responsibility to better that space. I asked him once how he could be so happy when life had been cruel to him. He said he believed God used his adversity for another good…to show others that true life shines from within. And you know, Scott, I know all those who met him are better for it, for they learned what I believe to be one of the most important lessons in life."

"And what's that?"

"That regardless of how wretched our past, it's no excuse for the path we choose for our future. At some point, we all have to take responsibility for our lives."

Scott sat expressionless. Brenna sensed that the tale of the scarred man made a deep impression on the unhappy boy. "Is he still alive?"

"He died when I was eleven. But his words have helped me withstand some pretty rough times for many years since."

"Like what?"

"Well, Scott, that's a bit of a long story. But, trust me, Saddleback changed my life forever."

From that moment, Brenna began to notice subtle changes in the boy. He started to interact more with those around him, including the house staff. He invited some of the area boys to their home, and for the first time, she heard him laugh. Slowly, she too began to feel differently, more comfortable in her position as his governess.

In addition to their studies, their days were filled with outings, including strolls through Queen's Square, picnic breakfasts at Sydney Gardens, visits to the markets every Saturday and Wednesday, and hot chocolate and the delicious Sally Lunn cakes. Brenna's favorite time was hiking through the hills surrounding Bath, and she was delighted by the stunning array of autumn colors. For Scott, who had lived his entire life in Bath and done little outside his home, their excursions revealed a new world of possibilities.

As Brenna and Scott left the theatre this day, her thoughts once again centered on the bulletin crumpled in her pocket. She glanced around and pulled her bonnet low, praying no one would recognize her as their ticket to fortune. She knew as long as the flyers were displayed, she would feel uneasy traveling within the city. When they arrived back at the Royal Crescent, Brenna was convinced her plan for handling the situation was short-sighted, but she hoped it would give her the time she needed to execute her longer-term solution.

Later that evening, after the rest of the household had retired, Brenna paced in her chambers. She opened an oak wardrobe and searched through the clothes the housekeeper had given her, garments the housekeeper's daughter had long since outgrown. Although the outfits were loose on Brenna, they were more than she had ever owned and she gratefully accepted them. Brenna found a plaid, wool cloak and hurriedly pulled it around her shoulders. She tiptoed down the back narrow staircase and felt the damp air envelope her as she silently closed the back door. Shivering slightly, Brenna tucked her hair inside the hood and fastened the silk frogs about her throat. She looked at the row of homes along the street and sighed. *Which way?* She hastily decided to set out eastward to find and destroy all the notices she could locate throughout the city.

At dawn's first light, a weary Brenna slipped through the back door of the house. Never would she have guessed how determined her pursuer was, for the notices were everywhere! She initially thought she might need to make five or six stops in her search but immediately discovered the folly in that reasoning. For although Bath was small in circumference, it was heavily populated with inns, taverns, and public centers—in nearly every one, she located another flyer.

He must know I'm in Bath, for he certainly would not have posted this many in all the surrounding cities! To do so would cost him a fortune in the men needed! The task of locating the flyers, she discovered, was much harder than she had imagined. For, as she walked, she was forced to continually dodge the city's night patrol. Brenna knew it was probable they too had seen the bulletins. Then, once inside the common room of the inns, she pretended to read all the posted notices. When no one looked her way, she quickly removed the notice and stuffed it into her pocket.

Since she had covered only a portion of the town, Brenna glumly realized she would have to spend the following evening in much the same manner. Exhausted, Brenna fell onto her bed.

Having slept less than two hours the night before, Brenna's tasks throughout the day were labored. It was all she could do to get through Scott's lessons, and she repeatedly had to assure the worried boy she was not ill.

Darkness settled over the city as Brenna, for the second time in as many nights, tucked her long braided hair into the hood of her traveling cloak and gradually made her way down the lit streets toward the central district of town. The sky was covered in low-lying clouds, but Brenna felt no raindrops. She hoped the rain would hold off until morning. This task was difficult enough. Her first stop tonight would be the baths for which the city was renowned. As she walked down Barton Street, she was again astounded by the abundance of construction in the city and although the street was quiet now, tomorrow it would be a flurry of activity with construction workers busy with hammers and saws. In every direction, Brenna could see a new building being raised or an old structure refitted.

She had learned too that *The Corporation*, which regulated most of the city's projects, had nearly all it could handle with the continual wave of visitors. From royalty and elitists, to the indigent and weak, Bath was inundated with people hoping to find relaxation and healing in the mineral waters of the spas. Often, the visitors decided to reside permanently in Bath. Brenna learned that the only recent strain on the booming Bath economy was during the war with the American Colonies several years earlier. Now, however, Brenna could see no evidence of that hardship.

She walked past the grand Abbey Church for the first time after dark and Brenna understood why it was so often referred to as the "Lantern of England." The church looked like an enormous, brilliantly lit lantern. Candlelight illuminated its endless array of windows. Like her first night in Bristol, Brenna was forced to cast aside an inexplicable urge to stop and enter the church.

Outside the King's Bath, Brenna quickly located the notice board, and as she expected, the flyer she sought was prominently displayed. She paused briefly to peer over the balcony of the open arena and into the bath below. The water was calm, unlike the other occasions when she and Scott visited. Always before, there was massive commotion as crowds of young and old people splashed, dove, and lounged in the warm water.

Pulteney Bridge was her next target, but she recalled Scott telling her there was another bath down the road that was usually reserved for the wealthy. Sighing with disdain, she realized that likely another bulletin would be posted there. As she approached the small, enclosed building, Brenna decided that, of the many baths in town, she favored this one. The Cross Bath, as its sign read, was a uniquely shaped stone structure with a series of small columns at its entrance. Brenna found no bulletin posted outside the sandy-colored building and turned to leave. She paused and changed her mind, deciding it prudent to check inside. She anticipated the doors would be locked, but as she tried one, she was surprised when the heavy door gave way. Once inside the small foyer, she retrieved a flyer plainly tacked to a notice board. Curious about the interior of the bath, Brenna pushed open a second set of doors and gasped slightly when the hot, mineral-laden air smothered her. A steamy mist clouded over the waters and made it hard for her to see. The water looked so warm and soothing that she wished she did not have such a long night ahead and could indulge her tired body. She wondered why the bath house doors were unlocked at this late hour with no staff in evidence. Brenna turned to leave but was startled by the sound of voices coming toward her.

"And did I not tell ye I had something special in mind?" a woman's light laughter filtered through the mist.

"A midnight swim was not something I even remotely imagined," chuckled a man.

Brenna's body went rigid as she recognized the voice. Quickly realizing the peril she was in, Brenna darted behind a curtain in the shower area as the couple entered the bath chambers. Since she was unable to see the forms of the two through the fog, she prayed her movement would be unseen as well.

Unbelievable! This is unbelievable! Of all places! Will I never be safe from him? What is he doing here? Why is he not off sailing? Does he ever work? If it's so important to him that I'm found, why doesn't he leave the task of finding me to someone trained in searches, giving him time to attend to his business?

Perhaps the woman he's escorting now is the true reason he's staying in port for so long. That must be it! That scoundrel! He's using the search for me as an excuse for staying here so long! That must be it! Of course! That makes sense! He has no intention of finding me or paying that ridiculous reward!

Brenna wanted to shout with relief at her new insight. Still trembling, yet curious, she could not resist a quick glance at the man and his mistress who were now standing at the edge of the water with their backs to her. Timidly, she peered through the mist. The woman was beautiful. Her flowing, black hair glistened, as did the dark, olive skin of her legs and arms against her red canvas bath gown. The captain was clad in black cotton swim trousers.

Brenna was not close enough to hear their whispered conversation. As they moved into the water, Brenna imagined it was she in the water with him. *No! I will not let you do this to me!* Not knowing whether she referred to the man or to her thoughts, Brenna gasped slightly, angry at her mind's betrayal.

The captain's companion turned her head sharply. Saying that she would be back momentarily, the woman ascended the bath steps and headed for the women's changing area.

Brenna froze, not breathing. Without warning, the curtain she was standing behind was pulled back. Brenna remained silent, face to face with the captain's beautiful companion, her body dripping with water. Brenna waited for her to shout, but to Brenna's surprise, the woman made no sound. Instead, her eyes narrowed, her face tensed as she looked first at Brenna's face and then to the handful of bulletins clenched in her hands.

The woman's expression changed from shock and surprise to a creeping recognition. In that moment, Brenna knew the woman realized she was the one for whom the captain was searching. The woman looked over her shoulder toward the direction of the captain and hesitated. When she turned her eyes again, Brenna saw something else in them, and for a fleeting moment, Brenna thought it was the look of jealousy. Puzzled, Brenna decided she must have imagined the look. Sensing the woman's continued indecision, Brenna bolted, clumsily tripping and slamming her knee on the uneven stone surface.

Brenna sprang to her feet and ran without looking back.

"What was that?" she heard the captain ask.

"Nothing of importance. Just a varmint of some sort."

"An alley cat, perhaps?"

Nathan Grant resembled a caged tiger pacing the small quarters aboard a ship that he knew had been docked far too long. First, the much longer than expected voyage here with uncooperative winds, and now, he was running out of options in his search for Brenna. His reward notices brought many responses, but all led nowhere. Well versed in the deceit of some, even he was dismayed by the tactics of those who tried to claim the reward. The message on the flyer had been vague, leaving open many possibilities. Most of the replies were from people who claimed to know Brenna and her location, yet they demanded the payment before they would release more information. Others used a similar tactic and stated that the girl was being held captive and would come to a tragic end were the messengers not given the immediate reward. In one such reply, a supposed blackmailer even provided Nathan with a scribbled note which said, "Help me, Nathan, or a grueling death shall be my end! Your beloved, Brenna." Nathan laughed aloud before having the man thrown off his ship.

The worst deception occurred as a man, hoping Nathan had never before seen the woman he sought, presented his cousin and claimed she was Brenna. With her eyes downcast, it was apparent the girl was deeply ashamed of her part in the charade. Had her plight not been so pathetic, Nathan would have found the situation humorous, for although she was young and blonde, the woman did not even come close to matching Brenna's beauty. When Nathan exposed their fraud, the man offered to sell his cousin, at the price of the reward, as a replacement for the missing Brenna. Nathan noted the pained look on the girl's face and sent the man fleeing the ship, fearing for his life. After he spoke at length with the girl, Nathan learned she had been orphaned several years earlier and left under the care of her cousin who used her in many such schemes. For the last year, she had been trying to secure a sound job and free herself from her cousin's hand. Nathan provided her with the name and address of the Gauleys to whom he had once intended to refer Brenna. Astounded and teary-eyed with gratitude, the girl left the ship with a smile that for Nathan was the only bright spot of this entire ordeal. He was later satisfied to learn the Gauleys hired the girl and they were all pleased with the arrangement.

However seemingly far-fetched each story was regarding Brenna, Nathan personally followed every lead. He began to wish he had never offered the reward, when Iestyn knocked on his door. His first mate entered and announced the presence of yet another courier with a supposed message from Brenna.

Nathan sighed deeply. "Bring him in." The courier placed the scroll firmly in the captain's hand and turned to wait outside the door while the captain read the message. Inside the brown paper, Nathan found a pouch with several coins and quickly read the neatly penned letter.

To Captain Nathan Grant,

It has come to my attention you are offering a surprisingly large sum for information leading to my whereabouts. I hope by writing this letter, I will be able to save you considerable time and expense, for I am certain you must be eager to resume your ship's command and duties.

I realize boarding your ship in the manner in which I did was unlawful and unfair to you and your crew. While it does not justify my actions, I believed at the time, sir, I had little choice.

Prior to seeing your bulletin, I intended to wait until I had secured the funds in total to pay you for the price of my passage. After realizing your determination in this matter, I feel it necessary to let you know of my subsequent plans for repayment.

Enclosed are a few shillings I have saved. I realize this, along with what I left in the cabin, is a mere fraction of the price for which I am indebted, but it is all I can secure at this time.

I know also that you may find this method of restitution not equal to the crime, and if that is the case, I apologize, for I know of no other options short of turning myself in…yet in such a case neither of us would benefit. From prison, I would be unable to repay you.

I plead to your sense of good judgment and character of which Iestyn has spoken so highly.

As I am able, I shall contact you again with payment. Until such time, I hope you will find my offer acceptable in hopes that we may rectify this peculiar situation.

Sincerely,
Brenna

Iestyn, who had patiently waited as the captain concluded his reading, was dismayed by the bellowing laughter of the captain.

"I take it from yer response the message t'was not of a serious nature, Captain?"

"Quite the contrary. Here, read this for yourself, for you'll never believe me."

Several moments passed. Iestyn handed the letter back to Nathan and shook his head in amazement.

"Well, at least we know the little twit is all right," said Nathan with a chuckle.

"Praise God for that!"

"And Emily and Weston will be consoled to learn their daughter has at least become an honest thief and stowaway."

"Captain," Iestyn spoke seriously, "she said she had little choice."

"Of that I am certain. And this note does make the reality of locating her much less arduous."

"And how is that, sir?"

"First, we know she must be in England, for she heard about the reward. Second, we know she has found employment of some sort, her earnings are evidence of that, and finally, we know she has hired or enlisted the trust of someone to pen her thoughts."

"Why do ye say so?" questioned Iestyn.

"'Tis obvious she would not have the skills to write the document herself."

"Beggin' yer pardon, Captain, but on that point yer entirely mistaken. I'm quite sure a woman who can read so fluently is definitely capable of writin' as well."

Nathan raised his eyebrow as if to doubt the words of his first mate, "Brenna can read? Are you certain?"

"Absolutely. I often saw her readin' yer books, even yer navigational manuals."

"My manuals?" asked the captain in disbelief.

"I saw her myself."

Nathan unrolled the letter and slowly shook his head as he again noticed the beautiful penmanship.

"Incredible! And how would she," he puzzled aloud, "a woman of such obvious poverty ever have gotten an education on St. Christopher?"

"I know not, sir, only that she did."

An education would explain her sophisticated speech. Then, shifting his thoughts, he asked Iestyn to quickly retrieve the courier. Moments later, the redheaded lad appeared before the captain. The captain spoke urgently. "'Tis of the utmost importance I know who hired you to deliver this message."

Fidgeting uneasily before the towering captain, he said, "Well, uh, normally such information is confidential, but seeing how I don't know anyway, I don't need to worry 'bout violating the rules."

"What do you mean, 'you don't know'? Didn't you speak with the party?"

"No, sir. An envelope addressed to us containing six pence and directions for delivering another to your ship was slipped under our office door sometime during the night."

"I told ye, Captain, she's clever, that one. She might be too much a match for even you," said Iestyn playfully.

Nathan ignored the remark and asked the courier, "From where does your company operate?"

"Right here, in Bristol, sir."

Nathan handed the lad a flyer and said, "You may take your leave, but if you hear or see anyone who fits this description, you must report to me immediately. You too are eligible for the reward, and be assured, it is only for her good we are searching. I give you my word. No harm shall come to her."

Once alone in his cabin, Nathan tapped the end of his quill lightly on his desk. *So, the girl's educated. That certainly changes the direction of our search.*

Brenna nervously watched as swollen raindrops streaked, one by one, down the outside of her windowpane. The storm, which had enveloped the city for nearly a week, prohibited their outings, and she was impatient. The added anxiety of not knowing whether the captain had received her message was almost more than she could stand. She had paid more than she wanted for the courier services, but she knew it was vital the captain not be able to trace her. She had addressed three envelopes and delivered the first one to a courier service in Bath. She had slipped it under the door and gave them specific directions to secretly deposit the next message, during the night, to another courier service in Bristol, giving no indication of where the note originated. That service was then to take the message to the captain of

The Grace. She hoped they were honest services and did not just take her money. The companies were both highly reputable and advertised confidentiality. She had no choice but to trust them. She regretted having to pay for more than one service, but she wanted to be certain she could not be traced to Bath.

Please, Captain, be content with my plan!

The street below was quiet. Brenna looked over the scene from her attic window and saw only an occasional passerby, so the sight of a lone peddler caught her attention. With overcoat and large-brimmed hat to shield him from the downpour, he slowly led his thin horse and wooden cart along the street. Brenna looked at the man struggling for existence and felt a kinship toward him. He so clearly resembled her in an earlier time, a time that now seemed so distant. The sight, though, was so familiar that she half expected to see a large, golden-haired dog trailing behind the cart. She attempted to ignore the ache in her heart about Honey and vividly recalled walking mile after mile in just such rain, trying to find anyone who would buy her goods before they spoiled. She remembered the weight of her soaked clothes and the smell of the rotting earthworms; the odor, combined with her often empty stomach, left her feeling queasy.

How different is my life now. Brenna thought of her abundance of food and her soft bed. She doubted whether the same was true for the peddler who was no longer in view. The sight below changed as a light brown carriage pulled to a stop in front of the home. Brenna did not recognize the elaborate carriage or its four magnificent sorrels whose heaving sides and sweat-foamed coats suggested they had just completed a long and hurried journey. Brenna's brow furrowed in dislike for either the driver or the owner who would permit such treatment of these fine animals, unless the situation life threatening.

A man Brenna had never before seen emerged from the carriage. The enormous man did not waddle as she would expect a person of his size; rather, he barreled toward the house. Far below, the loud closing of the door told Brenna that the head of the household was home.

Until this moment, Brenna had been eager to meet her employer and secure a permanent position, but during the last few days, she had the strong impression she was the only one who looked forward to his return. It was clear the rest of the staff was terrified of the man.

Nearly a week earlier, while she assisted Scott with his penmanship, Mrs. Stone entered the study. Glumly, she said, "I just received word. Your father will be returning next week."

Scott paled, then lowered his eyes, "Oh."

More brightly, his mother added, "The weather is taking a turn for the worse, so perhaps he'll be delayed."

Brenna's thoughts of that conversation were interrupted by the shouts of an unnaturally high-pitched man's voice. "You did what behind my back? Hired a what? And just who do you think you are to make such decisions?"

Brenna's eyes flashed with fury and she gritted her teeth. She realized how much Malcolm Stone sounded like Harley.

"I don't care how adept she is! If you hired her, then she's fired!"

Unable to hear Mrs. Stone's reply or listen to any further berating, Brenna decided to go to the aid of the woman and explain the circumstances of her employ. Mr. Stone, however, altered her plan with his boisterous announcement that he would rectify the situation himself. Brenna desperately hoped Scott, who had earlier gone to his room, had not heard the argument between his parents. Sadly though, she knew such confrontations were probably all too familiar to the boy.

"But she also tutors him," panted Mrs. Stone and followed her husband as he moved up the staircase toward Brenna's quarters. "So, she's good for your purse as well." The sound of the footsteps abruptly halted.

"What? You've allowed a woman to teach my son…in my home!"

"But it saves you money by not having to hire both positions," she argued pitifully.

"And brought the humiliation of the town! So help me, wench, if you've told a soul about this I'll…"

"Don't you threaten me!" cried the woman. Brenna heard her retreating footsteps down the stairs.

With temper barely in check, Brenna boldly prepared to face her employer, but as the huge man appeared at her door, Brenna fought the urge to run herself. Never before had she seen a more menacing sight as the massive ashen-haired man before her. His features were dark and exaggerated. His heavily feathered eyebrows enveloped a wide-sloping forehead and a pulsing vein trailed down the axis of his expanded nose that accentuated his thick lips. His pox-scarred skin, white and swollen, resembled curds of malformed cheese. Brenna's senses were assaulted by the horrific smell of an overly sweet perfume heavily doused over a pungent bodily odor. For Brenna, the combination was repulsive, as though it seeped into her skin.

Malcolm Stone's furious glare instantly changed when he saw Brenna. "Well, now," he huffed in an effort to catch his breath after his climb up the stairs, "this is a different matter…entirely."

Brenna's emotions raged as she noted the way his gray eyes openly covered her body. Brenna's initial reaction was relief, for at least in being fired, she could get away from the scary man. All her instincts told her he would bring only more trouble. His words seemed to confirm her fears. "Ah, so yer Miss…? I apologize," he licked his already moist lips, "I didn't catch yer name."

"Findlay," responded Brenna coldly.

"Perhaps my wife was correct in hiring you after all. She did say you work well with Scott, and I am so pleased to hear he is doing well with his studies."

Brenna trembled with rage at his willingness to use his son. It was all she could do to remain silent.

"Perhaps I may have been a bit hasty in my decision. I will need to give the matter further thought." He smiled as if he thought she ought to be grateful. "I give you permission to stay on. That is, of course, on a trial basis according to your…uh…performance." He looked directly at her bosom. There was little doubt as to his insinuation.

"Pah," spat Brenna, deciding to tell the monster just what she thought of him and his offer, when Scott appeared in the doorway. "Is it true, Miss Brenna?" he asked excitedly. "Is it true, you can stay?"

Aghast, she looked at the boy whose trust she had finally and completely won. How could she possibly tell him now that she was leaving because his father was a crude and vulgar man? The thought of Scott having to live this way, as she had lived with Harley, sickened her. Scott looked longingly at her with bewildered eyes. He momentarily reminded her of Honey. She left the dog alone to fend for herself and she still felt the guilt of that action. *No! I shall not abandon him too!* Although all her senses told her to get away, she knew she had to try to do something first to help the boy.

She pointedly ignored his father. "Yes, Scott, I will be staying after all." Without looking back, she walked Scott from the room. "I believe we have some studies to continue." *You may have won this battle, Mr. Stone, but you shall never control my life the way Harley did! Never!*

Malcolm Stone watched the gentle sway of her skirt as she left. *Ah, the boy has some pull on the girl. Excellent, excellent.*

Chapter Eight

"So, Miss Brenna?" asked Scott. He leaned forward in anticipation of his teacher's reaction to her first sip of the warm mineral water.

Brenna glanced in either direction, smiled discreetly, and whispered, "I can't believe anything that tastes this bad and smells this bad could possibly be good for you!"

Scott giggled with delight.

"I can understand swimming in the waters, but what I can't fathom is why people flock from all over Europe to drink this stuff! It's positively awful!"

"Mother drinks over two quarts a day!"

Brenna gagged at the thought and handed her full glass back to the man pumping the water, who frowned in exchange.

"Where now?" Scott asked enthusiastically.

Reluctant to return to the Royal Crescent for fear Malcolm Stone might be there, Brenna said, "Come this way. There's someone I want you to meet. He's a man I met when I first arrived in The Bath and haven't seen since."

"Who is it?"

"A baker over on George Street." She paused in front of a large building. "Scott, what is this?"

"The Upper Rooms. Surely you've heard of it."

"Isn't that where your mother frequently goes?"

"Yes, several days a week."

"What does she do there?"

"Mostly she goes for the dances. She says it is the finest ballroom in England. But Mother and the other paraders like to go there during the day, too. I went with her once. It was dull. They just sat around talking and eating."

"Does your father ever join her?"

"Not to the balls. He hates balls, but I know he goes to play faro and basset."

"I heard your mother say she was shocked to learn Mr. Dawson resigned as the Master of Ceremony of The Rooms. What does the Master of Ceremonies do?"

"A lot of nothing, according to my Father." He shrugged, "Mother says, 'the Master of Ceremonies insures proper etiquette of a high society.'"

"What happens now that he's resigned?" Brenna turned her head to better hear the music of what sounded like a small orchestra playing from within.

"There's an election. At dinner, Mother reads aloud the candidate's advertisements in *The Bath Journal*."

"Oh, I see."

"There's a bunch of fellows running, but Mother says Mr. Tyson will easily take the race."

"Why is the position so important?" asked Brenna, still puzzled by the society here and its strict rules of conduct.

Scott scratched his curly crop thoughtfully, "Whoever wins basically rules The Bath."

Brenna joined Scott in strolling up the cobblestone street. One at a time, Scott harmlessly tossed several small pebbles he had earlier picked up. "But the most famous Master of Ceremonies was Nash Beau."

"I've heard Mrs. Twedt mention him."

"Can't live in The Bath long without hearing of him."

"Did you know him?"

"Oh, no!" Scott laughed, "He's dead. He died, hum…well… Oh, my tutor before you would be angry I can't remember when he died, but, anyway, it was a long time ago."

"Why was he so famous?"

"Well, I guess he was sorta the king of The Bath, at least that's what he called himself, but I don't think he was royalty. Anyway, Mother said he changed The Bath from a 'socially inadequate town, to a superior, elitist center.'" Brenna grinned, imagining Mrs. Stone saying the practiced words.

Brenna jumped slightly at the unexpected sound of the Abbey Church bells ringing through the morning tranquility.

"Someone important must be arriving in town," said Scott loudly. "They ring the bell every time someone important comes to town."

"So you've said." Brenna wished they would stop. "There certainly must be a lot of important visitors here, for I've heard them ring every day since my arrival and often several times a day!"

"I know. It's been going on ever since I can remember. Father says it's just a gimmick at making the 'nobody's' feel important. He doesn't like tourists much."

"So I've gathered," shouted Brenna, the bells suddenly not ringing. "I would think," she said more quietly, "that the ailing who come to Bath, excuse me, The Bath, in search of healing and solitude, may be a little more than annoyed at the bells."

"Father doesn't have too many good things to say about the sick who come here either. Says he thinks The Bath is becoming a dumping ground for them. Says they're taking over the town. Says his gout is so bad because he can hardly find the space to sit in the bath houses."

"Mrs. Twedt told me she thinks over half the town has problems with gout," said Brenna absently.

"Yeah, well, my father sure does. It's so bad, he always travels by coach or sedan chair."

"He never walks?" asked Brenna. She realized she had never seen Malcolm Stone leave the house by foot.

"Only walks around the house and then only when he has to. That's why they built the Crescent with such wide doors and stairways, you know, so the sedan carriers can drop the riders off in bed. Their feet never have to touch the floor."

Brenna's mouth opened and closed. "Surely you jest!"

"No, it's a fact."

"No wonder so many suffer from gout!" exclaimed Brenna. "They never exert themselves!" She wanted to add, *and eating and drinking continually can't help either,* but she remained silent.

"Maybe, I've never thought about that, but anyway, Father says nothing good will come of all these people moving here. Except for their buying tea, that is."

"I see," Brenna said. She guessed his father rarely ever had anything good to say about anyone or anything, regardless of the topic.

Rounding the corner to George Street, Brenna was dismayed to see a 'For Let' sign hanging in the window of the empty bakery. "I can't believe it!" Brenna said sadly. She looked through the window at the vacant shelves and added, "He's closed his shop." Brenna found the door unlocked and opened it for Scott.

"Shop's closed," came the friendly voice from the back, "but I'll be with ye in a minute."

With broom in hand, the large baker appeared and beamed when he saw Brenna. "Glad to know yer still here!" Seeing Scott, he added, "And that ye got the position."

Brenna smiled at Scott, "So am I. What's going on here, anyway?"

"I'm returning home to Hull."

"Hull? Hull, England?" inquired Brenna.

"Aye, in the North Country."

"Why are you leaving now, after all these years in Bath?"

A distant look filtered across the old gentleman's face. "Ye sure ye want to hear it?"

"Of course!" exclaimed Brenna.

"Well, many…many years ago, a restless lad of fourteen left home to conquer the world. He told his mother he'd be back when he'd discovered the eighth sea. Twelve years later, realizing t'was time to settle down, he arrived in a small developing city and opened a bakery. The shop and town prospered well through the years, but the lad's fires are growing dim. Fifty-seven years after he first began his quest, the boy's going home, realizing finally that he'd crossed his seventh sea even before he kissed his mother goodbye."

As they walked from the shop a short time later, Scott said, "I'm worried about the baker. He seems so sad."

"Actually, Scott," said Brenna, putting a comforting arm around his shoulder, "I think he's very content. He's going home." As she spoke, a deep ache filled her. Even if she wanted, she had no home to which she could return. Brenna stopped walking, looked to the sky, and made a silent vow. Somehow, someway, she would find a place she could call home. If she could not find one, she would create it...and she would fill it with her love.

Brenna was surprised at the sound of someone crying when she walked down the basement steps of the Stone home nearly an hour later.

"What is it, Courtney? What's wrong?" asked Brenna to the housemaid as she entered the large kitchen.

"He hit me!" the young maid blurted.

"Who hit you?" demanded Brenna, her voice tense.

"Master Stone. 'Twas my fault, I guess, but..."

"Listen to me," Brenna said. She gripped the girl by the shoulders. "No one has the right to hit you! No one!"

"But he's my master!"

"No, Courtney, he's your employer. He has no hold on you!"

"Oh, but he does," the blonde girl cried. "This was the only job t'would hire both my sister and me."

Brenna glanced around the kitchen and looked for Courtney's sister. "Hard working as the two of you are, you'll have no trouble finding another job. Where's Heather, anyway?"

"That's the problem. She's got a terrible fever, so I did the chores alone this morning. Even though I started at four-thirty," she sniffled, "I hadn't quite finished when Master Stone came in at ten."

"And he hit you for that?"

"He requires all the chores be done before he gets up."

Having assisted the sisters once with their daily chores early one morning when she was unable to sleep, Brenna understood why Courtney had not been able to complete her chores on time. It took the two sisters and Brenna four hours to light the eight fires, polish the fire grates, shake the curtains and chair covers, dust and polish the furniture with oil, sweep the floors with damp sand, and brush the rugs. Brenna was amazed to learn those were the tasks of a typical morning, chores that had to be completed before nine-thirty. Brenna recalled what Mrs. Stone told her at the time she was hired—that she expected an orderly household. Brenna now understood what she meant.

"I don't care what the circumstances were, he was wrong to strike you!"

"Do ye really think so?" questioned Courtney. She dabbed her tear-swollen eyes.

"Yes, I do!"

"And if ye were me?"

"I'd quit."

"Oh…I," she stammered nervously. "Well, maybe I should talk to Heath…" Courtney jumped at the ringing of a bell.

Brenna noticed that the third bell, in a row of bells hanging high on the kitchen wall, was ringing furiously.

"That's the study's bell! The master's in the study! He'll 'ave me hide that the beds haven't yet been made and the chamber pots emptied!"

"He's not your mast…" Brenna's voice trailed off in frustration. She realized the girl had dashed up the stairs unhearing.

The cook entered and said warningly, "Ye'd better watch yerself! He ain't one to tolerate any back-talk from ye, even if ye is a governess."

"Ye'd be wise to heed her advice, Brenna," said Mrs. Twedt, following the cook and carrying a large cone of sugar. Setting the cone on a huge chopping block, she added, "He's not a man ye would wish to cross."

"And ye'd better tell her, Mrs. Twedt," the stout cook nodded disgustedly at Brenna, "that she'd best not be takin' the mutt out of the dog-wheel every time I turn my back! I'm tellin' ye, that the master will string me up if the meat is burnt again!"

"And I will gladly accept the blame," said Brenna. Her face flushed instantly with anger, "for any destruction to the main course!"

"She's right, Brenna," said Mrs. Twedt, trying to calm the ire of the two women in what had become an ongoing battle ever since Brenna first spotted the dog-operated spit. She, too, never enjoyed seeing the hound in the wheel, suspended high over the fire, but it was the type of spit the Stones had requested when the home was constructed, true for many homes in The Bath.

Brenna was unwilling to drop the argument. She faced the cook squarely, "Nay, I will not allow such treatment of an animal, and neither should you!"

"It gives the beast a chance to exercise!" argued the cook.

Brenna eyes flashed with anger, "At the sting of a whip and tip of a flame! With all the different types of spits available, it's inexcusable these are used!"

"Well, 'tis none of yer affair anyway!" cried the cook. "Why don't ye hold yer tongue, like every other governess!"

"June," said Mrs. Twedt uncomfortably, "why don't ye help me carry the laundry."

Brenna heard the cook's scowling words as she left the room, "I don't see why the Stones can't bring in outside help on laundry day like the rest of the families in the Crescent!"

Chapter Nine

Malcolm Stone was more hostile than ever following the sudden resignation of his two housemaids. Brenna tried to avoid all contact with him. She arranged for Scott's morning studies outside the home at public halls and libraries. They returned at noon, well after Mr. Stone left for the day. Following their late afternoon sessions, she immediately retired to her quarters and dined with the housekeeper and butler. She did not venture from the servants' area as she had done before Malcolm Stone's return.

One evening, reading her newly acquired copy of Henry Fielding's *The Life of Mr. Jonathan Wild,* Brenna heard a light rap upon her door. "Who is it?" she asked quizzically, skeptical it might be Malcolm Stone.

"It's me."

Brenna smiled and opened the door. "Scott, what keeps you up this late evening?"

He dropped into the chair across from her. "Why don't you ever sup with me anymore or come to my room to read to me like you used to?"

Brenna looked uneasily at the boy. "It's time I take my proper role as one of the staff. If you've felt abandoned, I apologize, it wasn't my intent."

"But, Miss Brenna, you're more than just one of the hired help!"

"I appreciate your confidence, Scott, but in truth, I am not."

"But even Father said he would welcome your company."

Alarmed, she replied calmly, "Oh, really?"

"He said so, just this afternoon at dinner. Oh, please, Miss Brenna, won't you join us when we dine tomorrow?"

"Thank you for the offer," she said uncomfortably, "but I can't."

Scott looked at the floor. "I know it's because you don't like him."

Brenna was sad by the boy's realization. "I don't know your father well enough to make that judgment."

"Aw, I know you're just saying that to be polite. Nobody likes him much, not even my mother, and he doesn't even care." His sad eyes turned toward the warm embers. "And neither of them cares about me."

After years of living with Harley, Brenna knew the anguish and guilt of a child who feels responsible for a parent's withholding of love. It angered and frustrated her to know there was little she could do to spare this boy from the same torment, yet she fiercely wanted him to understand.

"Scott," she said after a few moments, "sometimes people get so focused on their lives, they forget what's most important…the ones they love. But almost always…one day…they realize how wrong they've been."

"I don't think my parents love anyone except themselves," cried the boy softly, "not even me." Brenna knew his feeling had bothered him for a long time. "Why don't they love me?"

"I don't know," replied Brenna honestly. "I really don't. I can tell you this, and it may be hard for you to believe, but it's not your fault."

"But it must be!"

"No, Scott. I know, for I too was born to parents who cared nothing for me."

"Really? You?"

She nodded. "They sold me as a baby and I've never seen them since."

"Sold? They sold you?" The boy was incredulous. "Then who took care of you?"

"A very kind woman, and when she died, her husband who detested me."

"But how could he not have liked you?"

"I don't know."

"But that's so unfair! It wasn't your fault!"

"Precisely, Scott, just as you are not to blame!"

Scott's big, questioning eyes looked at her. "Do you think your parents, the ones who sold you, ever felt badly about what they did?"

Brenna squinted slightly and rubbed her palms. "I've often wondered that same thing. I wish I knew the answer. But I will never know. I don't even know their names." Brenna brushed aside a single tear. She tried to smile. "I know it doesn't make sense, but I used to stand on the shores of St. Christopher and it felt like…like…someone was thinking of me. Then later, I would think it had probably just been me wishing. But you know what?"

"What?"

"Sometimes even wishing feels good."

Long into the night, Brenna could not sleep. Images of Nathan Grant, Honey, Harley, Scott, Malcolm Stone, and her faceless parents twisted in confusion in her mind…*Why do you pursue me? How could I have abandoned you? Why did you despise me? What will happen to you when I can't be your nanny? Stay away from me! How could you have sold me?* Her eyes stung with hot tears. Brenna clutched a blanket. *Oh, please, let this stop!*

Brenna was impatient for Scott to appear so they could begin their later-than-normal morning lesson. She peered anxiously out the parlor window at the swirling flurries of snow. It was the first snowfall she had ever seen. The clock over the mantle struck half-past ten. She knew Scott must be tired from their discussion the night before. She turned quickly, startled at the high-pitched voice behind her, "I get the impression you may be trying to avoid me. That wouldn't be true now, would it, Miss Findlay?" An icy shiver ran down her spine by the closeness of Malcolm Stone.

Coldly, she responded, "I've been busy with your son's affairs, which was," she added, recoiling slightly, "the reason I was hired."

"Ah, but not by me. Regardless, you are under my employ and subject to my rules. And that being so, I request you continue your tutoring of Scott on the proper rules of etiquette at our table."

"I find nothing lacking in Scott's manners."

Mr. Stone ignored her and turned to leave. "Dinner is served at four o'clock. Your presence is required."

Brenna tried to concentrate on her meal, but it was all she could do to keep from exploding in fury at Malcolm Stone who openly leered at her. Worse yet, his wife made no attempt to hide her animosity and glared at her. Brenna felt trapped in the feud between the couple. Had Scott been absent, she would have made her feelings known. As it was, she was forced to remain silent.

The evening had started miserably. When she entered the dining room, Brenna was met by Malcolm Stone. The man rose from his oversized chair and motioned for her to take the seat directly opposite his; it was the chair normally reserved for Mrs. Stone. Brenna denied the gesture and said she might be better able to "tutor" Scott if she sat across from him.

"Obviously," snapped Mrs. Stone, who had entered the dining room followed by Scott. "And I will take my proper seat." She reached for her chair but stopped at her husband's words.

"We will have nothing of the sort! Tonight, Brenna is our honored guest. You, dear wife," he added sweetly, "shall take this seat here, across from Scott."

"Why I never…" she exclaimed, then loudly yanked the chair away from her husband's hand and sank into it.

With no alternative, Brenna moved to the chair where Mr. Stone openly gaped at her. Brenna was determined to concentrate only on her food and failed to notice when Scott unintentionally clanked his teeth on his spoon as he took a sip of his cheese soup. Mrs. Stone looked at

Scott and then Brenna. Scott's fork clanked. Again, she looked from Scott to Brenna.

She threw her napkin against the table. "It was my understanding, Miss Findlay," she erupted, "that you were to join the family here tonight to instruct the boy on the proper rules of etiquette! From where I sit, you seem to be ignoring your duties!"

Brenna put down her fork. "I'm sorry, but I was unaware I missed something."

"Missed something!" hissed Mrs. Stone. "Why Scott would have been turned out by all the boarding schools in England had he displayed such vulgar eating habits in front of them! And you're the one who is supposed to be training him!"

"I apologize for my oversight, but what exactly did he do?"

"Merely clanked his spoon with his teeth," interjected Malcolm Stone. He waved his fork, "An offense not worthy of such discussion."

"Not worthy!" Mrs. Stone hissed. "Why, I remember…"

"And your treatment of our guest," interrupted her husband, glancing icily at his wife, "would not win you any points with the ladies' society either."

"Guest?" screeched Mrs. Stone. She glared at Brenna. "May I remind you this 'guest' is our servant!"

Brenna could no longer listen to the full-fledged battle. She turned her thoughts and sympathy to Scott who was visibly mortified by the behavior of his parents. He sat with his eyes turned down. Brenna recalled his sad words last night of his parents not caring about him. Slowly, Scott's gaze met hers. Brenna mouthed the words, "It's okay."

She had never endured a longer meal. Regardless of the topic, Malcolm Stone and Mrs. Stone argued continuously, and all the while, Brenna was subjected to his degrading stares. When Mr. Stone said he thought it was time for everyone to retire, she immediately stood, thanked the family for the meal, and left.

Back in her quarters, Brenna jerked the ribbon from her hair, scrubbed her face vigorously with a large cloth, changed into her cotton night dress, and kicked back the covers. She fell on the bed and did not care how early it was to be retiring. Stiff from sitting so rigid at dinner and frustrated at what had transpired there, Brenna angrily tugged the blankets around her and tried to forget the entire affair.

She woke at a quiet knock on her door, completely unaware of how long she had been asleep. Brenna opened the pocket watch on her night stand and tilted it toward the fire. Puzzled at what Scott could want after eleven o'clock, Brenna drowsily put on her slippers and dressing robe and opened the door. Malcolm Stone was the last person she wanted to see standing there. Brenna pulled the gown tightly around her nightclothes, innocent of the lovely sight she presented standing in the glow of the firelight, with her golden locks cascading over her shoulders.

"Yes?" she asked plainly.

The man gasped from the corridor. His trek up the stairs left him breathing heavily. "I…ah, wanted to apologize for my wife's rude behavior this evening." Continuing to pant, he added, "It was most inappropriate."

Uncomfortable with his presence and the strong odor of brandy emanating from his breath, Brenna pushed against the heavy door, "No apology is necessary. Good night, sir."

Malcolm Stone wedged his foot against the door just before it closed, then kicked it open fully. His towering frame consumed most of the opening. He wiped the sweat from his forehead, his eyes unabashedly roaming the length of her body. Without warning, he grabbed a handful of her hair and stroked it between his thick fingers. She yanked it from his grasp.

"Oh, come now, Brenna," he slurred, the effects of his brandy apparent, "'tis late and let's be honest, we're both in need of a little company, aren't we now?"

Horrified, Brenna retorted, "'Tis obvious the lateness of the hour has affected your good sense. Now please, take your leave!"

"And you, Miss Brenna, have little say in the matter."

"Malcolm! Malcolm! Where are you?" bellowed the harsh voice of Mrs. Stone from below.

"Blimey, woman!" spat Malcolm Stone. He turned toward the sound of his wife's voice.

Brenna did not hesitate. She pressed hard against the door and secured the lock. Trembling violently, she fell against it.

With her suspicions confirmed, sleep did not come easily for her this time.

What am I going to do? I can't stay, yet how can I leave Scott in this terrible situation? The sun cast its early morning shadow over the frozen ground before Brenna finally found the sleep that had eluded her.

"Mercy," exclaimed Mrs. Stone sternly to Brenna, "if this weather doesn't clear soon, we shall have no guests at all!" The two women looked out at the row of icicles suspended from the window's frame.

"All the better," barked Malcolm Stone as he entered the parlor. "Guests are nothing but a bunch of bloody leaches!"

"Easy for you to say," cried his wife. "You aren't the one who has done all the work! You aren't the one who will be the laughing stock of the entire town! And you…"

"Hold yer tongue, woman!"

"Excuse me," interrupted Brenna, "I need to be getting back to your son." She turned to leave, but paused. "I realize you are both busy, but it would mean a great deal to Scott for you to look in on him."

"You mean to tell me he's still in bed?" interrupted Mr. Stone. "It's been four days!"

"He's had a raging fever. The doctor wasn't even sure he'd recover." Brenna felt her face flush.

"Enough!" demanded Malcolm Stone. "Don't you dare tell me how to raise my son!"

Brenna's eyes flashed. "How to raise your son? You've paid more heed to your horse!"

A dark, thunderous gaze consumed him. "No servant shall ever, do you understand me, ever speak to me that way!" He raised his arm to strike her.

"The first guest has arrived," interrupted a voice from the hall. Malcolm Stone stopped and pivoted angrily to face Stanford. The butler realized his announcement was ill-timed. He said sheepishly, "Shall I show him in, sir? It's your brother-in-law, the judge."

Malcolm Stone lowered his fist and turned toward his wife. "That's just wonderful," he said sarcastically. "And how nice that your brother is the first to arrive."

Brenna hurriedly left the room and mounted the stairs. She recognized she had crossed a dangerous line in speaking her mind. She knew better, and yet she felt someone had to be honest with them, if there was any hope for Scott. She understood her days here were coming to an end and this latest battle would not help. She wondered about Mrs. Stone's brother, the judge. It was obvious Mr. Stone did not like the man. Brenna decided that if Mr. Stone did not like his brother-in-law, then she most likely would.

She took a deep breath and turned the door to Scott's chambers. The boy's face lighted with a smile.

"Are my eyes playing tricks on me or is that actually the look of someone who is feeling better?" inquired Brenna, playfully moving toward his bed.

"Aw, Miss Brenna, you're funny."

"And you look so much better. It's great to see a little more color back in those cheeks." She reached out and tousled the boy's hair. "Since you're feeling better, would you care for some carrot and parsley soup? It's awfully good."

"No, thank you. I'm really not very hungry."

"You ought to be since you haven't eaten anything in days, and by the look of you, you'll waste away if you don't do so soon!" She realized he was not yet convinced. "And besides, I made it myself, especially for you."

"You did? Why?"

"Because I care about you." Brenna took his hand and sat beside him. "You gave us all quite a scare, you know." Brenna felt a surge of love for the boy. Until he became ill, she had not realized just how much he meant to her.

"Well," he said, interrupting her thoughts, "you might have been worried, but I think you were the only one who was."

Brenna did not see the judge standing in the open door behind her. "Everyone was very concerned."

"Was my mother?" Scott asked warily.

"Certainly!"

"Why didn't she stay with me like you?" His voice trailed off. "I think she was worried a lot more about her party than me."

Brenna thought of Mrs. Stone saying earlier in the week she feared exposing herself, thus disrupting the party. "Scott, she hired me to care for you, both when you're healthy and when you're not. And as for the party, she talked about postponing it, but when she knew you were going to be all right, she continued with the plans."

"But she never came to be with me."

"Well, it may be that..." Brenna stopped. Scott's eyes had moved to the door.

"Uncle John," beamed the boy obviously delighted, "you came!"

"Of course. Just as soon as I heard you were ill."

"You mean you didn't come just for the party?"

"Not at all, lad," he answered truthfully. "You know I don't care one bit for pompous socializing! It's you I'm worried about. And from the look of you, I arrived none too soon!"

"What do you mean? I'm feeling well now."

"You're skin and bones! I hardly recognize you!"

Scott's laughter filled the chambers. After calming, he asked excitedly, "Uncle John, have you met Miss Brenna?"

"Ah, so Brenna's the name of the lovely woman to whom I have yet to be introduced."

Brenna rose and introduced herself as Scott's governess. With the combination of the judge's laughing eyes and Scott's obvious affection for him, Brenna realized her first musings about the man had been correct. If Malcolm Stone disliked him, then surely she would like him, and she did so immediately.

"It looks like the two of you have some catching up to do. I'll be out of your way."

"Ah, come on Miss Brenna," sighed Scott. "Won't you please stay? I've been dying for you two to meet."

"From all of the things you have told me about him, I feel as if we already have." Brenna looked directly at John Charles and said warmly, "He speaks very highly of you. He's told me all about your wife and your chateau complete with horses and dogs. And he says you're the best player of bowls in England."

"A drastic overstatement, I assure you," laughed the judge, "but we would have a wonderful time if only his father would allow him to..."

Then, thinking more carefully about his words, he said, "If Scott were able to visit us more often."

"Yes," agreed Brenna. "I believe it would do him great good as well."

"Maybe," said Scott enthusiastically, "maybe Miss Brenna and I could visit you there soon. Maybe we could even go back with you when you leave!"

"Now that's an idea worthy of serious consideration," said the judge, smiling fondly at Scott.

"I really must be going back to my room now," said Brenna, placing a soft kiss on Scott's brow. "I'm so relieved you're feeling better. I'll be back to check on you later."

"Thank you, Miss Brenna," said Scott seriously, "thank you for everything."

Brenna mounted the stairs to her quarters. She could hear the gaiety of the party below. From the music and laughter, Mrs. Stone's much-worried-about party appeared to be a success. Once in her chambers, Brenna placed another log onto the hearth and sank down in her chair with a copy of William Shakespeare's *The Twelfth Night.* She had selected the book earlier in the day from the family library. Although she had not slept for any extended period during the four days Scott had been in bed, Brenna found it difficult to relax. The last week had taken its toll. First, the disastrous dinner with the family, followed by Mr. Stone's unwelcome visit to her room, and the day after that, Scott became ill. A light tap on her door interrupted her thoughts. She was almost afraid to ask who it was. To her surprise, it was the judge.

"I'm sorry to bother you, Miss Findlay, but I saw your lamp was still lighted, and I thought I might have a word with you."

"Certainly. Please come in," she said, offering him a seat on the chair across from her.

His serious manner frightened her. "What is it? Is it Scott?"

"Quite the contrary! I came expecting to see the old Scott, unhappy and following in the example of his father…thinking only of himself. Instead, I discover a happy, confident, and considerate young lad. I tell you," he shook his head slowly, "if I hadn't seen it, I would never have believed it! And I'm certain it's all your doing."

"Thank you, sir, but your credit is misplaced. Your nephew is a fine boy, one who was just in need of a little attention."

"I realize that. The lad and I have always been close, even though his behavior has been less than admirable. But raised in this home, it's a wonder he's kept his sanity at all! Excuse my frankness…and I don't mean to sound cruel," he continued, lighting his pipe, "I don't know what's gotten into my sister. Why she ever married the man will forever be a mystery to me! I tried to talk her out of it, but she would not listen to reason. And since her marriage, she has become more like the man, heaven forbid! But how she can ignore her own son is…well, it's just beyond my comprehension! Anyway, if it weren't for you, I don't know what would have become of him. I fear he would have become a replica of his cruel father. I honestly believe you have saved the boy from a very sad life!"

"You give me far too much credit!"

"And you give yourself far too little."

Uncomfortable with the compliments and uncertain just how to bring up the delicate subject, Brenna inquired, "Sir, forgive me. I know this is a private family matter, but have you ever considered," she hesitated, "caring for Scott yourself?"

"Believe me, there's nothing both my wife and I would love more, but my sister won't hear of it. She's too concerned what her so-called friends would say about her. We've considered taking legal action, but proving any wrongdoing on the part of a parent is exceedingly difficult, if not impossible, even for a judge!"

"Oh, I see," said Brenna disappointed. "I'm terribly concerned for him. I don't know how much longer I will retain my post here, yet I cannot, in good conscience, leave him alone here."

The judge inhaled his pipe deeply and studied the woman closely. "Well, perhaps, another reason for my visit today will help. I didn't mention it to Scott because I did not wish to give him false hope without first consulting his parents, but my wife and I are preparing to leave shortly for France and we're very hopeful he'll be able to accompany us."

"That would be wonderful!"

"We will be gone several weeks and Scott will need to continue his studies. I heard you are also his tutor. Would you be interested in joining us?"

Brenna nearly collapsed with relief at the prospect. "Oh, I can't tell you how thrilled I'd be!"

"Then it's set. I shall speak to my sister about it first thing in the morning."

"I am so glad," said Brenna, looking into the kind, brown eyes of the judge, "you are here and that Scott is well enough to enjoy your visit."

"And for that, I'm told, you are to be given the credit as well."

"I'm sorry?"

"Scott said you stayed by his side nearly four continuous days."

"I didn't want him to be alone. I remember when I was a child and ill, my mother stayed by my side, no matter what."

"She sounds like a good person."

"She was."

"She has passed away then?"

"Yes, several years ago."

"I'm very sorry to hear it. Where does the rest of your family reside?"

"I have no other family."

"Oh, I see," the compassion in his voice was evident. Then brightening, he said, "Since my wife was unable to attend tonight and I can see that you are in need of getting out of these cramped chambers, I have a request."

Brenna looked at him questioningly.

"That you escort me to the gala below."

"Me?" Brenna was astounded. "But it would not be fitting for a man of your stature to be seen with a nanny!"

"Ah, my dear, do you think I care one wit about what is proper or fitting? Why, I can't think of anything more enchanting than being seen with one of the great beauties in all of England, with the exception of my wife, of course," he smiled.

"I am very glad to hear of your loyalty and high regard for her, but truly, I cannot. I look a fright!"

"You, my dear, could not be more wrong."

"But I have nothing suitable to wear!" Seeing he was not convinced, she added, "Nor have I ever been to such an event. I would have no idea how to comport myself. Thank you for the offer. I am much honored!"

"Nonsense! You're coming and that's that. I shall be back in ten minutes." Not waiting for her reply, he left the room abruptly.

They walked down the wide stairs. Brenna held firm to the judge's arm. "I guarantee," he whispered, "that if you've never been to a ball in The Bath, you won't believe some of the ladies' outfits you're about to see!"

"I've seen some of the gowns the ladies parade in." She recalled one woman who wore a skirt that flared out several feet in one direction, which gave her a lop-sided appearance.

"Ah, then you've had a taste of the styles, but be prepared! The last party I attended here, a woman wore a birdcage, I jest you not, an actual birdcage with a bird in tow, as part of her hair coiffure!" He laughed. "It reminds me of the fable about the Emperor's New Clothes. If one person started to laugh, the rest would realize just how ridiculous they all look!"

Brenna wondered how ridiculous the people at the party would think her, wearing the plain blue gown the housekeeper had given her, with her long curls falling carelessly over her shoulders.

Brenna felt the eyes of many turning toward them when they entered the grand ballroom. She thought the level of conversation in the room momentarily diminished. Brenna blushed when the judge introduced her as his niece from London. She knew some of the neighbors knew better but none said a word. She guessed no one would risk questioning a judge.

Malcolm Stone cast a furious glare at her. The judge, guiding her toward the dance floor, whispered, "It's apparent my brother-in-law is quite perturbed at one of us. And although he doesn't care much for me, I cannot fathom what I've done recently to cause him such spite. Therefore, dearest niece, you must be the target of his anger."

Brenna bit her lower lip and looked away from Malcolm Stone. "You're right. I apologize. This is awkward. I ought to go before causing any more trouble." She turned to leave.

"Nonsense! I think we've just livened up this stuffy affair." Then more seriously, he asked, "Why is Malcolm so mad at you?"

"I'm afraid I failed to hold my tongue today."

"How delightful! What exactly did you say?"

"I told him I thought he ought to be more attentive toward his son."

"Oh my! I'm sure he was pleased at that! Malcolm is certainly not one who takes kindly to any criticism."

"So I've learned."

"And I take it you were protecting Scott today by telling him his parents inquired of him when he was ill?"

Brenna hesitated.

"You don't have to answer; I already know. However, I do appreciate your protection of Scott." He looked again at Malcolm Stone. "As much as I relish the thought of him being brought down a notch or two, I'm concerned for you." Quietly, he said, "I don't trust the man. He's full of anger. And, believe me, working with criminals all day I've come to recognize the signs. That man is trouble!"

"I agree," replied Brenna sincerely.

"I've been concerned for a long time for my sister, and lately, for Scott. While I don't believe he would harm his own family, a man like that is unpredictable."

The thought of Malcolm Stone hurting Scott filled her with terror. She remembered the hatred on his face earlier today. If they had not been interrupted, he would have tried to hit her. She had seen the same look in Harley, and yet, even he had never looked so menacing.

"Ah, well, let's not discuss such things now. There's a party here to enjoy. Now, what say you? Ready to give this dance floor a try?"

Rarely had Brenna known such gaiety. At first, she was self-conscious about her every movement. She recalled how Helen instructed her on various dance patterns. Helen told her that one day she would use her skills to attend socials. After her death, Brenna assumed those hours of practice had been wasted. She realized this ball might be the only opportunity she would ever have to put her mother's lessons to use.

She decided to ignore her fear and enjoy herself. After three dances with the judge, she happily accepted invitations with several other seemingly eager men.

The whole evening sickened Malcolm Stone. First, he had to put on a façade and greet the deplorable guests. Then, he was required to stand hour after hour on sore feet, in pants that were miserably tight, and watch his guests consume his food and wine. All he wanted was to go to his room and recline with a stiff brandy. The worst punishment was being forced to witness his brother-in-law, a man he detested, appear with and then flaunt about the room, the servant who had made a fool of him—the same woman who had become his sole obsession.

From the first moment he saw his son's nanny several weeks ago he tried to make her take note of him. At night, he envisioned her young, firm body lying naked next to his, and when he saw her, it was all he could do to control himself. Now, he was forced to watch her dance before him with other men. He wanted to shout that she was an imposter, yet he realized that doing so would bring himself embarrassment. Inwardly, he seethed. *Enjoy yourself now, Miss Nanny!! Soon…very soon…*

After nearly an hour and a half, Brenna once again danced with the judge. "Well, my dear," he laughed and twirled her, "I do say, you've been the talk of the party. I haven't heard of so much commotion happening in The Bath since Queen Anne visited in '02. Apparently, people talked of nothing else for years. I'd wager that after tonight, you'll need to brace yourself for the men who will be calling."

"Oh, Judge Charles, you quite flatter me with your exaggerations."

"And you, dear niece, are utterly too modest."

"Why did you introduce me as your niece? I'm certain to have been recognized by some as Scott's governess. I could prove a terrible embarrassment. And I'm certain my clumsy dancing has done nothing to promote your good name."

He squeezed her hand. "Nonsense! Never has my family been so well represented. I hope you didn't object to me introducing you as family, but I felt it might save you from tedious questions and quell any rumors that might have surfaced to hurt my wife. And as for your dancing, if I didn't know better, I'd say you've been doing so all your life."

"And you," said Brenna sincerely, "are overly kind!"

The judge beamed, glancing around the room at the flamboyant gowns and hairstyles. "I'm certainly glad the ladies haven't disappointed us tonight." Then in a hushed voice, he added, "Have you seen the woman with a built-in ship in her hair?"

Brenna threw back her head and laughed loudly, exclaiming, "How could I possibly have missed it?"

"These styles," he grinned, "are supposed to represent a woman's personality. What do you suppose the ship means?" Rippling with laughter, he said, "Wishing she could sail away from all this madness?"

Brenna laughed again. She was thoroughly enjoying the music from the lively, nine-piece orchestra. Throughout the evening, a variety of latecomers strolled in, their names announced as they entered. Brenna paid little attention to the introductions but she stopped cold when she heard, "Captain Nathan Grant, hailing from the American Colonies." Brenna froze, terror filled. "I…I'm sorry," she stammered once she finally could get enough air to make any sound, "I need to go…outside for a moment. I…I can't breathe." Brenna fled the dance floor and on to the terrace with the judge trailing close behind.

Once through the doors, the judge said, "My goodness, you're pale. Are you all right?"

"Yes," said Brenna visibly shaken. "I'm fine, I just felt a little sick." Brenna looked to make certain she could not be seen from within, then turned to the judge, "I'm sorry, but would you mind if I just stayed out here a minute and rested?"

"Of course not. You're not to move! I'll get you something to drink." He paused, "Would you also like a wrap? It's freezing cold."

"No, thank you, it feels good, but a refreshment would be fine." Once he was gone, Brenna steadied herself enough to cautiously peer from behind the green velvet curtain and through the French doors into the ballroom. She did not have to search far. Nathan Grant was a sight she could not miss. Attired in a black, short waistcoat, accented with a broad red cummerbund, the sea captain stood out from every man in the room. He and the judge were the only two men not wearing powdered wigs. Under different circumstances, and if she were seeing the captain for the first time, Brenna realized she would have been eager to meet him. Several women gathered around him, giggling, obviously trying to catch his eye.

She noticed that he appeared to have little interest in any of the women. He acted polite, yet she sensed a slight annoyance in him by their presence. Brenna smiled at the thought. Her smile quickly faded when she realized his lack of interest might be because his thoughts were with the beautiful woman from the Cross Bath. Brenna wondered if she would be joining him here.

"Brenna, I said, is this acceptable?" asked the judge from behind her.

"I'm sorry, I didn't hear you," she said, embarrassed. "Yes, this is fine, thank you." She gulped the punch and said, "Would you mind terribly if I retire to my chambers through the back door? I am," she said truthfully, "not feeling very well and would prefer not to encounter any of the guests."

"Certainly. I hope you're not coming down with whatever it was that made Scott so ill."

When she awoke the next morning, the uneasiness caused by Nathan Grant's unexpected arrival last night had not diminished. *What happened after I left? He obviously did not discover the truth or else I would surely not be waking here!*

The sound of angry voices from outside filtered through her partially open window. Brenna moved closer to the window to hear more fully. It was evident John Charles and Malcolm Stone were in the midst of a heated argument.

"Really, Mal," the judge was angrily saying, "I just don't understand your rationale!"

"And you're in no position to question it!"

Brenna felt a sinking feeling. Mr. Stone must have denied Scott the opportunity to travel to France. The judge's next words, however, clarified the subject of the argument.

"Just give me one good reason why Miss Findlay should not accompany her pupil to France?"

"As I've said, Scott has been studying very diligently these last few months and is deserving of a respite."

"Fine, then let her just come to look after him, and I'll see to it no formal studies are administered."

"You're missing the point!" argued Malcolm Stone. "Scott's been ill, probably pushing himself too hard with his constant studies. He will not be able to fully rest if she is present. She will be a constant reminder of his studies."

"That's ridiculous! Scott loves Brenna. Why I've never seen him more at ease than when he's with her!"

"My decision is not reversible!" shouted Malcolm Stone. "If she is to remain under my employ, she stays!"

After a long pause, the judge replied. Brenna could tell from his thin, low-pitched tone that he was struggling to contain his temper. "I have a mind to take you at your word and hire her myself, but in doing so, I would be taking away the best thing that's happened to the lad."

Brenna silently closed the window. Malcolm Stone had won the battle.

Chapter Ten

"I gather ye had no luck at last night's social in Bath," said Iestyn. He entered the captain's quarters and saw the familiar look of frustration on the captain's face.

"No. I found no trace of her."

"Well, perhaps," Iestyn said cheerfully, "the guests will have the opportunity this mornin' to again read the bulletin ye handed out. Hopefully, one of them may have a clue as to Brenna's whereabouts."

"If they read it this morning, it'll be the first time they've had the chance to do so."

"Really? Didn't ye distribute them as ye always do at these gatherin's?"

"No. As always, I approached the host, in this case, a Malcolm Stone. After giving him a bulletin and asking his permission to question his guests, he requested we discuss the matter in his study."

"And once there he declined to grant yer wish?"

"Not exactly. I was told his wife was overly concerned about the success of the party and he wanted nothing to jeopardize the festive atmosphere. He requested I say nothing to the guests but said he would see to it that each be given the notice as they left."

"And ye agreed?"

"I felt I had little choice."

"And do ye believe this Mr. Stone honored his promise and distributed them?"

"I have no reason to doubt him. But I'll tell you this, if we're ever asked to do business with him, I shall personally see to it that we decline."

"Really? That's surprisin' comin' from ye, sir. What did he do that bothered ye?"

"Nothing I can readily identify other than a vague sense that he's trouble. And besides," he grimaced, "he smelled…awful."

"Yer instincts are probably correct. An' did anything eventful happen at the party?"

The captain sighed, clearly disgusted. "It was the same as every other dreary social I've attended in this search these last couple months."

"Ye certainly didn't stay too long. Failed to attract the attention of any women, did ye?"

"It seems," said Nathan, ignoring the barb, "I missed all the excitement, for most of the talk was of a young woman."

"And ye mean to say," smiled Iestyn, "ye left the party without her? I must say I am worried about ye, Captain. T'would appear ye may be losing yer touch."

Nathan smiled pretentiously at his first mate. "Actually, I never got the opportunity, for she left prior to my arrival."

"Captain," said Iestyn much more seriously, "ye mean t' say ye never got a look at her? Isn't it possible one so admired could be Brenna?"

"Actually, the same thought occurred to me, knowing Brenna would cause such a commotion. I inquired into her identity. Unfortunately, this woman, a Miss Findlay, is the niece of a well-known judge from Winchcombe."

"What a pity! Wouldn't it have been somethin', t' find Brenna at an event like that!"

"T'would have been a coincidence! I'll tell you this, if Brenna is socializing, it won't be long before we locate her, for many a man will be eager to present her on his arm."

"And I assume yer speakin' from personal feelings?" Iestyn smiled broadly.

"Being with her, dear Iestyn…in the manner you refer…I assure you, has never entered my mind. As I've said before, I've an obligation to Weston and Emily to find her. And find her I will!"

Iestyn chuckled and closed the door behind him. "Whatever ye say, Captain."

Although the conversation had been in jest, Nathan was disgusted—disgusted because Iestyn's insinuations were the truth and Nathan could find no explanation for his feelings.

Although he tried to concentrate on the search for the daughter of Weston and Emily, his thoughts more and more turned to Brenna the woman. Every aspect of her fascinated him. Previously, he tried to convince himself the reason for his intrigue was purely to discover the facts of her mysterious past…her survival of the shipwreck, her childhood, the story behind an educated woman selling produce, and her reason for leaving the island. But lately, he realized that finding the answers to these questions and reuniting Brenna with her family were not his only motives for wanting to find her.

Since the day she ran from his ship, she was the center of his thoughts. Lately, he forced himself to admit his feelings were far more than mere concern about her safety. Although, God knows, he had done plenty of worrying. Never before had his thoughts been more consumed than during these past two months. From the moment he awoke, even before he opened his eyes, he thought of her. All day and into the long night he thought about her. Always one to be in control of his emotions, Nathan found these constant thoughts of her unnerving. When he ate, he wondered if she was able to find food. When he dressed, he wondered if she was warm enough. Never before had sleep been so elusive. When his exhausted body finally gave in to sleep, he saw her in his dreams. *What is wrong with me? Why does she haunt me? I barely know her!*

He removed her bracelet from his pocket and rubbed it between his hands. He remembered again the first time he saw her. Covered with mud and dripping wet, she still managed to hotly refuse his assistance. *How beautiful you were even then, Brenna.* He recalled his disappointment at having to leave the island without seeing her again and how he decided that on his next stop to St. Christopher he would make an effort to locate her. His second encounter with Brenna was just as vivid. Fragile and weak, she lay crumpled on the floor of the dark hold. Even now, the thought sickened him. She nearly lost her life aboard this ship. He closed his eyes to block the horrific image. *Why didn't you come to me, Brenna? Didn't you know I would never have let you suffer like that?*

Nathan stared out the small porthole to the hills of Bristol. *Brenna, where are you?*

"Hey, Captain," said a husky voice outside his cabin.

"Come on in. It's not latched."

"Hey, Captain," repeated the large man, grinning, "some of the men thought we'd stir this ole town up a bit tonight. Care to join us?"

"No thanks, Thatch. I don't really feel much up to going out tonight. Maybe next time, huh?"

"Yeah sure, Captain, maybe next time." The supercargo turned to leave but stopped. "Yer sure yer okay?"

At the captain's nod, Thatch added, "I don't mean to interfere, but some of the men have been concerned. Beggin' yer pardon," he stammered, unable to look directly at the captain, "an' I know I may be out of line, but are ye ill, sir?"

Nathan smiled at the burly man. "No, you can assure the men that I'm in the best of health, and unless I'm mistaken, both my physical and mental capacities seem to be intact." Stretching his legs upon his sea chest, he added, "I realize the men must have concerns about our delay in Bristol, and if so, please direct them to me. You have my word that as soon as we locate the girl, we shall make haste in weighing anchor."

"Thank ye for yer straight answers, sir," said the supercargo. "I've been with ye for a long time, and I just don't like to see ye suffering."

"I appreciate your concern, Thatch."

Thatch peeked his head around the outside of the door. "I'm certainly glad to know yer not ailing."

Maybe I am. Nathan thought, once alone. He locked his hands against the back of his neck. *I certainly must have been mad in my response to Launey at the bath house.* He was still puzzled by his reaction toward her. Before he began his search for Brenna, he had looked forward to seeing Launey again. Now, he possessed no desire to ever do so. His thoughts trailed back to what happened a month after his arrival in Bristol.

"Who is she?" Launey demanded and stormed into his cabin unannounced. Nathan was at his desk, cleaning his sextant. She flung the reward flyer at him and threw her satchel on his berth. "Two fortnights! You've been here well over two bloody fortnights and you didn't have the decency to let me know! I had to find out by my father showing me this ridiculous bulletin!"

Nathan looked up, surprised. "My apologies. I've been preoccupied with a pressing and unexpected matter." He had never before witnessed her anger and was surprised at its intensity.

"With what? Or whom? This Brenna woman?"

"Yes, mainly with Brenna."

"Why? Who is she?"

"She's the daughter," he said curtly, not in the mood for a confrontation, "of some close friends, and she's been missing for a very long time."

Launey looked at him closely. She twisted the silk ribbons from her bonnet around her long finger. Her tone went from loud to soft. "You were too busy to even call on me?"

"I've an obligation to find her," he responded dryly, "and the task has proved more challenging than I anticipated."

She moved to him and wrapped her slender arms about his neck. She stopped and waited for him to kiss her.

When he did not respond, she pulled away. "I…I can see your mind is on other things…for the moment." Then coyly, "But I do have something special to make you forget all your troubles. Just bring your carriage by my home late this afternoon and I'll see to the rest. I assure you, it'll be an evening you shall long remember."

Nathan opened his mouth to decline, when he thought of Brenna. Irritated by her continual intrusion into his thoughts, he changed his mind. "With an offer like that, how could I possibly refuse?"

Relief flashed on her face, then quickly disappeared. "By chance, while you were in St. Christopher, did you have an opportunity to visit that shop I told you about, the one that makes such exceptional gowns?"

The vision of Brenna in the yellow gown filled his mind. He'd had it tailored for Launey at her request. "I apologize, my plans changed. I don't have the dress."

"Oh, no matter," she said, obviously disappointed. "I have always admired the fine quality of the garments made by those islanders. How those primitive and barbaric people produce such high quality work, though, is beyond me."

Nathan realized that until now, he had never *really* looked at her, past her great physical beauty and into her heart. He did not like what he saw. "I suggest you broaden your knowledge about people and places before speaking your ignorance so freely."

Launey opened and then closed her mouth at his stinging reply. She had never heard him utter an unkind word before.

He mused back on what transpired later that evening and his response to Launey's not-so-subtle offer. *Yes, Thatch, I must be sick after all.*

In the carriage, Launey told him she had a big surprise waiting for him. The surprise, it turned out, was a private session at the Cross Bath. She had arranged every detail, complete with champagne on their journey to Bath.

Nathan was determined to force Brenna from his mind and enjoy the evening. He decided to give his courtship with Launey a little more time. *Hah! What a fallacy that proved to be!* When he stood in the warm waters of the Cross Bath and looked into Launey's dark eyes, it was Brenna's blue he saw. Instead of Launey's black hair, he imagined Brenna's golden tresses. And when Launey's body moved toward him in the water, it was Brenna he envisioned coming to him. He knew immediately he had made a mistake in being there. He refused to be with one woman while secretly longing for another. When Launey returned to the water after hearing a disruption, Nathan abruptly moved away from her. "I apologize for my wretched behavior. The fault is not yours but entirely my own. I'm afraid my pressing business will not allow me even the smallest of pleasures. If you'll excuse me, I think it best if we leave now." Nathan rose from the steaming water.

"But we just arrived!"

Launey looked bitterly out the front window of her home at Dowry Square in Bristol and thought about the disastrous evening at the Cross Bath. Her plans had been exemplary. She had been certain that by the end of the evening, he would ask for her hand. And if not, she had an alternative. Though she had not yet succeeded, she was determined to seduce him. She did not know the man overly well, but enough to know that if he believed her with child, he would marry her. It was all so perfect! She could leave Bristol with him. The fact that he was an American was inconvenient. She would certainly never consider living there, but she knew she could persuade him to build her a home in London. She understood he would be sailing most of the time anyway. She had always wanted to live in London. She knew precisely where her house would stand and how it would look. Her mother would be green with envy.

And now, because of his search for this Brenna, it's all ruined! I'd like to find the girl myself and wring her bloody neck! I wish I had done so when I caught her spying on us in Bath! He has to marry me! If not, I'll be forced to grovel before my parents and beg them to let me stay.

Launey hated the thought, yet her parents had given her three months to move out. If she worked hard enough, she thought she could get them to change their minds, but she was not sure, not this time. She had never seen them as angry as they had been these past two weeks. She feared they might make good on their threat to turn her out. She could not believe she had been so careless by getting caught stealing from them.

But it's their fault! They cut me off, saying I spent money on frivolities. Frivolities! How dare they? What did they expect? Do they really want the daughter of Bristol's most prominent judge to dress as a pauper?

Launey smiled at their foolishness. *They actually believed this was the first time! Her father...a judge...actually believed her tears!* She wondered what her parents would do if they knew she had been stealing from them for years. She almost wanted to tell them just to see their expressions. She could not believe how blind they had been…how always willing they were to blame the thefts on the housekeepers. She could not recall the number of housekeepers they had fired for theft. She smiled at her cleverness.

Launey fully expected Nathan to plead for forgiveness after his behavior in Bath. To her dismay, he did not. Finally, earlier this week, after deciding it must be his pride that prevented him from seeking her out, she sent a messenger to his ship with another invitation. "*Nathan. Thought we'd give it another try. Meet me at Fletcher's Inn, Thursday, seven p.m. I guarantee you'll forget your business affairs. Passionately yours, Launey.*"

Launey looked again out the window and smiled confidently at the sight of the returning messenger as he walked toward the front steps. She met him at the door and tore into the letter.

Dear Launey,

As you are aware, since my return to England, I have been dealing with a complicated issue. It has consumed nearly all my time and energy. With such preoccupation, I should not have accompanied you to Bath. To have done so was unfair to you.

I have since come to another realization for which I must be honest. I simply do not feel the level of enthusiasm in our relations to warrant continuation. It is my sincere hope that in the days ahead you find someone who will care for you wholeheartedly and unreservedly.

Please know this is sent with my deepest sympathies in trying to spare you further pain. Please accept my regrets also, that I will be unable to accept the fine invitation to join you at Fletcher's Inn and for my behavior the other evening. It was reprehensible.

Sincerely,
Nathan

Launey crumpled the note. She slammed the door and moved to the parlor. She looked furiously around the room. She spotted her father's prized crystal vase collection, grabbed the largest vase and threw it against the marble floor. It shattered. "How dare you! How dare you!"

The beautiful woman who had been hiding behind the curtain at the Cross Bath filled her mind. Launey reached for another vase, looked at it closely, and watched as it dropped from her hand. "I will not be discarded by you, Nathan Grant! I will not!" She screamed until she was hoarse.

She heard her mother's footsteps, running to see what had happened. Launey straightened her dress, looked at the shattered pieces of glass at her feet, and decided who she would blame for the mess. She had grown weary of the butler anyway.

It had been two days since she overheard the conversation between Malcolm Stone and John Charles. Brenna watched the carriage, drawn by two horses, slowly pull away from the house at the Royal Crescent. Scott's beaming face suddenly appeared in the open window. "Goodbye," he shouted exuberantly, "I shall miss you!"

"And I'll miss you! Have a wonderful time!"

"Oui! Oui!" came the boy's giggled response. The carriage rounded the corner.

Brenna slouched on the cold stone front steps. She felt her chest tighten with anxiety. Thrilled as she was for Scott, she knew she was not safe to stay here, yet she did not know where to go with Nathan Grant still in pursuit. The judge expressed his reservations for her safety as well. Shortly after dawn this morning he came to her chambers. Dressed in her night robe, Brenna ushered the man in.

"I beg your pardon to bother you at this hour, Miss Findlay," he said quietly, "but I wanted to speak with you privately before we leave today."

"No apology necessary. I wasn't sleeping." When Brenna saw his uneasy expression, she asked, "Is there something wrong? Have your plans changed?"

"No, we're still planning to leave after we sup, and unfortunately, we are still doing so without you."

"What's troubling you? Is it Scott?"

"No, Brenna, my concern is for you."

"For me?"

"To be perfectly frank, I don't believe my brother-in-law's argument for not letting you go. I have known him for a long time, and I know his motive is not Scott's well-being. No, there is definitely more to it."

"I know," replied Brenna truthfully, "but I shall be cautious."

"Nonetheless, I can't stop thinking of Malcolm's behavior toward you the other night at the party. He was definitely full of contempt."

"Don't worry," said Brenna, wishing she could believe her words with the same conviction she spoke them. "There are several staff members here who I'm certain will be willing to help should any trouble arise. As a matter of fact, I have been thinking to ask Mrs. Twedt if I can temporarily share her quarters."

"That would be wise. Still, I want you to be very careful. He's clever, Brenna. Be on your guard at all times."

"I will," said Brenna with much more enthusiasm than she felt.

Brenna sat with her knees huddled against her chest on the cold front steps and thought back on that conversation. Brenna wished she knew how to avoid Mr. Stone until she could decide where to go to be safe. To force her fears aside, she imagined Scott as he traveled with his aunt and uncle to France. She pictured his adventures. *What a grand time you shall have, Scott.*

Yesterday, she shared with him the knowledge she gained from Mr. Middleton about France. She yearned to join Scott on his travels, although she never let him know of her desire. She did not want to cause any further animosity between the boy and his parents, so she told Scott they had asked her to go but she declined. Brenna explained to him that she needed to further her studies in order to continue his tutoring. This time off would be the perfect opportunity to do so. Reluctantly, Scott accepted her argument.

I only wish you were going to live with them permanently, rather than just a holiday! Why is it that couples who would make such wonderful parents are so often unable to have children, yet those, like the Stones, can? It makes no sense! She thought of the parents who wanted her only for profit.

Brenna tried to create an image of her own mother and father, but nothing came. *Do I resemble either of you?* She hoped not, for she wanted no physical connection to them. She realized they could walk past her now and she would be none the wiser. Her brows furrowed as another thought struck her. *Are you even alive?* Brenna felt a wave of sadness rush through her. *Would I even know? Would I have any sort of sense if you had died? Probably not. But if you are alive, do you ever wonder about me or even care whether I'm alive? Do you have any regrets about selling me?* Brenna sighed. *No, likely not, for you never returned to St. Christopher to inquire about me.*

Brenna patted her knees and realized she had no time for such bitterness or musings. She had to decide what to do quickly.

She spent the day walking the quiet neighborhoods of Bath in deep contemplation. Reluctant to face the Stones alone, she delayed her return until well past sunset. Brenna slowly walked in the direction of the home and noticed Mrs. Twedt coming toward her.

"Oh, Brenna," she said, obviously surprised, "I thought everyone had left. Did ye forget something?"

"What do you mean, Mrs. Twedt, 'forget something'? I'm just returning."

"So ye haven't heard?"

Brenna looked at her blankly.

"Mr. Stone's given all the staff the night off!"

"Really?"

"That's precisely what I said when I heard of it. In all my years here, he has never given all of us time off at once." Then cheerfully, she added, "Whatever the reason, I'm so pleased! Oh, and I do wish you'd call me Carolyn. Well, I'd best hurry. I'm going to see Jill and the baby." Mrs. Twedt called over her shoulder, "Can't believe I'm a grandmamma!" Not waiting to hear Brenna's response, she scurried down the street.

Brenna dashed into the house. She took several steps at a time up the three flights of stairs. She did not know where she would go, but knew she would not stay here alone with Mr. and Mrs. Stone. Hastily, she stuffed the estimated cost of a night's lodging into her pocket and placed her remaining earnings back into a pewter canister. She secured the lid and slipped the small container under her mattress. *If I have to waste my coin like this, I'll never be free of my debt to the Yankee captain! But what choice do I have?*

She turned to leave and jumped. Malcolm Stone stood in her doorway.

"Oh! You…you frightened…" Brenna recovered slightly. Visibly shaken, she added, "I didn't hear you enter." She realized only then that she had smelled his awful presence a second before she saw him.

"My dear," he said sweetly, "I'm sorry if I startled you."

"'Tis' of no concern," her calm belied her fears. The sight of him in his night robe stretched tightly over his midsection added to her panic. "Now if you'll excuse me."

"And where, may I ask, are you going?"

"I was informed we were given the night off."

His eyes narrowed slightly. "Ah, that's correct, but where would you possibly go at this hour? My wife told me the tragic tale of how ye have no family."

"Well, I…I have friends who will welcome me," lied Brenna weakly.

"That is a relief," he toyed, "for I would hate to speculate on what might become of you, should you be forced to ah…wander the streets."

Brenna was desperate to get away from him. "If there is nothing else, I shall…" She instantly regretted her choice of words.

"Ah, but there is…so much else…and I believe you know precisely what those duties are." He rubbed his thick hands together. "That is, if you wish to remain working here."

Brenna flushed with anger and moved toward the door. "If those duties include compromising myself, then I assure you, I am no longer under your employ!"

Calmly, he extended his enormous arm and blocked her passage completely. "Oh, come now. Think of Scott's devastation when he returns and finds you gone." He licked his lip, as a lion about to devour its prey, and added, "You don't really want to go out in the cold when you've got me to keep yer flesh warm."

Repulsed, she hoped to appeal to his sense of loyalty. "I'm certain your wife also needs your warmth."

Malcolm Stone grinned wickedly, "Ah yes, the good Mrs. Stone. You need not worry about her, for since she's had so many fitful nights lately, I added a little ah…something extra to her toddy tonight. Rest assured she's sleeping quite soundly."

Her voice quivered, unable to hide her disgust. "I will never, never compromise myself to you!"

Forcefully, he grabbed and twisted her arm. "And just who do you think you are to deny me?"

Brenna jerked away. "Don't you touch me, or I'll..."

"You'll what? Run to your captain friend?"

Brenna's jaw sagged.

Malcolm Stone beamed. "Ah, yes, I know all about Captain Nathan Grant. How, you ask? Let's just say," he smirked and pulled out a reward bulletin from his robe pocket, "that one of our little visitors here the other night had a vested interest in you." He leaned casually against the door frame and continued confidently, "You do realize that if you refuse me now, I'll have no choice but to turn you over to him? And you don't really want that now, do you? Why else would you be using my home as a hideout?"

Terrified as she was by Nathan Grant, she relished the prospect of having to face the captain now. "I will not be blackmailed! Turn me over to him if you wish, but I will not be coerced! Never!"

"How confident you are! But 'tis evident you have no choice. Oh, you can rest assured, I'll collect the reward for you...and it will be so much sweeter...after tonight. I couldn't turn you over without a proper goodbye, now could I? If it's by force, all the better...for only I will be unscathed by such an encounter!"

Her heart pounded, her eyes were wide. She scanned the room for an escape, unaware she was biting her lower lip.

He laughed, reading her thoughts, "There's no other way out." She looked toward the window. "You'd never survive the fall." He widened his stance and said with a twisted smile, "Ah, my dear, you may fear me now, but after our...ah, escapades, you shall yearn for more of my bountiful body."

Icily, she stared into his gray eyes. "Even in death, my body would turn away from you repulsed!"

He lunged forward. Alert for his action, Brenna dodged low and fell to the floor in the opposite direction. She scrambled out the door. A wrenching grip seized her ankle and dragged her back into the room. Wildly, she clawed at the hall floor, unable to anchor herself. He forced her on her back and savagely tore the front of her gown and chemise.

Crazed by the sight of her bare breasts, he pressed his chest against hers. Brenna was being crushed. She gasped for air. The heaving, sweating animal smothered her lips with his. She slammed her teeth into his and pierced his flesh.

"Ah!" he screeched. His head whirled back. Blood trailed from his mouth. Enraged, the powerful man slammed his fist into her face. An anguished cry escaped her. Listlessly, her head rolled to the side. Several seconds passed before she was able to focus enough to realize he was on top of her, clumsily trying to pull aside the remainder of the sleeping gown at her waist. She reached out and grasped the base of her washstand and pulled it toward her. She heard the splintering sound of porcelain as it smashed his skull. With her last surge of strength, Brenna wiggled free. Glass, water, and jagged wood covered the floor. Blood oozed from his head. She crawled toward the stairs, clamored to her feet, and descended quickly.

Wicked, slurred words echoed from above. "You'll pay, wench! You'll pay!"

A delicate array of spider webs covered the beams, rafters, and walls of the decrepit barn. Piles of dead flies, contorted and stiff, littered the frozen manure and dirt foundation. The wood slats, warped with age and connected by crumbled mortar, were no match for the January winds. Brenna huddled in the corner of the half-standing stall and wept. She was oblivious to the surroundings and the temperature. Her body was evidence of the violent night past. The left side of her face and lips were twice their normal size and were a combined shade of crimson and coal. Her right eye was swollen closed. She rubbed her bruised and swollen ankle. Brenna shuddered at the thought of what would have happened if Malcolm Stone had completed his brutal act. She knew her battered condition was the result of a struggle that lasted only a few seconds. She realized she would not have survived much more violence. She thanked God she was alive and that the savage man had not the time to complete his violation of her. But even in her relief, Brenna could find no consolation.

Once again she had no home, no future. She might again serve as a governess, but the threatening words of Malcolm Stone boldly intruded into her thoughts. *You shall pay*! She knew he would never give her a reference and her chances of finding another household to take her without one were slim. She knew also he would see to it she was never hired in Bath or the surrounding areas. *And if he saw the flyer in Bath, the place where I tried to destroy them, I will surely never be safe to work anywhere else where they are still posted.*

Hot tears streaked down her swollen cheeks and lips. She stopped and half-smiled. The jesting words of a stranger caused her to smile despite her sadness. *T'would appear, madam, that your tears do little to aid in the soggy state in which you now find yourself.*

Funny, you of all people, Nathan Grant, should be the one to comfort me now! Oh Captain, I wish you were here! Brenna rubbed her pounding temples. *Why him? Of all people! Why do I crave him here now? What's wrong with me?*

Explosively, the images of the voluptuous woman on St. Christopher, the brunette at the baths, and the women gathered around him at the party flooded her thoughts. *What a fool I am! No, Captain Grant, I will not be added to your list of worshiping women!*

Her thoughts of the captain momentarily gave her a reprieve from the despair in her heart. She knew she had decisions to make. She was overwhelmed at the idea of starting all over. As she had the day her money was discovered by Harley and then again when she was near death in the hold, Brenna felt the deep ache of uncertainty.

She did not know where else to turn. She closed her eyes and whispered, "You gave me hope before, when I thought there was none. I am before you again asking that you have mercy upon me and show me the way, for I don't know what to do. Help me."

She rounded the corner and faced the house at the Royal Crescent. It looked particularly ominous. *I had so hoped that within your walls I would find peace and love.*

After her desperate flight from the house last night, she wanted never to return. Yet, after her prayer, she reached a decision. She would journey toward the country home of John Charles and wait for his return from France. She knew she would be on her own for considerable time and needed her savings. She prayed that since it was nearly noon, Malcolm Stone would be at his shop.

Reluctantly, she climbed the front steps and tried to push aside her terror of last night and the throbbing of pain in her face. Silently, she entered the house.

Brenna stood in the dark entrance and heard the pounding of her heart in her ears. She wondered whether the cold draft hugging her ankles was merely her imagination. The eerie quiet that greeted her was unexpected and unsettling. *Where is everyone? Surely, the staff ought to have been back hours ago. Is Mrs. Stone still sleeping off the effects of whatever it was her husband gave her? Why is it so dark in here?* It was then she noticed that the curtains were still drawn and shutters closed.

Well, at least I don't have to explain my battered appearance to anyone, thought Brenna, fighting the urge to flee. She assured herself she would only be there long enough to gather her belongings. Shakily, she tiptoed up the stairs to her chambers. Her bedroom door was ajar. She stopped in mid-stride at the sight of the splintered wash stand still on the floor. *Why would he have left it there? Surely it would have triggered numerous questions from his wife and the staff.* Then, the sickening revelation struck her. *He's expecting me! He's waiting for me!* Brenna no longer cared about the money. She spun and ran down the steps to the front door. As she jerked it open, Brenna froze. An unfamiliar voice spoke from behind her, "Aren't you forgetting this?" Brenna wheeled around and could see only the outline of two darkened figures in the parlor entry. One of the men quickly pulled aside the curtains. The two were in uniform. Holding her container of coins, one of the men repeated, "I said, aren't you forgetting this?"

Dumbfounded, Brenna stared at the men.

"Well, what are you waiting for? Aren't you going to arrest her?"

Brenna recoiled at the high-pitched voice of Malcolm Stone, only now visible as he rose from a wingback chair. A large bandage was draped about his head.

"Miss Brenna Findlay," said a man of small stature, "I am Constable Bannit. This is my assistant. The court of The Bath formally charges you with the murder of Mrs. Marigold Stone."

Unable to comprehend all of what he said, Brenna heard only, *the murder of Mrs. Stone.* Mumbling, she asked, "Mrs. Stone? She's dead?"

"Don't play the fool with us, Miss Findlay," said the constable smugly. "Mr. Stone told us everything."

Stunned, she asked, "What everything? What are you talking about?"

The constable cast a warning glance toward his snickering assistant. He then returned his gaze to Brenna. "Mr. Stone told us how, after he settled down last evening in his study to read, he was interrupted by an argument between you and his wife. When he entered your chambers, he saw you stab her with the fire poker."

"What?" Brenna was unable to believe what she was hearing.

The man ignored the interruption. "And after the murder, you tried to flee. In an effort to stop you, Mr. Stone wrestled you to the floor. You then pulled the wash stand upon his head."

"He's lying!"

"Come now, madam. The evidence is quite clear. Even a neighbor witnessed you rushing from the home as if your life depended on it."

"My life did depend on it," cried Brenna helplessly. She turned directly toward Mr. Stone and exclaimed, "He attacked me!"

The constable found her argument entertaining and wanted to know how she would continue with her tale. "I see," he said as he attempted to contain a smile, "and Mr. Stone tried unsuccessfully," he said dramatically, while looking at the size difference between them, "to attack you?"

"That's right."

"And that would explain your bruised appearance?"

Brenna rubbed her hand against her tender cheek. "Yes, yes, of course."

"Why then, Miss Findlay, if Mr. Stone tried to *attack* you, as you say, would you ever return to his home? Were you hoping for another encounter?"

"No! I thought he'd be gone. I was returning to collect my belongings."

"And included in your belongings were the earnings you thought too paltry. You did not feel you were being paid your worth."

"What?" asked Brenna, utterly confused by this new accusation.

"Mr. Stone told us he offered to pay you a higher salary, but when his wife found out, she encouraged him to reconsider. She then came to your quarters to explain her reasoning. The two of you quarreled, and in your fury, you killed her!"

"That's ridiculous! I was more than satisfied with my wages! I never saw Mrs. Stone last evening. Officer," she pleaded, struggling to speak through her swollen lips, "I'm innocent!" She desperately wanted him to listen, "If I committed this horrible offense, why would I take the enormous risk to return today?"

"Greed, my dear, greed. It is the root of many foolish decisions!"

"No! You're wrong! You're wrong about all of this! When I ran last night, I wanted to escape from that evil man!" Brenna pointed a sharp finger directly at Mr. Stone.

"Yet, if what you say is true, you ran away from an employer to whom you were indebted."

"How so?"

"He said ye were hired with no references. I have never heard of that being done. Yet, he took the chance with you."

"His wife was the one who took the chance. She hired me, not him."

Angrily, he turned on her, "And you rewarded her by stabbing a poker through her!"

"No!" screamed Brenna, sickened by the thought of Mrs. Stone dying so brutally.

"Why, then, did you have no references? Could it be that you were in trouble before? Possibly, this is not even your first arrest for murder!"

Brenna panicked. *Should I tell him the truth, but what then? He'll certainly find me even that more guilty! No, my past will only further incriminate me, and surely by the time they know the truth about me, Judge Charles will have returned. He will help them understand that Malcolm Stone is guilty.* Brenna tried to calm herself. She took a deep breath and said, "I had no references because I had no previous working experience, and I have no family. That has nothing to do with what is happening here!"

"And just what is that?" questioned the constable.

"I am being falsely accused of a crime I did not commit! And with your assistance, sir, the killer is being allowed to go free."

"And who do you propose is our murderer?"

She looked squarely at Malcolm Stone. She ignored his glare. "Mr. Stone is responsible for the death of his wife."

"And if ye were in fact accosted by the man, as you claim, why didn't you go to the authorities immediately?"

Trying to ignore the terror which Malcolm Stone sent through her, Brenna concentrated her attention on the officer and his question. "I needed the chance to decide my course of action," she said truthfully.

"Interesting theory," said the constable, "almost convincing."

"You can't be serious!" roared Malcolm Stone, who had remained silent to this point.

"Well, it appears it's your word, Miss Findlay, against his." Then, without warning, he said, "Brenna Findlay, ye are hereby placed under arrest for the murder of Mrs. Marigold Stone."

"No!" cried Brenna helplessly.

Eager for his chance to assume authority, the assistant quickly moved forward and placed heavy iron clamps about her wrists and ankles. With the assistant pressing her forward, Brenna shuffled down the front steps and into a metal carriage. The words of Malcolm Stone from the previous evening rang in her ears. *You shall pay!* Brenna realized he would try to see that she paid with her life.

Charleston, South Carolina

Emily's scream pierced the darkness. She grasped Weston's arm and wailed, "She's in trouble!"

"Wha..." Weston was startled awake by his wife's cry. He reached out to pull her toward him, but she shoved him away.

"You've had another nightmare?"

Emily did not answer. She moved from the bed and began to pace the dark room.

"Emily, what is it?"

"She's in trouble, Weston! She's in trouble!"

Weston struck a match and lit the candle on the nightstand. Even in the dimly lit room, he could see Emily's ashen face. He had not seen her this distraught in years. "Emily, come back to bed. It's just a dream. It'll be okay." He wished he felt so certain his words were true.

Emily, wide-eyed, nearly shouted, "It won't be, Weston, not ever! Not ever!"

Weston sat helplessly on the side of the bed. He knew of nothing he could say that would help.

"I'm telling you, Weston, she's in trouble! She needs me and I'm not there!"

Weston struggled to hide the fear he felt for his wife. "Emily, listen," he said firmly, "listen to me. She's not in trouble. She's dead! And there's nothing any of us can do to change that!"

"Oh, Weston," she sobbed, sinking back upon the berth. "I know it doesn't make any sense and I can't explain it." Weston wrapped his arm around her.

Unable to stand the confinement, Emily abruptly stood and dropped the sleeping gown off her shoulders and onto the floor. She walked to the large wardrobe, yanked open the heavy doors, removed a dress, pulled it on, and began to furiously fasten the buttons down the front.

"What are you doing?"

"I'm going back."

"What?"

"I'm going back."

"Back? Back where?"

"St. Christopher."

"Emily, this is insane!"

"I don't care! I'm going back!"

"Emily, why are you doing this? Why now?"

She turned to face her husband. Never before had he witnessed what raw truth looked like, yet he saw it now and was terrified.

She lifted her head and looked at him directly. "Because I don't believe she's dead."

Weston felt a wave of sickening despair. He sensed what his wife might be thinking, but to hear her voice the words was shattering.

"I used to believe she was dead. I no longer do."

"Emily, do you hear what you're saying?" At her silence, Weston dropped his head to his chest, defeated. His eyes swelled with large tears, and he looked with hatred at his own hands.

His fists clenched and his voice trembled. He looked at his wife. "Do you have any idea how I wish to God you were right? I want her back too! More than life itself, I want to bring her back to you! And I…I want that moment back!" Weston cried out in a pain so deep that he sounded like a wounded animal. "I had it in my hand, Emily! I had it in my hand!" Then, struggling to find the courage to continue, he choked back the tears, "Do you know what I would do for another chance…for one chance to have that moment back?"

Emily closed her eyes and bit her quivering lip. She saw for the first time what pure guilt could do to a man. She knew that although he never uttered them, his next words had been burning within, slowly tearing him to pieces for nearly twenty years.

"I let go, Emily! I let go of the rope!"

"You didn't let go!" Emily's eyes blazed with anger. "It was taken from you, Weston! Look at me, look at me! And you hear me, Weston, for it's the truth and you know it! No one…no one could have held that rope!"

Weston knew she spoke the truth but it was of little comfort. He still wanted another chance. By God, he would let his arm be wrenched from its socket before he would let go again!

Emily moved to the open window. The sea breeze drifted across her face. Suddenly, it was so clear. She knew no one would ever understand. But she knew the dreams…all the dreams…all the nightmares, over all these years, had been Brenna's way of trying to reach her. She was more certain of this than she had ever been of anything in her life. Whether from heaven or earth, she knew not. And it had taken far too long, but she finally understood the cries.

Emily turned and went to her husband. She took his trembling hand in hers. "I know how this must sound, Weston, but I'm not crazy. Something happened to me tonight. I don't know why or how, only that it did. She's in trouble. I know it. I can feel it with everything I am. And I don't care if I have to swim. I'm going back to St. Christopher! I don't know where else to look."

Bristol, England

"Captain! Captain! Read this!" shouted Iestyn. He ran toward Nathan, who stood at the foredeck conversing with the coxswain. Iestyn shoved a letter in his hand.

Nathan frowned at the stricken look of his first mate. He scanned the first few lines of the letter before he demanded, "When did you receive this?"

"Only moments ago." Visibly shaken, Iestyn asked, "Oh, dear God, what does this mean?"

Nathan did not reply. He flung the parchment on the deck, leaped down to the lower deck and onto the wooded gangplank. He jerked the reins of his gelding from the hitching post, swung into the saddle, and commanded the horse into a breakneck gallop.

Iestyn picked up and reread the horrifying letter.

Dearest Iestyn,

I know not my precise reasoning for writing this to you, yet in doing so, perhaps it may relieve some of my inner turmoil. While I pen this to you, I await with heavy heart, my execution for the crime of murder. As you read this, I will surely have felt the grip of the hangman's noose. Looking at the gray, stained walls of this Bristol prison, I face my greatest humiliation—leaving this life having made so little contribution, so little difference.

Your captain once vowed that his justice would be my end and perhaps it is for that crime I am now being punished. Yet, it is important you understand that for the crime of murder, I am wrongly convicted. Perhaps, though, in the law of God, punishment is irrelevant to the crime, and this then is mine. If dying this way is His heavenly wish, I will try to die with dignity.

While in Bath, I tutored a young boy named Scott Stone, for whom I have the greatest fondness. You spoke often of your captain as honorable and of considerable influence, even in England. If that is true, and I pray that it is so, I implore you to convince him to do whatever he can to secure the boy's future to the care of his uncle, Judge John Charles of Winchcombe. I realize this is asking a great deal of a man to whom I am indebted, but Iestyn, a fine young life depends on it. I die in peace knowing you and your captain will do all that is possible to see that Scott is well cared for.

When I began this letter, I was uncertain for my reason in doing so, but it has now occurred to me that, as self-serving as it may be, I simply wanted someone to know of my passing and for someone to care. This may be asking overly much considering my behavior aboard The Grace, yet throughout my silence, you continued to care for me. Whether you were acting upon the command of another does not matter, for you treated me with a compassion and kindness I have not known since I was very young. Please accept my sincerest apologies for my behavior toward you.

The knowledge that you are sharing in my final thoughts is of great comfort to me now, for I know I am not alone. Thank you for being the kindest of friends. I have one final request. Through a miracle in the dark hold, I recently became a believer in Christ and know you are as well. If you will say a prayer for me, I will be forever indebted.

Take good care, my friend, and may all your days be filled with blessings and joy.

Fondly and forever yours,
Brenna

"Where is she?" stormed Nathan, bursting through the front gate of Bristol's Newgate Prison.

"Who?" asked the lethargic guard. He rose slowly from his chair.

"Brenna," said Nathan as he leaned forward on the man's desk.

The man yawned and said, "Oh, her. Well if ye've come for the hangin', yer too late. She saved us the tro…"

Nathan jerked the man by his collar and with a deadly glare, he demanded, "What are you saying?"

The man pulled back from the looming figure. He saw a murderous look in the green eyes. "Yer too late, she's dead."

Chapter Eleven

Ye're too late! She's dead, she's dead, she's dead! With his head between his hands, Nathan squeezed his temple, trying to crush the hollow, relentless words. Violently, his arm swept the copper dish from in front of him. The owner of the wharf inn, a short stocky man, fidgeted nervously behind the counter. The disheveled patron had been sitting in the same spot for nearly seven hours, not eating or drinking, just sitting. Yet, it was clear he was battling an unseen demon.

Oh Lord, Brenna, if only I could take back my words! If only I hadn't appeared so callous, perhaps you would have sent word that you were in trouble! If only…

"Captain," interrupted Iestyn softly, "I'm glad I found ye. I've been lookin'…"

"What do you want?"

Iestyn had known Nathan Grant for a long time. He knew he would be riddled with guilt over Brenna's death, but nothing prepared him for the sight of the man before him now. Having scarcely eaten or slept in over a week, the captain's complexion was gaunt and pale, covered in part by a stubble of beard. His eyes were dark and sullen. Normally impeccably dressed, Nathan's clothes were rumpled and soiled.

"Captain," said Iestyn softly, "don't ye think ye ought to be gettin' back to the ship? Ye look like ye could use a good…"

"If you've come to lecture me, Iestyn, just leave."

"I'm concerned 'bout ye, sir."

"I don't need or want your concern!" snapped Nathan.

Exasperated, Iestyn said, "Well, t'would appear someone needs to look after ye, seein' that ye ain't doin' so yerself."

"You've said your piece, now get out!"

Iestyn had never before raised his voice to the captain. "Ye can sit here all ye want and starve yerself to death, but it ain't gonna bring her back! She's dead and there ain't nothin' we can do 'bout it now! Nothin'!"

Nathan flinched against the words and stormed, "That's right, she's dead, and the fault is mine! You tell me, Iestyn, how I am ever going to tell Emily I found her daughter, and because of me, she's dead!"

Unable to bear the sorrow in his friend's eyes, Iestyn looked away. "I don't know, but I do know that as hard as it is for ye t' realize, there are some things which not even ye are goin' t' be able to control." Iestyn moved into the booth and continued quietly, "'Tisn't yer fault Brenna took her own life. The blame is not with ye."

"She's dead because she was running away from me and because I was not there to stop her."

"Nay, Captain. She's dead because she hanged herself. If she wouldn't have done so, ye probably would have arrived before she was executed. The fault lies solely with her. She thought her situation was hopeless, yet as long as there is life, there is hope. Brenna failed to realize this and it cost her life."

"What kind of a life did she have? She had no one, Iestyn, no one! And worst of all, she knew it! Oh God! And she died in that stinkin' hellhole!" Nathan closed his eyes against the image of Brenna spending her last days in Bristol's revolting dark prison, a prison that was unquestionably the most wretched in the region, nearly as notorious as London's own Newgate Prison.

"Why did they bring her to Bristol?" he asked helplessly. "Was it asking too much to let her stay in the Bath prison where at least she wouldn't have to die surrounded by such filth? Where she could do so with some dignity?" Pausing, he straightened slightly.

"Dignity," he whispered, "*dignity*." Rubbing his hands over his rough beard, Nathan's tired eyes stared at Iestyn, "Tell me, is tying a dirty sheet around your neck, standing on a stool, then kicking it away, dying with dignity?"

"What?"

"Look at this." Nathan removed Brenna's crumpled letter, which Iestyn had given him after learning the terrible news of her death. Even though he could barely stand the sight of it, Nathan had forced himself to read it over and over these last few days, as if doing so might somehow change the outcome. Nathan's hands shook as he clenched the tattered letter. "Right here. She says she will 'try to die with dignity.' Does killing yourself sound like one who plans on dying with dignity?"

"Nay, but I don't see why any of this matters now. What's done is done."

"And another thing that bothers me about all this," said Nathan, ignoring Iestyn's answer, "does Brenna seem like the type of person who would kill herself?"

"I don't think there is any one type who does such a horrible thing."

"Perhaps," said Nathan, squinting absently at his first mate. "But the more I think of it, the more it just doesn't make sense."

"What doesn't make sense?" Iestyn was confused by the subtle change in the captain.

"Brenna. We always were certain of one thing about her; it was that she was a survivor." He pulled his coat over his shoulder and added, "I guess what troubles me the most is that I just don't believe she would do it."

"Captain," Iestyn said, worried, "that well may be the case, but the fact is we know she did."

"No," corrected Nathan as he rose, "we know the guard at the prison said that she did."

"Aye, but sir, you inquired about that, and the guard said he removed the body himself."

"Removed, yes, but he didn't say he knew for a fact she was dead."

"But Captain," argued Iestyn, "don't ye think he'd notice if'n she weren't dead?"

"I don't know, I never asked!" As Nathan headed toward the door, he tossed several coins at the inn's owner.

Surprised, the man responded, "Thank ye! This more than covers..." Nathan was gone before the man finished.

Nathan Grant leapt off his horse and ran toward the prison gate. Trailing behind, Iestyn said breathlessly, "I think yer being very unrealistic, sir."

Over his shoulder, Nathan snapped, "Perhaps, but one way or another, I'm going to get some answers."

Iestyn shook his head. He feared the captain was setting himself up for a heartbreaking disappointment.

The man stationed at the battered front desk was not the same man who had been on duty the previous week. "Where," demanded Nathan, "where's the turnkey who was on watch the night the woman hanged herself?"

"Let's see." He shuffled through some documents. "Ah, that would have been Stan. Stan Peterson."

"Where is he?"

"Probably at his place," he shrugged. "He lives in a room above the inn over there, across the street."

Nathan stopped and pivoted. "By the way, where were you that night?"

With ale in hand, the jailor opened the door. His face dropped at the sight of the man who, a week earlier, caused him to fear for his life. And from the look of his disheveled appearance, the stranger was even more menacing than the guard recalled. Nervously, he asked, "What is it?"

"There are a few questions I'd like answered." Nathan entered the room uninvited, with Iestyn behind.

The guard said gruffly, "I'm off duty now, and besides, I answered all yer questions the other day."

"Not quite," said Nathan. "You said she hanged herself?"

"That's right."

"Then you saw her for yourself?"

"Yep," replied the guard, visibly uncomfortable with the probe.

"And she was dead?"

"Bloody buzzard! Don't ye think I know a dead person when I see one?"

Acutely aware of the man's uneasiness, Nathan gambled, "It just seems that a man would not be sweating at such harmless questions unless he had something to hide."

"I've nothin' to hide," retorted the man angrily. "I jus' don't like someone accusing me of not knowing a dead person when I see one. Now, if ye don't mind…"

Nathan knew the man was lying. He abruptly drew his saber. With the point gleaming at the base of the jailor's throat, Nathan whispered through clenched teeth, "As a matter of fact, Mr. Peterson, I do mind. And I suggest, if you place any value on your life, you tell me exactly what you're holding back and why."

The man dropped his mug, his words spewed forth. "I didn't think t'would matter!"

"You didn't think what would matter?"

"Seeing how she was dead anyway, I let him take the body."

"Who?" questioned Nathan.

"The judge. Judge Charles."

"Judge John Charles?"

"Aye."

Stunned, Nathan let the sword's tip drop to the floor. "Judge John Charles came to see Brenna? Why?"

Exhaling loudly at the removal of the blade, the guard spoke more freely. "His sister was the one this Brenna woman murdered."

"Supposedly murdered," corrected Iestyn.

"His sister? Are you sure?"

"Aye."

"Then why," Nathan mused as he placed the saber back in its sheath, "would he come to see her?"

"He said he came to see her hang."

Nathan looked squarely at the guard and said sternly, "I want to know everything that happened that day, every detail."

"Well," began the man slowly, "it started when the prisoner requested a quill and parchment. As she hadn't asked for nothin' since she arrived, I agreed. So after ciphering awhile, she called me back to her cell and asked me if I'd hire a messenger. I used the coins she had when she arrived and paid a lad to deliver the letter. He said he'd deliver the message first thing the next morning."

"And kept the rest of the money for yerself, no doubt," interrupted Iestyn.

"Seeing how she wouldn't need it, I didn't..."

Irritated, Nathan demanded, "We know about the letter, now what happened next?"

"Well, not much, until late that evening. The judge came in. Said he had just arrived from France and heard 'bout his sister's death. Said he wanted to see the murderess for himself. He being one of our own, I gladly gave him the key to her cell."

"And he went to see her?" asked Nathan.

"Aye."

"He went alone?"

"Aye."

"And next?"

"He came running back a few minutes later and said she was dead. Said she'd hanged herself. I was just about to go see fer meself, when he went crazy."

"Crazy? How so?"

"'Bout the fact he never got his revenge. Said he wanted to see the fear in her eyes before she were to swing, and she spoiled that fer him. After giving it some thought, he asked to take her body. Gave me a fair profit too, he did! Said he would see to it that, dead or not, she would pay."

Skeptical, Nathan recalled the good-natured man he met at a party in Bath several weeks past. He did not seem to be the type who would seek such revenge.

"So you didn't see her body?"

"Not hanging," responded the guard.

"How then do you know she was dead?"

"I saw him carry her out."

"Covered?"

"Aye, with her blanket. Now, I know where ye are leading, but I tell ye, yer wrong. She was dead! And even if she weren't, she is now, for the judge was bent on seeing she pay fer killing his kin."

Nathan had heard all he needed. Spinning around, he darted from the room and ran down the steps.

The guard, relieved, yet worried he might lose his job, yelled to Iestyn, "Ye don't think he'll report on me, now do ye?"

"Serves ye right if he does," scolded Iestyn and followed his captain's lead.

Once back at the ship, Nathan hurriedly bathed in cold water, not taking the time to have it warmed. He shaved and changed his clothes. Once on the bridge, he quickly shouted instructions to his officers and crew.

Iestyn acted upon every command, but offered his advice. "Sir, even if yer assumption is correct, what possible motive would this judge have in lyin' and takin' her out of the prison, when she was about to be hanged for the murder o' his sister? It jus' ain't probable."

Nathan adjusted his tricorn. "I don't know his motive. But it's clear there's more to this story, and my hunch is that Brenna once again outwitted death."

"And I think ye are settin' yerself up for a terrible realization."

"Perhaps, but one way or another, I am going to learn the truth."

"But sir," Iestyn argued, "even if she were alive, surely the guard was right. By now he would have killed her himself."

"I don't think so."

"Why? What possible motive…"

"You recall me telling you about a party I attended in Bath and about a judge accompanied by his niece who…?"

"Left before you arrived!" exclaimed Iestyn wildly. "So you think it was Brenna?"

"I don't know, but I intend to find out."

The air was crisp and the dirt road frozen. The flat moon captured the darkened silhouette of a lone rider as he journeyed through the still night. In deerskin leggings, gloves, and coat, and with a tricorn fitting snugly over his ears and a scarf covering his face, the rider was well-suited to combat the frigid air. Forbidding his mount to break into a sweat, the rider kept the animal at an even trot, its hooves leaving prints in the snow that lightly dusted the countryside.

Nathan was acting upon a hunch. He had no proof Brenna was alive, nor that she had enlisted the aid of the judge for her escape, but such was the only conclusion his mind would allow him to accept. He made his way through the entrance of the judge's chateau, four miles from the village of Winchcombe. Nathan showed no sign of fatigue.

"Brenna! Brenna!" came the urgent, muffled voice of John Charles through the wall of her quarters shortly after dawn.

"What is it? What's wrong?"

"We have a visitor. The gentleman is just now making his way toward the house. I'll let you know when it's clear." Brenna could hear the sound of his feet hurriedly leaving the study.

A visitor at this hour? How odd! Without a window to the outside to gauge the hour, Brenna opened the pocket watch Mrs. Charles had left in the room. *Six-twenty? Why, it must barely be light!* Worried the traveler might be bearing bad news, Brenna impatiently returned to her vanity to continue the toiletries she had begun before the judge's knock.

Brenna had grown close to the judge and his wife Carrie over the past week. Since the moment John Charles rescued her from the prison and brought her to their home, they had gone out of their way to see to her comfort in the small, hidden room behind one of Carrie's large oil paintings in the study. The judge, knowing the realities of a magistrate's enemies, built the secret room when the home was constructed. He wanted a secure place where his wife and housekeeper could escape if necessary. The hidden room, although small and without windows, was comfortable. Several of Carrie's paintings brightened the walls. Brenna's favorite painting was one of an English country lane in spring. From the study, there was no evidence an extra room existed. To exit, Brenna simply slid the back panel of the painting away from the massive gilded frame and stepped through.

Brenna still found it hard to believe she was here and alive. She was astonished when John Charles came to her prison chamber. In a hushed tone, he told her he had a plan, but there was no time to discuss it. She was, he told her, to lie on the floor of her cell feigning death, should anyone look in. She had been surprised when he left her cell and returned moments later. He draped her soiled blanket over her and boldly hoisted her over his shoulder. With Brenna's arms dangling limply, he carried her out of the prison into his waiting coach. Once inside the moving landau, John Charles apologized for not coming sooner. He had just learned of his sister's murder and of the conviction. He said he knew Brenna was innocent. Then, after hearing her side of the story, he was convinced of Malcolm Stone's guilt. Not having been present for the hasty trial, the judge said her best chance of avoiding the noose and eliminating the threat Malcolm posed, if he were to learn of her freedom, was for her to escape with everyone believing she was dead.

When Brenna told the judge she was fearful of getting him in trouble, he shrugged. "Brenna, do you have any idea how responsible I feel for this entire tragedy?"

Brenna looked at his pale, sad face and protested, "But you had no way of knowing what Stone would do! Nobody could have foreseen such evil!"

He sighed heavily, "Don't you see, Brenna, it's how I've spent my life, trying to determine what motivates men and women and the dastardly acts they commit. With Malcolm, I saw all the signs, yet I did nothing."

"Judge Charles, this was not your fault. None of it was."

"I wish I could share your conviction. When my sister first met that man, I tried to stop her, but the more I protested, the more she gravitated toward him. Short of forbidding her to marry him, I don't know what else I could have done to stop her. Our parents were deceased, and I was the only one left to give her any guidance. She was very stubborn where Malcolm was concerned. But with Scott," he said shaking his head, "I should have intervened long ago. Unlike my foolish sister, he had no choice of living with the man. When I think of the danger he was in.... At any moment Scott could have been killed...by his own father! For that, Brenna, I am guilty." He looked at her directly. "And guilty, too, where you were concerned. I should never, never have left you with him! If I had been any type of a man, I would have demanded that you accompany us to France. If I had, none of this would have happened. I'll never forgive myself for leaving you there!"

Since her arrival, Scott was not told of her presence. The death of his mother had been a terrible shock, and although it was somewhat beyond his comprehension, the tragedy was still overwhelming. The boy had been shielded from Brenna's supposed involvement in his mother's death; instead, they told him Brenna had decided to return to St. Christopher.

She was heartened to discover the depth of love that not only the judge had for Scott but Carrie felt for the boy as well. When she ventured to the study, Brenna was able to observe the two on several occasions playing outside in the unusually cold English winter. It was clear Scott was also very fond of his aunt.

It would be hard for anyone not to like her. Brenna loved Carrie's warm smile and gentle manner. Although heavy in frame, the woman had a remarkable inner beauty that was immediately apparent. And it was evident the judge and his wife cherished one another. Theirs was the sort of relationship Brenna had only read about; she was heartened to witness such love. Brenna was overjoyed that Scott could experience it.

Caring as she did about this family, and despite the judge's reassurances, Brenna knew her presence placed them all in great jeopardy. She was a fugitive, convicted of murder, and anyone associated with her escape would face serious consequences. Brenna spent her days agonizing over this knowledge. She knew she must leave before she was discovered and she must travel a great distance to secure the family's safety. *But where?* John and Carrie, she knew, must also have been concerned, but they never voiced such fear. When she spoke of it, they told her not to burden herself. They were confident all would be resolved. Instead, they apologized for her having to stay hidden away in the tiny room, only able to leave when Scott left the house. She wanted to tell them that, compared to some of the places she had slept, this was high luxury. She yearned to confide the truth of her past and her time aboard the ship with them. But she decided otherwise, knowing such information only placed them in further danger if she were captured.

John Charles did not wait for the traveler to knock before he opened the door. He recognized at once the American captain who had attended his sister's party.

"Captain Grant, isn't it?" asked the judge, surprised.

"Yes. Nathan Grant." Nathan presented his gloved hand. "I apologize for the intrusion at this hour."

"It's no problem. I was awake. Won't you come in? You must be frozen."

"Thank you." Nathan brushed the snow off his shoulders and entered.

"By the appearance of your mount, you must have traveled most of the night. Would you care for some tea?"

"No, thank you, sir. This is not a social call."

"Oh?" said the judge, taking a seat in the parlor.

"This is a private matter and one I don't think you'd wish to have overheard by your family. May I suggest we discuss this somewhere else, your study perhaps?"

Not wanting to arouse his suspicion by hesitating, the judge frowned, "As you wish."

The judge lit his pipe and took his seat in the study. He motioned for the captain to do the same.

"Well, Captain Grant, you have my full attention."

Brenna covered her mouth, suppressing a gasp. *Captain Grant! Him? How is it possible? Of all people!* Then, recalling the note she had written to Iestyn enlisting the aid of the captain to help Scott, she sighed. *Ah, so that's it. He's here about Scott.*

"I won't waste your time, Judge Charles," Nathan was saying when Brenna calmed enough to listen. "I have reason to believe you may have had something to do with the escape of Brenna Findlay from the prison in Bristol."

The judge, completely dumbfounded by the accuracy of the captain's statement, paused in motion. He hoped his suddenly trembling fingers went unnoticed. Attempting to settle himself, he inhaled his pipe. "That's a very serious accusation."

"I realize that," said Nathan unapologetic. "You do know then of whom I am referring?"

"Certainly! She was convicted of killing my sister. I also know she died in prison before justice had dealt its hand."

"So I've been told," replied Nathan, raising his brow. "But I have reason to believe she's not dead and that you aided her in this fabricated story."

"Why would I help my sister's murderer? That makes no sense!"

"I know not the reason; only that you did."

The judge looked closely at the captain and asked slowly, "And just how is it you came to such a false conclusion?"

"I have my sources."

"I see. And just what is your concern in this matter, anyway?"

"My motives are unimportant."

"And proof of my involvement in this so-called escape? Bring forth what you have or take your leave!"

"The proof I can substantiate," bluffed Nathan, uncertain just how far to play out this charade. He knew he had too much at stake to retreat now. "But publicizing such information will undoubtedly bring a great deal of unhappiness to both you and your family."

Angry, but cautious not to show it, the judge turned his back on Nathan, fiercely staring out the window. *How? How could he have known? I was so careful! Obviously not enough, because he knows the truth! But why would he care? Blackmail! The bloke is blackmailing me! How wrong I was about this man! I actually liked him when we first met! And to think I have always considered myself a good judge of character!* He wiped the sweat from his brow and thought carefully. After a long silence, he turned and boldly faced Nathan, "What is it you want?"

"I want no more than to know where she is."

A flicker of surprise touched the judge's face, certain this Yankee was going to ask for a large sum of money in return for his silence.

"I give you my word, sir; no harm will come to her."

The judge sensed the captain was telling the truth, but he was not about to turn Brenna over to this stranger. "You are wasting your time. I know nothing of the woman."

"If that were true, Judge Charles, I believe you would have thrown me out immediately. I know your part in this, now, where is she?"

"And if I refuse…"

"And if you refuse," interrupted Brenna. She appeared from behind the large painting, "he'll do whatever it takes to find me anyway."

Nathan looked as though he had been struck in the head by the boom of his ship. His eyes grew wide, his mouth sagged, and he struggled for words, yet none came. His initial shock gave way to an explosion of laughter.

He rushed forward, pulled her high overhead, and spun her several times. Then, still laughing, he lowered her and gazed into the beautiful eyes of the woman who had been the sole object of his thoughts for the last several months.

"Thank God, Brenna!" he whispered. "You're alive!" Instinctively, his lips moved toward her open mouth. Like a dark storm cloud burdened under its own weight and hovering just over the sea, Nathan paused. Yet, the moment his lips touched hers, the cloud burst. No longer fueled by relief alone, Nathan was driven by an explosion of emotions. All his life experiences seemed to culminate in this moment. He realized everything he wanted, everything he was, was here in her. It was suddenly very clear. The sea had always offered him a means not to experience the excitement and adventures he had always believed he sought, but instead a means of sailing away from himself. Yet, until this moment, he had no idea he had been running. Now, here before him was the happiness he never knew he was missing. He had found

Brenna. He knew she would forever be his sail, his sea, and the wind at his back.

When he finally pulled away, Brenna was unsteady and shaken by the passionate, startling embrace. She could not believe she had not resisted his kiss but yearned for more. She flushed with embarrassment and avoided Nathan's gaze. She looked at the judge whom she had momentarily forgotten.

John Charles appeared not the slightest bit uncomfortable in the wake of the kiss. He grinned and said in jest, "I take it then that the two of you are acquainted?"

"Yes." Nathan hesitated, trying to form the best words to tell Brenna and the judge about her parents and his search for her. "To be precise, I'm more familiar with her pa…"

"Yes, we're acquainted. Actually, we're in love." Brenna interrupted without hesitation. She knew if the judge suspected she was fearful of the captain in any manner, he would protect her, regardless of his personal danger. She realized, too, that the next few minutes would mean the difference between safety and even greater danger for Carrie and John if the captain alerted the authorities.

Nathan studied Brenna's face, perplexed at her surprising profession of love, and wondered what game she was playing. Although she was good at disguising it, he sensed deep fear in her. He surmised she was trying to protect the judge. Not wanting to call her out, Nathan hesitated. "I've been searching for her rather diligently after we became…uh, separated." Then, before the judge could have opportunity to question him further, and eager to get Brenna out of England before anyone else learned of her escape, Nathan decided to forgo lengthy explanation. "My ship is to set sail shortly, and it's my intent to take her with me to the Colonies."

The judge was amazed by this unexpected turn of events. The solution about what to do with Brenna was now so clear. "You do intend then, fine sir, do you not, to take her back as your wife?" When he saw the look of astonishment on the captain's face, the judge added, "You certainly don't intend to destroy her reputation?" The judge's question was more a statement than a question.

Brenna nearly laughed aloud at the preposterous question of getting married and that the judge was worried about her reputation, for she was after all a convicted murderer! Her lighthearted musings evaporated when a wide smile spread across the captain's face. He looked at her squarely. "Yes, Your Honor, your point is well taken. I have every intention of marrying her."

The judge clasped his hands joyfully. "While I'm not a man of the cloth, I am, however, a believer…and being an appointee of the court…I've done many such pronouncements. So, if you are agreeable and so inclined, I see no reason why I shan't perform the ceremony, considering it'll be difficult enough to keep her identity quiet." He turned to Brenna. "How many days, my dear, will you need to prepare yourself for the affair?"

Brenna's mouth and eyes opened wide; she struggled to form any response. Before she had a chance, Nathan interjected, "My ship departs on the morrow. If there is to be a service, it must be done today, this morning if possible."

"That's very sudden," replied the judge, his brow lowering. "Are you certain this decision has not been made in haste?"

"I have no reservations." Grinning broadly, the captain again turned to Brenna and took her hands in his. "And you, my lovely…and evasive Brenna…are you sound in your decision to become my wife, confident that you can stay by my side, with no desire to…flee…and for us to faithfully love one another for as long as we both shall live?"

Brenna fought the urge to wipe away his grin and expose the charade. She longed to tell the judge the truth—that she barely knew the man, that he was only here to satisfy some twisted quest for revenge, and that the "ceremony" was nothing but a fraud. She was certain, once they left the judge's home, the so-called vows would be disregarded by the captain and she returned to jail or sold. Brenna knew the captain had no intention of taking seriously such vows. But she also knew she could not further endanger this family. She saw that the judge watched her intently and waited for her reply. Brenna swallowed hard. She squeezed the captain's hand hard and hoped it caused him pain, but said sweetly, "Of course, dear Captain. How could there be any doubt? For you must know, I have learned well your great tenacity for…securing…regardless of the cost in time or money, whatever your heart desires. And if your heart desires me, then there will be no question that together we shall remain."

The judge looked uneasily at the two, thinking the exchange rather odd. *There's something peculiar here. Perhaps I ought not*…then he recalled the kiss. He smiled. It was like no other he had witnessed, and he sensed that even the two young people before him might not be fully aware themselves of the passion between them. He felt a sense of well-being when he imagined the life they would share.

Satisfied, the judge said abruptly, "Well, then, it's decided. I shall don my robe, and we shall begin again, ah, let's say around noon?"

"Since we're all here, why don't we proceed now," offered Nathan eagerly.

"Nonsense," laughed the judge. "I know you're anxious. With a woman such as Brenna, any man would be, but you've waited this long. A few more hours to give the bride time to properly prepare is not asking overly much." He moved toward the door and added, "If you wish, Captain Grant, you may ready yourself in my quarters."

"That won't be necessary. I need to make some arrangements in Winchcombe, but I'll be back shortly." Then looking directly into Brenna's eyes, he said softly, "I shall return shortly. Meanwhile, dearest, I trust you will take care, for I wouldn't want to further burden the good judge and his family by involving them in another…search for you."

His meaning was deftly clear, "You needn't worry. I won't do anything to cause trouble for this fine family."

"As I suspected. While in the village, I shall do my best to find a wedding garment of sorts, but the village is small and on such short notice, it may be impossi…"

"That won't be necessary," interrupted Brenna, not wanting anything from him except her freedom.

"Very well, my sweet," Nathan placed his hands firmly on both her shoulders. "And until we are wed, may this remind you of what is to come." Boldly, his lips found hers. The kiss ended abruptly and she was aware of the judge looking at her from the doorway. Blushing profusely, she retreated to her quarters.

For Brenna, the next few hours were a blur. When Carrie learned of the impending wedding, she took charge. She arranged for Scott to leave the house by accompanying the stable-master to visit a neighboring farm to purchase a horse. Next, she prepared Brenna's bath, insisting it long and relaxing, complete with the perfumed oil and scented shampoo she had just purchased in France. She left shimmering French body powder for her to use after her bath. Brenna had just slipped into a dressing robe when Carrie lightly tapped on her door. She entered carrying a large box. Her blue eyes sparkled with delight. Noting the plain dress Brenna held in her hand, Carrie said, "You weren't planning on getting married in that?"

"I have nothing else," replied Brenna simply.

"Maybe you don't have anything else, but I do. Now, I know you couldn't possibly wear anything of mine, you being so small, but hopefully this may be a little closer to your size." Carrie opened the box. Brenna could not believe the sight of the satin wedding gown folded neatly inside.

"It's beautiful!" exclaimed Brenna, running her finger against the soft material.

"It was my mother's. It's old, but I believe it well preserved. I know she would be so pleased to have you wear it."

"Oh, but I couldn't!"

"Of course you can and you will. Here now," she said, pulling the garment from the box. "Let's see what condition it's in."

Two hours later, Brenna stood at the beveled glass mirror and could not believe she was looking at herself. Carrie beamed with delight, "My goodness, my dear, you look positively stunning!" Critically, she inspected Brenna's hair, combed and braided in an intricate coiffure and woven with a white ribbon. "Well," she smiled, crossing her arms with satisfaction, "not too bad, considering I'm quite out of practice."

"It's wonderful! I've not had it so styled since I was a child." Brenna's eyes filled with tears at the thought of the hours her mother used to spend combing her hair. She knew Helen would have loved how Carrie took the time to do so now.

The dress was simple, yet elegant. With minor alterations complete, the dress fitted snugly to Brenna's slender form. Her narrow waist was accented further by the flare of the gown's skirt. The creamy satin bodice, dotted with tiny crystals, was cut low in the front. It made Brenna slightly self-conscious. The back neckline was cut just as low and exposed her shoulders and back.

When she saw Brenna's expression, Carrie Charles teased, "Your captain will certainly be pleased my mum was not the least bit modest. In fact," she laughed, "she had a reputation for being rather scandalous in her time." Laughing lightly, she added, "Well, of one thing I'm certain—when you awoke this morning, you didn't have the slightest idea that today would be your wedding day, did you?"

"No," responded Brenna with a nervous laugh. "This has been a day of surprises. Seven days ago, Carrie, I thought I would not live to see the next sunrise, and now look at me…here with you…and wearing a wedding gown of all things!"

"Miracles really do happen, you know." Now it was Carrie's eyes that filled with tears. She patted her cheeks as if to ward them off and said, "Honestly! Enough of that. I just want you to tell me all about him, this Captain Grant. John said he is really quite a sight himself. Said he liked him immediately. Tell me, when did the two of you become acquainted?"

"On St. Christopher."

"Really? While his ship was in port?"

"Yes. We met only briefly."

"And it was aboard his ship that you came to England?" Not giving Brenna a chance to respond, she interrupted herself enthusiastically, "Oh how romantic! These are my favorite kind of love stories…like yours and Nathan's! I usually only get to read about them! Oh Brenna! This is so exciting!"

Brenna turned uncomfortably. Eager to change the subject, she looked again in the mirror. "I can't thank you enough…for this dress, for everything!"

"I'm so pleased you like the gown. I was certain I'd never live to see it used. You know, it's strange, but even though we've only known one another for a week, and I know you are a lot younger than I…but it seems…I don't know…you feel like a sister to me."

Looking at the woman eighteen years her senior, Brenna felt a tightening of her throat. "Oh, Carrie, you cannot know what that means, for I have no family."

Carrie hugged Brenna, "Well then, henceforth, we shall consider one another sisters! And starting today, Nathan's family will also be yours. Does he have many siblings?"

"I know it must seem peculiar, but I have no idea."

"Well, my dear, I sense you may be in for many surprises in the months ahead!"

If only you knew. She looked away so that Carrie would not see the tears threatening to come again, tears of the unknown. Regaining her composure, Brenna added, "I only wish I knew how to repay all you and your husband have done for me! When I think of the risk you both took, I…"

"Nonsense, we only did what was right. And as far as how you can repay us, you already have. You've changed the course of Scott's life. And…I might add…the best way you can repay us is by making this wedding day the happiest day of your life!"

Brenna wanted desperately to confide in her new friend that this wedding was not all it appeared. Such a disclosure, she knew, would certainly bring a halt to the ceremony, and once again, Nathan Grant would become a threat to the family.

"Just imagine," sighed Carrie, "it won't be long now, and you'll be the wife of an American sea captain! And tonight," she giggled, "will be your wedding night! A night ye shall forever cherish."

I wonder in which prison I shall spend this night. In Bath or Bristol? Or perhaps he won't be able to wait even that long, and he'll turn me over to the authorities in the first village we pass.

"Oh, forgive me, Brenna," said Carrie, seeing the color drain from her cheeks. "I didn't mean to upset you by speaking too personally."

"Carrie, you have no need to apologize."

"It's just that you're looking a little pale. Are you certain you feel well?"

"Yes, I'm fine."

"I guess the excitement has been a little much for both of us." Carrie turned to leave. "Is there anything else I can get you? If not, then I'll let you have a few minutes to rest and gather your thoughts."

"I'm fine, thank you. But, Carrie, before you go, may I speak to you about Scott?"

"Certainly." Carrie sat down on Brenna's bed. "What's troubling you?"

"Well, to be honest, I'm quite concerned for him. This may not be my place, but Malcolm Stone is evil and I fear for Scott."

"My husband and I both share your conviction." She became more serious than Brenna had ever seen her. "He's a terrible man and we're doing everything in our power to see to it Scott never spends another day with him. As you know, John bears terrible guilt over what happened to you and his failure to help his sister. Be assured, he will never allow anything to happen to Scott, never!"

Overcome with relief, Brenna cried, "I'm so glad he has you!"

"Brenna, you need not worry about Scott. He will be well cared for, especially after today." She smiled. "He doesn't know it, but that mare he's looking at now is one John purchased for him yesterday."

"Oh!" exclaimed Brenna, unable to hold back her tears of relief.

"And, for goodness sake, stop crying or your red eyes may give the groom cause for concern."

"Ladies," came the judge's voice at the door, "Captain Grant has returned and is eagerly awaiting his bride."

"Oh dear," Carrie said to Brenna, "and you've had no time to rest with all my chattering!"

The judge knocked again. "May I enter?"

"By all means," responded his wife.

Attired in his judicial robe and powdered wig, the judge entered. He was carrying a small, neatly wrapped package.

"Do my eyes play tricks on me," he smiled, "or do I behold the two loveliest women I've ever seen?"

Carrie laughed "Oh, John, how you tease me! But you're correct about Brenna."

"Brenna," said the Judge, "even the Royal Family would be honored to welcome you to their family this day."

"And you're overly kind," blushed Brenna, unaccustomed to such flattery. "But I think my background would be cause for more than a little concern to the crown!"

The judge laughed heartily. "Even so, my praise is not given without merit. In any case, that's not why I'm here. I've come bearing a gift," he said and handed her the small box.

"Nay! I cannot accept! You all have done far too much already!"

"Well, on such short notice, I'm sorry to say we have no gift to offer, other than our wish of happiness. No, dear Brenna, the gift is from your groom."

"What?" Apprehensive, she opened the package, unable to believe its content—a delicate gold necklace studded with what looked like diamonds, rubies, and brilliant sapphires. The judge and his wife looked equally astonished by the extravagant gift.

"Are you certain this is for me?"

The judge laughed at her skepticism. "I don't know why you're so surprised. It's obvious the man is quite smitten with you. I daresay, if I'm any judge of character, he loves you most sincerely."

Brenna felt her cheeks grow hot with anger. The captain was making a mockery of this day and increased it by further deceiving such fine people.

Brenna yearned to tell him the sad truth as Carrie fastened the gold necklace about her neck. *No, Judge. It's not love he suffers but rather triumph…for conquering the one who he thinks made him a fool…first in stowing away aboard his ship and then escaping him in his search…and now he's using this gift for even more deception. I don't know what it is he feels for me, but it certainly isn't love. He doesn't even know me!*

The judge clapped his hands once in anticipation. "Well, if you're ready, there's an eager groom in the parlor."

Eager to seal my fate, thought Brenna gloomily. She reluctantly followed the couple.

"I only wish it were spring and we could have decorated the home with garden flowers," said Carrie as they walked down the hall.

Carrie and John entered the parlor while Brenna paused in its entry. The captain's back was to her, just like it had been on the deck of the ship. She saw he had changed his clothes since this morning. When he turned, she could not deny that Nathan Grant was dazzlingly handsome. He did not fit the part of the rogue she knew him to be.

The captain's emerald eyes softened when he saw Brenna. A slow grin spread to his eyes. He moved to her quickly, taking her hands in his. "You're beautiful," he said, pressing her hand to his lips.

Brenna looked into his eyes. She wanted to believe him, yet she knew him capable of deception. She touched her finger against the smooth metal of the gift necklace. "I am perplexed by this gift."

"Be assured, it is offered in pure celebration."

"Celebration of what? This…wedding?" Brenna could scarcely say the word, knowing it to be a sham.

"Of course! That and…" shaking his head, he laughed, "that once again you have out-maneuvered death!"

Brenna looked closely at him, unable to determine whether behind the laughter he meant this as a compliment or an insult.

"As for the gown," said Nathan, unable to mask his surprise, "it's incredible." With white teeth flashing, he added, "If I didn't know better, I'd say you had been plotting this wedding for some time."

Brenna opened her mouth in protest, but stopped when the judge asked, "Well now, shall we begin?"

More than a little agitated, Brenna reluctantly accepted the captain's offered arm to the front of the room.

"I do," said Brenna ten minutes later, feeling as though she were performing a part in a play.

"I hereby pronounce you husband and wife," said the judge proudly. "What God has joined, let no man put asunder."

Nathan's kiss, like the service, was brief. But the mere brush of his lips on hers left her more affected than she wanted to admit.

A light lunch followed the signing of documents, and while Brenna picked uneasily at her food, she noticed the captain chatted with ease with the judge and Carrie, as if they'd been friends for years.

Brenna eyed him laughing gaily with the couple. *If only you knew the scoundrel for what he is, you'd throw him from your home!*

The meal passed without incident, and too soon for Brenna, her newly acquired husband presented his hand to assist her in stepping into the rented carriage. He checked his horse, now tethered behind the carriage, and took the seat across from her. Both the judge and his wife peered in through the open window to say their goodbyes. Tearfully,

Carrie handed Brenna a basket overflowing with the remains of the meal. "I noticed you ate very little, Brenna, so I thought this might help in your long journey. Oh, and here," she said, handing Brenna the large box containing the wedding gown, "you must take this."

"Oh, Carrie, I couldn't possibly accept, I…"

"I insist. I shall never have a daughter of my own, yet somehow," she said winking, "I think it very possible that you will."

Unable to say any more without breaking down, Brenna simply bit her lip, nodding appreciatively.

"Captain Grant," the judge said, "there is one matter which concerns me."

"Oh?"

"It's the matter of the proof you said you have implicating me and my family in the escape. I must ask that you…"

"There is no proof," interrupted Nathan. "To my knowledge, the jailor, my trusted first mate, and I are the only other ones who know how Brenna escaped the chambers of death, and I'm confident none will ever reveal the circumstances surrounding any of it."

Confused, the judge asked, "How then, did you know?"

"I didn't. Initially, it was a hunch, and a lucky one at that."

The judge shook his head in dismay at the way the captain had called his bluff when he first arrived this morning. "You've missed your calling, Captain Grant. With that art of persuasion, you should have been a lawyer."

"I'm afraid I have enough trouble reading the sea, let alone the minds of humans." Nathan nodded to the driver who had been standing in the entry of the barn inspecting the animals. As Nathan intended, the man had only a distant glimpse of Brenna and heard none of the conversation. Because she was a convict, Nathan took no chances. He had arranged for a private escort to Bristol. No other passengers would be allowed aboard.

Attired now in a cotton dress and wool cloak from Carrie's younger years, Brenna shivered slightly on this cold February afternoon as they traveled the uneven path toward Bristol.

"I think it possible," said the captain, looking at her quizzically, "you would freeze to death before requesting anything from me." Then without asking, he removed the metal foot warmer from under his seat and placed both her feet on it. He then covered her with a thick sheepskin and placed a hot soft-sided water bottle underneath.

"Thank you, but that wasn't necessary," said Brenna curtly, frustrated that the mere touch of his fingers against her ankles left her quivering. She was nervous riding alone with a man.

Brenna looked out the small window at the passing countryside while the captain's gaze remained locked on her. Without seeing his face, Brenna knew he was grinning. Finally, unable to tolerate his scrutiny, she said with irritation, "Is it your intention to stare at me for the duration of this journey?"

"Possibly," he responded nonchalantly.

"How is it," she asked curtly, "that a man of your position never acquired proper etiquette?"

The captain could not suppress another smile, "I'm afraid your beauty has given way to my coarser side. But rest assured, madam, that my mother, being quite an authority on manners, did her best to instill such qualities in me."

And failed miserably, Brenna thought bitterly, holding her tongue.

Knowing her thoughts, Nathan chided, "And you," he asked, trying to glean more about her, "who taught you such social graces of a lady?"

Determined to ignore him, she turned her attention once again toward the window.

"It won't help, you know," said Nathan after a couple of minutes.

"What won't?"

"Staring out the window."

Brenna again tried to ignore him.

"No matter how badly you wish to be away from this carriage, staring won't help. I'm afraid you're stuck with me."

"Until, that is," she snapped unable to contain her anger, "you hand me over to the nearest prison."

"Now, why on earth," he inquired as he leaned forward, "after finally finding you, would I do that?"

"Obviously you were not satisfied with the terms of my repayment for passage aboard your vessel."

"Ah, I see," he smiled, happy for the explanation. "If it will put your mind at ease, I fully intend to see that I am reimbursed sufficiently. But imprisonment and monetary compensations are not quite what I have in mind."

Having no doubt as to his meaning, Brenna angrily tugged the blanket over her shoulders. *So, you intend to make me your whore after all! 'Wife' or not, it will never happen, Captain Grant, never!*

In an effort to calm, Brenna looked out the window and pretended it was not the frozen winter ground she looked upon, but instead she imagined the landscape in spring, as it was in Carrie's painting where white lacy blossoms lined the roads and ravines. The rolling meadow beyond would be a lush, green blanket of grass, home to horses, cows, and goats that grazed contentedly in the warmth of the spring sun, their winter coats blowing away like the winter winds before them. Stone fences lined the valleys and hills, striking friendly boundaries between neighbors. Roses, peonies, lilies, and lilacs bloomed brilliantly, bringing life to the thatched roofed cottages. Brenna thought the land looked enduring. *Just as I must be,* she thought, as a jolt of the carriage reminded her of the struggle and winter before her.

Throughout the journey, Nathan wrestled with how best to present the news about Emily and Weston. He had no idea how she would react, but he was certain what he had to say would come as a shock. He sensed he must be careful and decided to start by finding out what she knew about her past. It had been nearly an hour since they had spoken. "I regret your family was not able to be present at the taking of our vows."

Brenna did not look at him as she answered. "I have no family."

"Your mother and father have passed away then?"

For a fleeting moment, Brenna yearned to confide in him about her sadness over the loss of Helen and the horror of learning she had been sold as an infant. She had not been able to tell anyone about that and not doing so was tearing her apart. She opened her mouth to speak when she remembered Helen's warning to beware of sharks covered in porpoise skin. She closed her mouth and looked at the handsome man before her. If ever there could be such a man, it might be Nathan Grant, for outwardly he appeared good-natured and kind, but she knew the man could not be trusted, and she could not bear the thought of having such a painful conversation with someone she could not trust. "I don't care to discuss it," she said finally.

"Why?"

"There is nothing to discuss. Please, speak of it no further!"

Nathan could clearly hear the pain in her voice, and yet he pressed, "And if you were to learn that there is much to speak about?"

Brenna's brow furrowed. She looked at him suspiciously.

He appeared not to have noticed. "What if you were to learn that whatever it is you think is the truth is, in fact, not so?"

"The truth?" Brenna's eyes flashed with anger. "You're going to talk to me about truth?" She uttered a bitter laugh. "Let me be clear, if in fact I have not been so. I don't trust you, Captain! Not you, not your words, and certainly not your motives! Nothing!"

Nathan knew he was well deserving of such wrath, but he was surprised by the intensity of the sting.

He rubbed his hand across his face and jaw and pondered how to get through to her. Somehow he needed to earn her trust, but he knew it would take time. He studied her closely and realized she was struggling not to cry. He sighed heavily with another realization—*she deserves to hear the truth from the only ones who have earned the right to tell her—Emily and Weston.* He would not rob her or them of that opportunity.

"Brenna," he said softly, "I know you believe I'm not deserving of your trust. I hope to one day change your regard of me. But until then, please know that things are not always as they appear."

Brenna was again struck by his ability to show such tenderness. And she wondered if he was referring to himself when he said that things are not always as they appear. She was about to ask when the captain reached in the inside pocket of his vest and said, "I meant to give this to you before we said our vows. I believe it's yours."

"My bracelet! I…I can't believe it!"

Its clasp was repaired and the metal brightly polished. Brenna's eyes filled with tears. She rubbed it between her hands. "I never thought I'd see it again, and I've never seen it more beautiful! I thought surely you would have sold it by now."

Amused, Nathan grinned. He gently placed the bracelet around her wrist and fastened the clasp. "I tried, but with the inscription, I was unable to find a buyer, and I didn't want to go to the trouble of having it melted."

Brenna eyed him suspiciously. She thought his words in jest, but she was not certain. She quickly decided it did not matter; she was just grateful to have the bracelet back. *First, the necklace, and now this. What's his motive?* Confused, but exceedingly pleased, Brenna smiled as she studied her wrist, thinking that once again it looked complete. After a long pause, she said, "Thank you, Captain Grant; it's my most precious possession. Actually," she laughed, despite her resolve not to, "it's my only possession."

His eyes narrowed as if bothered by her offhanded remark. Then shrugging, "I was only returning what was yours. And I think perhaps, now that you are *my wife*, addressing me by my given name would be appropriate."

Wife indeed! Brenna wondered how the same man who had just given her a gift could cause her such anger the next moment. *He knows this marriage is a farce! We're strangers to one another, no more!* She forced back her thoughts, "I didn't think you cared about propriety."

Nathan smiled broadly. "I just happen to have selective manners. And now if you'll excuse me, I fear the lack of sleep over the recent days has finally gotten the better of me." He crossed his arms over his chest and his muscular legs at the ankle, then closed his eyes.

Five minutes later, thinking he was asleep, Brenna was surprised when he opened his eyes slightly. "By the way, you didn't happen to accompany Judge Charles at a certain social gathering recently in Bath?"

"How did you learn of such?"

Rolling his eyes, Nathan said with a wide grin, "I should've known, I should've known!"

"And I, Captain, have a question for you. How did you learn of my escape?"

"Deductive thinking," he responded as he closed his eyes once again.

How is it that you seem to know so much about me? Relieved that she might be able to relax since she was released from his fixed attention, Brenna leaned her head back against the cushioned seat where she was able to study him freely. She realized her first impression of him on the island still held true. He was undoubtedly the most handsome man she had ever seen. She grudgingly had to admit that upon closer inspection, he was even more handsome than she realized before. *Why is it, that cads like you seem to be blessed with such looks?* It was easy to see how women could easily fall prey to him. Brenna pursed her lips, determined once again she would not be added to that list, especially when she noticed that even in his sleep his expression seemed to mock her, the edges of his mouth turned slightly upward.

I know so little about you, Captain Grant. What's your intent? If we had met under different circumstances, would things be different? Would we have been fond of one another? Instead, we find ourselves here, wed under false pretense. Unable to find any consolation in her thoughts, Brenna closed her eyes, but she was unable to rest. She could not stop wondering what manner of man was before her. Was his heart kind and thoughtful, like Iestyn and John Charles? Or was he like Harley and Malcolm, only better at concealing his true nature? Her mother had told her that she once believed Harley was a good and honorable man, but she had been blind to his true nature. She warned Brenna about making the same mistake.

Never one to need much sleep, Nathan was surprised when he awoke nearly four hours later. He found Brenna just as before, back straight against her seat, staring at the orange sun low on the horizon.

"Do you need anything?" he asked hoarsely.

"No, nothing, thank you."

"I requested this coach not make any unnecessary stops, but if you are in need, I shall ask the coachman to do so."

"That won't be necessary."

Nathan stretched his legs. "Several aspects of your imprisonment still baffle me. First, I understand from talking to the guards that after you were arrested, you were taken to the prison in Bath where you spent considerable time, and then, shortly before the hanging was to take place, you were transferred to Bristol. Is that right?"

"Yes."

"How long were you in the prison in Bristol before you escaped?"

"Two days."

"And that's when you wrote the letter to Iestyn?"

"Yes, I was scheduled to hang in a few hours when Judge Charles arrived."

Nathan closed his eyes, sickened at the thought of how close he had come to losing her.

Why does he look so relieved? He's the one who was personally going to see to it that 'justice was done.' He should have been relieved it was over for him, that justice was served.

It had bothered Nathan why, when she was in prison in Bath, no one from that city had seemingly made the connection between the "Brenna" on the flyers and the "Brenna" convicted of murder. There had been posters displayed everywhere throughout that city, yet no one from Bath ever came forward to ask for the reward. It made no sense. He could understand that since she had only been in the Bristol prison for two days, no one there made the connection, but there was plenty of opportunity while she had been imprisoned in Bath. The story of her "self-hanging" was carried in the Bristol paper, but no earlier account of her story had been covered.

"Do you know why the story of the murder of Mrs. Stone and your subsequent arrest and conviction were not carried in newspapers? If it had been, I'm certain I would have heard and come sooner."

"Judge Charles told me the newspaper reported only that a well-known resident of The Bath had been murdered. But until next of kin could be located, no further information was to be released. Judge Charles said he suspected Malcolm Stone did not want him to hear about the case before I was set to hang, for he feared that Judge Charles would have argued on my behalf. Stone wanted a quick trial and hanging before Judge Charles could return from France."

"But how was such information kept from the papers? Could Stone have had such influence?"

"I had the same question for Judge Charles. He explained that he was well acquainted with the presiding judge on my case, a man of apparent corruption. Judge Charles suspects Malcolm Stone either bribed that judge or had some sort of scandalous information to use against him to keep the story quiet and the trial in haste. It was by God's grace that Judge Charles returned from his trip when he did, which was far earlier than planned. He said he did so because he felt uneasy about having left me in Malcolm Stone's home."

"Hum, interesting," said Nathan, rubbing his thighs. "That would explain why neither I nor my crew ever heard about your arrest. But what I still don't understand is why, if you were in jail for as long as you were in Bath, why did none of the jailers come forward to claim the reward? We had bulletins covering Bath. Surely, those bulletins were seen by someone."

Twisting her finger around the small window fabric cover, Brenna looked uncomfortably out the window. She knew the bulletins in Bath were not seen because she had removed them. "Yes, it does seem peculiar."

Nathan eyed her suspiciously. He knew she was withholding something. He looked toward the ceiling of the coach. *Lord help me. What have I gotten myself into?*

Ten minutes later, Nathan opened the basket and held it for her. "Since we'll be arriving late, we might as well take advantage of Mrs. Charles' refreshments."

Three hours later, the coach eased to a stop. Brenna knew by the aroma of salt and fish, they were dockside. Stiff from sitting so rigidly, she accepted Nathan's arm in climbing out of the carriage into the bitterly cold air. Two watchmen nodded briefly to the captain as they walked up the gangplank. Brenna recognized one of the men as the one she slipped past months earlier. She nearly died in the hold after that. With nowhere to hide, she wondered what awaited her this time. Brenna stopped outside the captain's quarters, the quarters where she had previously spent a good deal of time.

She gasped when he swiftly lifted her into his arms with ease and opened the door. "I believe, Miss Brenna, this would be considered proper."

Unprepared for his action, Brenna opened her mouth to protest. Stunned, she stared at the sight that greeted them.

Scantily clad in a maroon negligee and lying on her side atop Nathan's berth was the brunette he had been with at the baths.

"Launey," said Nathan, still holding Brenna.

Launey's expression changed from surprise to blazing fury. "She's the one, isn't she? The one you've been searching for?"

Nathan did not respond as he set Brenna's feet to the floor.

"But I read she was dead!" she exclaimed. She rose from the bed and covered herself. "Just yesterday! In the newspaper! It said she hanged herself!"

Nathan was surprised Launey had made the connection. "I thought so as well."

"Then where did you find her?"

"It's a long story, and it's much too late to go into now. I can only ask that you keep this knowledge to yourself, for to do otherwise could have serious consequences for us all."

"Why, of course, love, you know how trustworthy I am." She smiled and approached the captain. Placing her arms about his neck and pressing her body seductively to his, she kissed him.

Embarrassed, yet unable to turn away, Brenna was shocked by her desire to tear the woman's arms away. Brenna saw the disappointment on the woman's face when the captain did not return the embrace, but instead moved away from her. Coyly, the woman twisted her finger around a long strand of her hair. "I hear ye are planning to depart shortly."

"Yes."

"Well," she said sweetly, "that's why I've come! It is such a long way for you to travel, and I…well…I thought you might like my company." She looked at his raised eyebrows and continued without giving him a chance to reply. "Now, you don't have to worry about a thing. All the arrangements have been made."

"I appreciate your offer, but that really won't be possible."

"Why?"

"It has nothing to do with you."

"What then?" she demanded. "You think you can write me a note and then discard me like some used sail?"

"I am sorry, Launey, but that's enough," said Nathan sternly.

"Enough! Enough of what? You've given me no answer! Or," she turned toward Brenna and jeered, "do I need to ask? It's with her, isn't it, that you intend to satisfy your needs on your long voyage!"

"Launey, she's my wife."

A long pause hung in the air. Brenna had experienced such an eerie calm only once—when her island was in the eye of a hurricane. And, like a hurricane, this silence was shattered.

"Your wife?" she screeched.

"Yes."

"How? When?" she demanded, her face red.

"Today."

"To…day! Why you bloody…you said you were…you were searching because…because you had to! Out of obligation, no more! You bloody lecher! You lied!"

"It wasn't my intent."

"You liar! How could you have done this to me? You've ruined everything!" Seething, she turned on Brenna and closed the distance between them. "You little hussy! Just what did you do to manipulate him into wedding you?" Launey raised her hand to strike.

Nathan seized her arm and stared at her with such intensity she feared he might strike her. Never before had she heard such menacing in a voice as when he whispered through clenched teeth, "I suggest you seriously rethink your actions."

Launey moved away and hissed, "I shall not forget this betrayal, Nathan. Never! Mark my words, you'll regret this day!" Grabbing her valise, Launey marched out of the cabin and slammed the door behind her.

Nathan was silent for several seconds. "I apologize you had to witness that."

"You owe me no apology," said Brenna, surprised by his apology, for in reality she was nothing more than his prisoner here.

"Captain? Captain?" came Iestyn's urgent knock.

"What's the matter?" Nathan opened the door.

"I know 'tis none of me business," said Iestyn as he tried to catch his breath, yet puzzled why the captain prevented his entry, "I was jes' returnin' t' the ship an' I spotted Miss Launey leavin' in a most unladylike manner, and frankly, I was worried she may have done ye bodily injury."

Nathan responded with a chuckle, "I appreciate your concern, but you needn't worry. She did me no harm, although she did try her hand at Brenna."

"Brenna?" asked a bewildered Iestyn, stepping around Nathan.

Iestyn stared, mouth agape at the two of them. It was several seconds before any sound came to him. When it did, he shouted, "Brenna! Saints above!" He recovered slightly and rushed toward her.

"I can't believe it!" He grabbed her, held her tightly, then pulled back and looked at her again. Tears rolled down his cheeks and his voice quivered, "Never has this ol' heart beat with more joy! I felt surely I'd never see ye again! This is astoundin'!" Turning to Nathan, he said humbly, "I must truly apologize, sir. Fer I certainly thought ye were chasin' her ghost!"

"I'm just glad that between your thoughts and mine, mine was correct."

"An' never in all my years…have I been happier to be on the losin' end! Ah, I'm bustin' t' 'ear all of this…but enough now of my ramblin', ye must be famished. I shall see that a special dinner be prepared immediately."

"That won't be necessary, Iestyn. My wife and I have already dined."

"Well then I shall…" Iestyn stopped. "Beggin' yer pardon, yer wife?" After looking at the captain, Iestyn turned to Brenna who made no attempt to contradict. Beaming, he added, "Well! 'Tis indeed an evenin' full of surprises! And how did that happen so suddenly? Ye were here only last night, captain."

"It's a bit involved and too lengthy to discuss at this hour. I'm certain my bride must be fatigued." Then, grinning at Brenna, he asked, "Perhaps a soothing bath would be in order?"

She wondered again how it was he anticipated her desire but wished he were not able to do it so readily. Brenna rubbed her stiff neck, "A bath would be lovely."

Iestyn, still obviously stunned, said, "I'll see to the bath immediately." Leaving, he added, "I surely wish I'd known ye was comin'. I would've planned a celebration the like o' which ye have never seen!"

"You're a lucky man," said Brenna after Iestyn closed the door.

"I would definitely agree," grinned Nathan. He looked at her closely.

She ignored his inference, "To have enlisted the aid of such a man as Iestyn."

"Yes, and for once, we are in total agreement."

"At least where Iestyn is concerned, you have good sense."

He smiled broadly and added, "More than just where Iestyn is concerned, I assure you. And now," he added reluctantly, "as much as I hate to leave, I've got a ship and crew in need of some final preparations before the morrow."

"Are we really departing so soon?"

"*The Grace*'s cargo will tolerate no further delays and her crew has been eager to get under way for quite some time…and given what transpired this evening, I think it best we hurry. If the tide was right, I'd have us do so now. As it is, we'll have to wait until daybreak. I informed the crew yesterday we might leave immediately. Is there anyone you want me to contact before we hoist anchor?"

"No, no one."

Nathan donned his tricorn and buttoned his coat. "If you need anything, inform Iestyn, and he'll see to it."

At least he has his priorities in order. Perhaps, his duties will keep him away all night.

Fifteen minutes later, Iestyn appeared with yoke and steaming buckets to ready her bath. Hurrying about, he talked continuously. "I'm certainly sorry, mum, 'bout any problem Miss Launey may have caused ye. She was insistent on waitin' for the captain and has been here since this mornin' orderin' me and the rest of the crew around like she were in charge. If'n I'd known the captain would be returnin' with ye, I'd a never let her step foot aboard this brig. I left no more than an hour ago an' had asked her t' be gone when I returned." Not giving Brenna a chance to reply, he added with glee, "Oh lassie, what I'd ha' given' t' see that look on her face when she spied ye! 'Tis no wonder she left as she did!"

Brenna poured into the bath several drops of the French oil Carrie had given her. "She was very upset."

"Ah, don't ye be worrin' 'bout that. She's been a lick of trouble from the first day I set eyes on her. I'm jes' glad the captain has finally come to his senses and given her the heave ho!" He picked up a kettle of steaming water from the stove and poured it into the brass tub. "Ah, Miss Brenna, I knew from the moment I saw ye that the two of ye were made for one another! And now, I jes' can't believe it, yer married! And without me havin' t' say a word! Incredible!"

Brenna longed to share with Iestyn that all was not as it appeared. She was convinced the wedding a sham and wondered what would happen once the captain realized she would not cooperate with his more heathen intentions.

"I tell ye, when I first read yer letter sayin' ye was t' be hanged, I prayed harder than I ever had that the good Lord would find a way t' spare yer life. Well, then we heard 'bout the hangin' and all…I jes'…well…I jes' thought t'would be like one o' those God things where we aren't t' understand until we're a meetin' the Almighty face t' face— an' I have t' admit, I better be gettin' down on me hands an' knees thankin' the Good Lord…an' offerin' a prayer o' forgiveness fer some o' the things I was a thinkin'…lettin' ye get t' the point where ye thought ye had no hope and had t' resort t' somethin' so awful as takin' yer own life."

"Thank you, Iestyn," said Brenna with a lump in her throat, "for everything…especially for your prayers."

"Well, I have t' confess, when the captain told me yesterday he was goin' in search of ye, I thought he'd finally lost his mind. An' I tried me best," he said shamefully, "t' talk him out of it. Said he was wastin' his time. But I'll tell ye, he would hear none o' it. Once he got the notion in his head that ye might be alive, he would believe nothin' else."

He obviously was anxious to find me, to personally ensure that I paid for my crime against him. Why else would he have pursued me? I was nothing more than a stranger to him!

"And now, if there be nothin' else, I'll leave ye t' yer bath."

"No, that's wonderful. Thank you again, Iestyn."

"'Tis my pleasure, mum. Believe me, my job had lost considerable interest since ye left this ship. I'm just so thankful yer back! I still can't believe it!"

Moments later, Brenna disrobed and immersed herself in the warm water where she tried to clear her mind and calm her nerves. Lying back, she let her hair flow long over the outside of the tub, soaking in the scented water. Like Iestyn, she could not believe she was back on this ship. *How did this happen?*

'*Your wedding night, a night ye shall forever cherish,*' thought Brenna of Carrie's word earlier today. *Instead, I await this night with angst and dread. What shall he expect from me? Certainly not to behave as a new bride who has married out of love? What will he do when I reject his advances?*

Nervously, Brenna scanned the berth where she had slept alone so often. She prayed silently. *Please, please let us adopt the same sleeping arrangements as before, in separate cabins.* But the words of the captain spoken earlier today rushed forth, '*I fully intend to see that I am reimbursed sufficiently.'* Wringing the sponge tightly in her fist, Brenna vowed angrily, *I don't care what you think I owe you, Captain! I will not repay my debt as a whore! Harley said I would resort to such tactics, but I will not! Captain Grant, you shall never succeed in forcing me to your bed!* Satisfied with her resolve, Brenna slipped low beneath the surface and enjoyed her bath.

Nathan stood silent in the portal, unable to enter fully, yet equally powerless to move away. Before him, Brenna lay with eyes closed in the warm water.

The glow of the fire's dying embers cast a soft light upon her. He thought the hues of her skin flowed within the water, as if dropped from an artist's brush.

Unable to resist a touch, Nathan moved toward her and slipped his hand beneath the water.

Brenna's eyes opened and locked with his. She knew she should resist, yet she was paralyzed to do so. She felt incapable of movement. In this moment, she just wanted comfort and peace. And she wanted someone to hold her. Before her stood a man who was like two sides of a coin, yet she could not see which side was facing her. *Was it good or evil? Malicious or loving? Cynical or kind?* Nearly within her grasp was the truth; she knew it. She could sense it, yet she feared if she moved or even blinked, the coin would rotate sideways and she would be left forever unknowing.

Nathan sensed her need. His gaze held hers and refused to let go until she saw the truth.

Within the brilliant green, she found no evil, no malice, and no wrong. Brenna no longer had the strength or the desire to resist.

Effortlessly, Nathan lifted her glistening body and laid her gently upon his berth. Casting aside his clothes, he lay down beside her and warmed her body with his.

He brushed his lips against the base of her throat and realized that for the first time in his life he was content. Gone was the void that had always existed. Silenced was the voice telling him there was another out there for him. Calm was the sea that had always urged him onward. Still was the driving force telling him there was more. Finally, he grasped what had always been out of reach.

Nathan loved as he had lived—confident, yet gentle. Brenna's body molded to his like the wind filling a sail.

After years battling for existence, she gave up the struggle and realized she faced no opponent. Gone were the limits, the bars, the island's end. In Nathan Grant's sheltering arms, she found freedom, and with it, passion—intense and pure. Years of frustration, fear, and relief came together in peace and perfection.

When the two, who had each struggled through a lifetime of challenges, joined together, it was as though the dark waters of the sea suddenly parted, briefly revealing the brilliant kingdom beyond. It was a world never before seen or touched. Neither would ever be the same nor fully alone again.

Chapter Twelve

The first rays of sunlight had yet to filter across the horizon. Nathan looked at the woman sleeping beside him. He fought the urge to trace his fingers along her eyes, lips, and throat. A wisp of her soft hair lay across her cheek as if she were standing against the wind. He wanted to grasp it, to pull it to his lips, to inhale her sweetness, to stay like this forever. He was overcome with emotion so intense he forced back his threatening tears. "Oh Brenna," he whispered, "Thank God, you're here. I don't know what I would have done if I hadn't found you." He recalled with sickening clarity the day at the prison in Bristol when he believed she was dead. He closed his eyes as a wave of anguish swept over him. He forced the thought aside. Opening his eyes, he found it impossible to believe she was actually here, alive, and in his bed. He had always been fiercely independent, yet he knew now he could not survive losing her again. He looked around his cabin where he had lived for so many years and realized it had never felt like home, until now.

He propped himself on his elbow and gazed at his bride. *From this day forward, my home, Brenna, will forever be wherever you are.*

Nathan needed to tend his ship. He forced aside the urge to pull her back into his arms and rekindle the love they shared last night. He looked at her closed eyes and relived every moment of the remarkable evening. He knew he would do so often for the rest of his life. He sighed with reluctance and drew himself from the warm bed.

Nathan buttoned his shirt and gazed at her. She was only partially covered by the white bed sheets. He could barely comprehend that the beautiful woman before him was his wife. Like lead pulled to magnet, he moved closer to her. He rested his head on his crossed forearms and knelt at her bedside. *What spell have you cast upon me, Mrs. Grant? When I look at you, I can't see or think of anything else. My head swirls and I feel as if I've consumed all the port in Europe. What have you done to me?*

He was the first man she had been with, there had been no doubt. And he felt an overwhelming sense of gratitude and admiration for the intriguing woman before him. She must have fought off pursuers in the past, yet she had waited. He lightly brushed his lips against her forehead and said hoarsely, "Thank you for the honor." She stirred but did not open her eyes. For the first time in his life, he regretted ever having been with another woman. *If only I'd known then what I know now. I never counted on you, Brenna. I never counted on you!*

He recalled their first meeting on St. Christopher and winced. He had suspected she was a whore. The memory filled him with shame. He wanted to remember this the next time he was tempted to pass judgment on someone. Gently, he lifted her soft hand and whispered, "In some way, Brenna, I'm going to make all this up to you and…" Despite his solemn promise, he could not help but chuckle, "If last night is any indication, we're going to share a remarkable life together."

She looked so innocent and pure. He decided Iestyn had been right about her—she did look like an angel. He wished their first time together had come with more trust between them. *Brenna, I know there's much you don't understand now, and it may get worse without me telling you everything, but please, please don't lose faith in me. Someday soon, it will all be clear.* He wanted to wake her, to explain everything…the shipwreck, her parents… But as much as he yearned to tell her, he realized again, as he had in the carriage yesterday, that she and her parents needed to discover the truth together. He smiled at the thought. *I suspect it'll be a moment that will be retold for generations!* Sighing heavily, Nathan reluctantly turned and left his sleeping bride.

She awoke at the sound of a door closing, but her eyes remained closed. Dreamily, she settled deeper in the warm bed. A smile touched her lips. She was filled with a contentment she had never experienced. Momentarily, she forgot its source. She felt the softness of the bed, yet there was something unfamiliar in its touch. She opened her eyes and gasped, quickly pulling the sheet over her. It was the first time she had slept without any clothes. Then the realization dawned. Fury filled her. She yanked back the covers and kicked them to the end of the bed. A rage more intense than she had ever known consumed her as she shoved herself off the bed. *You fool! You weak, pitiful fool!* She saw a small spot of blood on the sheet, evidence of her own body's betrayal and her lost virginity. Furiously, she grabbed the sheet and repeatedly stomped on it.

Is nothing sacred? Every vow I made to myself! Even ones that I just made! Everything I believed! It's all gone! Brenna kicked the cloth across the cold floor, grabbed her dress, and forced it on. "And Miss Brenna," she mocked aloud, her face flushed hot in fury, "did he force himself or was it blackmail he used in coercing you to his bed? Oh? You say you just gave yourself to him freely? What? You were tired and something inexplicable came over you? You were searching for what, the truth? And you thought the man who has been trying to destroy your life would let you find the truth? In him? Oh, you poor, pathetic girl!" Brenna moved back to the berth and stared down at the bed where they had spent the night entangled in one another. There was no release for her wrath. She fell on the empty mattress and sobbed. "When Brenna," she moaned, "when are you going to take control of your life? First Harley, then Malcolm Stone, and now Nathan Grant! They've all imprisoned you. When will it stop?" Unable to find any answers, Brenna wept until she fell asleep exhausted.

Brenna rolled to her back and noticed for the first time the list of the ship. *So, we're at sea.* She recalled the morning she awoke in the hold and discovered the ship had set sail. *I wish I were there now. Anything would be better than this! How could I have been so weak! I've let him slip into my life! Not only into my bed, but now into my heart!* She was gripped with despair at the realization that her own feelings had betrayed her. After their unbelievable night of passion he held her. Never in her wildest imagining could she have known how utterly perfect it would be to lie with him in the shelter of his strong arms and hear his soothing words. With her head pressed against his chest, she heard the even beating of his heart, and for the briefest of moments, she sensed that as long as his heart continued to beat so would hers. And when the warmth of his body filtered through her, she felt she would never be cold again. As she pressed her face against his chest, she smelled the salt of the sea and the leather of his saddle. She smiled inwardly and knew; even if she were ninety years old, blind and had not seen him since, she would recognize when he came near by his wonderful scent. In his arms she felt safe and protected.

She covered her face with her hands. *Brenna! You weren't safe. It was all a bloody charade! A game! And now he has twisted your heart and he knows it! He knows he*'s *won! He's mocking you! Oh God! How will I ever face him?*

She knew she was not strong enough to do so from the bed. Standing at the wash basin, she sponged her face and paused in front of the thick, leaded mirror. The pale face of a person she no longer knew or trusted stared back. *Why did you do it? How could you?*

Drained of all energy, Brenna moved to the small porthole. She stared, unseeing at the blue water beyond. *At least in prison, I knew what was to become of me. But what about now? Is it your intent, Captain Grant, to turn me over to the sharks when you've had your fill of me? Would your desire then for revenge be avenged? Would justice be complete?*

Distantly, she heard approaching footsteps. She wanted to run back to the hold. She wished he had left her there to die. Instead, she forced her shoulders back. She longed to be anywhere but here.

Nathan walked eagerly toward the cabin, his face red and stinging from the cold. They had gotten underway quickly but in light of what he heard earlier this morning, he prayed it was quick enough. When he emerged on the deck at dawn, he was met by Miles asking to speak with him…urgently. Nathan had never seen the man look so sheepish or so ill-at-ease.

"Certainly, what's the trouble? You look cold and tired."

Miles cleared his throat. "It was a long night, Captain. I have something to tell you and you may not be too pleased to hear it. I did something quite unbecoming of a gentleman."

"Really?"

"Well sir," began Miles, clearly uncomfortable, "when I saw you return last night and heard we would sail at daybreak, I walked down the street to the stable to retrieve our two goats. The only one around was a stable boy who was just leaving. Anyway, all the sudden I heard this commotion and Miss Launey of all people came storming in, half dressed! Although she had on an overcoat, those weren't no day clothes she had underneath! She didn't seem to recognize me from the ship…but I recognized her. I heard she had been aboard since morning giving everyone the what for. I'm just glad I was gone most of the day an' missed it.

"Anyway…Miss Launey grabbed that stable boy right by his shirt, she did, and starts talking to him. I say talk, but actually, she was yelling…yelling that she had to hire a coach immediately. He explained it was after hours, that all the carriage horses had been put up for the night, all the coachmen had left, and he couldn't help her because he had to go tend to his sick mother. And Miss Launey, she was furious…kept screaming at the poor lad…demanding he help her… that it was a matter of life and death…that she needed to get the constable…or her father the judge…that a murderer was getting away…and that she was gonna block the ship from leaving…that its captain…Captain Grant… had to be stopped. Anyway, all this and the lad still told her he couldn't help her.

"So, sir…I…ah…I told the boy to go tend to his mum. I would see that Miss Launey be helped…that I would harness a horse and take her myself."

"Miles, I have a strange impression that perhaps you didn't exactly help her."

"Not exactly sir. In fact, well sir, she wanted somewhere to change her clothes while I harnessed the horse…and I must say, she wasn't fit to be going anywhere proper in what she was wearing! And so I told her she could use one of the empty stalls to change…and well sir…

"…when she walked into the stall…I ah…I…closed and bolted the latch…from the outside." The man raised his shoulders and tightly squinted his face.

"She started yellin' and pounding…but nobody was around to pay her no mind…especially not as cold as it was.

"I would have come to ye sooner, but seein how we wouldn't have the tide nor the light until morning…I thought it better if I waited there…in the stable…just in case there was a fire or something…."

"That was…gentlemanly of you." said Nathan with a grin.

"She hollered for hours an' didn't even know I was standing watch. Oh, she had might nasty things t' say about you, sir…never heard a woman speak like that. I'm sure it was a cold night for her…but there was plenty of straw and no windows so I think she ought to be okay…well…maybe not okay by her standards." The man laughed despite his tension. Nathan knew when Miles started with the "anyways" he was nervous.

"Anyway, sir…I waited out the night there and just now returned. I don't think she will be found until the stable opens in a couple hours, but I think it best if we be getting outta here, right quick."

Despite the seriousness of the situation, Nathan found himself chuckling at the thought of Launey spending the night in the stall. He recalled the hatred in her voice and her raised hand to strike Brenna. He shuddered when he thought of what could have happened had Miles not intervened. He would have to find a way to reward the loyal man for his quick-thinking actions.

Nathan realized he should have taken Launey's threat more seriously and taken Brenna somewhere safe last night. The thought of more harm coming to his wife caused Nathan to experience a pain so intense; it was as though he had been kicked in the stomach by his horse.

They had been the first ship out of dock. He was not sure if a chase would be launched, but he was not about to take any chances. He had already put full sails to the wind to get her out to open water as quickly as possible. Nathan quickened his pace toward his cabin. He looked at the door, astounded at the intensity of his feelings for his new wife within. He barely knew her, and yet he realized he would stop at nothing to protect her.

He hoped she was awake and eagerly turned the latch. Instead of being clad only in a gown and lingering in berth as he hoped, Brenna was fully dressed, standing erect with her back to him. She made no acknowledgement of his presence. He sensed she might be self-conscious about their lovemaking. He went to her and wrapped his powerful arms around her waist and brushed the side of her neck with his lips. She had no reaction. Puzzled, he gently turned her around to face him. Emptiness was all he could see in her red, swollen eyes.

"Brenna, what is it? What's happened?"

Bewildered he need even ask, Brenna continued to stare at him blankly.

"What is it? What's happened to upset you?" Again there was no reaction, not even a flicker of the life he had seen there last night. Helplessly, he dropped his arms. "It's okay. We can talk later. Perhaps we ought to take our breakfast. You must be star…"

"That won't be necessary," she said listlessly. "I have no appetite."

"I would have thought," he jested, trying to lighten her spirits, "after last night, you'd be famished, m'lady."

Brenna found no humor in her degradation. "Last night, I made the gravest error of my life. I'm ashamed by my weakness. Be assured, Captain Grant, if it's your desire to take me again, it shall be by force, for I will never, ever willingly do so again."

He was stunned by her unexpected words and decided that trying to talk to her now might only do more harm than good. Reluctantly, he opened the door. "I've never yet resorted to force. And you may rest assured; I have no plans to begin now. Not even with you, Mrs. Grant."

"Mrs. Grant! Pah!" spat Brenna furiously after he left. "I'm not Mrs. Grant and you bloody well know it!"

Three hours passed before Brenna had any visitors.

"May I enter, mum?" asked Iestyn. He opened the door with a tray in hand.

"Iestyn, where I am, you're always welcome."

He placed the tray on the wooden table and said sheepishly, "I've brought yer lunch. Ye must be starved, havin' no breakfast an' all."

"To be honest, I am." Brenna had begun to regret her refusal of the morning meal.

"Honestly!" His voice was laced with an anger Brenna had never heard in him. "I don't know what's gotten into the man!" Brenna knew immediately 'the man' to be the captain. "I had in me hands a superb tray filled with the finest scones and tarts in all o' England. Set to bring 'em to ye earlier this mornin', when the captain spotted me and told me ye wished not to be disturbed. Well, knowin' last night was yer weddin' night an all," he blushed, "I followed his orders. Should've known where yer concerned, lassie, the captain's got little sense."

Brenna smiled for the first time all day. "Oh, Iestyn, you always seem to know how to brighten even the bleakest of days."

Iestyn's brows furrowed. He wondered what could have transpired on their first night that she now referred to this day as bleak. He had seen the captain was in no better mood. Iestyn suddenly felt great empathy for the woman. He remembered she barely knew the man to whom she was now wed. He tried to cheer her. "Well, mum, I must tell ye that when I first saw ye here last night, I thought I was lookin' at a ghost."

"I'm sorry, Iestyn! My appearance must have been a great shock."

"T'aint nothin' t' be sorry 'bout! Never have I been so happy than when I saw that ye were alive. After gettin' yer letter an' then believin' ye had taken yer own life, well, I don't know when I felt more miserable!"

"I'm truly sorry for misleading you. It was never my intent when I wrote to you."

"I'm jes glad t'was all a misunderstandin'! I can say in all honestly, though, t'was the captain that took it the worst. T'aint never seen anyone suffer like that!"

"Iestyn," a raspy voice interrupted from outside the door. "The cook is in need of yer services."

"Well, if you'll excuse me, mum," Iestyn said as he left, "I fear I've talked too much already."

"No," said Brenna honestly, "I've missed your conversation."

Iestyn grinned. "Well then, I'll be back shortly. Oh, and mum, ye said in yer letter ye thought I may have been actin' kindly t' ye on the command of another. Ye were wrong on that point. My friendship t'aint for sale."

Brenna gently blew her hot tea until it was cool enough to drink. She doubted Iestyn's interpretation of the captain's feelings when he believed she had died. She thought Iestyn ought to know better than anyone how little she meant to the captain. He was, after all, the one who told her when they docked in Bristol that the captain was going to make sure justice was done.

Was your pride so wounded, Captain Grant, that it wasn't enough you thought me dead? Her gaze settled on the bed, the images of the man who shared himself with her so tenderly there last night were irreconcilable against the images of a man who would despise her. *Why else, but for revenge, would he have been pained by my death? We were little more than strangers? And yet…I barely knew him, and for months he has possessed my thoughts and dreams. Is it possible, he could have been so affected by me?*

She moved to his painting of the sea at night. *Could Judge Charles be right?* She touched the necklace still around her neck. *Could the captain actually feel something akin to love for me? This would certainly explain his kindness after discovering me in the hold, his unyielding search, the gifts, and even the wedding.* She moved closer to the painting. *Have I been wrong about you all along, Captain Grant? Could it be this wedding is more than just a guise for you?* Explosively, Launey's words struck her and shattered her blissful daydreams. Until now, she had not given the woman's words any thought.

"You told me you were searching for her only out of obligation," Launey said.

So, it was only out of duty that you searched for me, Captain Grant. Your duty to see justice prevail! Nothing more?" Angry at her foolishness in once again wanting to believe otherwise, Brenna began to pace the small quarters. She thought of his tender words last night. They perplexed her until another thought occurred—that of Launey wearing only the thinnest of negligee and lying on his berth. *Perhaps it was her you imagined in your arms last night.* Brenna sank slowly down on the berth. She felt sick.

Why though, if he cared so much about Launey, would he have behaved as though he wanted nothing to do with her? It makes no sense. Is it possible she is somehow a part of this entire charade? Is that possible? When he went to Winchcombe yesterday, had he sent word ahead to have Launey waiting for us?

Was it all staged? But why? Why would they go to such lengths? No, that is not possible! I saw the surprise on her face…and Iestyn's later…neither were the reactions of an actor! So, Captain, is it that you merely had grown tired of Launey and were ready for your next conquest?

Brenna recalled the scantily clad woman on St. Christopher who tried to board the ship and bid the captain goodbye. Brenna ran her hand over the smooth wood of the ship's side. *Was this ship, The Grace, named for another one of his women?* Brenna frowned at the thought. She was tempted to ask Iestyn about it. *Who is she, this Grace? A woman in one of his many ports of call? Or perhaps…* Brenna jerked to her feet, thunderstruck by the possibility*, perhaps his wife! What if he already has a wife!* Brenna's heart pounded rapidly at the possibility. But she calmed when she realized that if this were true, Iestyn would never have been pleased by their marriage announcement. Disgusted for even worrying about any of his motives or other women, she flung herself down on the berth, angry that her name could now be added to his list of conquered women.

Brenna peered through the porthole. Darkness had long since settled over the water, allowing her a limited view of the starlit sky. She thought about venturing to the deck, but knew she should not do so unescorted. Uneasily, she wondered if the captain would be true to his word and not take her by force. She opened the pocket watch from his desk. Seven-thirty. She wondered if it was his punishment to order Iestyn to cancel all her meals. She was startled by Iestyn's knock. He entered, wearing a formal white serving coat and gloves. Surprised to see him so attired, Brenna grinned, "Are you planning to go to a ball?"

"Actually, yes. A private one of sorts. Your husband," said Iestyn, trying his utmost to sound proper, "has requested yer presence in dinin' with him in his...ah…temporary quarters, mum."

Brenna did not know how to interpret the invitation after their last encounter nor the revelation of the captain having taken up different quarters. Not wishing to spoil Iestyn's obvious elation, she said with far more enthusiasm than she felt, "Is he ready for me to join him now?"

"Aye, but first let me get this." Brenna watched with fascination as the man got to his knees, reached under the berth, and pulled out a large, flat box. "It's one o' six under here," he said, slightly out of breath. "When ye first fled this ship and we thought ye'd be easy to trace. The captain had a clothier in Bristol tailor ye some clothes." He grinned, obviously pleased with the gifts. "We guessed at yer size."

"Tailor me some clothes?" Brenna was dumbfounded. "Why?"

Iestyn looked at her seriously. "I think he knew ye'd be returnin' with us t' the Colonies."

"Why would he think such a thing?"

Iestyn shrugged. "Ye'll have to ask him. Now, I'll stand behind this screen, an' when yer ready, I'll help ye tie up the back of this gown."

Brenna opened her mouth, trying to form another question, but closed it as nothing came. *Obviously, the captain had been planning for some time to have me back aboard this ship. Why? So that I'd keep him company, as I did last night, his form of pressing me into service?* Brenna felt her anger starting again to mount, but it was tempered knowing that Iestyn certainly did not feel such motives of the captain. Brenna did not know what to believe.

Ten minutes later, Iestyn removed a cloak from the iron wall hook and pressed it around her shoulders. Silently, she followed him down the corridor, wearing a new, pale blue dress.

"Your bride is here," announced Iestyn proudly and entered the dim chambers. Brenna's eyes grew wide at the sight of the captain standing before her in the small room illuminated only by the fire in the stove and a single candle in the center of the small table lavishly set for two. Wearing a fine white waist-coat, complete with a white cummerbund and a crisply starched white shirt and stock, the captain tipped his hat and bowed.

He gave her the same broad grin she had first seen on St. Christopher, then pulled a chair out for her. "Thank you for joining me. I'm afraid I might appear a little more than foolish sitting here like this alone."

She forced their earlier encounter from her thoughts and held out the skirt of her long gown. "I fear the shock of all this has me at a bit of a loss of words. I wasn't expecting anything so stately."

"As for the details of this dinner, the credit belongs to Iestyn."

"Once again, Iestyn," said Brenna, "Thank you."

"T'was the captain's idea to celebrate yer return in style. I must say the cook had a whale o' a time once he got the nod for this dinner. May I pour ye a glass of Madeira? 'Tis Lisbon's finest."

Brenna hesitated, not accustomed to drinking spirits. Nathan sensed her uncertainty and said lightly, "You may want just a taste to see if you like it."

Iestyn filled their goblets. "It does this heart good t' see the two o' ye here together! And here's some warm bread t' hold ye 'til the main course."

"I must say," chided Nathan after Iestyn's departure, "if he was a few years younger or you a bit older, I think I might have had to vie with him for your hand. He's quite fond of you, you know? He was beside himself with grief at the thought of your death."

"That's precisely what he said of you," quipped Brenna. She looked squarely at the captain. "Although, quite honestly, sir, I'm rather puzzled at the reason."

Nathan looked at her directly, "I felt responsible for you fleeing in the first place."

She peered into his green eyes, looking for clarity in his expression. She could not read anything.

"For a woman who has lived her life in the tropics, you seem to have adapted quite nicely to the colder climes."

Brenna had vowed to keep her guard against him and not under any circumstances let herself forget her earlier anger. Yet, despite her resolve not to, she was completely at ease in his company. She decided that rather than fight her inner warnings, she would use caution but strive to find whatever enjoyment she could.

More confident, she returned her attention to him, yet the moment her eyes locked with his, her only thought was that of his loving touch of last night. She felt her resolve slipping as her face and neck grew hot. She refused to let him unnerve her and forced the intimate thoughts aside. "I have to admit I haven't gotten used to seeing my breath! It looks like everyone is smoldering."

They both laughed heartily. Calming, she asked, "Why do you presume I've lived all my life in the tropics?"

"You didn't?"

"Nay, Captain, you're not in error. Until I boarded your ship, I had never left the shores of St. Christopher."

"Your first venture away from home resulted in rather unhappy consequences, did it not?"

"If you're referring to the fact that I ended up aboard this ship…with you…under these most unpleasant circumstances," said Brenna, speaking the first thought that came to mind, "then I suppose I would have to agree."

Nathan erupted in laughter once again. "Although the verdict is still unknown in regard to these 'unpleasant circumstances,' I was," he said, still laughing, "thinking of your stay in prison."

Not able to help herself, Brenna laughed with him, but stopped abruptly when a thought struck her. Her tone turned solemn as she asked pointedly, "Aren't you curious about that?"

"About what?"

"You've never even asked whether or not I am guilty."

"Brenna," he said suddenly very serious, "if you'll recall, I took you for my wife yesterday. Believe me, had there been any…" he stopped as Iestyn returned carrying a heavy tray filled with an array of the most elegant food Brenna had ever seen.

"Iestyn," said Brenna breathlessly, "I've never seen anything like this! How in the world did you do all this?"

"Well, considerin' we had nothin' prepared on your weddin' night, 'tis the least we could do."

"Please thank the cook for me!"

"Certainly. Now, if there be nothin' else, I'll leave ye t' yer dinner."

Brenna looked wide-eyed upon the feast of turkey, finely cured ham, potatoes, and yams. "Do you eat like this on all your voyages?"

Nathan smiled, amused, "You had best enjoy it now. If you'll recall, by the time we docked in Bristol, to say the meals were repetitious would be an understatement."

After what I went through in the hold, Brenna wanted to say, *I thought all the food wonderful.* Yet, Brenna remained silent. Her stowing away was a sensitive topic.

Brenna's face was illuminated by candlelight. "How is it," Nathan asked softly, "that when we first met, you were selling produce on St. Christopher?"

"It was the trade of my fa—Harley—the man married to the woman who raised me."

"And he allowed you to sell, unescorted?"

"I wasn't usually unescorted."

"Oh?"

"My dog."

"I don't recall having seen a dog with you."

"The rain."

"Ah. Well, a dog may be helpful in some situations, but certainly not enough to protect a young…"

Brenna laughed, "You've never met this one."

"Still, I can't fathom a father letting you do so, hound or not."

"For the last several years, he had been unable…unwilling," she corrected, "to do so himself."

"Unwilling to do what himself?" asked Nathan incredibly. "The work?" Seeing her affirmative nod, he questioned, "Did he do any of it himself?"

"No, not in a long time."

"How long?" Nathan asked, his eyes darkening. "How long exactly had you been doing such labor?"

"Since I was twelve."

"What!" Nathan roared.

His anger surprised Brenna. "And how old are you now?"

"Just short of two score."

"Seven years!" he stormed. "You pulled that mule and cart for seven years?" Not waiting for her response, he demanded, "What sort of a man would allow a young girl to work in his place? What sort of man was he?"

Uneasy by his mounting ire and uncertain why this would bother him, Brenna hesitated. "He…well, his interest was more toward the bottle than anything else."

"I see," replied Nathan, the muscles in his cheeks grew visible as his jaw clenched. "And what, in addition to selling the produce, were you required to do?"

"Plant and harvest."

"By yourself?"

"Yes."

"Unaided?"

"Yes."

"There were no other siblings?"

"No, none."

Nathan wished he could get his hands around the coward's neck. He worried at the despair Emily and Weston would feel learning how their daughter had been robbed of a happy childhood. He hurt for them. Yet, when he looked at her now, so beautiful and sweet, he knew *that* alone would be strength enough for them. After all these years…after all the pain…the three of them together! Nathan could only imagine what that day would bring. It would be a day to end all days.

His abrupt change in mood baffled her. She could see that the man before her was suddenly very far way. "What were you thinking just now?" Brenna could not help but ask.

He straightened and said thoughtfully, "I was just thinking about your past and righting a wrong."

Brenna knew it was something more on his mind, but she was reluctant to press him further.

"You said he was the man who was married to the woman who raised you. What of the woman?"

"She was extraordinary."

"Yet she permitted you to work in this manner?"

"No, she would never have allowed it. She passed away just after my twelfth birthday."

"I see," sighed Nathan.

Brenna wondered why he was so clearly bothered.

"How was it," he asked, struggling to keep his ire at bay, "you came to live with these people? What of your birth parents? What do you know of them?"

"The people to whom I was born did something reprehensible." Brenna then closed and opened her eyes. Her expression changed from pain to a cold resolve. "However, neither they, nor their actions, are of any importance to me now. They are dead to me."

Nathan pursed his lips and wondered if he should tell her the truth, right here, right now, regardless of whether or not she believed him. He thought about their conversation yesterday in the carriage. She had told him she did not trust him or any of his words. His actions with her last night clearly had not helped.

"For as long as I can remember, I believed Harley and Helen were my parents. It wasn't until the day I boarded your ship that I learned I had been born to another couple."

"Really?" Nathan was surprised. "Is that why you were crying when first we met?"

Brenna shook her head. "No, after completing my work later that day Harley told me the truth."

Incensed, Nathan demanded, "After all you had done for him?"

Baffled by his anger, Brenna contemplated the surprising man. Of one thing she was certain, his wrath was not fabricated.

"When you learned he was not your father, was that when you learned of my identity as a ship's captain and boarded *The Grace*?"

Laughing aloud, Brenna finally settled enough to ask, "Is that what you honestly believed? That I came looking for you? Why would I have done so?"

"You didn't?" exclaimed Nathan. "It was the only conclusion I could surmise! Why don't you enlighten me?"

"When I knew I could no longer stay on the island, I remembered seeing an American vessel docked, so…I took my chances."

"Having no idea it was my ship?"

"None."

"It appears," chuckled Nathan, "that we were both amiss in our assumptions."

Brenna's laughter eased slightly. She could never remember a time when she so enjoyed herself. The man she thought to be vengeful sat laughing with her now, as if he truly welcomed her company. He appeared to be a compassionate listener, one who cared enough to learn of her childhood and who seemed genuinely upset by its darker aspects. She wanted to believe him. She wanted to believe in the best in him, and yet, when she felt herself being nudged toward doing so, she remembered Helen's words, that she too had believed the best of Harley. Then the images of Malcolm Stone and the parents who sold her filled her mind. She should have been able to trust them too.

"Tell me about growing up on St. Christopher," Nathan said and crossed his arms. "Where was your favorite place on that beautiful island?"

"A hidden mountain pool," she spoke without hesitation, yet she was surprised, for she had never told another about it, not even Helen.

Intrigued, Nathan propped his chin in his hands and leaned closer to her. "Really?"

Brenna described every detail she could recall of the mystical pool, encased by high cliffs, flowers, ferns, and a thunderous waterfall.

"This was your private place, wasn't it?"

Brenna looked into his warm eyes and wondered how he could have realized this. "To my knowledge, no one else knew of its existence."

"Brenna's hidden mountain pool. It sounds nice. I'd like to see it."

Brenna looked at him directly, "It was nice. It was perfect."

In sharing her secret, Brenna feared a glib response. Instead, he said thoughtfully, "It seems that you needed such a place…a place where you were free."

Who are you, Captain Grant? You seem to understand so much.

"I'll take yer dishes, if yer finished," said Iestyn, reappearing in the doorway. He realized immediately his intrusion was ill-timed. Inwardly, he cursed himself for the disruption and quickly gathered the dishes. He set a plate of truffles before them. "These are England's finest," he added before he quietly retreated.

Nathan lifted the plate and offered it to her.

"They look wonderful," she responded as she took one. "Even though I'm afraid I overdid a bit on the meal, I can't pass on this. I've never had one."

Nathan could not suppress his amusement at Brenna's so obvious enjoyment of the sweet chocolate. "If the cold will not overly vex you, would you care to join me for a brief walk about the ship?"

"I can't think of anything nicer after spending the day in the cabin," said Brenna and slipped her arms through the cloak which he held open for her. "I fear I'm in need of a little exertion."

"Oh really," Nathan grinned broadly, "why, I would have thought, m'lady, you would still be fatigued from last night."

Brenna tried to ignore the jest by looking away, but not before Nathan glimpsed her smile.

"That's just about the extent of her," said Nathan later of the ship. He followed Brenna up the five steps to the foredeck. "Generally, when I escort guests, I take them through the holds, but in your case, I don't believe that's necessary."

Unable to detect any bitterness in his tone, Brenna smiled innocently, "Whatever do you mean, Captain?"

"If my information is accurate," his voice was laced with sarcasm, "I did hear of a clever young woman who managed to survive in just such a hold for weeks…and while the poor ship experienced the slowest crossing voyage in its history."

"You mean to say," Brenna jested, "the woman managed to live right under the nose of the captain and his crew? However did she accomplish this with such ease?"

"Precisely what I'd like to know."

She wondered again if he truly felt no animosity toward her for having stowed aboard his ship. *If not, then why did he want justice for me having done so?*

When he realized she was not going to answer, the captain asked, "Are you cold? If so, we can take our leave."

"No, actually, I like it."

The two stood quietly at the ship's rail. The moonlight showered its rays upon the water and overhead the huge sails rustled in the easy breeze.

"Brenna," said Nathan gently. He simply spoke her name, yet it was said with such tenderness that it surprised her. "Why were you crying that day…on the island?"

Her voice sounded frail when she answered, "I had lost all hope."

Brenna sensed profound sadness in him. She wondered if it was merely her imagination. Then, without warning, he took her hands in his. His voice was barely above a whisper, "I'm sorry."

"For what?"

"For not taking the time to even ask."

Brenna closed her eyes. She could not think clearly when he behaved this way. *Why is he saying these things? Is it possible for him to be this convincing and yet feel nothing for me? Why is he doing this?* Not knowing what to believe, Brenna pulled her hands from his and looked out at the glimmering water beyond the rail. She regretted having done so. She wanted his touch. She wanted to fall into his arms and to believe everything he was saying, yet she realized she was treading on dangerous ground.

Abruptly, she said, "I can see you have a great love of the sea. That's something we share. I find the sea is so comforting and yet…" Uncertain of her words, she paused.

"And yet, what?"

Brenna laughed. "I'm not really sure. I know this may sound strange, but it's as if the sea is yearning."

"For what?" asked Nathan, as his voice deepened.

"I don't know exactly. Perhaps...for a truce between the forces that continually battle within its depth."

Intrigued, Nathan leaned on the rail and asked, "And which forces are those?"

Having known only a few people in her life who cared enough to take interest in what she had to say, Brenna found it difficult to continue. He sensed her reluctance to speak. Nathan turned, lifted her chin, and looked directly into her moonlit face. "Brenna, the sea has always been part of me, and I feel the same may be true for you. Despite what you might think, your attitudes toward it are of great interest to me." Then, tenderly he brushed aside a wisp of her hair that had blown across her face. "Please continue. You were talking about the sea's battle."

Acutely aware of her body's response to his casual touch and the memory of him lying next to her, Brenna trembled slightly. *No, Brenna! You are not going to become weak to him again!* It took effort for her to cast aside the memory of his touch. "Well, similar to man," she began, still amazed by his willingness to listen, "the sea seems to contain all the opposing forces of nature. Within it, one can experience fear and humiliation, yet also peace and triumph. It is roaring and it is silent. It brings pleasure and it brings despair. And stranger still, its salty water sustains life for so many, and yet it is poison to just as many others. Continually, it seems the sea is at war with itself, a war that it can never win." Brenna realized she had spoken more than she intended and stopped. The sky darkened, a cloud blocked the moon's light, and while she was unable to see the man so close to her, his presence was undeniable. She felt her pulse quicken.

"You, madam," he murmured, "have spoken my exact feelings."

"Then perhaps," Brenna said without thinking, "we have finally found one subject we can mutually enjoy." Realizing instantly the folly of her words, Brenna blushed and hoped he would spare her any embarrassment.

He did not. "Need I remind you so soon, sweet Brenna, of yet another area where I can assure you, we both find complete enjoyment?"

Brenna's face grew hot. She turned her back to him. "Do you have no honor?"

Nathan spun her around and covered her lips with his. Her anger drained away. She could think of nothing but his warm, eager kiss. She wanted him to lift her in his arms and carry her back to her quarters where they could resume their lovemaking from last night. Yet, as quickly as he pulled her to him, Nathan withdrew.

"Now that we've reestablished *that* topic of mutual satisfaction, I think it best I bid you goodnight."

Like the first day she met him on the island, Brenna was once again too furious to speak, only tonight, the anger was toward herself. *The same day,* she wanted to scream, *the very same day I vowed I would never do so again, I fell victim to him! I was actually praying he would take me to his berth! And worst of all, he knows it!* Inwardly seething, she followed him.

Moments later, Nathan opened her cabin door. Flashing a white grin, he gallantly tipped his hat. "Goodnight, dearest wife. Stay warm."

Later, Iestyn knocked on her door and asked if there was anything she needed. Her terse, but polite, reply left little doubt that she was clearly upset. He found it hard to believe the couple who had been so obviously enjoying themselves an hour earlier could end the evening in such disarray.

Grumbling under his breath, Iestyn made his way down the passageway. "It's beyond me how the captain would let a thing like this happen! An' I don't much care if he doesn't like me bringin' it up. Brenna's well bein' is my business!" Certain he would find the captain in a similar dark mood, Iestyn was amazed when he entered the captain's quarters.

Nathan sat on the edge of his berth and tugged on his boot. Grinning, he said casually, "Why, Iestyn, how nice of you to drop by."

Iestyn noted with pleasure the difficulty the captain was having in removing his right boot. He said indignantly, "Well, I'm certainly glad ye at least enjoyed yerself tonight, sir."

"And why wouldn't I have?" Nathan paused momentarily in his struggle.

"From what I gathered, yer wife was not in the most pleasant of moods."

"Oh, really?"

"Aye, can't remember ever seeing Miss Brenna quite so upset."

"Ah, well," Nathan said nonchalantly, "I'm certain she'll recover before long. Here," he asked and extended his long leg, "would you mind?"

Iestyn ignored his request and said boldly, "I find yer flippant attitude puzzlin' at best, sir!"

"Why?" Nathan questioned when he realized his first mate had no intention in assisting him.

"For one who was so anxious t' find the lass an' besieged with guilt over her death, ye act as though ye've grown tired of her already!"

Nathan raised his eyebrows and chuckled. "Tired of Brenna? Hardly!"

"Glad I am t' hear it, but if'n ye ask me…"

"Brenna," said Nathan, preventing Iestyn's intended lecture, "is really most intriguing. Her insight on a variety of subjects is fascinating. In all honesty, I've never met a more…remarkable woman!"

"Precisely what I tried t' tell ye on the last voyage! An beggin yer pardon, sir," he stammered, "why on earth," he blurted out the question that had been eating away at him all day, "are ye allowin' yer new bride t' sleep in separate quarters?"

"I assure you, Iestyn, the decision was entirely hers."

"Glad I am t' hear ye've not lost yer good sense entirely! Although perhaps," he jested, "ye've finally lost yer touch where the ladies are concerned."

Brenna's words earlier in the day that she had made the biggest mistake of her life still stung more than he cared to admit, but he was not about to give Iestyn the satisfaction of knowing the accuracy of his jest. Instead, Nathan said casually, "Brenna needs a little time to adjust to me…and to being married. I'm simply honoring her request."

Satisfied the captain seemed to have the girl's best interest at heart, Iestyn lifted Nathan's boot and forcefully yanked it off. Setting the boot down, he asked, "What was her response when ye told her 'bout her parents?"

"I've decided it best for me to steer clear of that topic."

"What?" exclaimed Iestyn incredulously. "Didn't ye tell her the truth?"

"No. At this point, Brenna has nothing but misconceptions about her parents…and me for that matter."

"Why then don't ye straighten her out and be done with it?"

"You have no idea," sighed Nathan, "how much I desire to do just that. But hearing the truth from anyone but her parents would rob them all of something they have dearly earned."

Iestyn started to protest but stopped when Nathan added, his tone laced with regret, "No, she doesn't trust me…not that I've given her much reason to…and she has so much hostility toward them. Believing her parents love her is something I don't think she will accept from anyone but them, and even they may have a tough time convincing her. The pathetic, evil man who raised her fed her all sorts of lies about them. She hasn't shared the particulars of the offenses, but whatever they were, she is devastated by them. No," said Nathan. He rubbed his chin as if to convince himself, "After her reaction the last two times I've attempted to talk to her about it, I think it best if she discovers the truth herself."

"Even so," added Iestyn, "seems t' me yer makin' a big mistake by lettin' her sleep alone."

"That topic," said Nathan as he yawned, "is also closed for further discussion."

"Since the hour is late, I'll take my leave." Then, just loud enough for Nathan's ears, he grumbled, "Sleepin' alone, and only the day after the weddin', unthinkable!"

Nathan smiled at the man's good intentions. He folded his arms behind his neck and stretched out his legs. Although fatigued, he knew sleep would be slow in coming. As it had been all day, the recollection of Brenna's warm body pressed against him was all too vivid. He yearned for her, not only physically, but emotionally as well. The thought of her lonely childhood sickened him, and he craved to hold her now for all the times she had been alone and frightened.

He blew out his bedside lamp. *How is it I feel so bonded to her when all the women I knew before were merely a brief diversion from the sea? And now, I don't care if ever I sail again! When I came to England on this voyage, I could imagine myself doing little else, and now, all I want is to be with her. What sort of hex have ye placed on me, Brenna Grant? And why, when I barely knew you, did I blurt out to the judge that I intended to marry you?* The answer to that question had escaped him from almost the moment the words were out of his mouth. Until they were spoken, he had no intention of such a proposal! He knew he could have persuaded the judge to let him take Brenna simply by telling the man the truth about her parents.

For one who generally weighs all his options, Nathan, you certainly behaved irrationally on this one!

Nathan closed his eyes and tried to sleep, yet he found himself chuckling aloud when he recalled her laughter. Several times during the evening she threw back her head—her long, blond hair flung wildly over her shoulders—and laughed. It was unlike any laughter he had ever heard. It was not the polite cackle of so many women, nor the giggle of a shy lass, but Brenna's peal of laughter came as if from the depth of her being. It encompassed and shook her entire body. The thought struck him of how that one small aspect of her…her laughter…was in itself a great tribute to who she was. For, after all she had endured and all that brute of a stepfather did to destroy her childhood, he did not take away her laughter. Somehow, remarkably, she was still filled with joy. Nathan had been right about her from the very beginning; she was a fighter and a winner. And Emily and Weston had also won. He was certain their strong spirits had carried through in her.

Once again, Nathan closed his eyes and tried to release his mind from all thought. It was to no avail. The picture of Brenna lying in the steaming bath was etched upon his mind. "Lord help me," he groaned miserably, "this may be a long voyage."

Huddled next to the stove for warmth, Brenna dined alone. Unlike every other evening for the past three weeks, when she ate with the captain, tonight he sent word through Iestyn that his duties would not allow him to do so. She looked at his vacant chair and realized how much she looked forward to their evening meals together. She tried to justify her loneliness without him, thinking that anyone who was confined as she was would be eager for company, regardless of who that company might be. As she thought the words, she knew she was not being honest with herself. She had spent the better portion of her life alone and was well-accustomed to it. Brenna sighed with defeat. It was the captain she missed.

Brenna tore off a small portion of freshly baked bread and smiled. She pictured the captain sitting before her now; undoubtedly, his teasing remarks would be coming forth in an endless stream. Flashing his stunning white smile, he would wait for her response. If there was one thing Brenna had learned about him, it was that he discovered humor in nearly all facets of life. Regardless of how dull the topic, Brenna continually found herself immersed in laughter whenever he was near. In truth, she had never known such joy. She learned also that while the captain was quick with a grin, he was an exceedingly perceptive listener as well. Repeatedly, she confided in him as she had with no one, and to her amazement, he genuinely appeared interested, regardless of the topic.

He had a never-ending stream of questions regarding her childhood, and she sensed his relief when he learned of her close relationship with Helen. He wanted to know how she received her education and what her favorite subjects of study had been. When she informed him she had always been fascinated with the Colonies and of her lifelong desire to go there, a strange expression swept across his face and his response was one that still puzzled her. "Your destiny, Brenna, has always been in America, and although it's much later than intended, you're finally going home." When Brenna pressed him for further explanation, he casually shrugged, saying, "One day soon it will all be clear to you."

Oh, Captain, she thought, staring across at the empty place before her now, *nothing is clear. You said my destiny is in America. But what will that destiny be? Who are you? Are you the sensitive, funny, and caring man you portray? If not, could this all possibly be a façade? If so, why? To what end? Has convincing me of your sincerity really become some twisted desire of conquest? Are you simply playing out this charade to its fullest? And, if so, what will be the finale?*

Is it really possible you are still trying to see that justice is done? If so, is death on the American frontier to be my justice? Or is prison still where you intend to see me live the remaining days of my life? And then, Captain Grant, would the price of my life be enough? Would your revenge then be complete?

When she thought it through, her doubts sounded preposterous. *Could his resentment be so profound that he would go to all this effort just for revenge? Was that truly possible? If not, why did he pursue me for months? Why did he spend such tremendous time and coin in the search…and then when at last he found me, took the vows of marriage to someone he knew nothing about? He's a man who could have nearly any woman of his choosing! And yet he chose a stranger and a convicted murderer at that? It makes no sense!*

Brenna pressed her hands against her pounding temples. *Oh, Captain, is it possible you have no resentment toward me and this marriage actually means something to you? Were it true!*

Brenna slapped her napkin on the table in disgust. *No, Brenna! Have you forgotten what happened before—the last time you trusted him?* She hated to remember, for it forced her to see what she so desperately wanted to forget. Yet she knew she must never be so careless as to cast aside what happened after she was rescued from the hold. She was given his quarters and his clothes, slept in this very same berth, and tenderly nursed back to health. Even then, she wanted to believe Iestyn's kind words about the captain; yet none of it turned out to be true. None of it! It had all been a lie. While he played the invisible, yet ultimate caring host, he plotted to see that when she landed in Bristol 'justice would be done.' *He didn't care about me then, nor does he now!*

Brenna rose to add a log to the smoldering fire and brushed aside her angry tears when she heard a light knock on her door. She hoped the captain had completed his tasks early and decided to join her. Brenna pinched her cheeks to bring color to them and ran her hands over her skirt in an effort to settle the wrinkles. "Come in, it's not latched." Iestyn entered, carrying a steaming kettle. Brenna said slightly downcast, "Oh Iestyn, it's you."

"Ah, lassie," he jested, "that wouldn't be a touch of disappointment I hear? An' here I brought ye my special tea."

"I'm sorry," she replied sincerely. "It's just that I thought you were the captain."

With eyes twinkling, Iestyn beamed, "Ah, so he's gotten t' ye after all. Well, glad I am t' know it! I was beginnin' t' worry." He winked at her, poured her a cup, and then placed the kettle in the suspended ceiling tray over the table. "He does grow on a person after a while."

Indeed, thought Brenna wistfully. "Iestyn?" she asked, growing serious. "There's something I've been wondering about."

"What's that mum?"

"Well, you've been with the captain for some time now."

"Aye indeed," he said proudly, "I've been his manservant for more than a decade."

"The captain seems reluctant to speak of some aspects of his past. And I know so little about him. If it isn't betraying anything too personal, I was wondering if you could tell me a little more of his history?"

"His history?"

"Yes, about how he was awarded command of this ship."

"Oh that! "Well now, 'tis one area where I can tell ye just 'bout anythin' ye be wantin' t' know, for I was there through it all."

"He must have been quite young to become a sea captain. It was my understanding for most men it takes years of working one's way through the ranks, and even then, few attain the title of captain."

"Aye mum, yer right. An' Captain Grant was the youngest I'd ever seen. Yet, from the moment he took command, a more competent leader I've yet t' see. He has what other captains often seem t' lack…good sense. He also has an uncanny ability t' read a situation, whether it be guidin' a ship through the most violent o' storms or knowin' a gifted crewman when he sees one. From the very beginnin', the captain was a born leader with a sharp business eye as well. He knows exactly what t' buy and how 'twill sell overseas. In fact, a more skilled sailor, captain, and owner ye will rarely see."

So, he does own The Grace. Brenna surmised after the long delay in Bristol that he must be at least partial owner, for certainly no owner would have allowed it—stowaway or not.

"Aye, and not 'jes this here packet…but a small fleet o' 'um."

"You mean he owns more than this one vessel?" Brenna was incredulous.

"Yea, this one an' four others like her." Iestyn was clearly enjoying her enlightenment.

She had never heard of a captain owning his own vessel, let alone several of them.

Amused by her look of disbelief, Iestyn added, "Aye, I saw the entire event unfold many years ago."

"When I asked the captain about his becoming a captain, he told me it was merely being in the right place at the right time."

"Is that what he said? Hardly!"

"I had a feeling there must've been more to the story," said Brenna, motioning for Iestyn to sit at the table with her.

"Ah, an' a fascinatin' story 'tis! Well, let's see, it all started 'bout thirteen years ago, I guess. I was servin' under a Captain Waugh on a tradin' voyage toward the southeastern coast of China. Aboard the Colonial ship was a crew of 'bout sixty, includin' seven apprentices, among them, eighteen-year-old Nathan Grant. Little did we realize what an impact this young, Princeton-educated man would have on us all."

"The voyage started routinely enough, but when we were 'bout five weeks out, another American vessel hailed us an' their captain came aboard. He said that Thomas Gage's men, under the orders of George III, had clashed with a small band o' Colonists in Lexington, Massachusetts, and that we were at war. We were all stunned at the news. We knew tensions were runnin' high, but we hadn't believed t'would come t' war so soon. This captain told us the Patriots were commissionin' privateers t' attack enemy merchant vessels, fer t'was thought t' be our only hope in defeatin' the mighty British fleet. Captain Waugh was warned we'd best stay on our guard against the British, fer the Patriots had taken one British vessel an' in retaliation, the Redcoats were out fer blood.

"Well, unbeknownst t' the rest of us, a handful of our crew was sympathetic t' the British, an' a week after learnin' we was at war, the Tories aboard waited 'til t'was dark an' tried t' take the ship, wantin' t' sail t' England an' commission her t' the British. The mutiny was unsuccessful, but a bloody battle t'was, lasting over four hours. When the smoke cleared, nine men were dead, four Tories and five Patriots. An' t' complicate matters, the ship had run aground on a small, abandoned island's sandy reef. An' let me tell ye, all heck broke loose when we bottomed out. Tories ended up on the badly damaged ship with all the stores and most of the guns, but not enough hands t' push her off the sand, an' even if they got off, not enough of 'em were still alive t' crew the vessel. Captain Waugh, with the rest of us, ended up on the island with no food or fresh water, an' 'twas none t' be found on that forsaken island neither.

"Not wantin' t' wait 'til we were all dyin' of starvation, Captain Waugh ordered a raid, but with no shelter, guns, or ammunition, we knew t'would be a slaughter. Nonetheless, fer a day and a half, under Captain Waugh, we plotted a strategy fer our assault. Whilst all the rest o' us were arguin' 'bout how t' attack, this young apprentice stepped forward suggestin' we reason with the Tories. After all, he argued, we 'ad all been ship mates. But as ye know, war can secure man's loyalties right quick. An' the men nearly busted their guts at the notion that a man could jes' approach the enemy an' talk without his head bein' shot off. Yet 'fore we knew what happened, that's jes what that apprentice did! He walked straight toward them Tories, their guns pointed dead-center at his heart.

"I thought fer sure t'would be the last time I'd see that young man. I remember thinkin' what a shame t'was too, fer he was a sight walkin' with shoulders pulled back an' staring into the eyes of death. I knew then t'was somethin' extraordinary 'bout the man. Ye can imagine our surprise when he climbed aboard but even more so when he emerged twenty minutes later in one piece. He convinced the Tories that although they had supplies enough t' last them several months, if another ship happened by, they'd best say their prayers they were British. Bein' we were in water so near the Colonies, t'weren't likely. He told 'em they could bet his would be the only offer of help they'd get from an American-sidin' crew.

"The young apprentice persuaded both sides they had no choice but t' help one another. The Tories would be put ashore at the nearest port an' the Colonists would keep the ship, in exchange for not turnin' in the Tories as traitors.

"Once back aboard, the Tories refused t' serve under Captain Waugh, an' the Colonists refused t' take orders from the Tories. After a vote by both sides, the apprentice, Nathan Grant, was appointed interim captain. An' let me tell ye, t'was not an easy crew to manage, for the two sides hated an' distrusted each other. But, all hands were needed t' get the vessel t' water an' then sail her. The young captain brought the crew together in bringin' in the crippled vessel. To this day, I don't know how he managed it. The owner of the ship was so impressed, he gave the lad command of another one of his ships. T'was then I signed on with him.

"Four years later, Captain Grant purchased his first ship, one that t'was so badly in need o' repair nobody thought she could be salvaged, nobody 'cept Captain Grant. He had that vessel overhauled an' when she was finished, she was one o' the fastest, sleekest ships I'd ever seen."

With door ajar, he stood in the shadows of the moonlight and stared at the sight of his sleeping bride. The vision took his breath away. He had hoped he might return before she retired for the evening. He was surprised to find the cabin in darkness but, seeing her now, he was not disappointed. Even in her sleep, she was captivating. He longed to slip beneath the sheets and hold her tenderly, to cover her now slightly-open mouth with his. The last few weeks had been torturous, for he wanted her more than he had ever desired anything in his life, yet he kept himself at bay. She had made it clear she wanted nothing to do with him in that regard.

How can I blame her after our wedding night? I never intended for it to go that way and yet, I felt powerless to stop it. Cursing himself at his foolish excuses, Nathan found it hard to even believe his own thoughts. *Powerless to stop? Idiot! That may be the weak argument waged by a young lad coming of age. But me? Hardly!* Still, Nathan could find no justification for his lack of control. *All I wanted, Brenna, was to earn your trust and to prove I'd wait for you as long as you desired. Instead, I alienated you and drove the wedge deeper between us.* Thinking he should leave before he once again cast aside his better judgment, Nathan turned to leave, but paused. Brenna stirred.

"Honey," she murmured. "I didn't want…I didn't want to leave you."

Nathan felt as though he had fallen off his horse and the wind knocked from him. It had never occurred to him she might be in love with another man. He walked to her and sat on the edge of the berth. He stared down at her helplessly.

Brenna's eyes opened quickly, softening when she saw who it was. "Captain," she smiled as she wiped the sleep from her eye. She liked the scent of the salt spray he brought with him.

Using the tinderbox to light the lamp next to the bed, he asked gently, "Sleeping well?"

Brenna squinted while her vision adjusted to the light and said softly, "Hum yes, thank you." When she could see clearly, she saw his pale face. "You look fatigued. Are you all right?"

"Brenna," he asked solemnly, coupling her warm hand in his and ignoring her question, "who was it you were dreaming of just now?"

"What?"

"Just now, who were you dreaming of?"

Brenna smiled and said without hesitation, "My dog."

"Your dog? But you called him 'Honey'."

"Yes…her name."

Nathan laughed, relieved. "And I thought for a moment you were pining away for another."

"And if I had been?" asked Brenna. She yearned for the truth of how he felt.

"I don't know," he answered. "I suppose I would have given you the opportunity to choose."

In the soft light, she was unable to detect any trace of deception.

Nathan sensed her skepticism. His eyes darkened, "I will not have you spend your life with me while loving another. With you, Brenna, I will play second to no man."

Puzzled by his sudden display of possessiveness, Brenna could find no explanation. "And what of me?" she asked, unable to suppress the question that had been nagging at her for some time. "Am I to go through life knowing your heart is with another?"

"Another? Who?"

"Launey."

"Launey?" said Nathan surprised. The tightening about the corners of her mouth was not lost on him. "Where she is concerned, or anyone else for that matter, I assure you, madam, you need not worry, for you have captivated my heart completely."

Brenna wanted desperately to believe him. "And what will the title of 'husband' have on your sea-roving heart?"

A look of puzzlement showed in his eyes, "I apologize, your question is lost upon me."

She tried to hide her unwelcome jealously. Rising to her elbows, she said testily, "As I attempted to board your ship on St. Christopher, one of your…guests…made it clear that a certain captain had kept her company every evening while in port."

Nathan grinned like a dolphin and laughed, "Brenna, please! Your lack of regard for my discretion wounds me deeply!" When he realized Brenna did not share in his merriment, he added, "My men told me of the incident at the St. Christopher quay. Unfortunately, it wasn't the first time I'd been the target of that particular woman's pursuit."

Nathan chuckled. He recalled sitting in the port tavern earlier that same day, eating a mincemeat pie, when the woman approached and offered him a quick romp. He remembered she splashed the contents of her mug at him when he politely rebuffed her offer. His quick head-dodge was all that prevented the flying ale from hitting him squarely in his face.

Nathan looked at Brenna a little more seriously. "I assure you that although I've not lived the life of a monk, I'm not nearly so indiscriminate as you seem inclined to believe! Oh, and speaking of the quay, you never did tell me how you managed to get aboard this vessel."

"Let's just say your guest was of great assistance."

"What? Surely you jest!" Then, realizing she was serious, he slapped his knee. "And to think, I was actually aggravated by her advances! I need to remember to thank her one day!"

"Iestyn told me tonight the story of how you became a sea captain."

"Did he?"

"He said you saved the lives of an entire crew at the risk of your own."

"Iestyn does tell a dramatic tale, especially where my past is concerned."

"Is it not accurate?"

Nathan was puzzled that such details about his life seemed important to her. He smiled, thinking this was a good sign. "I did nothing that any other person in my position would not have done."

"Not according to Iestyn. He said all of the other men had the opportunity, but it was you who took the risk. He said if you hadn't been there, he is certain they all would have died. He says you're the only one he knows who is considered a hero by both the Colonists and the British."

"And Iestyn has much too loose a tongue." He suppressed a smile. "That is, when it comes to you. There was a time when he was a most trustworthy manservant, but I'm beginning to have my doubts."

Brenna sat up quickly. "You must be joking! Why I've never seen a more loyal man!"

"It seems you have won the hearts of my crew as well. Remarkable really, for it's been my experience that most crews are quite leery of having a woman on board. It seems you have changed their minds. As it is, my men are continually urging me to leave my post and tend to you, and every day the cook is drumming up his finest dishes for your palate. Tell me, my dear, how is it you've managed to complete this coup when you so seldom leave this cabin?" Nathan looked at her bright smile and pushed her gently back against the pillow. "I can see all this pleases you greatly. Need I, in fact, begin worrying that your next plan will be to convince my men to mutiny and put you at the helm?"

"Well," said Brenna excitedly, "if you'd give me access to your sextant and charts, perhaps..."

"Henceforth," he interjected lightly, "I shall take note to keep them under lock and key."

Folding her arms, a playful defiance danced across her face. "And do you believe a mere lock and bolt would deter me?"

Nathan locked his eyes with hers and said without humor, "Knowing your ability to maneuver out of seemingly impossible situations, I would never underestimate you Brenna...never...to make whatever you want yours."

Except where you're concerned.

Interpreting her silence for fatigue, Nathan said reluctantly, "I can see you're tired, so I'll let you go back to sleep." He grinned playfully, adding, "Since I am already here, and the hour late, why don't we just..."

"Goodnight, Captain."

Sighing, Nathan pressed his lips gently upon her forehead. "Goodnight. And I do wish you'd call me Nathan." When she did not respond, he rose to leave, "Oh, and Brenna, competing with a canine for a woman's affection has, until now, eluded me, so I would gladly accept any advice on how I might get in the race."

"It's trust, Captain, nothing more," answered Brenna seriously, pointedly ignoring his request to call him by his given name. She refused to do so as long as she was unable to determine if he was anything more than a captain, one who pledged vengeance against her. The warmth of his kiss lingered on her forehead, conjuring memories of their one night together. She had long since given up trying to forget it happened, for that was one battle she was unable to win.

Brenna pulled the covers tightly around her. She was grateful she was not spending the night in the cold hold but was beginning to regret banishing him from her bed. *At least he would have kept me warm.* She knew full well he would do much more than that and her fleeting willpower would have been no match for his.

Oh, Captain Grant, if only your feelings were sincere! She thought of the gentle look in his eye when she first awoke tonight. *Is it really possible you are the vengeful man my mind has created? When you said you were going to see that 'justice was done,' could there have been another meaning behind your words? Could this all have been a misunderstanding?*

Brenna sat up quickly. She had to speak to him and find out. *Once and for all, I must know the truth!* She could not wait until morning. She tossed her warm bedcovers aside and hurriedly got dressed.

When Nathan entered his quarters, he found Iestyn stoking the fire. "Ah, 'tis ye sir," said Iestyn, the disappointment was heavy in his voice. "'Twas me wish not t' be seein' ye this evenin'. Was hoping," he added coyly, "that ye and the misses might be actually awakenin' in the same berth on the morrow."

"It was my wish as well, Iestyn." Nathan looked uneasily about the room. He did not want to be here. He turned to his first mate and friend. "Iestyn. I've come to a decision. Brenna spoke to me this evening of the importance of trust. And she's right. If we are ever going to have it between us, she needs to know she has the freedom to be with me or not. I hoped by now she would have understood the sincerity of my heart. But she still does not trust me…and as long as that is so, there can be no true love."

Nathan thought of their first night aboard. "And while some of my behavior is to blame, there is more to it, a lot more." Nathan turned to face the dark sky through his small window. "The only reason she agreed to our vows was out of fear and duress. She believed she was protecting the judge and his family." Nathan hated his next words, but knew them necessary if he were ever to have a future with the woman he loved. "Iestyn, I must offer her a choice. A true choice…and I pray to God she chooses me."

At that moment, Brenna walked up to the captain's door and raised her hand to knock. She halted when she heard the captain's next words.

"As soon as we lay anchor, I want to have annulment papers ready and drawn. I will present them to Brenna before we deboard."

"But, sir, I think yer makin' a big mistake."

"My resolve is firm. This must end, and it must end soon."

Brenna heard no more. She ran back to her quarters and felt as though the dorsal fin of a shark had been driven through her heart. She never heard the captain's next words.

"Our vows…taken by charade on her part…need either be reaffirmed…and not under duress…but rather freely and with love…or they must be disavowed."

"But sir, 'tis obvious the lass loves you."

"Loves me? Hardly! If only that were true! And even if it were, I am convinced Brenna is not aware of it. Truly, I don't think she knows what her feelings are for me. How could she, if she feels she was coerced into marrying me? No, for her sake…and for mine…we both need to know she is free in her choice of me."

Nathan ran his finger down the inside of the cold window. "Once she knows I am serious in honoring her freedom from her vows, then I pray beyond words that she will tear up the annulment documents."

"And if she does not?"

"It will kill me, but I will sign them."

"And then?"

"Then I will do everything in my power to win her heart…and her hand. I shall never stop loving her."

Iestyn could not stop a huge smile from consuming his wrinkled face.

Chapter Thirteen

The sun rose slowly on the horizon. The ocean's swells reflected brilliant orange and yellow hues. Two porpoises, oblivious to the cold, took turns playfully diving and springing upward, proudly leading the vessel. Any observer would find this to be the start of a glorious day, but Brenna, who looked at the scene from the quarterdeck, found no solace in the beauty before her. Her mind was dark; her body ached with the knowledge of last night. She had feared his abandonment from the start, but having heard his words left her with a cold, empty despair. She could no longer deny an even greater terrifying truth. She was with child. For some time, she sensed it was possible, and Brenna now found no joy in having to admit the truth. *A baby. What kind of a mother will I be, when I cannot even care for myself? A baby conceived of malice and deception.* Brenna closed her eyes, the pain of it more than she could bear.

A different image pushed through her consciousness. She felt the captain's sheltering arms as he lifted her from the bath. She remembered his eyes gazing softly into hers and his hands touching her gently. *No, this child may have been conceived in deception, but not malice. Surely it wasn't that, for not even he could have masked such feelings.*

What's to become of us, this baby and me, once this marriage is annulled? What then? Brenna saw herself standing for the first time on the American shore. *Where will I go?* A more horrifying picture came to mind. *It can't be prison he wants for me!* She bowed her head and begged. *Please God, not prison! Please don't let this child be separated from me! Don't let this child ever know the abandonment I have known! Not that! Anything but that! God, give this child a chance—a chance to be loved!*

From his post on the upper deck, Nathan was surprised to see the slender form of his wife below him on this chilly early morning. He started to call out to her and then paused. He could sense she was crying. It reminded him of the first time he had seen her on St. Christopher. *What is it, Brenna? Is it something I've done?*

He squinted thoughtfully and realized again how strong his feelings for her had grown. *Every day is exceptional knowing I will be spending it with you. When we are apart, my hours are empty.* He decided to go to her but stopped when he saw her leave the rail and slowly move away.

Twenty minutes later, Nathan cheerfully tapped on her door and entered carrying a tray of warm tea and biscuits. Brenna stood at the portal window. Nathan frowned. "What is it, Brenna? Are you ill?"

Brenna turned and marveled at his skill in deception. On his face, she could see only compassion. She considered telling him the truth and wondered what he would do when he learned she was with child. She had considered every glum possibility.

Not willing to risk any threat to her child, she had no plausible answer. "No," she responded flatly. "I am not ill."

Nathan studied her pale and drawn face for any indication of what troubled her. Unable to discern an answer, he set the tray on the table and decided not to press her. The cold draft of the compartment struck him. He nodded to the dark stove. "It's freezing in here. Why has this fire been permitted to die? It's no wonder you're not well!" In voicing his frustration at his inability to console her, he spoke more harshly than he intended.

Instead of seeing the usual spark in her beautiful eyes, Nathan saw only emptiness. He was puzzled by the profound change in her behavior from last night and moved closer. Nathan took her hands and again asked, "What is it, Brenna?"

She pulled her hands away and did not respond.

"How can I help, if I don't know what's wrong?" He waited, but again, no reply. "Is there any way I can be of help?"

"No," she said and turned her back to him. "You've already done enough. Please leave."

As winter ebbed into spring, the ship continued its steady trek toward the Colonies. Time passed slowly for Brenna. Her body nurtured the life growing within while her mind continued to search for a solution for her child's future. Unlike the bright, brisk days outside, Brenna was encased in darkness, nearly incapacitated with worry.

Nathan did his best to lighten her mood, but she made it clear she wanted nothing to do with him. Their evening dinners together ceased as did nearly all conversation. When Nathan tried to reach her, she closed him out. Frustrated by his inability to help, Nathan repeatedly left the room before he lost his temper. On one such morning, Nathan was unable to contain his ire. He took her by the shoulders and said, "Brenna! How can I help if you won't talk to me?"

"The only way you can help is to leave me alone!" Brenna hated her words. What she wanted was for him to pull her into his strong arms and assure her that everything would be all right. She wanted his words of annulment to have been nothing but a bad dream. She wanted him to love her and to love their child.

Nathan dropped his hands in helpless defeat. More frustrated than he had ever been in his life, he left her alone. Iestyn met him in the corridor.

"Captain, may I have a word with ye?"

"Certainly!" The two entered the captain's temporary quarters.

"I'm mighty worried 'bout Miss Brenna," said Iestyn without hesitation.

"That makes two of us."

"I know we've talked 'bout it before, but seein' how bad off she is, don't ye think it's time ye told her the truth about her parents?"

"I've thought of little else. I've asked myself a thousand times if I'm making a mistake in not telling her. She has more distrust of me now than ever, although she will not tell me why. And you? Has she given you any reason for the abrupt change in her behavior?"

"No sir. She's quite distant. I don't understand why…an' I've tried everything I can think of t' bring back her shinin' smile, but tis all been fer naught. I jes' don't understand it…things seemed t' be going so well between the two of ye and fer so long."

"I know. It doesn't make sense."

"Knowin' about her folks may help."

"I'm sure it would, if she would believe me. But my instincts tell me she wouldn't even if I tried. She knows I'm aware she was terribly hurt by something she thinks her birth parents did. And my hunch is that Brenna would convince herself I was just telling her of her parents now for my own advantage."

'Sir, I know ye t' be quite persuasive when ye set yer mind t' it. I think ye could convince her."

"I'm not so sure…it's Brenna we're talking about! Have you forgotten how stubborn she is?" He did not wait for Iestyn's reply. "Regardless, I made an inner pledge to Weston and Emily that she hear the truth from them…and as hard as this is…I need to honor that pledge." Nathan moved to the stove, poured two cups of coffee, and handed one to Iestyn. "I'm just grateful we've made such excellent time. If I'm correct, we ought to be docked within the week. The truth will be made known very soon."

Later that night, Iestyn turned down Brenna's bedcovers and confronted her directly, "The captain an' I are mighty worried 'bout ye, mum."

Brenna bit her lip and struggled to fight back tears. She felt she might die if she did not talk to someone soon, yet she knew Iestyn was deeply committed to the captain and would argue that even with the annulment, the captain would honorably take care of his child. Iestyn had mistakenly believed no harm would come to her when they arrived in Bristol. He had been wrong then about the captain and there was no telling what the captain might do if he learned of the child now. If Iestyn told him now and was wrong, it might not only cost her life but that of her child. It was a gamble she was unwilling to make.

"I appreciate your concern, but there is nothing you can do." She continued to stare out the porthole.

"Ah, lassie, I jes' hate t' see ye this way. I know I'm one with a big tongue, but I've also got might' big ears, so if'n ye want to talk 'bout whatever 'tis that's got t' ye, I'm listenin'."

Brenna faced him directly. "Thank you, Iestyn, but even you cannot help me with this."

Iestyn said with exasperation, "If it's the blasted sailin' that's gotten to ye, mum, the captain informed me today we should be seein' shore within three days hence."

Brenna felt a sudden knot tighten in her stomach. Her masquerade with the captain was drawing to a close. She bit her lower lip and tried to keep her tears at bay. "Three days, are you certain?"

"That's what he said." Iestyn was pleased by her interest in something. "An' the captain's rarely in error."

"Oh, I see," she said glumly.

"I know ye are not wantin' t' talk t' anyone here…but I left ye something on yer bed. It's the captain's, but I've had it fer the last year or so…been tryin' to read it clean through. I think ye could use it now more than me." Hesitant to leave, he moved to the door, opened then closed it behind him.

Brenna picked up the book from the bed. The Bible. Tears filled her eyes as she held it against her chest, remembering the light from the hold. She felt nearly as lost now as she had then. She still did not understand that light, but she knew it had been a light of God. *Please God, you gave me hope then. I have no right to ask, but please, give me reason to hope once again.*

Brenna opened the front cover and saw a neatly written inscription:

Dearest Nathan,

We've cherished watching you grow from a small boy into a remarkable young man.

May the Lord bless you and keep you. And as you journey across the seven seas, may you never lose your way.

Lovingly yours,
Emily and Weston Emerson,
Luke 19:10

Brenna looked hard at the inscription, then at her bracelet, and then again to the Bible verse. *How odd, that of all the verses…* Her thoughts trailed absently, an odd sensation filling her. She realized it was the same feeling she had when she woke from a dream, knowing it was important she remember what it was she had just experienced, yet unable to do so. *How strange, to experience it now while I am yet awake.*

Frustrated that she could not recall what it was she wanted to remember, Brenna held the book tightly, reluctant to part with it. She found comfort in it. She wondered how Weston and Emily Emerson… whoever they might be…could have been as fooled by him as she.

The following afternoon, Brenna was roused from a fitful nap and heard the sound of a gull. Moving to the porthole, she wiped away the moisture that had formed on the glass, unable to see anything. A thick fog had settled about the ship. She heard the squawk of the bird again and knew time was running out. Iestyn appeared and cheerfully confirmed that two hours earlier the captain announced they were near landfall and would continue to sail the coast. Iestyn said they estimated they were two days north of their destined Carolina harbor.

For longer than she could remember, Brenna had yearned to see this land. Despite her dark mood, she was deeply saddened that her first view of America was obscured by a blanket of fog. Several times she ventured on deck to see if the vision might be any better there, but to her disappointment, she was only able to glimpse an occasional shadow of what appeared to be a distant forest. She was amazed the captain and his crew were able to guide the ship with such limited visibility. Yet, two mornings later, while she put a kettle on the stove for tea, Iestyn appeared and gleefully reported they were preparing to drop anchor in forty fathoms of water. They had reached *The Grace's* home port of Charleston.

Overcome with worry, Brenna paced the corridor between her quarters and that of the captain's. She could no longer delay in pleading a case for her unborn child. Neither the captain nor Iestyn appeared to have noticed the change in her appearance, though to her it was fairly obvious. She wondered what would have been the captain's reaction had he discovered the truth on his own. *What will you do to me when I tell you? Will your contempt for me finally be clear?* She said a quick prayer, took a deep breath, and moved to his door.

"It's open, Iestyn," said Nathan. He was completing the last of his calculations for the estimated sale of his cargo when he heard the light knock, "however, I'm not yet hungr…" He halted, realizing his error.

"I have a matter of the utmost importance to discuss with you, Captain," she said coldly.

"Certainly." He stood quickly, amazed she had sought him out. He offered her the chair across from his desk. His brow furrowed at the sight of her trembling hand. "And is this the matter, Brenna," his green eyes looked boldly into hers, "which has been the cause of your great unhappiness these past several weeks?"

"Yes," responded Brenna solemnly.

"I must tell you I've been…"

"Excuse me, Captain," interrupted Iestyn as he opened the captain's door. Surprised to see Brenna, he added sheepishly, "Beggin' both yer pardons, but Captain Neal has come abridge in a longboat."

Nathan sighed heavily. "Tell Thomas I'll be with him shortly. Brenna and I have something to discuss."

"Aye," said Iestyn obediently.

"It's all right, Captain. The matter can wait until after your meeting."

He sensed her hesitation at having anything preoccupy their discussion. Nathan reluctantly turned to Iestyn in the corridor, "Very well, show the captain in."

"If you'll excuse me then," said Brenna. She started to rise.

"Actually, I'd like you to join us." Nathan walked toward the door. "I'm certain Captain Neal will be most pleased to meet you."

"Taken up new quarters, has he?" inquired a tall, lean man of Iestyn as he followed the manservant into Nathan's temporary chambers. "And why is that?"

"None of your bloody business," smiled Nathan while he sheltered Brenna behind him. It was obvious from his tone Nathan considered the man a close friend.

With a lopsided grin, the curly, dark-haired man spoke mischievously, "Some wench you brought aboard undoubtedly has had her fill of ye…huh…I beg your pardon, ma'am, I…I didn't see you there," he stammered, blushing profusely.

"Obviously not," mused Nathan, "and I can see your manners haven't improved overly much since my departure."

Brenna smiled for the first time in weeks at how close Captain Neal's jest had been to the truth. The expression was not lost on Nathan who was heartened to know she at least had not lost her sense of humor.

With a hint of smile still apparent, Brenna bowed her head slightly, "No offense taken, sir."

Impressed by her gracious reaction, the other captain's embarrassment ebbed, "And by whom am I so quickly forgiven?"

"Captain Thomas Neal," said Nathan quickly, "may I present Brenna Grant…my wife."

The stranger was unable to mask his dismay, "Your wife!"

"Indeed," smiled Nathan. He placed his arm around Brenna's waist.

Thomas Neal looked closely at Nathan and then Brenna. His eyes were as wide as his grin. "I never thought I'd live to see the day this bachelor married!" He chuckled and shook his head. "Your wife! That would explain *The Grace's* delay. Married! I can't get over it! And to think, we were all concerned for your safety! I'm just glad you were able to return before I depart."

"Are you still on schedule?" asked Nathan.

"Aye. *The Southland's* hull is fully loaded, and we were prepared to set sail three days hence, even without your order."

"Ah, good," said Nathan. He poured the captain a brandy. "And is port London still your destination?"

"Aye, just as planned, with a stop on Antigua, of course."

Nathan turned to Brenna. "*The Southland* is Captain Neal's vessel."

"Owned by none other than your husband, of course," added the captain. With the corners of his mouth turning upward, he winked at Nathan, "And I may be detained as well if stopping in England will bring me such good fortune."

"Sorry, Thomas, but Brenna hails from St. Christopher."

"Really?" he said surprised. "Then perhaps when we dock there I ought to have a closer look. I had no idea…"

"St. Christopher?" asked Nathan. "I thought Antigua was your only West Indies port of call this voyage."

The captain looked uneasily at his hands, then back to Nathan. "I wanted to speak to you about that, but it can wait for a more appropriate time."

Nathan looked at Brenna, then back to Thomas. "It's all right, we've got a moment. So what takes you to St. Christopher?"

"Of course, you know Emily Emerson."

Nathan froze. He wished he'd taken Thomas up on the offer to discuss this later. He forced his voice to remain steady and replied nonchalantly, "Yes, certainly. She's my mother's closest friend. I hadn't realized the two of you were acquainted."

"Well, we aren't. But her husband, Weston Emerson, recently paid me a visit and requested that he and his wife be permitted to sail with us. He offered a handsome fee if I would dock on St. Christopher."

"Really?" asked Nathan cautiously.

"Aye, and although I don't know the details, they apparently are on some sort of quest."

"Really?" said Nathan again, looking at Brenna who appeared genuinely interested. "And you've agreed to take them on?"

"I'm not exactly keen on the idea and neither, I gather, is Weston, but he made it clear Mrs. Emerson is determined. He said while many have tried to talk her out of it, she will not be deterred. I heard that for the last couple months she has tried to hire aboard every outgoing ship, but her husband would not hear of it unless it was aboard one of your vessels. Evidently, they had a bad experience on a previous journey and yours are the only ships he trusts."

"Ah, this is rather…unexpected," said Nathan slowly.

Brenna wondered about the odd expression on Captain Grant's face.

Captain Neal continued, "That's only the half, they…the Emersons that is, have left open the possibility they will stay indefinitely on St. Christopher until they find whatever it is they are searching for. We might have to retrieve them on some future voyage."

"I see. Well, if she's that determined, I don't see why we can't accommodate her. When exactly do you intend to leave?"

"Captain Neal," interrupted Brenna. "Do you have any idea what they are searching for? You see, I've lived there my entire life, and I may be able to help."

"No idea, ma'am. But I suspect with such determination, they must be searching for someone they love very much."

"And somehow lost," murmured Brenna, a distant look filtered through her eyes. She realized both men were staring at her. She turned and said softly, "Perhaps, I might have the opportunity to meet them before they leave. For truly, I might know the one for whom they are searching."

Nathan lost the battle to contain a large grin. "I think perhaps you very well might." He pulled out a stack of charts from under his desk. "We'll see if we can arrange a meeting with you and the Emersons before they depart. But, before then, I need to go over some charts and ledgers with Thomas."

Brenna could see that the captain wanted some time alone with his friend. She smiled at the newly acquainted captain and said honestly, "It was a pleasure meeting you, Captain Neal. I wish you Godspeed on your journey."

Thomas Neal beamed and pressed his lips to her hand. "The pleasure has been entirely mine. And, if by the time I return, you've grown tired of this rake, I'm certain we can make some sort of arrangements for another of his long voyages abroad."

Both Brenna and Captain Neal laughed heartily at his jest.

Nathan found it hard to understand the ease at which Thomas was engaged with his wife when she had so recently been closed to him. "I'll be with you shortly, Brenna, and we can complete our discussion, which has been…" he eyed Captain Neal playfully, "so rudely interrupted."

Back in her chambers, Brenna paced uneasily. It crossed her mind to try and escape once off the ship. She had learned the folly of that action before, however, and it would be nearly impossible here on his home land. *Nor would I subject my child to a life of flight. Nay,* she thought on the verge of tears, *I'm done running! I will face whatever consequences come my way! With every ounce of strength I possess, I will fight for this child!* She gently rubbed her hand over her expanded waist and thought of Iestyn's many proclamations about the captain. She prayed this time he was right. If so, perhaps he would be man enough to see his child well-tended. She did not know what else to do but tell the captain the truth.

More than an hour later, Brenna held her breath when Nathan turned the latch and entered her chambers. He carried a large box and put it down on the sea-chest. He said seriously, "I told you once I would see to it that 'justice is done,' and today I intend to fulfill that promise."

He saw her stricken expression. "I beg your pardon, Brenna, I was merely…"

"You were merely stating the truth," said Brenna. She shook uncontrollably, unable to contain a torrent of tears.

Dismayed by her reaction, Nathan moved to her and wrapped his arms around her. He pulled her close. "Brenna," he said tenderly, "why are you so troubled?"

She freed herself from his embrace and cried, "Do you really need to ask? In Bristol, you were escorting me to prison, and now you're just completing the task!"

"Brenna," he said and wiped away the tears from her cheek, "you are my wife. I have no intention of…"

Brenna did not hear his words. All the pain and fear she had so long contained poured forth. "I know I deserve punishment for my crimes, whether the punishment be desertion by you on this American soil or imprisonment, but this child," she sobbed, touching her hand to her abdomen, "your child does not!"

Uncertain he had heard her correctly, he whispered, "Child? You're carrying a child?"

Unable to look at him, Brenna nodded.

Nathan sank into his berth. A slow smile spread across his face. "A baby? Are you certain?"

Unable to speak, Brenna simply nodded.

Brenna had not known what his reaction might be, but she never expected this expression of pure joy. He lifted her trembling hands and gently pulled her to him. "So this is what has been upsetting you?"

Brenna felt suspended in time. She could see nothing but warmth in his emerald eyes. She realized his warmth had been there all along. It was her fear and anger that prevented her from seeing it. Before her, she saw not the evil and cunning villain of her nightmares, but instead, the kind and compassionate man she had dreamed all her life she would find.

"Desert you?" he whispered, comprehending her earlier words. "Brenna, do you not know? I love you!"

Her tears of pain became tears of relief and joy and spilled down her cheeks. She could scarcely believe what she heard. "You love me?"

"Yes," he answered hoarsely. "I think I've loved you since the first time I saw you digging through the mud for that shoe!"

"But you told Launey you were searching for me out of obligation!"

Nathan studied her closely and realized how much she needed to understand the truth. "That was merely to appease her and…partially…to justify to myself my feelings for you."

"Then you're not in love with her?"

"Brenna," he said and cupped her chin gently in his hand, "only once have I been in love and it was to that woman…the only woman…of whom I have asked for a hand in marriage."

She looked into his warm eyes. She knew he spoke the truth, and yet, she needed to understand more fully. "And at the port in Bristol when you were taking me off the ship?"

"I planned to escort you to the home of some close friends for your employment."

"You were securing me a position?" Brenna sank down in her chair. "It didn't matter that I had been a stowaway aboard your ship?"

"Hardly!" laughed Nathan aloud.

"But you said you were going to see that 'justice is done!'"

"And so I was." Nathan stroked her cheek. "It was obvious life had been less than fair to you. I was trying to find some way to ease your plight."

Brenna could barely comprehend what she was hearing. "And the annulment? I heard you!"

"Heard me? Oh Brenna, no! How?"

"I came to your door and heard you tell Iestyn."

Nathan looked shaken. "I only desired to procure the papers so you would know I would never bind you to a marriage for which you did not want to be held."

"Oh, Nathan," sobbed Brenna and fell against his chest. "What terrible misunderstandings we've had!"

"I don't think we could have had the truth more muddled if we tried." He pulled away to study her face, then asked seriously, "I've told you my feelings for you, but I still don't how you feel about me."

Brenna was unable to stop smiling. "I've thought of little else but you since our first meeting. You've consumed my dreams and my waking hours, yet I was so fearful of you. I couldn't make sense of any of my feelings. It wasn't until just before I was arrested, when I awoke in a broken-down barn, that I realized how much I really cared about you. Yet even then, I was convinced you were trying to trick me."

"I knew you were distrustful of me, an offense for which I'm ashamed to admit I was guilty. But a trick? Why then did you agree to marry me?"

"I was fearful of what you might do to the judge and his wife if I did not."

"As I suspected. And was that the only reason?"

"No," Brenna admitted honestly, "but I thought you were marrying me as part of your quest for vengeance."

"You thought this marriage was all part of a scheme?"

"Yes. I believed you were planning to either send me to prison or abandon me."

"But I would only have abandoned myself!" He laughed, "And been murdered by Iestyn!" He hugged her tightly. "Do you know how happy I am you're my wife? And how happy I am that we're going to have a child? I can hardly believe I'm going to be a father!"

"Then you have no others?"

"Most definitely not."

"I can't believe it's so."

"What? That I have fathered no others?"

"No."

"What then?"

"That you love me."

"Could there really have been any doubt after our wedding night?"

Brenna felt the heat rise in her cheeks. "I was so wrong about you, Nathan. I thought you had other sinister motives."

"As much as I would like to prove otherwise to you now, a carriage and driver are waiting for us." He moved away. "Brenna. I can't tell you what relief and happiness it brings to see your smile again. I have spent many sleepless nights worrying about your despair."

"Forgive me. I was just so concerned for this child."

"A child," he said thoughtfully. "I imagined many possibilities for your mood, but a baby never crossed my mind!" He heard the distant ringing of a church bell marking the hour and Nathan smiled. "The hour's late and we need to depart, but before we do so," he said and retrieved the box from the sea-chest. "I have something of yours which I thought you might like returned…to carry on the tradition of deboarding *The Grace*."

He opened he box. Brenna gasped at the sight of the yellow gown she traded in Bristol. "Is this…the same gown?"

"One and the same," chuckled the captain. "And I must say, for spending your life at the docks, you bargain rather poorly."

"You're right. T'was an awful trade, but I was desperate." She unfolded the dress and held it against herself, hoping it would fit with her expanded waistline. "How did you find this?"

"A woman with one of the reward flyers came to us claiming that a young woman of suspicious circumstances, and who fit your description, was in her neighborhood the day *The Grace* arrived in Bristol. She said that she and a friend had directed you to the shops of Christmas Steps. So, we traced you to the shop. The shopkeeper showed us the yellow dress. She told me she was going to resell it, and I just couldn't fathom anyone else but you wearing it."

"I'm sorry you had to purchase it twice."

"'T'was of sentimental value. And I know my mother and sister will be beside themselves with delight to see with their own eyes the dress that aided me in the search for you."

"Your mother?" asked Brenna. Brenna had started to undress but stopped at the realization that she knew very little about her husband. "It never occurred to me I'd be taken to your home, let alone introduced to your family! I may come as a very big shock to them!"

Nathan's green eyes sparkled, his laughter barely contained. "You have no idea."

"And your father?"

Sadness crossed his face. "He died several years ago."

"I'm sorry, Nathan. If he was your father, he must have been a good man."

"Yes, he was. He was the best. And I know he would have been most pleased by you. And by the fact," he grinned, "that you have finally chosen to call me by my given name."

"I was reluctant to do so sooner, for I feared getting too close to you."

"As I suspected."

"My apologies, too, for neglecting to even inquire about your family. In all honesty, I feared learning anything about them, believing I was never going to be a part of your life, let alone theirs...and such thought was painful. Forgive me for not even asking."

"Brenna, it's I who needs to apologize for all you've been through in which I've had a hand."

Brenna knew if she allowed herself to dwell on such kindness, she would dissolve again into tears. And there was too much she could not wait to know about her husband. "And siblings? Do you have any others besides your sister?"

"No." Then, noticing the difficulty she was having to fasten the many hooks on her gown, Nathan finished the task himself. The touch of her soft flesh against his fingers sent a rush through his veins. "Misunderstandings have kept me from your bed far too long." He pulled her hair away from the side of her neck and kissed her satin skin. "You, Mrs. Grant, are most tempting, and if we don't leave now, I'm afraid we'll not do so for a very long time."

Arm in arm they made their way toward the longboat waiting at the ship's side. Brenna loved the pressure of his strong arm.

"No bolting this time?"

She tightened her grip on his arm. "Nay, Captain Grant, I'm afraid you're bound to me now. You may later regret having searched so diligently for me."

"Never!" he answered honestly.

Iestyn stood on the deck and noticed immediately the change in the two. Nathan's grin and wink was all he needed. *Congratulations, Captain, it seems ye may not be in need o' those annulment papers after all!*

The small longboat moved slowly through the busy harbor littered with vessels of every shape and size. Nathan explained that flour and bread came in from Philadelphia and were exchanged for leather, potatoes, oranges, rice, and turpentine. Cheese, rum, and beer were imported from the northern cities, while inexpensive furniture came from Newport, sea coal from Nova Scotia, and wine from Spain and Portugal. From the tropics—rum, sugar, molasses, cotton, and salt. In return, Charleston traded mainly staves, shingles, tar, beef, pork, rice, tallow, butter, and peas. As was true of *The Grace's* load, many manufactured goods were brought in from England. It was immediately clear to Brenna that Charleston was a prominent city in the world of trade and not the remote and insignificant outpost about which she had been taught in her earlier years.

The craft moved closer to shore and Nathan motioned to the city ahead. "As you can see, Charleston is nestled on that peninsula between the Ashley and Cooper Rivers. I'm glad the fog has lifted so you can see it. It's really quite a remarkable city. If you look over there, you can see the spirals of St. Philips. And do you see that white steeple over there? That's St. Michaels. Whenever a fire alarm is raised, a lantern is hung from it pointing in the direction of the blaze. I don't know if you saw it as we sailed in, but back there is Sullivan's Island, where Fort Moultrie is located. And straight ahead is 'White Point' where *The Grace* will eventually be unloaded."

Nathan stood tall and explained each landmark. The wind was at his face and his green eyes captured the color of the sea. Brenna was reminded of the first time she saw him on St. Christopher and thought again that he and the sea were inexplicably intertwined. Yet, it was clearly evident that the land, this land, meant a great deal to him. She looked at him and knew he was the essence of this new country—wild yet refined, bold yet tender. She knew that in her husband stood America.

An open-aired carriage with no shield on its door and two powerful-looking buckskin horses stood at the end of the pier. Unlike

Mr. Stone's ornate landau, this carriage carried no adornment. Instead, it spoke of strength and simplicity. "Welcome home, sir! I was awfully glad to get word of your return."

"Thank you, Earl. And may I introduce my wife, Brenna."

Earl shook the captain's hand hard at the unexpected announcement. "Well now, this is cause for a celebra..." He froze.

Nathan anticipated the man's reaction of Brenna's resemblance to Emily. "Earl, as you can see, since this will all come as a bit of a surprise to the family, I would ask that you say no more of this for the time being."

Earl understood immediately what was being asked, but he was still shocked beyond words at the implication. He kept his eyes focused on the captain and said slowly, "Aye, sir...yer secret's safe with me."

Brenna thought the conversation odd and glanced uneasily at her husband. Nathan did not seem to notice. He placed her valise into the boot and assisted her into the interior. "Move out," shouted Earl with a flick of the reins. Lurching slightly, the coach rolled forward.

The jingle of the harnesses announced their presence as they rode through the fine city on this beautiful spring day. Several passersby yelled, "Welcome home, Nathan!" He smiled through the open window and returned their greetings.

The city was alive with activity. Shops of all kinds lined the wide, neatly laid out streets, from saddlers to clock makers, selling everything imaginable from hoops to fine crystal. A multitude of smells filled the carriage—smoked meat, fish, pitch and tar, flowers, leather, and tobacco. On nearly every post, pack horses waited patiently while their wagons were loaded for the long journey into the back-country. Everywhere there were people, horses, and livestock. And had it not been for Nathan's compassion, the city would have had one less tortoise. As they rounded a busy corner on Meeting Street, Nathan shouted for Earl to halt the coach. Immediately, Nathan opened the door, stepped out, and lifted a large turtle tucked tightly in its shell from the middle of the busy cobbled street. He carried it to a grassy dune.

Nathan shrugged when he returned to the carriage and saw Brenna's look of astonishment. "I saw him get clipped and spun by a passing wheel."

Brenna smiled. She was only now beginning to realize how drastically she had misjudged him.

They moved deeper into the city. Brenna was amazed by the large, vibrant-colored homes. Many were enclosed by tall wrought-iron gates which, according to Nathan, led to beautiful secluded gardens. Brenna noticed that most of the homes were two and three stories high and consisted mainly of brick. The majority of houses were narrow but deep. Nathan explained that most of the kitchens were detached to keep the heat from carrying through the entire home. Carriage houses and slave quarters sat behind many of the homes. She saw that many had piazzas; the balconies faced the ocean to capture the sea breeze.

They journeyed inward. It was evident that not all the city had prospered. Nathan explained there was one area, just south of Boundary Street where more than sixteen thousand people resided on a narrow peninsula in shacks and tenements.

Brenna looked forward to returning to the city and exploring its many streets and shops. Brenna could hear the distant chimes of St. Michaels' bells as they traveled away from Charleston. She smiled. "It reminds me of the day I fled Bristol. I was utterly terrified that day, you know."

"As was I…and also baffled at how you could have simply vanished so completely." He squeezed her hand. "I must say, you've perfected the gift of resourcefulness to a fine art."

"Well, I am not all that resourceful. I ended up in prison, if you'll recall."

His voice shook with emotion. "I'm just so thankful, Brenna, that you're safe and here with me now."

"And I with you," said Brenna, equally emotional.

It was several minutes before she regained her composure enough to absorb the sights before her. Although patches of fog remained, the day was, for the most part, clear on their journey inward. She had not expected the vast beauty that surrounded them. "It's odd, Nathan, for I feel so comfortable here. Somehow, I expected to be threatened by it all, but instead, I don't know…I know it may sound strange…but it seems this is where I belong."

"You do. More than you could ever know."

"Where exactly is your home?" asked Brenna excitedly.

"Ten miles north of Charleston, along the Ashley River."

Brenna bit her lip nervously, worried about the reception she would receive. "Are we going directly to your home?"

"Yes."

"And do your mother and sister live there as well?"

"No. My mother lives two miles down the lane from me in the home my father built for her. It was there I was born. My sister, her husband, and their three children live in town."

"And you," she asked innocently, "when did you purchase your cottage?"

"I purchased my home, not for myself actually, but for an elderly couple several years ago."

"Oh?"

"The couple, the Burgasons, lived in the home for quite some time, but they fell under hard times. They were at risk of losing their home. When it looked as if they would forfeit all they had worked for, I merely helped them out a little."

"That was very good of you, Nathan."

Nathan responded casually, "Mrs. Burgason saved my sister's life once when she was four. She pulled her out of a pond."

"She nearly drowned? That's horrible!"

"Yes it was. Mrs. Burgason wasn't much of a swimmer herself and nearly lost her life saving Laurie. Buying their farm back for them was the least I could do."

"How then did you end up living there?"

"Having no children of their own, they had, unbeknownst to me, willed the home to me."

"And they've passed away, then?"

"Yes, within a year of one another."

"How long ago was that?"

"Well, let's see," he said rubbing his chin, "it was just after the British evacuated Charleston, eight or so years ago I guess. The land is fertile, and the farm and stable are in good shape, but the house itself, I must caution you, will need some attention."

"Do you harvest any crops?"

"Indigo mostly."

"And slaves?" Brenna asked, fearful of his reply.

"No, I need to be able to sleep at night. From my perspective, outside of our Creator, man belongs to no one. Besides, two years ago a bill passed here to prohibit the slave trade. There have been numerous violations of it, and it's due to expire next year. I expect it'll face another bitter battle, but, nonetheless, it's on the books."

"You mean slavery doesn't exist here at all?"

"Unfortunately, no. Slave labor is rampant. The ban applies only to the buying and selling of slaves. And I must caution you. Although I'm not alone in my conviction against the use of slaves, it certainly isn't the predominant view here."

"I'm glad you have no slaves."

Nathan laughed, "And even if I did, I have the feeling you'd have them freed by day's end!"

"How is it you already know me so well?"

"Because, dear wife," he said and kissed her cheek, "you remind me a lot of another woman I know."

Brenna raised her eyebrows. "And I thought you said I had no competition for your heart?"

"You need not fear, for she's old enough to be your mother."

Contentedly, Brenna laid her head back against Nathan's shoulder, amazed at how comfortable it was there.

"By the way," he asked suddenly, "do you ever have a sense about what is going to happen…before it happens?"

Brenna looked at him, puzzled. "Why do you ask?"

"I'm just curious, for I've heard," he said nonchalantly, "of people with the gift of sensing when something…let's say ominous…is about to occur. I was wondering if perhaps you…inherited such ability."

Brenna laughed. "No, thank goodness. I've had enough to worry about as it was." She saw the relief spread across his brow and asked suspiciously, "Why? Is something bad about to happen?"

"Nay, m'lady," he chuckled, "I was just wondering."

Brenna thought the conversation peculiar but turned her attention to the passing countryside, enthralled by the scene before her. Nathan said the area was known as The Low Country and appeared to be a mixture of marshes and thick pine forests. Cascading over the lane was an arching treetop canopy. It reminded Brenna of one of Carrie's paintings.

As interested in the land and the neighboring plantations as she was, Brenna was even more captivated by the man who sat next to her. With his legs stretched out in front of him and his arms folded across his chest, a smile of satisfaction danced across his face.

"Tell me, Nathan, is there anywhere you're not at ease?"

"Well, I'm afraid I wasn't much at ease when I was searching for you," he replied seriously.

"You seemed to enjoy yourself without me when you escorted Launey to the baths."

"What?" frowned Nathan and sat forward. "How in the world would you know about that?"

"I have my ways." Brenna looked playfully out the window.

"Iestyn?"

"Nay," smiled Brenna, enjoying the game.

"How then? No one else knew except Launey, and I'm certain she didn't tell you."

"It wasn't Launey either."

"Then, there's no other way unless you were there yourself, which of course is impossi…" He stopped. Her head was back, her body rippled with laughter. "What? Brenna! There is no possibility!"

When her laughter did not subside, Nathan's eyes grew wide with disbelief and a thought struck him. "I seem to recall," he said distantly, "hearing a noise and thinking it some sort of varmint."

"An alley cat, I believe were the words you used."

Nathan stared at Brenna with his eyes and mouth agape. Now, it was he who erupted with a thundering laughter so violent it shook the carriage. It was several minutes before either was calm enough to speak. When she did, Brenna explained her presence there.

Nathan was astounded when she confessed her ventures to confiscate the flyers in the city.

"Why, you little minx! You unbelievable little minx," he said, shaking his head, yet unable to keep the admiration from his eyes. "Who knows what might have happened to you out like that alone! It never occurred to me, never in my wildest dreams, you might resort to such tactics! Heaven help me!" he cried. He squeezed his hair in mock panic, "I didn't have any idea what I was getting into when I offered to marry you!"

"Offered," jested Brenna, "you mean coerced! You know when I heard your voice at the Charles', I…" Brenna stopped as the coach turned sharply. Before her was a sweeping field, alive with a breathtaking array of wildflowers. Sitting atop the gently crested hill was a beautiful white stone home.

"This is it."

"This is your home?" whispered Brenna incredulously.

"No," he corrected, "it's ours."

"Nathan, it's…it's beautiful. I've never seen anything like it!" She had guessed that in owning several ships, he must live comfortably, but nothing prepared her for the stunning plantation before her. "In buying back their home, Nathan, you more than helped the couple out *a little!*"

"Well, I caution you, the interior is in need of much attention."

Nathan stepped from the coach and took her arm. Together they mounted the steps of the large front porch. "I don't believe this, Nathan," sighed Brenna softly. She ran her hand along one of the carved columns.

Suddenly, as he had done aboard *The Grace*, Nathan swept Brenna into his arms. "As I recall," he said and squeezed her tightly, "this might be considered proper."

"And this time, Nathan, will there be another woman in your bed…awaiting you?" chided Brenna.

"If there is," he teased, "I'm afraid she'll have to wait a very, very long time."

Brenna recalled her anxiety the last time he carried her across the threshold and how she had dreaded the future on the other side.

"I didn't bite, now did I?"

"No, actually…you were quite wonderful."

"Oh, how I would have loved to hear those words then, dear wife. Instead, I thought I had been banished from you forever."

"Somehow, Nathan, I don't think you would have let that happen." She ran her finger against his neck at his open collar and said coyly, "I've heard of men like you, Captain Grant. You were just biding your time until your maiden in distress beckoned you back to her bed."

"And glad I am you did," he laughed, "for I think I would have had to fall upon my own sword if you hadn't."

Nathan tenderly kissed her lips, then entered the home. "I hope you won't mind, fair maiden, but I sent word ahead that the staff be given the next two days off."

"Oh?"

"My motives are purely selfish and many would say scandalous, but I simply wanted time alone with my bride."

Flattered by his romantic affection, Brenna wrapped her arms even tighter around his shoulders, "Actually, truth be told, milord, nothing could please me more." She gazed into her husband's eyes and felt an overwhelming sense of relief. She fought the urge to cry when she thought of how her terrible fears about him had all been false. "You know, Nathan," she smiled through her tear-filled eyes, "if you hadn't been such a scoundrel, I might have recognized the true you much sooner."

"Ah, but a true swashbuckler can never reveal his hand too soon, lest a woman take full advantage."

"I knew it! I was right about you all along!"

Nathan's lips again briefly brushed hers before he reluctantly set her down.

"Nathan!" Brenna gasped at the staircase before her. It rose majestically and curved to the second story without touching a wall. She gripped the mahogany balustrade and exclaimed, "Nathan, I've never seen anything like this!"

"'Tis unique. I know of only one other like it in the world, and that's here in Charleston."

Still awestruck, Brenna's voice was filled with the excitement of a child, "It soars to the sky as if it were on the wings of a gull."

Nathan shook his head. "It's frightening you know."

"What?"

"How two people can grow up…thousands of miles apart and yet think so much alike."

Brenna's brow arched in question.

"The first time I saw that staircase, my exact words were that it reminded me of a soaring gull."

Brenna smiled a knowing smile.

Next to the staircase, Brenna saw that the home's most distinguishing feature was its gently rounded construction. Nothing, including its hallways, was straight or square. In each room, the walls, door frames, moldings, and wainscoting were fitted perfectly in one unbroken curve. Brenna had never seen any home more beautifully designed.

The common room, with its series of bay windows that overlooked the meandering Ashley River, was Brenna's favorite. In its corner was a carved tulipwood fireplace. Brenna thought the room, like the rest of the house, was both charming and elegant.

"As you can see, most everything is too dark and in need of fresh paint and new furnishings. I've been here so little that it was never a priority. In a few days," he said as he wrapped his arms around her shoulders from behind her, "I must leave to attend my long-neglected business duties here and I will probably be away for a few weeks."

"What!" cried Brenna. "Oh Nathan, surely not so soon! I will miss you!"

"I have the distinct feeling that over the next few days you will have little time for much thought about me."

"Nathan, that's impossible! You're the only thing on my mind."

"I believe that will all change very shortly." He saw her look of uncertainty. "While I'm gone, make whatever alterations you desire to the home. The staff will help you secure whatever changes you please."

"But, Nathan, I have no qualifications for such a task."

"Brenna," he said, his voice laced with affection, "this is your home. I want it to reflect you, not some stranger's idea of what appeals to their tastes."

"What if you don't like my choices?"

He lifted her chin in his hand and said seriously, "I can assure you, m'lady, that if it pleases you, it will please me."

Nathan led Brenna to their bedroom on the second floor. He moved across the large room and opened the heavy, dark drapes to expose a wall of windows that ran floor to ceiling and showered the room with sunlight. A set of French doors opened to a broad veranda that overlooked a stunning flower garden ablaze with azaleas and camellias.

Brenna immediately noticed there was no meshing around the bed.

"Do you not have problems with insects here in Charleston?"

"Hardly," laughed Nathan. "Actually, they're just as much a nuisance here as on St. Christopher. However, it appears to be more practical to drape the windows and doors instead of the bed chambers."

"Nathan, it's brilliant! I can't believe I have never heard of such a thing."

"The idea isn't mine. I'm only surprised it isn't more prevalent as well. I suppose it's only a matter of time." He pulled her close to him. "My housekeeper, Mrs. Stritzel, is continually telling me how the home is in need of a woman's touch. I've tried to persuade her, to no avail, that she could decorate the home as she pleases, but she always declined, saying one day it shall be the duty of my wife to decorate it as she desires. I have to say, I was never as optimistic as she about there ever being a Mrs. Grant. She will be most overjoyed to learn she was right and that you are here."

"What if she isn't, Nathan," she added, gently biting her lower lip, "what if none of them are? They had no idea you were returning with a wife. My presence may be shocking."

More than you'll ever know, more than you'll ever know. "Cast aside your fears, my dear. I know my family well, and they will love you, every one."

"And the baby? How will they react when they learn of the child?"

Nathan could not contain a bright smile. "I can assure you, madam, a child will be an answer to a much requested prayer. I fear my mother was beginning to believe she would never have a grandchild by me."

"Still, this will be a lot for them to take in at once."

"For you as well, Brenna. And before you know it, you'll have more family surrounding you than you'll know what to do with."

"When will I meet them?" she asked, unable to hide the uneasiness in her voice.

"Tomorrow night. Iestyn is traveling to my mother's home now to inform them. I'm certain Mother will invite their close friends for the gathering as well."

"Do you think that's wise?" she asked uneasily. "Perhaps it would be better for me just to meet your mother and sister first?"

"No, I think in this situation, we'd better let everyone see you at once." He led her toward the four-postered walnut bed, "Besides, my mother will definitely want her closest friend to meet you."

"Why?"

"And you, good wife, ask too many questions. You'll have all the answers you need tomorrow, but tonight, you're all mine."

Brenna rolled over and was disappointed to find Nathan gone from the bed. She did not know the hour, but guessed it to be close to three in the morning. A slight movement on the veranda caught her attention. She watched him unseen on the balcony with only a towel wrapped at his waist. She knew his keen eyes were scanning the sky beyond. With legs apart, arms crossed, and hair blowing in the wind, he looked like he was standing on the bridge of his ship.

Brenna took Nathan's robe from the base of the bed and slipped it on. Silently, she came from behind and wrapped her arms around his bare shoulders.

"Storm's brewing." He nodded in the direction of the sea and stroked her warm arms.

She rested her cheek against his back. "Do you wish you were out there? Preparing to battle this gale?"

Nathan chuckled. "Actually, I was thinking how glad I am that I am not!" With rain beginning to fall, Nathan turned to face her. "There's no place, not anywhere else on earth, Brenna, I'd rather be than with you."

Relief showed in her eyes, but she was still concerned. "You said in the carriage, now that you are a husband and a father, you have no desire to continue sailing and that you plan to concentrate on developing your businesses here. But Nathan, I'm fearful you'll grow tired of your landlocked life with me. I know how you feel about the sea and I…"

"How I feel about the sea is nothing compared to how I feel about you. I hope you understand that as long as I'm with you, it matters not where I am."

"I know you feel that way now, Nathan, but what about a year from now, ten years from now? I don't want you having to substitute one love for another."

"Brenna," said Nathan seriously, "I know who I am and what I need. And what I need is you. What I will always need…is you."

Brenna's face glowed with joy and knew he spoke the truth. "Well, do you remember when we were at sea and I asked if I might have access to your sextant and charts?"

"How could I forget?" he said, the rain coming down harder.

"Do you think it possible you could teach me to guide one of your vessels?"

He laughed loud and hard. "Heaven help me sea mates of the world! I can see it now, 'Attention crew! Captain Brenna Grant on the bridge!'"

"I'm serious, Nathan!"

"I know! That's what scares me the most!" He put his arms around her and grinned. "And who, pray tell, shall take care of our children while their mother is out sailing the seven seas?"

"Well, actually," said Brenna coyly, "I thought we could go together, at least when the children are a little older."

"And when we're off on one of our little excursions, what of the children's studies?"

"You and I can teach them! And think of what they will learn," exclaimed Brenna excitedly, "by the places they will see! And…"

"I see you've thought this all through."

"Of course!"

With a crooked grin, he said, "You know, Miss Brenna, I get the distinct feeling life with you is apt to be filled with all sorts of surprises."

The warm rain blew against them and neither cared that they were getting drenched. Nathan stepped back and looked at his wife with a keen eye. He wound a lock of her wet hair around his finger. Nathan grinned mischievously, "Do you know who you remind me of?"

"No," said Brenna apprehensively, "Who?"

"You! That day on St. Christopher when I first set eyes upon you. Now if only we had a little mud…"

Brenna threw back her head and laughed. "Nathan Grant! You are the cad I first believed!"

"Aye, but thickheaded would be more like it! If I had any sense, I would have done this then and there." Instantly, his mouth was upon hers.

She pressed her body to his and she felt his muscles tighten. Brenna loved the feel of his warm body enveloping hers.

Abruptly, he pulled away. "Just a minute, I have a brilliant idea." He went inside the house and returned moments later with the cushions from the settee. Nathan placed them flat on the balcony floor, secluded by a half wall.

"But, Nathan, they'll be ruined."

He grinned. "I've been wanting to replace these for the longest time!"

Lightning flashed in the distance. Brenna's eyes locked with the man she loved above all else. He guided her gently down onto the pillows. With thunder rolling across the night sky and rain pouring upon them, Nathan and Brenna became one.

Brenna awoke the next morning feeling as if she were standing on the peak of a mountain with God holding her hand. Beside her was her husband, a man whom she loved and within her, his child.

"Oh, Nathan," she beamed and kissed him over each closed eye. "I still can't believe this is happening! I prepared myself for an awful end and instead, I awake to this glorious day with you!"

He grabbed her playfully and pulled her on top of him.

"You know," she laughed and rose, "had I known the nights we'd share would all be like this, Nathan, I would have married you the first day we met."

"What," he teased, "and miss the excitement of running away from me?"

"What would you have done," she rolled to her side so she could face him unobstructed, "had someone located me and tried to claim the reward?"

"Paid them," he answered nonchalantly.

"Surely you jest!"

"I would have given much more than that, every penny I had, if it would have brought you back to me," said Nathan, speaking the truth.

"Why? You barely knew me."

"I knew enough to realize I wanted to spend the rest of my life with you."

Brenna's eyes narrowed and studied him closely. She was just now beginning to glimpse the complex man she married.

"You know, Mrs. Grant, you might forever be in trouble whenever it rains. I dare say, I'll never be able to look at a storm the same way again."

"Or that balcony," blushed Brenna.

He took her in his arm. "I love you, you know. More than life itself." Before she could respond, Nathan asked, "Are you hungry?"

"Very." She started to rise.

"Well, then," he said and pushed her back down gently, "I'll be right back." He walked from the room but stopped in the doorway. "And Brenna…I'll teach you to sail anywhere, anytime. You just give me the word."

The happiness he saw in her eyes spoke more than any words she could have uttered. He smiled and left the room. When he returned, he carried a tray with bread, cheese, and a yellow rose.

"It's the first one I've seen in ages," she exclaimed and touched a soft petal against her cheek. "Where did you get it?"

"Behind the house. Actually, I think it bloomed just for you."

"Nathan, I had no idea how hopelessly romantic you are." She looked at the tray. "Nor did I imagine the chef I was getting in the bargain."

"Don't worry," he laughed, "my specialties do have a price. In fact," he said as he put the tray on the floor, "I think payment is already overdue."

Nathan walked into their bedroom several hours later. "I thought I might bathe," said Brenna as she opened the wardrobe.

"I'll help you draw the water, but first, I need to talk to you."

"What is it?" frowned Brenna, troubled by his serious tone.

He took her hand and led her to the settee. He cleared his throat. "There's something you need to know before we go tonight."

"What is it?" She realized she had never seen him so uneasy. "Is it something I've done?"

"No, of course not." He stroked her hand and began gingerly, "Since the moment we met, there have been many misunderstandings between us, which for the most part were innocent mistakes."

"I realize that," interjected Brenna slowly.

"But there's something I've deliberately kept from you."

Surprised by the confession, Brenna waited for him to continue.

"Do you remember in the carriage after our wedding, I told you that sometimes what we think is the truth about something might not be the truth?"

"I recall it well. I was cruel to you in my response. I told you I didn't trust anything you had to say."

"I dare say your mistrust of me was understandable, but in all seriousness, Brenna, I'm not exactly certain how to say this, or for that matter, how you came to believe what you do about your past, but what I do know is that you're in error."

"In error? About what?"

Nathan held his breath, then let it out slowly. "About your mother, for one thing."

"Helen?"

"No, Brenna. Not Helen."

Brenna jerked her hand away from his. "Nathan, what are you talking about? I don't understand."

He struggled to hold his voice steady, "I knew the truth when you removed your bonnet in Bristol."

"The truth? The truth about what?"

"Who you are."

Brenna said slowly, "Are you saying…you know my birth mother?"

"Yes. And your father."

"That is not possible!"

"I know how far-reaching this must sound, but it's the truth."

"How could you," she demanded, "when I don't even know myself?"

"I will say no more, as you deserve to hear the rest from them."

"Nathan, you're mistaken! Tell me you're mistaken!"

"There's no mistake, Brenna. Tonight you will meet your parents."

Chapter Fourteen

They traveled the dark path in silence. Brenna heard only the rolling of the carriage wheels, the soft breathing of the two horses, and the steady rhythm of their hooves as they moved down the narrow lane. She shifted slightly, unaccustomed to the polonaise skirt gathered at her back. The dark violet gown was one Nathan purchased for her while his ship had been docked in Bristol. Nathan had helped braid her hair into a series of loops and pinned them together with a pearl clip. At her neck, she wore the necklace he had given her their wedding day. Nervously, Brenna rubbed the veil of her hat.

No matter how strong your conviction, Nathan, you're wrong! It's not possible you know my parents! How could you? Brenna had asked him question after question about his claim of knowing her birth parents. He flatly refused to answer any of them. Instead, he told her that after tonight all would be clear. For her, nothing was clear.

Brenna trusted Nathan implicitly, but on this matter, she knew he must be misguided. The idea that he knew the people who had abandoned her as a baby was unfathomable. And if by some far-fetched twist of fate he did know them, how could he want to reunite her with the very people who disposed of her in such a cruel way? What had they told him to cover up what they'd done?

In the soft lantern light, Brenna watched Nathan closely and saw the ease at which he rode the bumps. Even in the dimly lit carriage, she could see his eyes twinkling. If he was apprehensive about introducing her to his family, he did not reveal it. Rather, he had the look of a young lad eagerly awaiting the moment his parents would give him permission to open his Christmas gifts. She was about to ask if everyone in his family was as content in life as he, when the carriage turned a sharp corner.

Nathan's mother heard the carriage. She rushed out the front door and down the steps of the high wooden porch. A radiant smile lit her face.

It had been the surprise of her life when Iestyn brought word yesterday of Nathan's marriage. Although she had never previously had the pleasure of meeting Iestyn, she recalled how highly her son thought of him. She knew she must trust the accuracy of his announcement, and yet, she had been so stunned by the news that her eyes remained open with excitement and questions until nearly dawn. For more years than she cared to recall she had prayed for a loving woman to come into his life. She had begun to fear it would never happen.

Where did they meet? When were they wed? Where is her family? Do they approve of this union? What will Nathan do now that he is married? Will he and his new wife settle in Charleston? Most of her questions were of the bride. She could not wait to meet the woman who had finally won Nathan's heart. As eager as she was to meet his new bride, though, she did not worry overly much about whether she would like the young woman. She knew if her son loved her, she would too. *I only hope she feels welcome here. I can't imagine how intimidating this must be for her!*

She tried to see the woman Nathan assisted from the carriage. She frowned. His bride's face was shielded by the veil of a large hat. All she could observe was how well the tall, slender woman carried herself. Unable to contain her excitement, she rushed forward and grabbed Nathan into her arms. The hug was prolonged and tight. When she pulled away, her face was awash with tears of joy.

Brenna could not contain her smile. She knew the lovely woman before her was Nathan's mother. With her short, sandy-blonde hair, lightly streaked with gray, and warm brown eyes, Brenna thought the woman looked very stately yet kind.

Nathan's sister, with her three children following behind, rushed forth next. Each expressed their pleasure with hugs, kisses, and shrieks of delight, except for a little girl who looked to be about three; she immediately pounced on Nathan's back when he stooped to scoop up her brother in his arms. A man, whom Brenna presumed to be the girl's father, retrieved the clinging child and welcomed Nathan home with a hearty handshake. With the greetings complete, everyone turned to Brenna in eager anticipation of Nathan's introduction.

"Mother and family," said Nathan with a bow, "may I introduce my wife, Mrs. Nathan Grant."

"Really, Nathan," scolded his mother playfully, "have you been away at sea so long that your manners have left you completely? Cannot you at least present your bride by her given name?"

"No, mother," he said, flashing a mischievous smile, "I can't. It's a surprise."

"A surprise? Good heavens, what on earth are you talking about?" she chided again.

"Nate," interjected the father of the young children, "and why the veil? Or is her face a surprise as well?"

"As a matter of fact, Jim," smiled Nathan to the slender yet muscular man, "that too is a secret."

"This is preposterous!" exclaimed his mother, intrigued with the game and unable to hide a smile. She turned to Brenna and asked in exasperation, "Are you going to let him get away with this, my dear?"

Nathan looked closely at his wife and wondered if she would lift the veil and put an end to the mystery. He was pleased at her response.

"I, too, shared the same reluctance about the veil," said Brenna, "but your son is not easily dissuaded once he puts his mind to something."

His mother pointedly ignored Nathan's broad grin, looped her arm through Brenna's, and led her toward the house. She stopped suddenly and turned to Brenna. "Since my son seems to have lost all his good sense, we were not properly introduced. I'm Grace. Grace Grant."

"Grace!" Brenna laughed aloud at her earlier jealousies. "I'm glad to meet the ship's namesake!"

"One of the few respectful things he's done," said Grace and winked back over her shoulder to her son.

When they entered the elegant foyer, Brenna exclaimed, "Your home is lovely!"

"Thank you. I do love it so. And now, my dear," she said as she motioned for Brenna to have a seat on the comfortable settee in the sitting room, "why don't you tell me all about yourself?"

"Well," stated Brenna while glancing about for any sign of another couple, "I…"

"Excuse me, Mrs. Grant," interrupted a woman who Brenna assumed was the cook, "I'm sorry to trouble you, but I need your advice on a matter in the kitchen."

"Very well," she sighed and patted Brenna's knee. "You stay where you are. I'll hurry. I cannot wait to learn more about you!"

Brenna watched the congenial woman leave the room and smiled to herself. "Nathan's mother!" She could not believe she was here meeting his family.

Nathan's sister looked happy for the opportunity to speak with Brenna and moved to sit next to her. She smiled brightly and said, "I'm Laurie."

"I'm so happy to meet you," said Brenna warmly. She thought Laurie very closely resembled Nathan's mother.

"And I can't tell you how happy I am to meet you!" She nodded to the two boys wrestling in the corner, "the one in the red shirt is Dave, he's six, and the other is Bob, seven. And let's see," looking around she saw her daughter nibbling on a cracker, "that's Alison, three and a half."

"They're darling!"

With a look of affectionate resignation, she said, "Well, I'm not sure that's the term I'd use, but life would surely be quiet without them!"

"Ma'ma," squealed the girl when she saw her mother look at her, "I have to go to the privy."

"One moment, sweet girl, I'm visiting."

"But, mama," she said and crossed her legs, "I have to go now!"

"Excuse me," laughed Laurie, "but some things just can't wait."

Brenna laughed too, amazed by how welcomed she already felt. But her fears of meeting her supposed parents loomed heavy. She looked about the drawing room and surmised that many of Grace's fine furnishings were gifts from her world-traveling son. Above the mantle was a gilt-framed portrait of a man Brenna decided must be Nathan's father. She looked from the portrait to Nathan who stood laughing with Laurie's husband next to the hearth. She decided Nathan's dark hair had come from his father.

Nathan took a sip of his brandy and caught Brenna's gaze. He motioned for her to join them. "I don't think you've met Jim. But I have to warn you, he's a lawyer, and sly too."

"The pleasure's mine," said the handsome man, grinning. Brenna estimated that Jim was three or so years younger than Nathan. He had a square face with jovial brown eyes. "Ma'am," he said cordially, "'tis a pleasure to meet the one who's finally managed to catch this sea-rover." He turned to Nathan. "We were beginning to think there wasn't a woman anywhere in the world who would take you."

"Well, let me tell you," teased Nathan as he looped his arm through hers, "it wasn't an easy battle."

"So, Nathan," Jim asked, "what are your plans for *The Grace* now that you're a married man? Going to continue sailing her yourself?"

"Not unless I can convince her to join me." He squeezed Brenna's arm. "Somehow going it alone does not have quite the same appeal it once did. So at least for the time, I thought I might ask Evan Kelleher if he would be interested in taking over her command."

"Well," exclaimed Jim, "I can tell you, everyone here will certainly be relieved to have you home for a good while. Oh good," he said abruptly and nodded toward the foyer, "there's Weston."

With her back to the door, Brenna's heart pounded. One of the few things Nathan had shared when she questioned him was his belief that Weston and Emily Emerson were her parents. Unable to move and incapable of looking at the man Nathan believed to be her father, Brenna stood frozen with her back to him.

Nathan moved quickly to greet Weston.

"You're looking fine," beamed Weston. He shook Nathan's hand heartily. "You were gone so long, I was beginning to fear you might have fallen victim to one of the pirates we heard about in Britain. We were all a little worried."

"As I've heard," responded Nathan. He looked over Weston's shoulder. "So where's your wife?"

"You know Emily with children," said Weston. "She's outside with Alison who's singing her latest rendition of a song she wrote about a bear. And, speaking of wives, congratulations!"

"Thank you," Nathan said graciously.

"Yes, Nathan," said Emily enthusiastically. She entered the common room holding Alison's hand, "we were thrilled with the announcement!"

Nathan placed a supporting arm around Brenna's waist. "Honey," he said cautiously, "I'd like you to meet Emily and Weston Emerson."

Slowly Brenna turned. Her world was silent, void of everything but the face of the woman before her, a face that in an earlier time would have been the mirror image of her own. She felt nothing, heard nothing, but her own uneven breathing. Then darkness consumed her vision.

Nathan quickly grabbed Brenna as she collapsed and lifted her into his arms. "If you'll excuse us, I believe my wife may be in need of a little fresh air."

He set her down on the white porch swing and gently lowered her head. Moments later, slightly revived, Brenna raised her head and shook uncontrollably.

"Oh, Nathan, it was her!" she gasped, barely able to breathe. "It was her!"

"I know," he said calmly, "I know."

"How could they have done it? How could they?"

"Brenna, listen to me. I don't know what it is you think they've done, but whatever it is, you're wrong. They are good, fine people. Two of the best…"

"No!" she wailed and pushed him away. "They sold me, Nathan! They sold me!"

Concerned by her unnatural breathing, Nathan stroked her shoulders. "It's all right, Brenna. It's all right."

"Oh, Nathan," she cried, clenching her hands, "it will never be all right! How? How will I ever be able to go back in there when all I feel is hate?"

"Are you all right?" asked Emily who appeared in the door. She offered Brenna a glass and said pleasantly, "I thought perhaps a little water might help."

"Emily," said Nathan, "I think she could use you here now more than me."

He whispered in her ear as he rose, "Give her a chance, Brenna. Give her a chance."

Concerned, Grace stopped Nathan when he entered the house. "I hear your wife's not well."

"She'll be okay."

"I'll just go to her and see if there's…"

Nathan blocked her way and said firmly, "No, Mother. She needs some time alone with Emily."

"Emily?" asked Grace, clearly perplexed as she followed her son.

Nathan walked directly to Brenna's father. "Weston, I had wanted my wife to be able to hear something from you directly, but given her state of shock I'm concerned for her health…and that of our ba…" Nathan stopped abruptly and said instead, "I don't think she can absorb any more right now. Let's retire to the library. There's something I'd like to discuss with you."

Brenna could not find the courage to look at the woman next to her, and she despised herself for it. Over and over she had imagined what she would say to this person if ever she had the opportunity, and now that it was upon her, she was speechless. She held the cup with both hands and trembled violently. Slowly, she sipped the water under her veil. *Give her a chance.* She forced herself to concentrate on Nathan's words.

"Has that helped any?" asked Emily of the drink. Brenna nodded. "I know when I was with child, there were times I felt poorly too."

Brenna nearly choked. After regaining her composure, she mounted the courage to speak. Weakly she confessed, "You're the first one who's noticed, or at least admitted it."

"I'm sorry, I didn't mean to pry. If you desire, your secret will go no further."

"Thank you. I thought I'd let Nathan make the announcement when he's ready."

"He's a good man," said Emily thoughtfully and looked toward the house. "One of the finest I've ever known. Actually," she laughed lightly, "he reminds me a lot of Weston, strong yet never above helping another. He'll make a wonderful husband…and father."

"Yes," said Brenna. She imagined him cradling their child in his arms. "I know he will."

"You were married in England then?"

"Yes." Brenna was still unable to look at the woman.

"Your parents must have been heartbroken to see you move so far from home. Where in England do they live?"

"I never knew my parents," answered Brenna curtly. "We were… separated," she swallowed, "when I was very young."

"Oh, I'm sorry," said Emily, the steadiness of her voice failing. "Life without a father or a mother must be nearly as heartbreaking as a parent without their child."

Brenna sensed she had been terribly wrong about this woman, yet was still unwilling to forgive. She hesitated, "And you? What of your children?"

Emily looked away in an effort to mask the quivering of her voice.

"I had a child, a daughter." She trembled hard and dabbed her eyes with her handkerchief. "I apologize. I still can't think of it without…" Emily was unable to finish.

In the soft glow of the porch lamp, Brenna turned to the woman whose eyes matched her own. Within the depth of blue, Brenna saw the unmistakable shadow of despair deeply etched with time. The overwhelming suffering the woman had endured was very clear.

"How long," Brenna asked hoarsely, "how long has she been gone?"

"Nearly twenty years."

"Twenty years? And still you grieve?"

Emily wiped her tear-laden eyes and struggled to remain composed. She whispered, "There's some pain even time can never heal." She broke down and cried, "I'm sorry, it's just that I miss her so very much. I miss not knowing what she might have become."

Without thought, Brenna reached out and touched Emily's soft hand. In doing so, an inexplicable peace settled upon the two women. For Brenna, the peace came in the feeling, for the first time in her life, that she belonged. For Emily, the touch filled her with a sense of tranquility she had not known since the days she had cradled her infant daughter in her arms.

For both, it was a touch that eroded time. The bond had not been severed.

Explosively, the moment ended. Emily saw the bracelet. She felt her breathing cease. Nothing else existed. She was aware only of the bracelet and the wrist. She was living her dream, only this time, there was no fog. She seized Brenna's wrist and demanded, "Where? Where did you get this?"

Brenna dropped the glass. It shattered. The realization dawned. *My bracelet is from her! All this time, it was from her!*

Frantically, Emily scanned the veiled face for an answer. "Where did you get this?"

Brenna pulled her hat slowly from her head and cried, "From you."

"Wha...?"

"It's me, Mother. It's me!"

The pain was gone. For the first time in twenty years the pain was gone. The truth was before her. Before the words were spoken and the veil removed, Emily had known. As if cut loose from an anchor pinned to the bottom of the sea, Emily burst free and screamed, "BRENNA! BRENNA! WESTON! SHE'S ALIVE! SHE'S ALIVE! SHE'S ALIVE!"

Weston ran from the house and grabbed them both.

Five minutes later, the sobs of joy had not diminished. With a tear-stained face, Emily gazed at her son-in-law, "You brought her home, Nathan. You brought our little girl home!"

Chapter Fifteen

The air was sweet and the night unseasonably warm for the twenty-ninth of June. Launey rubbed her hand against the smooth bathstone framing the front door of the Royal Crescent. She smiled coyly. *After tonight, you shall be mine.*

Once again, as she had so often before, she rehearsed in her mind what she would say. Her presentation must be flawless. She had no room for error. Satisfied, she raised her hand and knocked.

Although she had followed him for months, it had always been from afar. Launey was unprepared for the huge, menacing man who opened the door. His face and its grossly exaggerated features stared back at her in the dark shadows of the moonless night.

"Launey Stephens, I assume," he said, his voice unnaturally high-pitched. He shifted his eyes toward the direction of the street. "Where's your coach and driver?"

"I'm staying at a nearby inn and saw no need of a coach."

"A trifle warm for a cloak," he observed suspiciously.

"I wanted no one aware of my presence here."

"Then by all means," he bowed in mockery, "be quickly inside."

Launey closed the heavy door behind her and followed Malcolm Stone into the study. He sank into a worn, leather chair. His eyes narrowed at the dark-haired woman as she removed her cloak. Not since Brenna had he seen such beauty. Although she lacked the natural grace and purity of his son's governess, Malcolm Stone imagined the strumpet would be well worth his time once between the sheets.

Launey sat across from him and looked disgustedly around the cluttered room. "I must admit, if this is any indication of the talent of the staff of The Bath, I am not impressed! I would have thought a man of your stature would expect more from your service maids."

He murmured through clenched teeth, "I released my staff following my wife's…death." Testily, he added, "Why have you come?"

"You have no idea?"

"I can only assume that the daughter of the honorable Leonard Stephens is here to inform me there's been some development in catching the pirates who have been terrorizing our fine community. Have the culprits been captured?"

"You might say so," smiled Launey at the man's composure. She dropped a thick leather-bound packet on the table between them. "And the evidence is all here. Evidence against you, Mr. Stone. Enough to see you swing."

The vein on Malcolm Stone's nose immediately darkened and pulsated visibly. "If what you say is true, where is your father with his mighty judicial committee?"

She looked around the house and envisioned what she would do once it was hers. She stretched her feet across the small table between them. "This has nothing to do with my father. It concerns only you, me, and money of course."

He shoved her feet off the table and the packet of papers with it. With his anger barely contained, he roared, "You speak in riddles. Tell me what you want or get out!"

More uneasy than she cared to show, Launey left the scattered papers on the floor and tried to appear unaffected. She reached casually over to the cheese caddy, sliced off a piece of cheese, and slipped it in her mouth. With a slight smirk, she settled herself into the chair again. "I really don't think you'd want me to leave, Mr. Stone, not with what I know about you. I'm certain the authorities would love to hear of your…involvement…in the pirating activities that have been plaguing the seas. In fact, it was quite an operation you masterminded. I dare say, you may go down in history as one of the most brilliant schemers of our time."

"So help me, wench, if you..."

"What I had the most trouble learning was why a handful of the local merchants, including yourself, were able to prosper so vastly in The Bath and Bristol when others were struggling terribly."

"You know bloody well that only the best were able to survive by their superior management."

Launey raised her brow. "Superior management? Yes, I guess you could call it that since you, Mr. Stone, are the sole owner of at least five of these lucrative shops. Tell me are there more than five?"

"That's preposterous!" He ignored her question.

"No, sir, not preposterous." She took another bite of the rich cheese and added, "Your name, of course, has been cleverly concealed. It's actually quite a brilliant plan...so tidy and neat. Your men pilfer incoming vessels. Subsequently, those very same supplies appear in one of your shops, repackaged of course. You are then able to inflate the prices exorbitantly because of what you claim is 'just' reimbursement for the price you've had to pay for the goods. Meanwhile, your competitors, who are unable to obtain the goods they need, go under and none are any the wiser. Really, Mr. Stone, you're to be commended for your resourcefulness."

"Did your father put you up to do his dirty bidden'?"

"Nay, actually, I came upon my information quite by chance."

"Chance?"

"Several months back, in January to be specific, I came upon some information I thought might have been of importance to you. So, I came calling."

"I've never before set eyes upon you. What possible information could you have had that would have been of value to me?"

Launey decided it best not to burden the issue now by telling him that his wife's murderer did not hang herself but instead had escaped. She wanted to momentarily put aside her vow for revenge against Nathan and concentrate on the matter before her. She would have time enough for her planned revenge later. "That's inconsequential now; you might say I've bigger fish..."

"Stop yer bloody jabberin' an' say what you've come to say!"

She ignored his taunts and continued. "When I arrived at your home on that cold, January night and was preparing to knock, to my surprise I found that your front door had been left slightly ajar. I must say I was completely captivated by the conversation coming from within. It was an interesting discussion between you and a Mr…Jade.… Yes, I believe that was his name." Launey smiled confidently, noticing Stone's darkening features. "Oh, surely you remember the night as well. Why, I'm certain the conversation took place in this very room. As I was saying, since the open door gave me an invitation, I simply entered the hall. I must say, what I learned was quite fascinating. It sounded as though Mr. Jade, or as he referred to himself, the Executing Officer in charge of the raids, felt he deserved more than twenty-five percent share in the profit. Tsk, tsk, I must say, your temper flared then. Really, Mr. Stone, a man of your status needs to learn to control such violent tendencies. Why, I'm surprised all the other Crescent residences didn't hear. You must really learn to be more cautious."

With his rage obvious and barely in check, Malcolm Stone spat, "What is it you want?"

"Half," responded Launey simply. "Half of all your profit."

"Half! Why you little…"

"And this," she said. She motioned to the room, "this lovely dwelling you now call home." Confidently, she patted the back of her chair. "Yes, I think I will rather like living in the Crescent."

Every vein in Malcolm Stone's face and neck bulged. He glared at the woman. "I think you ought not to overly concern yourself about where you shall live! You shall be lucky if you survive the night!"

Launey picked up the thick packet and some of the scattered papers. "I thought perhaps you just might feel that way. So I've taken a little self-protection you might say. Should anything…unfortunate…happen to me, written copies of everything I have here shall be turned over to my father's committee."

The huge man leaned toward her. He paused, then whispered, "You have no idea who yer dealing with. I guarantee you'll rue you ever crossed me!"

Launey fidgeted slightly. Things were not going as planned. She had assumed that when he heard about the copies, documents she had spent weeks tracing, he would be more agreeable. She quickly decided on another tactic. "Come now, Mr. Stone, why don't we look at this rationally? Now, 'tis true your share in the profits might be slightly reduced, but think of the benefit I can be to you. After all, my father is leading the commission in charge of bringing the thieves to justice. 'Tis only a matter of time before they, too, learn the truth. With me on your side, I'll be invaluable, for I can detour their investigation at every turn."

Nervous at his lack of response, Launey continued, "Now, while it's true that my father and I are, at the moment, slightly at odds, still he loves me and will keep me abreast of any new developments in the case." Launey smiled inwardly at the thought of her father's reaction if he ever learned his own daughter was sabotaging his efforts. *Oh, what a fitting and just reward for a father who threatened to turn out his own daughter and then ignored her pleas to go after Captain Grant and his murderous wife! Father said he had no proof a prisoner had escaped! No proof! How dare he! My word is proof enough! The captain and his entire crew should have been arrested for kidnapping me and locking me away in that frigid barn! I nearly froze to death! How dare Father tell me he didn't have the resources or the desire to instigate an open-water chase for someone who was already dead! Already dead? I saw the murderer Brenna with my own eyes! Oh, how Father will rue the day he ever treated me this way!*

Malcolm Stone walked over to the cheese caddy and sliced off a large chunk. In her musing, Launey paid no attention. When he moved toward the back of her chair, she failed to notice that the knife was no longer on the tray. But she let out a startled cry as the tip of the sharp instrument pricked the skin at the base of her neck.

"So, you thought we might be partners, did you, Miss Stephens?" He panted; his foul breath hot against her face. He stared down at her heaving bosom. "Well now, perhaps we might be able to work out such an arrangement after all."

Forty-five minutes later, Malcolm Stone stood over Launey's bruised and beaten body; blood trailed from the corner of her mouth. "Wench," he muttered, "you deserved it."

She had put up a fight, but in the end, her body satisfied him well enough. Yet it was her words, spoken in a desperate attempt to spare her life that affected him most. She had spoken of Brenna.

Brenna, whose face still seared his memory and for whom his lust had never died. For all the great achievements of his life, she was his greatest failure. Her death had left him bitter and unfulfilled. Every day it continued to eat away at him, a nagging sense that she mocked him. Now tonight, Launey said she was not dead but living in the Colonies in some God-forsaken place called Charleston.

Was it a lie? Launey's last ploy at trying to save herself? She had cried out in desperation that she had information about his wife's murderer. He had laughed aloud at that, telling Launey her attempts were futile, for it was he who had killed his own wife.

Was that all it was, an effort to save her neck? Or could she possibly have been telling the truth? Malcolm Stone ran his tongue over his rough, cracked lips and thought about the possibilities if she were still alive. Sweat formed on his upper lip.

His eyes moved to Launey's bloody body and his smile quickly disappeared. She had spoiled his plans. He was a fool, he knew, to have killed her, but he had done so in a moment of rage just as he had his wife. His temper often got the better of him, but he had always been able to minimize the damage. A quick glance through the copies convinced him she had not exaggerated the extent of the evidence against him. If in the wrong hands, some unknown henchman was certain to be busy, and his neck would pay the price. He had to leave. No time could be spared. He would have to put into action the escape plan he had hoped to never use.

Minutes later, Malcolm Stone emptied the contents of his safe into a large leather bag and left the house. He knew he would never return. Angry at being forced to leave behind all that he had worked for, he was not entirely disappointed. He now had a destination and a purpose. This time he would silence her laughter forever.

In the pre-dawn hours, a linkboy prepared to snuff the lamps of the Royal Crescent, when he heard a groan. He moved toward the steps and stopped. A woman lay sprawled in the open door frame. Blood pooled beneath her. She had left a red, oozing trail down the corridor where she had slithered toward the front door. A quarter of an hour later, the lad returned with the constable. With her dying breath, she spoke to the officer.

Chapter Sixteen

The bright sun was high overhead. Brenna shifted in the softness of the down-filled bed sheets. Above her, a rose pattern was etched in the ceiling of her parents' guest chambers.

"My parents," sighed Brenna softly. She gently rubbed her tender, swollen eyelids, evidence that the previous night's reunion brought laughter, tears, and continuous questions until well past four o'clock in the morning. What an emotional night it had been!

After the initial shock and exuberance, the remainder of the night was spent sharing events of their lives. Emily and Weston asked endless questions about her childhood and life on St. Christopher. They rejoiced in the knowledge that Helen had loved Brenna as her own child, yet they were horrified and heartbroken as she told them about Harley. The muscles in Weston's cheeks visibly tightened and his eyes flashed with anger when he heard of Brenna being told she had been sold. Emily cried aloud at the agony of how these words must have tortured her daughter.

"Oh Brenna, surely you know that was not true! We would have given our lives for you!"

"I realize that now and how foolish I was to ever have believed him!"

Last night, as she looked at her beautiful, gentle mother, the bitter memories of another night filtered to her conscience. She was on St. Christopher, having just been told about being sold. She had looked at the stars that night and tried to envision her birth mother. The only thing that came to mind was a cruel, evil woman. Brenna discovered last night how wrong she had been. When she thought of the sorrow she had suffered since Helen's death, Brenna knew it was nothing compared to the anguish Emily had endured these long twenty years. Brenna thought of the baby growing within her and shivered. She could not fathom losing a child or her mother's pain of having done so.

Emily and Weston peppered Nathan and Brenna with questions about this miraculous reunion. Everyone was stunned to learn of Brenna and Nathan's chance meeting on St. Christopher, her survival in the hold of his ship, her escape from Nathan in England, and their hurried wedding ceremony.

"Your daughter is quite resourceful," Nathan chided, his eyes twinkling. He put his sturdy arm around his wife's shoulder and said, "Both in surviving in *The Grace's* hold and in dodging me. I must say this reunion would have occurred much sooner had it not been for her creative wiles in escaping me."

"That may be true, dearest Captain," said Brenna, pinching him gently, "had I not been led to believe I was being escorted to a gruesome death."

Weston cast aside the jesting banter of the couple and said seriously, "We'll never be able to repay you, son, for bringing her back to us."

"And I, sir," said Nathan, his voice heavy with emotion, "will be eternally grateful that you were able to keep her safe during that terrible ordeal at sea so many years ago."

Weston closed his eyes and shook his head, still not able to comprehend that his daughter had survived.

"You know it's so strange," Emily said with a distant look in her eye. "My nightmares began in earnest almost exactly the same time you say you boarded Nathan's ship. And when you were imprisoned, that's when I was consumed with the feeling you were in real danger…but none of it made any sense."

"Oh God!" Weston cried. "I should have listened, Emily! It's just that I thought..." He choked back his tears, unable to finish.

Emily took his hand and said gently, "You had no way to know, Weston. None of us did."

With sad eyes, he said hoarsely to his daughter, "I don't know how you can ever forgive me! I didn't believe her! All these years! All these wasted years! Your entire childhood gone! I don't think I will ever forgive myself for what I've done to you." He looked at Emily, "To all of us."

Brenna could not bear to see his pain. She moved closer to him. "Dad. Me forgive you? I've spent the last year and a half despising you...both of you. I should be begging for your forgiveness."

Weston pulled his daughter into his arms. Trembling hard with emotion, he stroked her soft hair. Moments passed before he allowed himself to pull away to view her face. "My God," he said tenderly, "Brenna, look at you! Never in my wildest dreams did I imagine this night possible! I just can't believe it! Any of this!" Weston was barely able to say the words before he broke down, which brought forth a new wave of crying in everyone.

During the early morning hours, Brenna told her parents about Malcolm Stone, the charge of murder, and her escape. She wanted no secrets between them.

"Oh Brenna," Emily cried, "I can't stand to think how you've suffered! If only we had known! If only I had listened to my heart!" She covered her face and sobbed, "I feel exactly like Weston. I will never be able to forgive myself!"

"Mother," Brenna said softly, "neither you, nor anyone else, could have known I was alive."

"Oh, but when I think of all you have suffered! I can't bear it!"

"Emily," Weston looked into his wife's guilt-ridden eyes, "Brenna is right. It was all a terrible twist of fate. And somehow you and I are both going to have to accept what happened, and whatever guilt we feel, we can't change the past. Not ever. But by some unfathomable miracle, she's been given back to us."

"At what price?" Emily whispered. She did not wait for a reply. "At the price of Brenna's lost childhood and misery!"

Brenna considered her response carefully. "The price of you losing your only child was perhaps the greatest tragedy, but it was not all in vain. A lonely woman named Helen was given a daughter she desperately needed." Brenna turned to her husband and added softly, "And by some sort of other miracle, which I cannot fathom, it brought Nathan and me together."

"No doubt you would have known each other since childhood and probably united long ago had none of this happened," Weston interjected.

"Yes," Nathan chuckled, "but I would have missed the opportunity to discover just what a clever wife I had."

"And," Brenna smiled, gazing into Nathan's warm green eyes, "I would never have known the length my husband would go to pursue me."

"I might add, this miracle had another advantage as well," Nathan said, "for I know of at least one person whose life Brenna improved dramatically."

"Oh?" questioned Emily.

"A boy named Scott Stone. And as Judge Charles said, Brenna may well have saved the lad's life."

Emily struggled to comport herself and said thoughtfully, "I've always believed the Lord challenges us to find and build on the good amidst even the most horrific of adversities, and so it seems such is true now. But regardless, Brenna, you must understand that had we known you were alive, we would have devoted our lives to find you."

A gentle knock on her door ended Brenna's musings of the night before.

"It's open," she said pleasantly.

Emily entered. She carried a tray of scones and tea. Her face was aglow with happiness. "Oh good, you're awake! I didn't think I could wait a moment longer!"

"Good morning, Mother!"

At the words, Brenna and her mother looked directly into each other's eyes, a quiet knowing between them at the significance of the simple greeting.

Emily set the tray on the table, moved to the bed, and embraced her daughter.

"Oh, Mother," whispered Brenna, "I still can't believe any of this!"

"Nor can I."

"I was so afraid to fall asleep. I feared when I woke, last night would be only a dream."

Emily took her hand and looked at the bracelet. "I had the same fear. I still can't believe you're alive and that you're here! Never in my wildest dreams, if someone would have told me yesterday that today I'd be serving you breakfast, I…" she could not complete the sentence. She was engulfed by tears.

With her own spilling forth, Brenna cried, "It's a miracle, Mother! There is no other explanation for Nathan finding me!"

"It really is," agreed Emily, dabbing her eyes. "Now, we really must find a way to stop crying. As it was, I could hardly pry my eyes open this morning, they were so swollen!"

"Mine also!" Brenna threw her head back with laughter. Then more seriously, she added, "When I tried to sleep, I couldn't stop thinking about something."

"What, Brenna?"

"Something I did so many times ever since I was a little girl."

Emily remained quiet and let Brenna continue.

"Sometimes I would wake, before it was even light, and knew I just had to go to the shore. I'd take my lantern and stand there…and just listen."

"Listen? Listen for what?"

"I always had this sense…this unshakable sense…there was something out there…something I needed to find…or hear. And I kept thinking if I listened hard enough, through the wind and sea, I would hear it."

"Oh, Brenna! I can't tell you how many times…" Emily struggled to speak, "…how many times, I stood on the shore here…and on the porch at night…willing my thoughts to you."

"I could feel it, Mother…somehow…I could feel your love."

The two women collapsed against one another. Later, Emily recovered enough to bring Brenna a damp cloth from the basin to soothe her eyes. Then, the two women sat holding hands and prayed. Their prayer was not planned. It happened naturally, as an extension of their tremendous gratefulness. As their whispered prayers of thanksgiving poured forth, a peace and contentment filled both of them. Brenna had known such perfection only once before…when the warm holy light in the hold touched her. She experienced it now again with her mother holding her hand.

Later, Emily asked Brenna if she could brush her hair.

The question brought forth new tears to Brenna. She recalled how much Helen had loved to do so. Brenna closed her eyes and basked in the strokes of Emily's hand through her hair. She sensed Helen's presence and knew that somewhere Helen was rejoicing because once again her daughter was feeling the loving touch of a mother's hand.

"Are you up to joining me on the piazza for breakfast?" asked Emily. She opened wide the double doors to the small balcony.

"No amount of words can express how much I would love that." Brenna smiled, lifted her dressing gown from the end of the bed, and slid into it.

The March air was warm and fragrant with the budding of an early spring. Brenna looked over the terrace railing from the third floor of the home. She breathed deeply and enjoyed the sweet scent of wisteria filling her. From this uppermost vantage point, she could see the luscious Spanish moss that covered the large trees beyond and ferns of all sizes growing in abundance throughout the grounds. In the distance, she spotted the tiled roof of Grace's home and the road she, Nathan, and her parents had traveled in the early morning hours to bring them here.

"It's a miracle, Mother. All of it." She rubbed her hand over the gold chains at her wrist. "Just like the bracelet. And just like this bracelet, the link between us remained strong."

"You've worn it all this time?"

"Every day. Except," grinned Brenna, "when Nathan…had it."

"He's an extraordinary man, Brenna. We'll never be able to repay him for bringing you back to us. Never!"

"His search for me in England was unrelenting. Now I understand why he was so determined to find me."

"No, Brenna," smiled Emily knowingly. "There was much more to his determination to find you than merely this reunion."

"Do you really think so?"

"It's obvious he loves you a great deal."

Brenna smiled at the thought and knew it was true.

"I've known Nathan since he was a boy and I've never seen him so happy. I've always said he's the most resourceful young man I've ever known. Believe me, Brenna, he could have easily brought you here without marrying you. There's no doubt." She poured a small amount of milk in her tea and asked, "He got off then?"

"He left at dawn."

"At dawn? He'll be exhausted. He was up nearly all night with us."

"I don't think he slept at all, but after the long delay in Bristol, he was eager to tend to *The Grace's* cargo."

"He's a wonderful man, Brenna. If I had chosen the man to wed my daughter, Nathan would have been the one."

"I'm so glad you feel that way." Brenna looked over the sweeping grounds and sighed softly, "Oh, Mother, it is so peaceful here."

"Yes, it is. I love it." Then a sadness touched her face. "But t'wasn't always so peaceful."

"The war you mean?"

Emily sipped the warm brew. "It was terrible. My heart fills with sorrow every time I think of it. Did you know that Charleston, or Charles Town as we called it then, was taken by the British and controlled by them for over two years? The taking of this town was considered the biggest victory for the British during the war."

"I know only a little and that from my British tutor."

"Well, Sir Henry Clinton led thousands of men against us. When word came that Fort Moultrie had fallen, we knew we were in trouble, yet we were unprepared for just how bad it would be. The fighting lasted over forty days…forty terrifying days. It seemed as if the city was being continually bombarded. The fire brigades raced from one blaze to another. Not only was there constant fighting, but there was little food to be found. The city was starving and nearly every home, ours included, was full of the wounded and dying. Although we had stockpiled a lot of provisions, we hadn't been prepared to feed so many and depleted them quickly."

"And when the battle ended, what happened to all of you?"

"It was bad. While the British controlled the city, area families and friends were pitted against one another. British loyalists from all over the Colonies flocked to Charleston, and many here, including several of our most prominent citizens, signed a pledge of allegiance to the King. Some did so out of political conviction, some out of financial necessity, and others under coercion. But to this day, much bitterness exists among those who signed and those who did not."

"And those who refused to sign?"

"We were all, Nathan's family and ours included, labeled as 'rebels' and considered prisoners on parole. Needless to say, our lives were made very difficult during those two years. Financially, it was disastrous. We were prohibited from participating in any sort of business. Every transaction we made had to be done in secret. But, we were the fortunate ones. Many other patriots lost their lives."

"Praise God that you didn't!" exclaimed Brenna. "It must have been heartbreaking to see the Colonies at war with England."

"'T'was awful knowing we were fighting my homeland, but we felt we had no choice. First with the Stamp Act and then the Declaratory Act, we were being strangled and believed we had to fight for our rights. War was the tragic result.

"What exactly was the Stamp Act?"

"It forced us to pay for a stamp before we could conduct any official business. Without it we were not allowed to buy or sell property, marry, or even collect debts. The tax was so burdensome, it was destroying us."

"Why were the British determined to so heavily tax the Colonies?"

"The taxes were a means of reimbursing the British for the heavy expenses they incurred during the French and Indian War. They believed the Colonies ought to pay their fair share. And I can well understand their sentiment, for vast fortunes and countless British lives were lost in that war. But we argued that such a heavy tax could not be sustained, and if we were to be taxed at all, we must have decision-making input. After much resistance, the King finally repealed the Stamp Act…but replaced it with the Declaratory Act, which was even worse for us, and war ensued."

"Did you and Father support the Colonists from the beginning?"

Emily nodded. "Yes. In fact, Weston and Robert were among those who gathered in July of '74 here in Charleston to protest the Boston Port Bill and demand representation. After that meeting, we were more convinced than ever that war would most likely come."

"I can't believe that so recently you were living under such hostilities."

"It does now all seem very hard to believe."

"And Father's leg?" Brenna recalled asking her father about his limp. "He told me he was injured during the war, but we were interrupted before he could finish."

"Not in the fighting, but in a related incident."

"What happened?"

"Shortly after the British took control of the city, Weston traveled into town for a meeting of patriots. His timing could not have been worse, for as he passed Mazyck Street, we think a rifle accidentally discharged in a nearby powder magazine, setting off a massive explosion. Many homes and businesses were destroyed and more than two hundred people were killed!

"Two hundred?" Brenna was shocked.

"We think it might actually have been as many as three hundred. No one knows for sure, but it's a horror I hope never to witness again. Most of us still have nightmares about it. I heard the explosion from here and saw the smoke. When I got to the area…well…it was beyond description. Scores and scores of people were burned, bodies were everywhere…draped even over houses and trees…and the cries…oh, I can't think of it!"

Brenna covered her mouth, sickened at the tragedy. "And Father was one of the injured?"

"Yes. His leg was pierced with iron from a nearby gate."

"If it hadn't been for Robert, Nathan's father, your father would certainly have lost his leg, if not his life. Several area doctors wanted to 'let his blood,' but Robert would not hear of it. He continually argued that he had never seen anyone improve after a blood-letting treatment. In fact, he believed it might actually do a patient harm. For this view, he was ostracized by some. I don't know if blood letting is a good thing or not, but I'll tell you this, he saved more lives around here than anyone else. Weston's was one of them."

"Nathan told me his father died during the war. I know he's still hurting over the loss."

Brenna noticed a quiver in Emily's voice. "Nathan took the death of his father very hard, as did we all."

Brenna sighed deeply, pained at her husband's sorrow. "What was his father like?"

"Robert was truly the finest doctor I've ever known…and he was brilliant. I'll wager that no one he ever treated will forget their gentle, soft-spoken doctor. Robert never had anything but a kind word toward everyone. And," smiled Emily, "he never met someone he did not want to converse with. He would meet a person for the first time, and the next minute, he would invite them over to dine with his family. You would have thought they had been friends for years. Robert would go out whenever he was needed, regardless of the hour or the weather, to treat his patients. And I never once, not once, heard him utter a complaint in all the years I knew him. Even in the end, he died as he had lived, saving lives."

"How did he die?" asked Brenna, partially afraid of the answer.

Emily's voice grew unsteady once again. "He saved the lives of many of Charleston's best, yet in doing so, lost his own. When the British took control of the city, many of the Continental troops were imprisoned aboard British transport ships anchored in the harbor. Their plight there was wretched. Smallpox and dysentery swept through those prison ships. Needless to say, there were not many doctors eager to care for these men."

"Except Nathan's father?"

"Precisely. He said he was fully aware of the risk. Being a father himself, he argued, he was accountable to do no less than he would do if his own son were aboard one of those ships. Robert said if he died doing only what his conscience would permit, then so be it. And do you know what his final words were? He told Grace that if he had saved one of those men's lives, then he was leaving this world fulfilled. To the very end, he was consumed with healing."

Brenna's eyes were damp with tears. "I wish I could have known him."

"Oh, how he would have loved meeting you! He would have been thrilled about you marrying his son! Has Nathan told you anything about the war and what he did during it?"

"Iestyn told me he saved the crew of a ship that had run aground at the start of the war."

"Well, that was just the beginning. Have you ever heard of Francis Marion?"

"The Swamp Fox?"

"That's him."

"I've heard of him but I don't remember the particulars."

"He was feared tremendously by the British, for he and his group of men fought and harassed them in the backwoods of the Low Country. After his father died, Nathan was determined to join the fighting here at home. So, he temporarily gave up his sea command and traveled with the Swamp Fox. We later heard that Marion himself once told a reporter how Nathan proved invaluable to him. Nathan knew every detail of these swamps and forests, for this is where he spent most of his childhood. During the war, Nathan divided his time between fighting the British at sea and in the backwoods here."

"Weren't Marion and his men finally defeated?"

"Yes, near the Santee."

"And Nathan?"

"He was at sea at the time, involved in a battle of his own.

"He's never told me any of this."

"No, that doesn't surprise me. Nathan has always been modest and private." Emily smiled warmly at her daughter. "Yet, I have the feeling that in you he's found a confidante. He's a fine man."

"He is," said Brenna confidently. "So what happened to all of you after the war?"

"The city was left in virtual ruin, but it has been slowly rebounding ever since. That's the way with Charleston. Since its beginning, this city has been recovering from one disaster or another…wars, fires, plagues, and hurricanes. There's a resiliency here that's unequal to any place I have ever seen." Emily laughed lightly, "And, with the end of the war, Charlestonians weren't about to let their social life suffer any longer. We were tired of war. Now, clubs and dancing assemblies abound."

The sweet smell of magnolias filled the air. Brenna, her mother, and five other women worked diligently stitching the draperies for Brenna and Nathan's home. The three weeks since Nathan's departure passed quickly for Brenna who divided her time between her parents, Nathan's family, and redecorating the Ashley Meadow Plantation. In every aspect of her life, she was showered with warmth and welcome. She was filled with an overwhelming sense of belonging.

She recalled her fear; when, from the small porthole aboard *The Grace*, she glimpsed her first view of America. That vision had been obscured by a veil of fog and uncertainty. Now, the veil was lifted. Unexpectedly, she had found her family. Yet, strangely, it was as though she had been a part of them all her life.

"These colors are beautiful," said Emily of the drapery fabric, interrupting Brenna's musings.

"I think so too." Brenna had purchased the material several days earlier in Charleston. Initially, Brenna anticipated it would take her several weeks to complete the draperies. That was before she understood the meaning of cooperation Charleston style. Emily, who loved to stitch, asked to help. On the first day of their task, they had been at work for a couple of hours when Grace and Laurie appeared with sewing baskets in hand.

The four women continued to work in earnest when two black women and a girl of about sixteen appeared with sewing baskets of their own. The first woman who entered had a vibrant smile and introduced herself as Liz; the girl was her daughter Leis. Liz explained how Nathan bought her husband's freedom five years earlier and then hired him as his foreman. When she heard his new bride had undertaken the task of sewing her own draperies, she wanted to help. The older woman, Janie, timidly explained that Nathan's father once battled through a hurricane to tend to her ill baby. She said he was the only doctor willing to risk his life for that of a slave child. A family bond was created that night. Since then, Nathan had bought freedom for their entire family.

A week and a half had passed since the day Liz, Leis, and Janie first introduced themselves. Working together to make the draperies became a daily ritual. Every morning, shortly past eight, the seven women gathered to continue in their work. They decided when the window coverings were complete, they would begin sewing table linens next.

While the women stitched, the men, Weston, Jim, Earl, and his nephews Brandon and Randy, earnestly set about repainting the home's interior. Brenna selected the paint colors of the hues of St. Christopher—the sea and lagoons, the flowers, and the sunrises.

Brenna could not wait to begin each day knowing she would be surrounded by her loving family and friends. She cherished the easy rhythm of working with those who cared so deeply for her and for each another. Several times a day, tears of joy consumed her in the realization of how quickly they had all become a part of her life. There was a stark contrast between this tender love and that which she had experienced in her life on St. Christopher where she worked every day in solitude…a life which now seemed distant and even hard to fully recall. Brenna was determined she would never forget the value of such love. She would teach it to her children.

Weston leaned heavily against a massive cypress tree, contentedly watching his wife and daughter as they leisurely made their way down a flowering meadow slope toward him. They were returning from a flower-gathering expedition, neither aware of his presence. Their overflowing baskets attested to their success. He watched their long skirts billow in the gentle breeze. Emily wore a wide-brimmed hat and Brenna's shimmering gold hair was pulled back in a loose ribbon, a few strands fell free of the tie.

He realized Brenna must have said something funny, for Emily stopped walking, looked at her daughter, and then was immersed in bursts of laughter. Brenna joined her. He could not believe how much their laughter sounded alike nor could he help laughing himself. It occurred to him that he had not heard Emily laugh this hard since before they lost Brenna. The laughter now consuming her sounded as though it came straight from Heaven.

Weston knew he would never forget the vision of the two women before him. Thinking of it would bring a smile to him even in his darkest of moments. No matter what might happen in the future, he knew he could endure it, for he had this memory. He would treasure it for the remainder of his life, as he would the moment he first learned Brenna was alive. Though three weeks had passed since that extraordinary evening, he loved thinking of it, reliving each moment. He knew he would revere it until his last breath. Even now, his mind could not help traveling back to it.

"What is it, Nathan? You look so serious. Is your wife okay? I heard she fainted?" Weston asked the question after Nathan returned from the porch and pulled him aside to the study of Grace's home.

Nathan filled two glasses with brandy and handed one to Weston. "I think you might need this after what I'm about to tell you." He took a quick gulp of the warm liquid. "Something extraordinary happened on this voyage, Weston. So extraordinary in fact, that were I in your position hearing this tale, I would doubt the stability of my mind."

Weston looked intently at Nathan but remained silent.

"The first time I saw her," began Nathan, "I saw the resemblance, but I was unable to connect the two."

"The first time you saw who?"

"My wife. The second time I met her, she was so ill that I again failed to notice."

"Failed to notice what?"

"Yet it wasn't until we landed in Bristol that I knew the truth."

"Nathan," said Weston uneasily, "would you please start from the beginning? I have no idea what you're talking about and it seems to be important."

Nathan took a deep breath and began again more slowly. "The first time I met my wife was while we were docked in the West Indies. I was returning to my ship after a meeting with a plantation owner. It had been raining all morning. I found her with her produce cart stuck in the mud. I helped to free her cart."

"Your wife was selling produce?"

"Yes."

"Alone?"

"Yes."

"That's remarkable, Nathan. I've never heard…"

"My exact words." A distant look touched Nathan's face. "She's a remarkable woman. Anyway, after speaking with her briefly, I thought she looked vaguely familiar."

"Yet, you had never met her before?"

"No."

"Why then did she look familiar?"

Nathan glanced briefly at Weston and then to his hands. He said without answering, "When I saw her again, we were nearly seven weeks out. I found her near death in the hold of my ship."

"You mean your wife was a stowaway?" He saw Nathan's nod and exclaimed, "Nathan, this is astounding!" Still puzzled, he quickly added, "Yet why is it vital for you to tell me all this now?"

Nathan again avoided the question and continued. "For numerous reasons, I did not see her again until we anchored in Bristol. It was then I learned the truth."

"What truth?"

Nathan stared out the window and said evenly, "Briefly, even after I removed her hat, I thought it was a coincidence, believing that somewhere in the world we each have a near double—a close replica of our image. I simply thought I had found hers."

"Whose?" asked Weston. He was growing slightly agitated.

Nathan paused as if remembering Weston, "Emily's."

"Emily? You found someone who looks…"

"I thought the island where we met was also a mere coincidence."

"What island? Where did you meet?"

Nathan hesitated before he answered. "St. Christopher."

"St. Christopher," murmured Weston. An idea brushed his conscience, so remote that he had never before let himself entertain such a possibility.

"But it wasn't until I saw her bracelet that I knew."

As if speaking from underwater, Weston struggled with each word of his next question, "What is it you're trying to say, Nathan?"

For the first time Nathan's green eyes faced Weston squarely. "My wife. She's your…well, sir…my wife is…"

"BRENNA!" came Emily's distant cry.

Weston still could not take in all he heard that night.

"Dad," beamed Brenna and moved toward him. She kissed him gently on his cheek. "Have you been here long?"

"Not long enough. I could have stayed here all day watching the two of you. You and your mother together. It's still too incredible to believe!"

Emily joined them and hand in hand the three walked through the meadow.

"It looks as though we'll have bundles of flowers hanging throughout our homes this winter."

"And considering it will be nearly winter when our granddaughter is born," said Emily, "we'll want her surrounded by spring…even if it's dried."

"Her?" questioned Brenna.

"Believe me, Brenna," grinned Weston, "if your mother says you're having a girl, go ahead and paint the nursery pink; she's rarely in error. And speaking of grandchildren, Brenna, how are you feeling?"

"Wonderful."

"Do you feel up to going for a short ride?"

Brenna's bright smile was all the answer he needed.

"Weston, do you think it wise?" asked Emily. Brenna said she has had very little riding experience.

"I asked Doc Hildebrand about it. He said it's permissible since she is still not far along and provided she not overdo."

"That sounds lovely!" exclaimed Brenna. Then tentatively, "It's true. I've only ridden once…on my mule on St. Christopher…and that was not something to behold. He refused to take even a step with me on him."

"You need not worry, Brenna. Dusty is as gentle as they come and his gait is as smooth as any horse I've ever known."

"I just hope he's not as stubborn and ornery as my old mule!"

Brenna looked about her new home with satisfaction. She was amazed how quickly it had been transformed. Gone were the dark walls and curtains, replaced with lighter draperies and fresh paint. The curtains behind the sweeping staircase were removed and the greeting of sunlight was dazzling.

The fireplace stones had been white-washed and the woodwork and floors polished. In the kitchen, the silver and brass cookware glistened. The beams were newly varnished and the walls painted a light gold.

Brenna's choice of soft turquoise for the walls of their bedroom created a stunning backdrop for the white marble fireplace. A vase of freshly cut flowers filled nearly every room of the house with color and sweet aroma.

The only new purchases were five plush rugs and a few small decorative items. Despite the disbelief and urging of the housekeeper, Brenna opted to have most of the furnishings recovered as opposed to replaced.

She decided to use the spare bedroom next to theirs for the nursery. Emily was overjoyed to help in decorating it. Grace brought over Nathan's bassinet and rocker. Laurie donated many items in anticipation of the infant.

Brenna hoped Nathan would be as pleased as she with their home. She wondered about his reaction to all the changes and realized again how much she missed him. She longed to feel his arms about her. The house, although lovely, felt empty without him. His absence created an unexpected void in her life. She knew she would never again feel whole without him.

Brenna entered his study. This and the bedroom were where she felt closest to him. The study was the only room of their home she had not changed. In many ways the room reminded her of his cabin aboard *The Grace*. She sat at his large wooden desk and touched his quill and parchment. A brass fender and screen covered the fireplace and a large free-standing globe stood in the corner. A grand Charleston-made clock ticked rhythmically. She imagined it saying, "Nath-an…Nath-an" with each tock. From his father's black leather saddle with his physician's bag still strapped to the side, to the carved ship's eagle mounted above the mantel and bookcases full of leather-bound journals, the room captured the essence of Nathan. She loved the walls paneled completely in the soft tones of the native cypress wood.

Brenna closed her eyes and recalled the uneasy days aboard his ship and how wrong she had been about her husband. She smiled as she remembered his Bible, wondering who Weston and Emily Emerson were. She had been inexplicably comforted by the book and its inscription. Never in her wildest imaginings could she have dreamed the truth of who they would turn out to be.

He had ridden all night, but Nathan was not tired. The countryside became more familiar, and he had difficulty restraining himself to not force his mount into a break-neck gallop. The horse, though, sensed the nearness of home and quickened his gait.

The time Nathan had spent away proved to be productive but far too lengthy. Brenna had dominated his every thought. Over and over, he envisioned the sweet fragrance of her hair and the warmth of her body molding to his. The time at sea, when she held him at bay, was nothing compared to the agony of the past few weeks, for he knew she now awaited him willingly. Yet, it was more than just her physical presence he longed for. He missed her as a confidante. Her absence made him acutely aware of what a valued friend she had become. Never before had he wanted to share with anyone his innermost feelings, yet now, he experienced a sense of loneliness at being unable to do so. Despite his determination not to, Nathan pressed his mount to move faster.

He was eager to hear of what had transpired while he was gone. He veered from the road and guided his horse through a narrow opening in the tall brush, a shortcut to Weston and Emily's home. He had a strong suspicion he would find Brenna there. He ducked to avoid a low branch and then urged his horse to the top of a steep, grass-covered hill where he pulled him to a gentle halt. A smile consumed him. His hunch had been right.

In the valley below was a small riding arena. In the center, with hair tucked beneath a dark green bonnet and wearing an equestrian habit of the same hue, was Brenna atop Emily's brilliant golden palomino, his white mane and tail blowing in the wind. Unobserved, Brenna guided the horse in a very slow and even trot around the arena. Nathan watched with admiration. She was not sitting sidesaddle as was customary, but instead, she rode astride. Brenna tossed her head back and laughed. A breeze caught her bonnet and her long, golden strands fell over her shoulders. Even from this distance, Nathan was intoxicated by her.

Brenna's gaze swept across the valley to the hill and settled on the rider.

"Nathan!" she shouted joyously. Nathan urged his horse toward her. Brenna slid off her mount and ran toward him.

Nathan leapt from his horse and effortlessly swept Brenna into his arms and kissed her warm lips.

"Oh, Nathan, I've missed you!"

"And I you, you little vixen," he squeezed her playfully, "more than I dare admit." He pulled slightly away. She giggled when he grinned at her. "I must admit, you've once again surprised me with another hidden talent."

"Oh?"

"I was unaware you were so adept at riding."

"I'm afraid I put her up to that," interjected Weston. He extended a gloved hand to Nathan. "I hope you don't mind I've taken the liberty. We talked to the doctor and he approved so long as she be given a gentle mount and do nothing more than a slow trot. And I must say," he beamed, "she's done beautifully."

"I have little doubt. I'm sure you've learned there's no stopping your daughter once she puts her mind to do something."

"So I've seen! It seems she and her mother have more in common than just their looks," laughed Weston. The three walked the horses toward the stable. Weston turned to Nathan, "How was your business?"

"*The Grace's* cargo turned a nice profit. But I spent most of my time on another matter a couple hundred miles inland."

"Doing what?" asked Weston as he pulled the bridle off Dusty and replaced it with a halter. "What's in that virgin territory to interest you?"

"Land."

"Land? In the North?" Weston was surprised.

"Yes. We just purchased several thousand acres, milady. I hope you don't mind."

Brenna smiled, amazed that he cared about her thoughts regarding business concerns.

"Whatever for?" asked Weston intrigued.

"You'll probably not believe me when I tell you, so for now, I'll hold off on the details. I'm certain if you knew, you'd question my suitability for your daughter and probably call for an immediate annulment of our vows."

Two hours later, after recounting the events of the past few weeks with Brenna, Weston, and Emily over tea and shortbread, Nathan and Brenna rode home by carriage. When he stepped into the foyer, Nathan's eyes and mouth grew wide at their home's transformation.

"Brenna, how in the world did you accomplish all this?"

"If it weren't for the help of a lot of people, it never would have happened."

"It must have taken nothing short of the entire Colonial army! It's absolutely remarkable!"

"Then you approve?" Brenna hesitated.

"Approve? I'm utterly astounded!" They walked the home hand in hand. "Although this house has been in my possession for some time, I've never felt more at home than I do at this moment."

"Oh, Nathan, I'm so pleased."

"And you will be pleased, my lord," announced Mrs. Stritzel upon entering the study, "that your purse is only a little lighter than when you left."

"Oh? I thought I left explicit instructions that no expense was..."

"Believe me," interrupted the housekeeper, "the mistress here is determined. And she has good sense about her, she does." She tied the ribbon on her bonnet. "You're mighty lucky." Now, enough of my prattling. The table's set and there's plenty more vittles in the kitchen."

"Are you leaving, Mrs. Stritzel?" the captain asked with a grin.

"M'lady Brenna said this would be a grand time to visit my sisters. Actually," she winked at Nathan, "I get the impression she wants a little time alone with you."

Nathan looked mischievously at his wife, then to his housekeeper. "Give Janet and Connie my regards."

Once in their bedroom, Nathan pulled the ribbon from Brenna's hair. "Oh, it's nice to be home!"

"I'm so glad you're here! Though, I must warn you. I found a new love while you were gone."

"Really?" laughed Nathan as he ran his hands through her hair.

"Yes. He's really quite stunning and I've spent hours with him."

"And does this suitor have a name?"

"Yes…and four legs. Since Mother is not overly fond of horses, they want me to keep Dusty."

"You do seem to have a knack lately of acquiring whatever you desire, don't you?"

"And far, far more," she said sincerely.

"You deserve every bit of it, you know."

"Do you have any idea how happy I am, Nathan? How blessed I am?"

Nathan looked at her in wonderment. "Do you ever complain, Brenna? After all you've been through?"

"All I've been through led me to you. And I would not change one thing in my past…not one thing…if that meant anything different than being here with you now."

His white teeth flashed as he pulled her into his arms. "Now, what was that I heard earlier about your hidden talents?"

Chapter Seventeen

"A picnic today was a lovely idea, Brenna," said Emily. Their small, open-air buggy made its way down a winding path. Earl was at the reins.

Overhead, the sky was a brilliant blue with an occasional wisp of cloud. The smell of burning leaves and dried pine needles filled the air. Brenna closed her eyes briefly and allowed the essence of fall to embrace her senses.

"'Tis a lovely day," commented Emily, expressing Brenna's exact thoughts.

"It's just so bright and beautiful. I couldn't stay inside for another moment. I never dreamed any season could compete with springtime in Charleston, but this comes close."

"Each season in Charleston holds something special for me. As you know, many of our residents go to New Port or New York for the hot summer months. But I've never minded the heat overly much."

"Nor I. This past summer was not all that much different from St. Christopher."

"Are you certain you're up to going into Charleston? We could stop here."

"Let's keep going. This may be the last time I get out for a while. I hope Nathan can still join us for a picnic by the shore."

"Okay, if you're certain you feel up to it. I don't want you to become overly tired. The doctor said he believes you've scarcely got more than two weeks."

Brenna ran her hand over her large abdomen. "From the way I look, surely it will be sooner."

"Perhaps this isn't such a good idea. Earl, why don't you turn ba…"

"Don't worry, Mother. Today is not the day."

"Brenna," said Emily with a sudden sense that something was happening with her daughter, "I really think we ought to go back."

"It's okay, Mother. If I start having any contractions, I promise we can leave immediately."

Emily looked at her closely and said uneasily, "Are you sure you don't feel anything now?"

"Absolutely!"

Reluctantly, Emily agreed. Twenty minutes later, the buggy headed toward the wharf at the mouth of the Cooper and Ashley Rivers where *The Grace* was docked.

Earl presented his hand and then remounted the seat to await their return.

"Permission to come aboard, Captain."

Nathan emerged from the companionway. "Well, ma'am," he chided and rubbed Brenna's protruding belly, his boyish grin bright, "perhaps you ought to wait until I call back my crew to adjust the ballast. I'm not certain *The Grace* can accommodate your immense load."

"Nathan, you rascal, I've a mind to take my daughter and leave this instant," laughed Emily. "And to think, she even brought you a basket of goodies in case you couldn't join us!"

Nathan kissed Brenna's forehead and turned to tease Emily, "Just trying to complete my work here so your grandchild can have my undivided attention. In the future, I'll remember not to bite the hand that…"

"Nathan!" shouted Brenna. A large amount of fluid drenched the boards beneath her feet.

All three gaped wide-eyed at the fluid, then to one another. Several seconds passed before the silence was shattered. Husband, wife, and mother erupted simultaneously.

"Brenna!" shouted Nathan.

"My baby!" exclaimed Brenna.

"You said 'not today'!" cried Emily.

Nathan was the first into action. He scooped Brenna into his arms and commanded Emily, "Get Doctor Hildebrand!"

Emily ran toward the gangplank and Earl.

"Mother!" Brenna gasped. "Bring him quickly!"

The doctor was not easily located. Emily eventually found him at a meeting in the Charleston Exchange Building. It was nearly an hour and a half before he, Emily, and Earl barged through the door of Nathan's cabin.

Nathan grinned more broadly than any man Emily had ever seen. Brenna lay calmly on his berth with only the top of a tiny head visible in her nestling arms.

"Mother," said Brenna softly, "meet EmilieGrace Helen Grant, your granddaughter."

Later, the doctor declared baby and mother fit. He patted Nathan's back, "You're darn lucky, my boy, that your daughter decided to take the easy way into this world."

"It was all Brenna's doing," beamed Nathan as he put a cool cloth on her forehead.

"That's not true, Nathan! You were wonderful! I would not have survived this without you! And of all places! I can't believe we had this baby here, aboard *The Grace!* From the first moment I awoke in this room so many months ago after being in the hold, I have always felt safe here."

Nathan was about to say he could think of no more fitting place for their baby to begin her life than aboard the ship that had brought them all together, when the doctor interrupted his musings.

"You even got the tying of the cord right," said the doctor to Nathan.

"My father always said the laces of shoes work just about as well as anything. Luckily, Brenna chose to wear these and not her buckles!"

"The Lord was certainly with you today," the doctor replied happily.

Emily's eyes filled with tears. She said a silent prayer. She had prayed all through her search to find the doctor for the safety of Brenna and the baby. Emily struggled to regain her composure. "I'm so grateful you helped your father with an occasional delivery, Nathan!"

"So am I. Otherwise, I would have been of little use." Nathan lifted up his snugly wrapped daughter and placed her in Emily's arms.

The infant opened her eyes and looked directly into Emily's. Tears streamed down her face. She whispered, "She looks just like you, Brenna—just like you looked!"

"And, like the three generations of women before her," said Nathan, "she has her great-grandmother's beautiful Irish eyes."

The turnout for Nathan and Brenna's Christmas ball on December 17, 1789 was larger than anyone had anticipated. Word had traveled quickly of the incredible and unlikely tale of separation and reunion for Brenna and her parents. Throughout the region, people were eager to meet the great beauty who found her parents and had managed, in the process, to capture the heart of one of the most sought-after bachelors in the Colony.

Since coming to Charleston, Brenna had little opportunity to meet many of her neighbors. She had spent most of the spring and early summer with her parents and the restoration of her home. The remainder of her summer and fall had been consumed in preparation for EmilieGrace's birth.

Brenna glanced at the hall clock; it was nearly eleven-thirty. Despite the lateness of the hour, the guests showed no signs of weariness. Laughter filled the air. Never had the home looked more festive than it did this evening adorned in its Christmas finery. Garlands climbed the stairway balustrade, garnished with red bows and shimmering golden balls. A brilliant Christmas tree was adorned in silver and gold and berries and cones. A delicate porcelain nativity scene rested over the fire's mantle. At every turn, the home spoke of love, warmth, and welcome, none of which were lost on the guests.

Brenna was surprised at how comfortable she felt with her newfound friends. She understood easily why her parents, twenty years earlier, had decided to make Charleston their home. Over and over this evening, she told the story of her life on St. Christopher, her chance meeting with Nathan, her escape from him, and her reunion with her family. Always they wanted to know more. Weston, Emily, Nathan, and Grace stayed equally busy recounting the tale.

"If you looked any more irresistible, I'd have to bring out my saber in your defense," whispered Nathan from behind and kissed her on the neck.

"Nay, Nathan. I'm afraid 'tis you who has caused the disruption. I've been consoling brokenhearted women…and their mothers…all evening!" She tugged on his cummerbund. "You know what you remind me of dressed in black with this red cummerbund?"

"No. What?"

"The party at the Royal Crescent when I watched you from afar."

"Had I known you were paying such close attention, I would have dressed in my best finery."

"As it was, you appeared to have your hands full with the attentions of plenty of the ladies."

"And that bothered you?" He grinned. "Perhaps I might be able to use such tactics to my advantage after all."

"Iestyn warned me that you always were a cad. Where is he anyway? I've barely seen him all evening."

"In the kitchen."

"In the kitchen? Why?"

"Let's just say I have a feeling that the good widow, Mrs. Stritzel, may not require such a title much longer."

"So your suspicions are confirmed?"

"I've known both for a long time and I've never seen either one acting so peculiar. I'm just happy they finally got the chance to meet over these last few months. For years I've wanted them to become acquainted."

"I had no idea I was marrying a matchmaker! Iestyn told me he no longer desires to go to sea now that you are land-locked and there's a 'wee little one around who needs his attention'."

"He's very fond of EmilieGrace, but I think his motives are a little more complex," he smiled and nodded toward the kitchen.

Nathan knew he should attend to their guests, but he could not get enough of his wife. He loved everything about her and doubted she had any idea just how consumed he was with her. She was radiant. Her hair was pulled up in an elegant array of braids, exposing the soft, satin skin of her neck. She wore a wine-colored velvet dress draped low off her shoulders, its skirt wide. At her wrist, her special bracelet sparkled. On her neck was the necklace he had given her on their wedding day. Motherhood only seemed to enhance her beauty.

"You caused quite a stir earlier this evening, Nathan, when you finally disclosed your reason for buying so much land to the north and west."

"I know. They all think I've lost my level head for thinking there might be a profit in short-staple cotton."

"Do you really think there is?"

"Not yet, but there will be. With as many people working on a way to separate the seed from the cotton, it's only a matter of time before some young inventor comes up with the solution. If they can do it with sea-island cotton, then eventually, it will be done here as well. When that happens, I suspect there will be a flurry of buyers trying to obtain as much land as possible for production."

"And you just want to be ready."

"Of course." He placed his arms about her neck. "Besides, if my prediction does not hold, it's lovely country where our children may decide to reside one day."

"Speaking of children," said Brenna, "I think I'll go check on EmilieGrace. She may be hungry."

That's odd, thought Brenna moments later when she opened the door to the nursery and found the interior in darkness. *The lamp was burning when I left less than half an hour ago and there was plenty of oil.*

She jumped at the sudden squeak of someone rising from the corner rocking chair. She calmed quickly, "Oh, Mrs. Stritzel," whispered Brenna, "you startled me."

"I'm so sorry, my dear, t'wasn't my intent."

Brenna was paralyzed by the voice.

"And before you think of calling out, please know that I hold your wee precious one in my hands."

Brenna could not breathe. She was instantly covered in a cold sweat. Her body shook violently.

"Tsk, tsk. I'd forgotten just how tiny they really are."

Her vision adjusted to the darkness. Brenna could see EmilieGrace between enormous hands. He rolled her over and the baby began to cry. "If I weren't careful, one so fragile could easily be…crushed."

"Please, Mr. Stone, please don't hurt her."

"That decision is entirely up to you, dearest Brenna."

"What is it? What is it you want?"

"I saw you the other day, you know. In town, walking down Tradd Street, I believe. And for a moment, I thought I was looking at a ghost. Launey told me you were alive, though I must confess, I doubted her."

Brenna opened her mouth to speak, but a lump in her throat choked off all sound.

"That's right…Launey. You remember her, don't you? I believe your husband was actually quite smitten with her at one time. But you don't have to bother yourself 'bout that none. I've taken care of her for you." He moved closer. "You ought to be thanking me."

"What is it you want?" Brenna managed to whisper again.

"Come now, Brenna, you're a smart girl. Isn't it obvious?"

His presence was stifling. Brenna felt she was going to be sick. She could not bear the thought of him holding her baby.

"Please, I'll do whatever you want. Just leave her alone!"

"Ah, now that's more like it. A bit more conciliatory than you were in my home, now aren't you? Perhaps I owe yer husband my gratitude after all. He's warmed you to the idea of a man between your loins."

Nathan, thought Brenna wildly, *Help!* She knew though that he believed she was nursing the baby and would not be alarmed by her absence.

"All right, Miss Brenna, we'll play it your way." He yanked Brenna by the back of her hair with his free hand. Viciously, he pulled her with him toward the baby's crib and dumped the child within. He removed two scarves from his pocket. He stuffed one into Brenna's mouth and tied the other over the first scarf at the back of her head. Before she had time to react, Brenna was dragged out onto the piazza. "Your daughter is still easily reached, my dear, so I suggest you do not resist me now."

With the tip of a sharp knife at her throat, Brenna clumsily climbed over the iron railing and down his makeshift rope ladder with Stone following after her. Once her feet touched the ground, Brenna started to run, but powerful arms grabbed and restrained her.

Malcolm Stone breathed heavily when he caught up to them. The man with the strong arms held her while Stone removed a rough piece of rope from his pocket. He jerked her arms behind her back and cinched it tight. She felt the cut of the rope and her warm blood trailing into her hands. Despite her violent kicks, her feet were tied next. Then Stone grabbed her ankles while the other clenched her shoulders. They carried her toward a cluster of bushes where a worn-out seed wagon was concealed. Roughly, they dumped her on the wooden bed and covered her with branches.

"What took ye so long?" said the low voice through the darkness.

"Shut up, Jade. Just shut up and drive!"

"Brenna, Brenna," whispered Nathan. He opened the door of the dark nursery. "What's taking you so…" He stopped when he saw that his wife was not in the room. *That's odd,* he thought and lit the lamp's wick. *I didn't see her come downstairs.*

At what had now become a habit, Nathan moved to the crib to check his baby. "EmilieGrace? How did you get turned around like that?"

Mrs. Stritzel entered the room. He frowned. "Did you see the way EmilieGrace is sleeping? She never sleeps with her head at that end."

"How on earth did she manage that?"

"I don't know, but at two months, she certainly didn't do it on her own. And Brenna never puts her down that way. By the way, have you seen her?"

"Brenna? Nay, sir. Not recently."

Something was not right. Nathan could feel it…smell it. "Mrs. Stritzel, to your knowledge, have any of the guests been in here?"

"I don't believe so, why?"

"Do you notice a peculiar odor or is it just my imagination?"

"I don't smell anyth…well wait, there is something, a bit...well… foul."

"Exactly. I've smelled it before. I just can't quite place it."

Captain Thomas Neal burst into the room.

"Thomas!" smiled Nathan jubilantly, "this is a surprise! I didn't expect you back for another…"

"Nathan, where's Brenna?"

Nathan was immediately alarmed. "I don't know. Somewhere here. Why?"

"Are you certain she's here?"

"What is it, Thomas?"

"This," said the captain and handed Nathan a letter. "But don't take time to read it now. I can tell you of its contents."

"Oh?"

"It's from Judge Charles."

"Then you checked into the matter of trying to clear Brenna of murder?"

"Aye, and believe me, she's cleared!"

"What! That's incred…"

"We've no time for celebration now. Brenna's in danger!"

"How? From whom?"

"Malcolm Stone!"

"Stone!" gasped Nathan. "The smell! Oh my God, he's been here!"

Malcolm Stone could barely contain himself. The urge to pull over and take the wench was almost unbearable. She was even more alluring than he'd remembered. It had taken all the strength he could muster to not throw her to the floor of the nursery and relieve his pent-up lust, but it was too risky. As badly as he wanted her, he certainly was not about to ruin everything now.

He used a dirty handkerchief to wipe the sweat from his brow. He could think of nothing but the moment when he would rip the red velvet dress off her body.

Ahhhhh, how I wish we were already aboard my ship! Ten more minutes! Just ten more! I ought to be able to hold out that long! Possessed with desire, he tried to calm himself and imagined how many times he would take her tonight. *Let's just see how high and mighty you'll be once we're out to sea!* A wicked laugh filtered through the night air. *And to think, I won't even need to waste time tying you up! You don't have a prayer! Not a prayer!*

Thomas Neal shouted to Nathan, as they peeled from the house toward the stable, that shortly after he arrived in England, he was met by Judge Charles who had been waiting for the next America-bound ship. The judge told him he was trying to get an urgent message to a Captain Nathan Grant of Charleston. The judge was shocked to learn that Thomas worked for Nathan and had come to England seeking to clear Brenna of the murder charge. The judge gave Thomas a letter with the formal court ruling exonerating her for the murder of Mrs. Stone.

The judge explained that the daughter of a local Bristol judge had been murdered in June but she lived long enough to tell the authorities that Malcolm Stone was responsible and that Stone claimed also to have killed his wife.

Judge Charles said a massive hunt had ensued the night of the murder and the port had been closed immediately.

Judge Charles told Thomas that one of Malcolm Stone's men had been arrested two days before Thomas' arrival. The man confessed that Stone and his small band of men had been hiding out in the tunnels beneath Bristol since the murder and they had, only days before, commandeered another vessel and thrown overboard its crew. During that fight, one of Stone's men had been captured. He admitted that Stone was headed for Charleston, obsessed with finding a woman named Brenna.

Upon learning of this threat to Brenna's life, Thomas immediately set sail. His fears were confirmed earlier today when he arrived in Charleston and found that a ship of the description of Stone's stolen vessel was anchored off shore just two piers away from *The Grace* on White Point.

Nathan heard nothing but the pounding hooves of his steed. Like thunder echoing through a tunnel, horse and rider roared down the path. He gave no thought to how far behind him were Weston, Iestyn, Thomas, Earl, James, and half a dozen other men who dashed from the party. His all-consuming thought was how far it was to the wharf and Brenna.

Hatred, such as Nathan had never known, welled within. Ferociously, he clenched the reins, his fingers white and numb.

With her hands still tied behind her back and her feet roped together, Brenna was taken from the wagon and thrown into the bottom of a small boat. She landed so hard the wind was knocked from her lungs. She could not move and was paralyzed by terror—pure terror unlike anything she had ever known. She knew where the longboat would take her. She knew what he would do to her.

Please, God, please! Not like this! Not after I've finally found them! Please! Not like this!

Brenna gasped for air through her nose and screamed through the scarf.

"Won't do you a bit of good," laughed Malcolm Stone. He stood on the dock and tried to steady the craft long enough to climb in. "You're mine now." His look of pleasure was brief. He turned and shouted, "What the...?"

"Someone's comin', an' fast!" exclaimed Jade.

"That's impossible! We weren't followed!"

"Yeah? Try tellin' him that, ye bloody fool!"

Desperately, both men searched for a quick escape from the vision barreling toward them. Their ship was too far for their men to be of any help and the wagon and horse were fettered to the far end of the dock. They had no time to ready their muskets. Malcolm Stone had no choice. He dropped the boat's rope and reached for his saber. Jade did the same, but he lost his footing and fell sideways off the dock and into the water. Unattended, Brenna's craft began to move with the outgoing tide.

Malcolm Stone panicked. There was no time to remove his saber from its sheath. His only option was to jump into the water. As he turned, his foot slid into a wide groove of the slatted wooden surface. Frantically, he tried to free his foot, but he only wedged it tighter. He saw the face of the man charging toward him. Time seemed suspended. For the first time in his life, he knew true fear and what it was to be insignificant. All the power he had wielded, all the intimidation he had instilled over the years now meant nothing. The rider before him looked through him as though he were not even there.

Raw determination lined the captain's face, his jowls clenched and his eyes blazed. All Nathan could see was the boat drifting out to sea. Neither the man nor mount paused when they reached the pier. The horse's hooves pounded against the wooden planks.

The black whirlwind descended upon Malcolm Stone. Stone shielded his face and screamed, "No!"

The horse and rider barreled into his chest. He fell backwards and the back of his head slammed into the pier. He was dead before horse and rider soared over him, off the dock and into the water.

Jade climbed back onto the dock and saw Nathan off his horse, starting to swim toward the small boat. Jade jumped into the water and onto Nathan's back.

Weston had ridden furiously to try and keep Nathan in sight. Thomas was at his heels. By the time they reached the dock, Weston saw the boat floating away. Nathan was in the water struggling with another man. "You help him," shouted Weston to Thomas.

Without hesitation, Weston dove headlong into the cold water.

A rope brushed his face. He grabbed it. It was his lifeline to the boat, to Brenna. Suddenly, the years vanished. His leg was not injured. There were no streaks of silver in his hair. The waters were not those of a calm Carolina sea but of a raging West Indies storm. The rope ripped the flesh from his hands. His muscles were weak with fatigue. The rope was his only link to his baby. The waves swelled over his head and tore the rope from his hand. The boat was slipping away. *No! I won't let go! I won't let go!*

As quickly as it had begun so many years before on the St. Christopher shore when his cries splintered across the rocky cliffs, Weston's battle ended. His inner demon that had mocked and blamed him was gone.

"Brenna!" he screamed and pulled himself over the vessel's side.

There, just as he had left her twenty years before, was Brenna lying in the center of the boat. She was safe.

Postlude

Brenna looked at the gathering of family and friends at her home Christmas morning. She could scarcely comprehend the warmth she felt. They all were there—Iestyn, Mrs. Stritzel, Laurie, James, their three children, Thomas Neal, Grace, Weston, Emily, Nathan, and resting in her arms, EmilieGrace.

They had attended a Christmas Eve service the night before and baptized EmilieGrace. Brenna had looked upon the cross, illuminated by candlelight at the front of the church, and was reminded of a light that had reached her in the very dark hold of a sailing ship. She had asked God then that if He really did exist, to save her and give her reason to hope.

She knew last night with more clarity than she had ever known that when Helen died and she thought she too would die from grief, when she fell upon the sands of St. Christopher believing she had been sold, when she wanted to give up her struggle in the hold, when she awoke that terrible morning in the old barn after being attacked, when she faced death by hanging, when she despaired for her unborn child and feared abandonment, and even in the whispered longings of a mother's love willed across the sea to a shore far away, God had been there. He had always been there.

Helen had been right. Through it all—her sorrows, loneliness, pain, and joy, He had comforted her, wept with her, encouraged her, and forced her to find the strength to continue.

On this Christmas morning, surrounded by the human gifts of love around a massive hearth, Brenna knew she had been blessed with the greatest gift she would ever know: *God's* love, fully and completely. It was a love without bounds, without end.

"Brenna," said Emily." I have another gift, but before I present it, I need to say something." Emily struggled to keep her voice steady. "I used to live in fear of all the unknowns. My father told me we must believe that the Lord has something good in mind for us…whether while on this earth or beyond. I was never very good at trusting that.

"But now," Emily could not hold back the tears, "as I look around this room and think of all that has happened…all that transpired to bring us together, I know this could not possibly be just some random act of fate. It's a miracle…all of this…all of you. And I don't pretend to understand the why of it…none of this still makes sense…why have we been blessed when so many others who lose their children will never know such a miraculous reunion? Are we more worthy somehow? No, I don't think that's how God works. But I know one thing…Brenna, Weston and I…through all these years and the miles apart…we felt each other's love…which has taught me something…something very important…that separation…no matter the cause…death or the loss of a baby in a small boat a quarter of a world away…though we are separated…love can win…and it did.

I know, while this is the most extraordinary and emotional Christmas any of us have ever known, it's also especially painful for you, Grace…Laurie…Nathan, because it magnifies even more the void of Robert…and oh, how he would have loved to join in this celebration!

And Brenna, I know it's also true for you…of how you wish Helen were here. I can only imagine her joy to see you surrounded by so many who love you…and Weston…your father and mother…my father and mother…oh, what we would give to have them all here. But I know with everything that I am…somehow, some way, they are feeling the love in this room right now because they were a part of its creation…our love is a part of them and it's a part of us…and no matter the cause of the separation...love has conquered the divide."

Emily moved to EmilieGrace and lifted her from Brenna's arms and handed her to Grace. She removed a large, delicately wrapped box adorned with a large yellow bow and presented it to Brenna.

Brenna looked from her mother to her father. "I can't possibly accept anything else!"

"We've a lot of years to make up for, my dear," smiled Weston. "But I'm afraid I can't take credit for this one. Emily has kept it a well-guarded secret."

"It's a gift for EmilieGrace," said Emily softly.

Brenna could tell the gift was very important to her mother. Tenderly, she removed the ribbon and opened the box.

It was a yellow handmade quilt.

"The same one?" Weston's voice was hoarse with emotion.

"The same one. Remember when you found it?"

"How could I forget? It was the worst moment of my life." He walked over to the quilt and lifted it from the box. "I never thought I'd see it again. I remember not wanting you to bring it back with us, but you gathered up the pieces anyway. I assumed you had long since discarded it."

"Just tucked away in my trunk. I was able to salvage the individual blocks. I've re-quilted it and added three additional blocks. One, as you can see portrays the story of a young island girl standing on the shore with her lantern in hand, another of a very lonely Carolina couple, and finally, the tale of a family brought back together."

"I can't believe it," said Weston. He shook his head, "The yellow quilt."

"Weston, it's the one that helped keep her safe after all."

"I just can't get over any of this!" exclaimed Brenna, her emotions bursting forth. "I can't believe I'm here…Christmas with all of you! How? How could this be true? I can't believe I found all of you…that we have EmilieGrace…and even..." she laughed wiping her face, "…even that John and Carrie are coming to visit this spring and bringing their newly adopted son, Scott! It is all just too impossible to be true!"

"Well, my dear wife," grinned Nathan broadly. He moved to Brenna, took the quilt from her, and handed it to Weston. "I've got one more surprise to add to your list."

"It's got to be something big," laughed Laurie, "I haven't seen that sly look since he was ten and duped the schoolmaster into believing the town had voted to forgo classes for the year!"

"Actually, it is big…or rather, she is big!" Nathan opened the hall door. A large, yellow dog bounded into the room.

"HONEY!" cried Brenna as the dog leapt onto her lap. "Honey! Nathan! It's impossible! I can't believe…"

"I told you, you wouldn't!"

For the next several minutes, Nathan was unsure who was wailing and yelping louder—Brenna or Honey. After nearly ten minutes, Brenna stopped crying long enough to ask, "Nathan, how in the world did you do this?"

"Actually, the credit is all with Thomas. I simply told him about your dog before he left on his voyage and asked if he would stop on St. Christopher and have a look."

"And let me tell ye, ma'am," laughed the captain whose eyes were also moist with tears at the joyful reunion, "it wasn't any problem. Nearly everyone I spoke to knew of the large golden dog with the tip of its tail missing. They said she sat by the pier every day waiting for her mistress to return."

"And his finding Honey alters our plans this spring of traveling to St. Christopher to look for her. Although I must say, I was rather looking forward to seeing your mountain pool. Maybe when EmilieGrace is a little older we'll give it another try."

Thomas shared with Brenna news of Harley. He had learned that the man's badly decomposed body was found in his shack four months earlier with empty liquor bottles scattered around him.

Brenna was not surprised but she was saddened to realize the only emotion she felt at the news of his death was pity. The poor man had created the ultimate tragedy and one she once feared for herself, a death about which no one cared.

That evening at dinner, Grace lit a candle in Robert's honor. She told the story when Nathan and Laurie were young and Robert left Christmas morning to tend to a sailor who had broken his arm. The sailor's military ship made an unplanned stop in Charleston to seek medical aid for him. Grace was in the kitchen preparing the Christmas dinner for the four of them when Robert appeared with 127 men to join them. Grace laughed as she recalled the way the ship's galley chef and several of the men rummaged through their kitchen and cellar…and the feast that followed. Grace said although their cupboard was bare when it was over, it was the most meaningful and delightful Christmas she had ever known…until this day. Soon the rest of the group joined in reminiscing about their favorite past Christmas memories with loved ones no longer here. Emily and Weston lit candles and shared stories of their parents, as did Brenna in honor of Helen.

After the meal, the family gathered around Grace at the piano to sing Christmas carols. Brenna stroked Honey's soft fur and thought of their goodbye at the dock when she wondered if the Lord saved some of his blessings for lost dogs too. "I guess it's true old girl," she whispered with a laugh, "even for those with four paws."

Brenna's gaze moved to the tender faces of those she loved so dearly. Tears of joy trailed down her cheeks. She took Nathan's hand and the flash of her bracelet caught her eye. She thought of the circle it represented…the connection of this family…with God at the center… and of their bond…a bond that had endured and overcome so much…a bond that had never been severed. "I've found it, Nathan."

He looked at her puzzled and she said softly, "My eighth sea. I've found it. I've come home."

Later, with darkness settled in, Nathan and Weston stood on the front porch. Nathan grinned. "Weston, did I ever tell you about the time, while enjoying myself at one of Bath's finer pools, I thought I heard an alley cat?"

Acknowledgements

City on the Hill poem written by the author's great, great grandmother, Kansas pioneer Lydia Evans Davies Charles, shortly before her death in 1904 in Republic, Kansas.

A special thank you to my family and friends, especially my husband Doran whose patience and love knows no end, our three children Crystal, Hallie, and Natalie, and my parents Robert and Lucretia Sprowell for their many years of love, encouragement, and the support needed for me to complete this novel.

Many thanks and appreciation to numerous family and friends for their thoughts and input on this story, including: Sara Hunt, Sharon Forssman, Clare Sprowell, Cindy Frost, Betsy McDermott, Erika Nossokoff, Jane Penoyer, Jane Goding, Kay Collins, Angela Waugh, Sally Robinson, Denise Gardner, Erin Bergstrom, Coral Sowl, Randy Lamb, Hallie Geise, and Dale and Carolyn Geise.

A special note of gratitude and place in my heart for John Forssman and the late Grace Bauske, two high school English teachers extraordinaire from Ames High School in Ames, Iowa who never stopped teaching this student. Without their special care, editing suggestions, and encouragement, this novel would never have found its wings.

A tremendous note of gratitude to Doran Geise for the book's title and other key novel segment suggestions. Thanks, too, to Lucretia Sprowell, for her help (and laughter) in researching Bath and Bristol, England and navigating round-a-bouts!

As always, sincere thanks to Rich McDermott, the Senior Pastor of First Presbyterian Church in Fort Collins, Colorado, for his guidance in helping me find my way to the Lord.

A loving thanks to cover artist Susan Jenkins of Valrico, Florida, for bringing Brenna so fully to life on canvas and for creating a cover that my husband described beautifully as *"A Hope and A Promise."*

A note regarding the cover and a lantern: The artist, Susan Jenkins, and I worked closely to develop the cover. We wanted to portray Brenna holding a lantern, which signifies so much of what this story is about…searching, finding the light of life, etc. I had sent Susan photos of various old lanterns, but never felt any captured the right look. On a Friday of the weekend she was to begin putting paint to canvas, I sent her an idea for a lantern we were settling for but not thrilled about. The following Sunday, I attended services at the lovely, historic First Presbyterian Church in Topeka, Kansas. Its remarkable Tiffany & Co. stained-glass windows, installed in 1911, were reportedly designed by Mr. Tiffany himself. As we entered, my husband remarked that the lantern in one of the windows would be a wonderful model for the cover. I agreed; this particular window has always been my favorite. It shows Nicodemus holding a lantern while speaking with Jesus. The lantern's remarkable design, with no artificial light, allows it to appear "lit" even late in the day when the other windows darken. So, with lanterns on my mind, you can imagine my surprise when Senior Pastor Bradley Walker said in his sermon that day, "Today we are going to do something a little different. We are going to turn down the lights and I want the congregation to focus on that window and that lantern!" I have commented several times that I believe God has shown his presence (and his sense of humor) throughout this writing process…and the lantern and the sermon were no exception! I immediately contacted Susan, who was just about to begin painting the lantern portion of the cover. (If you view the video link, listed on the next page, of the painting coming to life, watch to see what happens to the lantern.) I am so grateful to Mr. Tiffany for this wonderful lantern design and to artist Susan Jenkins for bringing it again to light.

Author's Note: While the characters in this book are fictitious, I have strived to reflect as accurately as possible the places and events of the era. I have, on occasion taken creative liberty; for example, to my knowledge, there was no extensive pirating activity occurring in the

Bristol, England area at the time of this novel. And the Cross Bath, a unique and lovely structure in Bath, England, was apparently closed for restorations during the time portrayed.

I would like to thank the good people of Charleston, South Carolina; Bath, Bristol; and London, England for their work to preserve history in such wonderful detail through their many museums, libraries, and cultural attractions. And while eighteenth century Bath was famous for its ostentatious ways, I found it is not the case today. The people of Bath could not have been more warm and welcoming during my research.

I was blessed in my early research to discover a remarkable and invaluable book called *Journal of a Lady of Quality* by Janet Schaw, whose writings presented a vivid glimpse into the daily life of an era long ago.

I would also like to **thank the professionals who helped make this book possible**: Trai Cartwright, Donna Mazzitelli, Brian Schwartz, and Veronica Yager.

Author's photo by photographer Crystal Geise.

For more photography by Crystal Geise: www.crystalgeise.com

For more art by Susan Jenkins: www.susanjenkinsart.weebly.com

To view a three minute YouTube video cover painting demonstration bringing Brenna to life, accompanied by ***"The Eighth Sea Theme Song"*** visit: **www.theeighthsea.com** or scan the QR code below:

"The Eighth Sea Theme Song" was written from Emily's perspective, willing her thoughts to Brenna over the seas and through the wind. Words and music by Nancy Geise; Vocals-Gyll Perkins; Piano and Score Translation-Matt Baretich; Cello-Heidi Nagel; Tin Whistle-Pamela Robinson; Orchestral Enrichment-Jerry Palmer; Technical Engineering-Russ Hopkins; Recorded and Produced-KIVA Recording Studio/Russ Hopkins Productions, Fort Collins, Colorado.

"For the Son of man is come to seek and to save that which was lost."

—Luke 19:10(King James)

The Eighth Sea
Discussion Questions

Chapter One

1. Brenna felt great despair over her future. When in your life have you felt there was little or no reason to hope? How did you find the strength to continue?

2. When Brenna finally allowed herself to pray, Nathan appeared, though she is not aware there is any connection between her prayer and his presence. Describe a time in your life when you thought your prayers were not answered and yet later you came to know differently? Has there ever been a person who came into your life as a gift of God? What transpired to convince you they were such a gift?

3. A grave digger said, "If you don't stand for something, you stand for nothing." Has there been a time when you did not take a stand on something and you later wished you had? Once you realized your "missed opportunity," what additional action did you take, if any?

4. Brenna was told falsely that she had been sold as an infant. Have you ever been hurt by something that you later learned was not true? What did you do once you discovered the "untruth"?

5. Nathan stopped to help Brenna when her cart was stuck in the mud. Have you ever stopped to offer your help to a stranger? What was the result?

Chapter Two

1. Weston's father James, a coal miner, felt he had no choice in what he did with his life. Yet, with his dying breath, he told his son he had been mistaken. Have you ever felt that you were "stuck" in doing something you believed you were powerless to change? If so, what or who helped you see the choices available to you and what actions did you take?

2. Emily experienced a sense of foreboding before their sea voyage? Have you ever experienced anything similar? If so, how do you deal with such feelings and not allow your life to be guided by fear?

Chapter Three

1. Brenna realized that in order to save herself she had to leave the island, even if she died trying. Have you ever reached a point where you were willing to risk "everything" for something? What happened and how did it turn out?

2. Brenna felt that what was good in her was being destroyed by the life she lived with her stepfather. Have you ever experienced a relationship that was destroying you? If so, how did you recognize what it was doing to you and what did you do about it?

3. If you had been Brenna, would you have left the island? If so, how? What would you have done differently?

Chapter Four

1. Helen felt betrayed by the man she had married. Have there been times when you have been let down by those close to you? How did you deal with such situations?

2. As she was close to death in the hold, Brenna realized her death would mean the victory of Harley's evil. Have you ever been inspired to triumph over evil? If so, what inspired you and what was the outcome?

3. When Brenna was in Nathan's quarters, she could not understand why she was being treated with such kindness from a stranger. Have there been times in your life when you felt undeserving (or mistrusting) of the kindness of someone you barely knew? Were you able to overcome those feelings? If so, how?

4. Have you ever struggled, like Emily, and wondered where God is amidst tragedy? In what ways can you identify with her struggle to understand why bad things happen to good people?

5. When Brenna was in the hold, she prayed for a sign of hope to continue living. She found it in the warm light of a cross overhead. Have you experienced a time when you believed that a prayer had been answered? How did you know? Was there a clear sign?

6. Emily's father told us in his journal entry of his belief that the Creator of all the beauty around us has something even more wonderful in Heaven for us. Do you find comfort in this as well? In what ways can you relate to this belief?

Chapter Five

1. As she reflected on her island childhood, Brenna felt that Harley had acquired their farm unethically. As a result, she could find no comfort in living there. Have you ever been unable to fully enjoy something because of your feelings of guilt? What were the reasons for your feelings?

2. Nathan felt responsible for Brenna's well-being. Have you ever felt responsible for someone you barely knew? Why do you think you felt this way? What transpired and what was the result?

Chapter Six

1. In Bath, Brenna was looking for a new beginning, and yet, with many issues of her past unresolved, she found she was unable to do so. In what ways has your life been affected by your past, either positively or negatively?

2. Brenna had issues of trusting those around her. To trust is to love. How much do you trust people? Have you ever been disappointed when you trusted someone? What happened to create that disappointment?

Chapter Seven

1. Brenna told Scott he had a choice in how to proceed…either by making himself miserable or deciding to make the best of a bad situation. How has your attitude affected the outcome of your experiences?

2. Saddleback Sam said he believed God used his adversity for another good. Have you seen examples of this in your life? If so, in what ways?

Chapter Eight

1. Brenna experienced profound loneliness at different times in her life. When do you feel most lonely? How do you deal with it and what do those struggles teach you?

2. The baker said he realized that everything he had been seeking was at hand prior to ever leaving home. Have you ever failed to recognize happiness until you later had time to reflect back? What helped you see the source of your happiness?

3. Throughout her journey, Brenna wrestled with the questions "Why am I here? What is the point of my life?" Can you identify with her struggle? If so, in what ways?

Chapter Nine

1. The judge knew his sister was making a mistake in marrying a cruel man. Have you ever experienced watching those you love make a decision you knew was unhealthy? How did you handle the situation? Was there something in hindsight you wished you would have done differently?

2. Scott blamed himself for his parents' shortcomings. Can you relate to such feelings?

Chapter Ten

1. After she was attacked, Brenna awoke in a dilapidated barn wondering if she would ever be in control of her life. How much of what happens in your life is within your control? How do you reconcile God's will and yours in determining the outcome of your life?

2. Throughout the story, when Brenna was in grave danger, Emily experienced increasing nightmares about her lost daughter. Have you ever experienced anything similar? Have you thought of someone you love and later learned they were thinking of you at nearly the same time?

Chapter Eleven

1. Brenna said she was determined to "die with dignity." What does dying with dignity and having lived a good and full life look like for you?

2. Nathan said that until he met Brenna, he felt there was something more out there for him. Do you think it is part of the human condition to forever yearn for something more than we have to complete us? If so, how do we recognize contentment in our lives? Is contentment possible in your life without God at the center?

3. As Nathan's love for Brenna grew, he realized he found a part of himself that he never knew was missing. What do you think he meant by this? Have you ever experienced anything similar?

Chapter Twelve

1. Nathan recognized that Brenna did not trust him. Have you ever experienced having someone not trust you? What did you do (or could have done) to help them overcome their distrust?

2. Until he met Brenna, Nathan's one true love was the sea. Have there been things in your life you thought were of primary importance that you later realized were not as important as you once thought? Why do you think this was the case, and how did you grow from it?

3. Brenna talked of a secret hidden pool where she felt safe. Do you have a place where you feel most secure and rejuvenated? Do you go there physically or simply in your mind?

Chapter Thirteen

1. Brenna feared bringing a child into the world without a father. How have you benefited from the guidance and love of a father (or a father figure)?

2. Brenna realized that she had many misconceptions about Nathan that hindered her ability to see the fine man he was. Have there been times when you were surprised to learn you had been wrong about someone you thought you knew?

3. The morning Brenna awoke after realizing Nathan's true love for her, she felt like she was standing on a mountain with God. Have there been times in your life when you felt such joy and completeness?

Chapter Fourteen

1. Were Brenna and Nathan destined to be together…does God put people together? Or do we participate with God's presence in our lives to the point of discovering what is true and meaningful? Does it always take an eighth sea voyage to truly learn this completing perspective?

2. Why do you think Nathan never gave up on Brenna, despite her mistrust of him?

Chapter Fifteen

1. Emily had struggled with the feeling that something was unresolved. Have you ever experienced anything similar?

2. Have you ever found yourself, like Brenna, struggling to find your way home? If so, what does home represent for you?

Chapter Sixteen

1. Once reunited with her parents, Brenna realized she had inexplicably felt their love most of her life, even though they had not been with her physically. Have you ever felt the love of someone even though they were not physically with you?

2. Emily expressed feelings of not knowing if she could forgive herself for having left Brenna behind. Is there something in your life for which you have (or have had) difficulty forgiving yourself? Is there a way to rectify this conflict of your heart?

3. Have you ever experienced, like Brenna did while standing on the shore, that there was something in life waiting for you to discover? Did you find it or are you still searching?

Chapter Seventeen

1. Weston experienced God's redemptive love when he found himself in the water reliving the time he had let go of the rope connecting him to his child. Have you ever experienced God's redemptive love in your life?

2. What qualities in the main characters of Brenna, Emily, Nathan, and Weston do you most admire?

3. How did you see evil most manifesting itself in this book? Was it overcome, and if so, how? Systematic evil is bigger than any individual. Does it always take a Nathan in our lives, at a minimum, to insure our spiritual survival in the face of evil? Can we ever survive without some form of a life raft?

4. Were there common characteristics that most helped Brenna, Emily, Weston, and Nathan in overcoming adversity? If so, what were they?

5. What character do you most relate to and why?

Postlude

1. In what ways was God's transforming presence with Brenna and Emily? Have there been difficult times in your life when you later realized God's presence with you? If so, in what ways?

2. The theme for The Eighth Sea is universal…the search to find our place in the world, our way home. How do you see this struggle as a universal search? Does searching keep life open to finding? Does searching keep spiritual disclosure eternal and personal?

3. In what ways did you see God at work in the lives of these characters and does this spiritual reality relate to your experiences?

4. Brenna's life story shows how our experiences are evidence of God's transforming power. The story shows ways in which God is able to redeem tragedies. In what ways in your life have good things come from bad?

5. What was the most moving portion of the story for you?

6. Brenna later recognized that God was with her throughout her struggles. How do you know God loves you? What evidence do you have of God's transforming presence in your life experiences? What were the redeeming gifts?

7. What do you see as your own Eighth Sea?

Please share your thoughts on your experiences with this book with the author Nancy Geise: 8thSeaAuthor@gmail.com

Nancy Sprowell Geise

Nancy was raised in Ames, Iowa and is a graduate of Iowa State University. She and her husband Doran have lived in Austin, Texas; Fort Collins, Colorado; and Topeka, Kansas. They have three remarkable daughters. Nancy currently divides her time between Fort Collins and Topeka.